BURN
PATTERNS

Michelle Johnston,
without whom.

BURN
PATTERNS
RON ELLIOTT

 FREMANTLE PRESS

For I have sworn thee fair and thought thee bright,
Who art as black as hell, as dark as night.

Shakespeare, Sonnet 147

Chapter one

The police came for Iris at 8.55.

She had spent half the early-morning consultancy session in a stalemate with Hannah and Donna.

Hannah slouched on the green leather couch, her chin and lips thrust in mute protest. She wore a white t-shirt covered in smiling panda bears. She was sixteen, with the body of an eleven year old. It had been another difficult session, and only their second with Iris. Donna, Hannah's mother, sat rigid, often answering for her daughter.

Iris got up from her desk, where she'd been taking notes, and sat in the armchair, a friendlier distance from the couch. 'Did you read the article I gave you, Hannah, in the magazine, about Ed?'

Hannah shook her head.

Donna said, 'I haven't had time. Work has been so ... Why didn't you read it, Hannah? We're spending money here.'

'Lots of people have found it useful to give the problem a name. Once we give it a name that works for you, it's easier to tackle the sucker. Work out what its tricks are and how we can overcome it. Some girls your age have written about this. They called their eating problem "Ed" and explained how when Ed came into their lives, Ed started eating up their relationships, isolating them so Ed could keep them weak and to himself.'

'That's why I didn't read it. Ed is a stupid name. Like a dumb boyfriend.'

'Well, you won't have one of those if you don't start eating!' said Donna.

Iris glanced at her watch. They were only twenty minutes in. She needed to get past Donna, to Hannah, so she could draw out some positives to highlight and build on. Iris said, 'How much do you weigh?'

'Thirty-eight kilos.'

She knew. Exactly.

'Tell me about that number,' said Iris before Donna could criticise.

'What about it?'

'Thirty-eight kilos.'

'It's a lot.'

'What should you weigh?'

'Less.'

'Do you exercise?'

'Every day.'

'Must take a lot of discipline.'

'It does.'

'Do you get hungry?'

'Sometimes.'

Hannah remained guarded, answering quickly, perhaps trying to better Iris. Or her mother.

'Must be hard not to eat at those times.'

Hannah shrugged.

'Do you think you're a strong person?'

'No, I'm not. I'm weak.'

'Getting your weight so low must take a lot of time and effort, surely.'

'I'm pathetic. A baby. I can't do anything.'

Donna raised her eyebrows as she reached over and patted her daughter on the shoulder. 'We muddle through.'

Hannah smiled up at her mum leaning into her.

'I see two loving people. I see a mum and a daughter who want to do what's right for each other.' Iris also saw enabling and co-dependence, but shut out those thoughts.

They nodded.

'My job is not to make judgements.' And I struggle with that.

'But ...' said Donna, defensive.

Iris tried to summarise some of the basic tenets of narrative therapy. 'I am not the expert on your life. I don't have a pill. The first thing I think we need to do, Hannah, is talk about what is good in your life and what isn't working best right now and how we might change it. I need to find out more from you. You're the expert. I can help work out strategies we can try. We can set some goals together. We can do things to help change the behaviours and habits. I can also put you in touch with other approaches, so we can all work together on this. If you want to.'

'Of course she wants to,' said Donna. 'I'll find a way to pay for it.'

Iris needed to deal with Donna, too. Each alone, as well as together. 'Okay, then ...'

Someone knocked at the door, which was most unusual. Mary, Park Psychology and Healing Centre's upstairs secretary, opened the door, looking as startled as Iris felt.

Mary said, 'I'm so sorry, Iris. I'm sorry,' she said to Hannah and Donna. 'Iris, it's the police.'

Iris stood as two uniformed policemen pushed in past Mary.

'Dr Foster,' said the older one. Iris noticed sergeant's stripes.

'I'm not a doctor,' said Iris. 'I'm a clinical psychologist, which doesn't ...'

'We need you to come with us, Dr Foster.'

'What's happened?'

'An arson attempt.'

'There's been a mistake. I don't do that anymore.'

'Superintendent Richards sent me.'

'I have another job now. Other work.' Iris pointed to Hannah and Donna, then gestured beyond the doorway. 'I'm a civilian, demobbed.'

The sergeant stepped forward to whisper to Iris, 'It's a high school. I've been ordered to bring you.'

Iris blinked. Saw Patricia Calligan enter the office.

'What is the meaning of all this?' Patricia wore a sack-like dress of violent orange covered in little black Zulu shields.

Before Iris could explain, the sergeant interrupted. 'I'm sorry, Dr Foster, you can't say anything.' He gave Patricia a steady look. 'An emergency ma'am.'

Patricia measured the sergeant. Patricia kayaked. Worked

out. She and the sergeant would be well matched. The younger police officer looked from one to the other as though drawing the same conclusion.

Iris said, 'Patricia, they've requisitioned me, it seems. Out of my control.' She gave Hannah and Donna an apologetic smile and grabbed her handbag.

Iris led the police out of her office. She caught sight of her next client, Meredith Marsh, a woman battling chronic shyness.

Iris said, 'Not to worry, Meredith. Mary will have to reschedule, I'm afraid.'

Iris heard Mary as she headed down the stairs. 'It's all right, everyone. She's not under arrest. She's helping the police. You know she used to be the Fire Lady, don't you?'

Patricia called, 'Mary, that's enough sharing.'

*

The practice, in a converted two-storey federation style house at the edge of the CBD, was surrounded by eight-storey office blocks. A marked police car sat across the driveway, another officer behind the wheel. They pulled away as soon as Iris got in the back with the sergeant, the siren moaning.

Iris said forlornly, 'I don't do this anymore.'

The sergeant gave a sympathetic grimace.

Iris had left the fire service years before. She'd folded her private consultancy after the attack. Was that a year ago? Now she was a narrative therapist. Well, she struggled to fill in for Dr Chew, the practice's usual narrative therapist. She'd remind Superintendent Richards of this. She was no longer at his disposal. She'd demand a ride back to the office. She'd throw herself on Patricia's inexhaustible understanding, if not mercy.

The policemen did not talk. They were tense, listening to the unfolding events on the police car radio. A high-school evacuation. Units present, gathering. A device.

They pulled into the driveway of Barnard Christian College, going slow to edge past parents, police and the media. Journalists looked for people to question, camera folk climbed onto uplink vans for vantage points.

Iris said, 'This looks big, Sergeant.'

He nodded, but said nothing.

Closer to the school gymnasium, they drove past a police incident control vehicle. The brick gym stood apart from the rest of the school, surrounded by grass sports grounds and extra bitumen carparks, where three fire appliances had taken up position, their hoses deployed. The firefighters didn't have their breathing apparatus on, but otherwise stood in full gear, yellow against the red of the trucks.

Iris was led to the front of the gymnasium where a thousand students milled, hemmed and surveilled by a cordon of uniformed police officers. The co-ed students wore uniforms too, but contrived their own tiny acts of defiance. Some shirt collars were raised on one side, some jumper sleeves rolled to the elbow. Expensive haircuts trumped egalitarian school clothes everywhere.

At the entrance stood a uniformed policeman guarding a large plastic storage bucket full of mobile phones. Iris paused to scan the students again before moving inside.

Knots of chairs were gathered in archipelagos on the shiny pine floor, with detectives interviewing students. An assortment of civilians, possibly parents, teachers and probably child welfare protectors, formed semicircles of audiences around each interview.

Forensic police were dusting a closed side door. Another uniformed group was gathered at the side of the stage apron. More police forensics, fire service and police Arson Squad investigators were disappearing through a small hatch door at the side of the stage. Each got down on all fours to crawl in backwards, their air cylinders barely clearing the top of the hatch. A tight man in a tight suit who Iris would bet as ex-, possibly current, military, talked into a portable handheld radio. Whatever was going on, it had been going on for some time and it was big.

Iris was shepherded to Superintendent Richards who stood with a group of police and civilians watching a schoolboy who sat in a school chair facing a detective. The boy wore a school uniform, grey socks, no shoes. An ambo finished bandaging his right hand.

'Come on, Brent, tell us who helped you do this, then we can sort it out.'

'No one.'

'So you did do it yourself.'

'I told you. I found it.'

'I'm sure it was just meant as a joke. A prank which got out of hand.'

Superintendent Richards turned to Iris, edged her away from the interview. He was a tall, thin man, nearing sixty, pleasantly greying. 'Iris, glad you could make it.'

'Superintendent, I don't do this anymore. I can't help here.'

'A couple of quick questions about whether he's a pyromaniac or angry or a sociopath. You know, do your stuff.'

'You have people, Superintendent. Any number.'

'I need you, Iris. This is important. We've found an ignition device down there, disarmed, some accelerant poured about. Completely foamed now.' He pointed towards the stage. 'The side doors of the gym ...' He put his arms out, pointing to both sides of the gymnasium. 'They are all either padlocked or superglued. The fire suppression system, disabled – no sprinklers. And over one thousand two hundred schoolkids about to sit down to a school assembly. It would have been a catastrophe.' He pointed at the polished wood of the gymnasium floor. 'It's sprung, which means lots of air space under the floor. It would have spread pretty fast.'

'Tell me about him.' Iris pointed back towards Brent.

'Came stumbling out from under the stage as everyone came in for the assembly. Burnt his hand quite badly. We assume it went off too soon, while he was setting it. Look, I know you've kind of retired. Will you listen in, see if you get any impressions of him? Please. We need to know as quickly as possible if this might be an organised attack. A bunch of angry kids or something bigger. Are there more devices? We've got the whole school in lockdown. You know how important time is in this situation. We're rushing – in an orderly manner.'

Iris acquiesced. She'd give them an hour. Extract a promise to be left alone.

Iris said, 'Where are his shoes?'

Richards pointed at a uniform, repeated, 'Where are his shoes?'

'On it,' said the policeman, hurrying off.

Iris moved in to listen to the interview.

'The big metal kettle gizmo started sparking.' Brent had a nice haircut, a good watch. He was a handsome, fit-looking boy.

'I got it out and I climbed up and I yelled out and Mr Theolakis went down and yelled for everyone to get out. I put the fire out, you know!' He waved his bandaged hand dismally.

'Why were you down there, Brent?' The lead detective's coat hung on the back of the school chair. His sleeves were rolled up. An older detective took notes.

'To put some gear away.'

'Who told you to?'

'Nobody. I was being a good citizen.'

The detective leaned forward, dropped his voice. 'Brent, do you understand how much fucking trouble you are in? Do you know the terrorist squad are on their way? They don't talk, those guys. They'll shoot your friends in a split second. This is all real, mate. Not a computer game. Real people, real consequences. And you're going to give me cheek? Really?'

Brent blinked. Lost his fake confidence. He wasn't a bad kid. Assertive, although not angry or resentful beyond the obvious circumstances. He glanced away, his voice neutral. 'I went down for a cigarette. In secret.' The faintest start of a smile flicked his mouth, before he controlled it. He peered up at the detective, his eyes firming as he said, 'I smelled smoke and saw these sparks coming out of the gizmo. A wire was glowing. It glowed white, and the papers and torn-up gym mat caught fire. It spread onto the floor, catching on the petrol.'

'Petrol?'

'It wasn't petrol, but it smelled, you know, not kerosene ... anyway, the fire caught that and it started to run across the floor towards the boxes. I grabbed this other gym mat and I, um ...' Brent did the actions, pushing downwards as he clearly remembered what he had done. 'I pushed and pushed and the fire went out and I pushed the mat onto the gizmo and saw some of the petrol stuff on my hand.' He held up his bandaged hand.

He focused on a woman a few police away from the detective. She had tears in her eyes. He shook his head. 'I didn't do this bad thing. I didn't do the fire.'

His mother. She'd come from work. Brent wanted his mother to know of his innocence, yet had used an odd turn of phrase. A slight evasion. 'This bad thing'? Nearly a confession – to something. He was telling the truth about putting out the fire. What bad thing wasn't he telling?

The detective noted Brent's mother, but moved on. A young, smart, confident detective doing his thing. 'Brent. I smelled your breath when I got here. I don't smell cigarettes.'

'Gum, so no one smells.'

'See the thing is, Brent, the police officers have found no gum. No cigarettes. No butts. No lighter.'

Brent blinked. He tossed his head, sending his thick fringe flopping to the side in a reflex gesture as he went into himself to construct a new lie to shore up the one exposed.

The detective kept him off balance. 'Sweeney, you find any of those things?'

An officer in forensic overalls shook her head. She held up two clear plastic evidence bags. One held a pair of black shoes. The other contained a diaphanous material Iris thought could have been stockings.

'You didn't go down to smoke, Brent. You went down to start the timer on the ignition device you and your buddies had set up, didn't you? You were going to be outside or away somewhere when the floor caught alight. Was that it?'

Brent looked at his socks.

'This can all stop, Brent. We can stop the whole thing right now. You can go home with your mum. We can find a way to fix things.'

Brent didn't reply.

The interviewing detective checked to Richards who nodded, turning then to indicate Iris. The detective examined her; a quick appraisal. He would be clocking Iris's lack of uniform, noting her age, gender. Three strikes already.

Iris read it all, not offended in the least. She was used to confident young men, their open priorities. She stared back.

Superintendent Richards whispered in the detective's ear. He shrugged, gestured towards Brent, offering him to Iris as though he was lunch.

She moved to the front of the circle. She suspected she would not be given a lot of time. 'Hello, Brent. My name is Iris Foster. I've got a couple of general questions if you don't mind?'

He glanced up, clearly relieved to get a fifty year old woman instead of the tough detective.

'So your full name is?'

'Brent Leon Hughes.' He raised his chin slightly. He liked his name, was used to hearing it said.

Iris turned to the boy's mother. 'Mrs Hughes?'

She seemed startled.

'Sorry you've been brought from work. What do you do?'

'I work in an insurance office, Mrs Foster.'

'How are Brent's grades?'

Momentarily confused, Mrs Hughes answered. 'He could do better in human biology.'

'So he's in year –?'

Brent replied, 'Eleven.'

'Tell me about your dad, Brent.'

'My dad?'

'Yeah, tell me something good and something bad about your dad.'

Brent scanned his audience, defiant again. 'He farts when he's watching TV.'

Iris smiled, went on quickly. 'Name your four best friends.'

'They had nothing to do with this. Or me.'

'We can easily find out, Brent,' said the detective. 'From teachers. From your mobile phone. She's doing a personality test on you. Not solving the crime.'

'Well, yes,' agreed Iris. 'It's kind of a party game, really. So, no thinking. Your four best friends.'

'Chiko, Roosy ... Jane, Frances.'

Brent had paused before Jane, then thrown in Frances too quickly, thought Iris.

'You didn't let me say something good about my dad.'

'You did. Good and bad. You watch TV together. You can joke about him. Your parents love you, Brent.'

Brent appeared embarrassed.

'Thank you for your time.' Iris nodded to Mrs Hughes, then Richards, finally to the detective. The detective and Richards came after her as she stepped away from the interview group.

'You don't think he did it,' said the detective.

'Honestly, I don't think he did. He certainly doesn't tick any boxes on the firelighter scale. He's smart, loved, and socially confident. I suspect he's quite brave too, by the way.'

Richards said, 'You think he's telling the truth.'

The detective interrupted, 'He's not.'

'I think he told the truth about putting out the fire. I think he went under the stage with his girlfriend, Jane. Fooling around.'

Richards said, 'Because?'

The detective thought fast, putting it together. 'Why he took so long to put the fire out yet described it in detail.'

Iris watched him turning over the elements of her theory. She let him own it.

He said, 'Putting his pants back on. Forgot his shoes. Someone else forgot their pantihose. Bagged. Got her out in the confusion.'

'I think he's being loyal. He's probably a bit of a hero.' She shot a look at Superintendent Richards. 'On the other hand, I've been wrong before.'

The detective said, 'No, it all adds up. Good detective work, Mrs Foster.' He actually patted her on the shoulder before striding back towards the boy. 'Brent, the lady just read your mind. I'm going to whisper what she told me and you can decide how far that secret gets shared.'

Brent did not seem eager.

'So, stud, you ready to hear our theory?'

Iris started to make her way towards the open doors of the gym, when Richards caught up with her. Iris said, 'I hope he doesn't say it in front of his mother.'

'He won't. The kid's going to have to tell her eventually.'

'He'll tell his father and leave it to him to pass on.'

'We'll hire you for the counselling. Now, can you prepare a bit of a questionnaire for this lot?' They'd reached the door. Richards pointed to the barely contained mob of students on the oval.

'I can't.'

'Aren't there multiple choice questions?'

'Yes. There are. Superintendent, I don't know whether Brent has helped set the fire, even if he doesn't fit the profile. It wasn't profiling that excluded him. Most of what I discovered came from watching and listening. As you know, it's the pauses. The body language. The little glitches.'

'You can't get that from a questionnaire. All right. So give us one day. Stay and help us find who did this.'

'Superintendent.' Iris could feel herself pleading, hated herself for the weakness, him for pushing.

The superintendent was studying her.

Iris said, 'Ask the teachers. Ask for the withdrawn ones. The non-mixers. Also, the secret snickerers, the nerdy ones who are unloved by their fellows yet act as if they have some special secret. The secret may be their intended revenge. Or it might be a secret from their other life on the internet. Or it might just be they are a fourteen year old boy. Because ninety-nine point nine nine nine will have the fantasies. Including their fantasies about girls. Powerful mixed-up thoughts are not bad deeds.'

'No girls?'

'Soon, I'm sure. I have no current data, Superintendent. Not my field.'

'It's all your field, Iris. Part of your gift. The breadth.'

'Out. Out. Everyone out now!' A technician by the stage shouted.

The fire investigators and forensic police tumbled from beneath the stage like angry ants.

Police began shepherding. 'There are pipes running under the floor. Tanks of chemicals!'

'Don't use your phones. No mobiles. Don't use your phones!'

'Out now. Out!'

They evacuated with haste rather than panic.

Iris became caught in the crowd on the school sports ground, pushed back onto the oval, watching across the asphalt as a fully suited bomb disposal officer tottered into the gym like a fat child learning to walk. Police continued to herd them further back on the grass.

A couple of officers started poking at a garden delivery truck parked out the front of the gymnasium, possibly looking for a way to move it.

The fire crews were back on full alert, running out their hose lines once more. Moving purposefully, assessing where they might direct the water stream. The station officer signalled for one of the appliances to move back. His hands were up, miming a push-back motion, when he was engulfed in the sudden blossom of explosion.

The gymnasium spread in yellow and orange flame from its base, a billowing golden gush, like a big balloon of water bursting with a whoosh of hot air rushing, followed by the grind of brick splitting.

Someone ordered, 'Down!'

Schoolkids, police and Iris were dropping, trying to get under the sweet hot air, the brick fragments rushing towards them. A new silence lasted for a good two seconds before new noises came, scattered cries and moans, joined by sirens. Fire alarms started away in the other school buildings, car alarms began calling from all directions. Iris could hear it all through the ringing in her ears. She gazed up over other heads bobbing up to see two fire appliances burning, the school beyond seemingly untouched. They could see more of the school. The gymnasium had gone. A large pile of bricks smoked whitely with no fire.

Iris caught a flash of red flame. She saw Georgina at the upstairs window, fearful on the other side of the security screen. Iris smelled the nasty plastic smell. She recognised the image of the flashback, of the fire at her old practice. She saw Georgina again, her hair on fire, bashing at the locked window screen. Black smoke billowed from the roof. Iris hadn't moved then. She'd stood watching her secretary burn to death twelve months before. She couldn't seem to move now. Only bend her head down to look away from the burning fire trucks to her hands, to watch the drops of blood falling on them, dribbling into the grass.

Chapter two

Iris sat on a gurney in a corridor. She could hear a dull murmuring, the occasional moan. A doctor examined a girl in school uniform four or five beds down the corridor. A nurse pushed an empty wheelchair in the other direction. Iris stared at an air-conditioning vent near the ceiling when it whirred. She saw her dead secretary Georgina again. It was the earlier fragment, when her hair was not on fire. It was the moment Iris thought Georgina saw her down in the carpark holding her coffee. In the hospital, Iris smoothed down her skirt. She saw a scratch on one leg. She felt for her temple, touching dried blood, which she supposed meant it wasn't a deep cut. Her mind jumped to the school, to the station officer trying to get the fire appliances to move back. He was gesturing with his arms up, like surrender. She searched the gurney for her purse but became distracted by the smear of blood on the pillow.

'The truck,' said a voice.

'What?' Iris looked to the man next to her. He was one of the fire investigators, still dressed in his scene overalls. He sat with his back against the wall in a tiny space between Iris's gurney and the next.

'There was something in the truck, a secondary ignition device.'

'What?'

'I think he was going to back the truck up to the front doors, when everyone was inside. They open outwards. I think the gas cylinders were for later. I think he wanted a slow fire first, with smoke and kids finding all the doors locked, and only once the heat reached a critical point, did he want the whole thing to go. The truck was a failsafe.'

He was in his mid-fifties, overweight, blotchy, balding on top with longish hair at the back. 'You don't recognise me, do you?'

'I'm sorry, no.'

'We've worked similar cases. You're the Fire Lady.'

'No.'

'Yeah, I heard. Sorry.'

Iris stood, shaky at first, having to hold the gurney. She didn't want this conversation. They had taken her shoes.

'They won't believe me,' he said. 'This was him. I found the big zeds down under the stage. I got photographs. They were there, before it all blew.'

'I need to find my handbag. Get to work.'

He stood up with difficulty, putting all his weight onto one leg, grabbing the gurney. He saw her looking. 'No, I didn't get a scratch this time. Old wound. I saw you at the school. I wanted to touch base. Charles Koch. You can call me Chuck.' His hand was out, to shake.

Iris fled down the corridor, where parents were starting to crowd around the lying and walking wounded. Uniformed police were taking statements. Others were sitting in blood-stained clothing. She heard tones of comfort, of teasing, forced laughter. She heard someone say into a phone, 'The burns victims are being sent to St Clement's.'

The foyer was crowded. Mostly school students, with nicks and cuts. Others were dazed, distant, sitting in the waiting-room chairs, or three abreast on more gurneys, the side rails down. They'd be in shock. The television sets in the waiting area showed news from the school. Helicopter shots of the two burnt-out appliances next to the hole where the gymnasium had been. They might want to turn those off, thought Iris. It was too soon for perspective. They would need counselling. A program to move them through the trauma, individual enough to allow for the different resilience or frailty of each child's psychological make-up. They'd all need support, mostly, importantly, from their families. If the fire investigator upstairs was correct, this was not the work of a group of sick kids, which would mean less self-blame. On the other hand, the human mind did not cope well with the random. Until the cause could be discovered and fixed, fear was natural. The mind would try to find ways to connect selected dots. The human mind craved the comforts of cause and effect because it suggested the world was understandable, controllable and therefore safer next time.

The police at the truck would need more support. If they'd accidently set something off, they would need serious rebuilding. Especially the person who told them to investigate the truck. 'I thought ...' 'You thought what?' Blame. There are no accidents, only gross negligence. Someone would need to be blamed, not merely the perpetrator. An American word, perpetrator. Offender. Transgressor. Killer.

The group of people around the booking area was seven deep. Iris wasn't getting her purse any time soon. She considered the dried blood on the back of her hands. She thought of Lady Macbeth, the quote about spots, then considered her own mind striving for the distance of irony. The healthy brain could put layers of ideas and points of view between itself and hurtful things. She took a plastic cup of water from amongst many others on a table, taking a sip before splashing some on her hands, wiped them on her grimy skirt.

Iris went out of the foyer past the arrivals, through parents asking an incident officer how to get to their children. Mildly injured people were still being led into the hospital. Ambulances were still arriving. Kids in wheelchairs, with blankets over their legs, answered roaming doctors and nurses. Two soldiers were in the drive, sending off the empty ambulances, the occasional police car, like an aircraft carrier jumping its jets. Another large press pack was being held way back amidst parked cars. A woman reporter, vaguely familiar, called, 'Iris, what's happening? Give us a comment.' Some cameras swung towards her. Someone called, 'Hey, Fire Lady!'

Iris walked barefooted along the curb of the hospital emergency driveway to the street. Delivery trucks rumbled past. Business folk were purposeful. Shoppers meandered past another line of media vans with satellite uplinks aimed to the sky. She found a taxi. The driver looked Sudanese. Iris didn't ask him about the traumas of civil war or driving taxis in her country. She explained her plan to pick up money, her spare car keys, a pair of shoes, before heading back to the practice to pick up her car. His eyes flicked to her in the rear-view mirror as he drove. Too much information, thought Iris.

According to the radio, the explosion may have been a gas leak, yet police were questioning students about a possible student link to the fire trap. Early reports suggested that no schoolchildren were badly hurt. There were cuts, bruises, very few broken bones. Nine firefighters were dead and two members of the bomb response unit were missing, presumed perished in the explosion. The question was asked as to why people had gone back into the gymnasium after the first evacuation.

Iris didn't listen to the answer. They wouldn't be able to say, yet. She asked that the radio station be changed to something bland without news. She watched lawns being mowed, children being picked up from school. Tradies were packing up. The traffic was building towards peak hour. The local IGA had a special on tomatoes and mangoes.

Iris promised the driver she would not abscond, although he seemed more mollified by her prestigious street address than her assurances. She went round the back to get the spare key from under the pot by the pool. It was nearly four pm according to the oven clock. She wrote a note to Mathew who would have heard about the explosion, but not know her connection. She decided to leave that until later. 'Retrieving the car. Not working late.' She added 'possibly'. She went upstairs to find cash, comfortable shoes, a reasonably stocked handbag. She checked herself in the mirror, deciding she could repair most of her face in the taxi. A headscarf would hide the blood in her hair until she could take a bath. A long bath.

*

There was a parking ticket under the windscreen wiper of her car. Iris left it there. She headed into the practice, thinking she might write up Hannah's case file.

Downstairs were a couple of smaller consulting rooms, various amenities including a largish conference room, cramped kitchen, clerical office, reception alcove. A lone patient still sat in the waiting room, not one of Iris's.

Anna, a severe Dutch matron, looked up from reception as Iris tried to creep up the stairs. 'Iris, you're here.'

Pamela, who did accounts, watched over her narrow glasses.

'Good evening ladies,' said Iris breezily, tramping up the noisy wooden stairs.

'I'll let Patricia know,' Anna called after her.

I wish you wouldn't, thought Iris.

Mary stood up in her island at the end of the waiting room. 'Iris!'

'Mary.'

'Oh, I've just sent the last patient home. Another one is with Gillian. I didn't know ... You were at the school weren't you?'

'They wouldn't let me call. Then I lost my handbag with my phone in it.'

'Was it awful? Was it just awful?'

'But here I am, back. Could you unlock my door? My keys were in my bag too.'

'OMG.' Mary, in her mid-twenties, sometimes spoke like a tweet. She came around with her spare keys.

'I know I've missed the clients and I'm sure you've rearranged things beautifully. I have "thickening letters" to do and I thought I should write up Hannah.'

Mary opened the door. 'You've got a cut, Iris.'

Iris tugged her scarf forward. 'Only a nick. Not even stitches.'

'There's blood on your shirt.'

'I should have changed. All good, Mary. I don't need anything. You're good to go. Night.' Iris stepped into her room, closing the door, before she flicked on the light. It was not her room. It belonged to Dr Irene Chew, a champion of narrative therapy who was currently on sabbatical interstate, collating newly discovered papers from Michael White's estate. Dr Chew's honours degree, doctorate and other qualifications hung on one wall next to an enormous painting of a tranquil sea.

The desk faced the door. Two soft-backed chairs sat before it, one still facing the green couch where Iris had left it in the morning. Behind the couch hung a painting of orange and yellow hibiscus. Irene clearly favoured colourful pictures of neutral representational detail.

In a large, colourful box were children's toys. During counselling, a child could demonstrate certain things using dolls, and secrets might be told to a teddy bear. There was magic in the box too. Wands, fairies, toy cats could witness private victories or help defend against scary things. A toy dog could be named, borrowed to defend against 'the problem', whether it be night terrors or bedwetting or problems with fighting at school.

Iris looked back towards the couch, trying to conjure Donna and Hannah, to return to the morning before 8.55 when the police came for her. She marvelled at the hibiscus painting, how similar the colours were to the moment the gymnasium exploded. Iris imagined the gymnasium superimposed, saw the station officer too, fixed in the frozen time of the painted canvas on the office wall.

That's how Patricia found her, still standing in the middle of the consulting room, when she entered in a flurry of impatient concern and jasmine scent.

'Sit,' commanded Patricia, pointing to the couch.

Iris did, watching Patricia inventory her wounds and dirt.

'Is your head cut, Iris?'

'We were very lucky. Firstly they'd moved us all back, quite a long way. Also, there wasn't much glass. Very few windows. The brick pieces which reached us were all quite small. They'll need trauma counselling. The schoolkids, especially. I should have stayed at the hospital, I suppose. I could go back. I can talk to the relevant hospital staff.' Iris tried to get up, but Patricia laid her hand on her shoulder, pushed her back down onto the couch.

Patricia had strong arms, Iris supposed, from the kayaking. She favoured dresses with lots of colour in ethnic themes – African, South American, Australian Indigenous. Iris tried to focus on the Zulu shields rather than the orange.

Patricia sat down at the other end of the couch. 'So, the doctors have seen you?'

'Yes,' lied Iris.

'Do you want time off?'

'No.'

'Counselling. You need to talk about this.'

'Patricia. It's nothing. I mean, compared to ...'

'Which is exactly why you should talk about this one. To Frank?'

'Okay. Yes, good idea.'

Patricia studied her.

Iris smiled.

Patricia patted her hand.

Iris smiled a real smile. She could see Patricia trying to think of a way to chastise her for being a problem, without saying it.

'When you came to us, Iris,' she finally began, 'what was the plan? What was the journey we decided to embark on?' Patricia was a practising clinical psychologist as well as the manager. Her areas of expertise were relationship counselling and life-potential actualisation.

Iris didn't want to play. Yet she tried. 'I'm sorry, Patricia. I want to work in an area where I can make a difference to people. I want to treat people who are only mildly ill, who can be nudged to a better life. I don't want to be part of the life-and-death stuff anymore. I really want to make this work.'

Iris watched Patricia struggling to stay neutral, her lips tightening ever so slightly at the corners.

'I mean all people's lives are, of course, life and death to them. I do value this opportunity. The sanctuary here, the chance to work ...' Iris stopped. She wouldn't plead. 'You saw what happened. They kind of nabbed me, Patricia. I was dragooned. Shanghaied, kidnapped. I tried to say no, but, you know, it was the police after all. You saw. Talk about flight or fight, I keep trying to flee these guys and they keep dragging me back in.'

Patricia remained grim and focused.

Iris said, 'From their point of view, it was an emergency. Well, from any point of view, as it turned out. They still regard me as useful. Just to give them some quick profiles, but then things ... escalated. As they do sometimes. I explained they can't keep doing this. I explained I don't do that kind of work, any number of times. I was leaving when things really went pear-shaped.' The building did go pear-shaped, thought Iris. It took on the shape of a pear as it began its evaporation.

'Of course.' Patricia squeezed Iris's shoulder. 'I'm sorry, Iris. This isn't about the practice. It's your welfare. This is exactly why you wanted to move away from dangerous work.'

'Yes. Ditto.'

'Will you go home now?'

Iris bowed.

'Will you not come in tomorrow?'

'I have a lot of work. I feel fine, Patricia. I mean, sure, a bit bent out of shape. No worse than a spill on the rapids, I imagine.'

Patricia smiled.

Iris thought she'd finally reached her.

Patricia headed for the door, stopping to say, 'I think it's one of the ways we're different, Iris, and I need to learn to understand. You see, I never go on the rapids. I have enough trouble paddling on the flat stuff. You take care.' She winced, then was gone.

Chapter three

Frank's Jaguar was parked on the front verge outside Iris's house. He was waiting for her on the front step under the movement sensor light, which shone whitely on the veranda.

Frank Silverberg was a rumpled man of sixty-something in a rumpled coat, shirt, corduroys. With his unruly beard he reminded Iris of Francis Ford Coppola. He raised a hand at her, still sitting on the top step.

'Jesus Christ, Frank. Give me a fuckin break.'

'You offend, Iris. Firstly, you reject my concern. You do it by reaching for your firefighter register and swearing at me? You also hit me with Jesus, even though you're not religious and you know I am. Are you angry with me?'

'Can we not do this? I've had a big day.'

'Patricia telephoned.'

'Of course.'

He stood with a great show of effort as Iris went up the steps. Before she could move past he hugged her to his big soft body. She started to pull back but he wouldn't let go so she let her head rest on his chest. She smelled dog and the faint whiff of cigar. The security light timed out and it was dark for a second or two before it switched itself on again when Iris stepped out of the bear hug.

'Not supposed to touch the clients, Frank. Boundaries.'

He gave a hurt look.

She moved away from him to unlock the front door.

'Let's go out and have something to eat,' he said to her back.

Iris punched the security code. 'Come in. Let me get cleaned up.'

She went through to the kitchen, turning on lights. Her note remained untouched on the kitchen bench.

Frank called from the lounge room, 'How's Mathew's campaign going?'

'Campaign?' She could hear glass clinking.

'Process. Ascension? The road to the judiciary.'

Iris poured herself water. Added ice from the ice-maker.

'Slow and steady. A patient game.'

'Can I have some of his good scotch?' he said as he came into the kitchen with a tumbler already filled. He moved past her to get to the ice. 'How's Rosemarie?'

'You know: study study study.'

'Have you called her?'

'Yes.'

Iris went out into the hall.

'You promised me you'd call her, Iris.'

'I will. When there's time. Back soon. I'll get changed.' She headed up the stairs.

He called, 'Yesterday was Sunday!'

Was it? Where had the day gone? Mathew had been playing golf somewhere in the country. She'd been in the garden. She remembered transcribing, writing up casenotes. She recalled television later. A cooking contest program. Hilary Mantel in bed, or was that Saturday?

Iris headed for the ensuite where she considered herself in the mirror. No wonder everyone was so concerned. She looked like she'd been involved in an explosion.

Frank insisted Rosemarie was of an age where her life consumed her. He felt it important for parents, at this time of their selfish children's lives, to have scaffolding still in place, so when they inevitably came back, usually, mostly when they were having children of their own, the lines of communication were still open. Iris recalled being evasive; asking Frank if the lines of communication were attached to the scaffolding, like party lights, perhaps. Frank had a theory about mixed metaphors. He felt they were not only excusable but necessary in a postmodern, multiple media–bombarded world. Or was it multiply mediated? Frank could justify any grammatical error or moral choice. Was the world really, merely, linguistic? A critic referred to narrative therapy as a therapy of literary merit.

Frank had been the one to get her back into narrative therapy, although 'back into' was a bit of a stretch. He had decided she was sufficiently well. 'A job has come up, Iris. I think you might find it amusing. What else are you doing right now?' Recovering? She'd spent months recovering. She had recovered. Frank pressed, 'As I recall, you have done some training in narrative therapy.' Which was true, in her travels, somewhere between her work with post-traumatic stress and hooking up with the fire service, she'd done a month's training and six months as a therapist. 'Hardly expert and far from practised, Frank!' But he knew she was considering it. 'Excellent. There's a psychology practice in the city. The replacement for their resident narrative therapist has fallen through. Decided to trek in Katmandu or raft down the Amazon or some such selfish, sanity-saving, life-threatening nonsense. You meet Patricia in the morning. You'll get on like a house on fire.'

Iris dabbed at her temple. A glancing blow. Her hair was a mess. No. She could not do this.

She went back to the top of the stairs. Frank was sitting at the bottom, on the steps with his back to the wall. He always resembled a discarded cleaning rag.

Iris said, 'We have chairs, Frank.'

'It's a great staircase.'

She didn't go down. 'Listen, I don't have any acute distress. I'm fairly sure I'm not in shock, although I was. Just tired now. A post-adrenalin low. I can't do dinner.'

He nodded, didn't move.

'Frank, in spite of me being a little manic when Patricia saw me, I don't need any help. There's no emergency debriefing to be done. I'm good.'

'You thrive on trauma where others succumb?'

'Apparently.'

'Well, we shall see,' he said, looking down into his empty glass. He stood again with difficulty. 'I'm not here to heal you, Iris. I want to ask a favour.' He gave an odd smile. Slightly chagrined, if Iris were pressed to categorise it along the smile scale. 'Step into my office. I'll have a splash of my best scotch ready for you.'

Iris's shoulders sagged. He wasn't going to go. 'No. Wine. Open a bottle of red. I'll be down.'

Iris took off her shoes, bloody blouse, her bra, her skirt, tossing them into a corner. She would throw them out. She changed into a t-shirt, sloppy windcheater, tracksuit pants. She didn't bother about her hair or her face. Frank had seen her battered before.

Frank liked to flirt, had once seemed to toy with taking it further, against all professional or ethical considerations of course. Iris had never been interested in him in that way. She liked his wife, Janine, and his four children, whom she'd known for life. Frank and Janine held rambling lunches at an enormous table under a jacaranda tree. He had been a colleague and a mentor for a long time before he became her shrink.

Frank had poured the wine. He sat with his glass on the far couch.

'I hope you're not thinking of driving,' she said as she took a look at the bottle. 'Cheeky, very cheeky.'

'Mathew can afford it.'

She took her glass, settled on the other couch, her legs tucked up under, so she could see Frank past the Bailey's Red roses in a vase on the table. He'd switched on a couple of lamps instead of the overhead light, creating a soothing and restful mood.

'So, a favour,' she said guardedly.

'An assessment. A second opinion really.'

'Is this a project to distract me from thinking about today? Or are you going to tell me about this case, while you're really assessing me?'

He smiled. Of course. 'It involves fire.'

'Oh.'

'I know you're not doing that, only ... I'd like your expert second opinion.'

'Not tonight, please.'

'No, not tonight. Recharge your glass and I'll tell you a story.'

'I'm not lying down on the couch.'

'Sitting can work.'

Iris gulped the last of her wine. She poured more, aware he

was waiting until she was ready.

'Two girls.'

'Girls?'

'Our witnesses. Two girls driving towards Candonin on a dark and stormy sunset.'

Iris made a face.

'True. A thunderstorm. Wheeling white cockatoos – like live, angry snow.'

'Are you about to present me with an allegory?'

'Reporting. I've talked to them on the phone.'

'Where's Candonin?'

'It is about nine hundred kilometres from here. Permanent population of nine. Petrol station, caravan park of sorts, motel. At the start or end of ninety kilometres of straight highway, depending on which way you're travelling. Importantly, perhaps, it's very near where Skylab fell from its orbit.

'Our two girls, Ilsa and Helen, are Norwegians. Ilsa is a university student studying here and her friend Helen is a tourist. They were driving across the country, mostly to get to the other side, sightseeing while playing their music loud in their hired Volkswagen. They had been watching a thunderstorm to the south, which appeared to be travelling with them. The clouds were black and lightning flashed, yet on their left, to the north, the sky was clear, sunny. Helen found this particularly surreal.

'He came walking out of the desert, the dark clouds and lightning and a cloud of birds swarming and darting and careering about him. It was as though he'd emerged from a rookery, said one of them, just out of his shell.'

Frank was enjoying himself. His sense of drama. Showing off his excellent memory for the details told to him, the embellishments of his own.

'They stopped. It was strange, this man, walking out of the storm in the desert. No car, no truck, no motorbike nearby. The girls kept interrupting each other at this point to describe him. Mid-thirties but acting younger. Helen felt Anglo-Indian; Ilsa thought Eurasian, smidge of gypsy. Lightly dark; tall, thin. He wore jeans and a white shirt, good walking boots, all dusty. He carried a sports coat and a kind of shoulder bag. Ilsa described him as like a university lecturer, on his way to class. They thought he was younger, the way he walked, until he got close.

'"What are you doing out here?" they asked. "I am looking for my spaceship," he replied. He spoke well. Educated English, Australian accent.'

'Oh,' said Iris, flatly. 'Where's he from?'

'Mars, according to the Norwegian girls,' said Frank.

'Schizophrenia,' said Iris.

'Not so quickly.'

'Schizophrenia and substance abuse.'

'So, the girls think this is funny. He says things with a grin. A sparkle, it's a joke. It's getting dark, coming on for dusk. They give him a ride. They explain they are from Norway. He explains he's from Mars. Ilsa has been in the country for over a year, Helen for only a few months. He has been on Earth for some time. It's a game. They came here by plane, he by spaceship, which crashed. They talk of Norway and snow and skiing and mountains, and he of Mars and heat and aridity. They all talk of the desert and the flatness and the vast horizons and the sunset behind them, where you can see the edge of the Earth.

'The girls talk Norwegian together. The Martian, who says they can call him James, refuses to break out of his "act". Ilsa starts to find it annoying. Helen finds him most amusing. He knows about music, film, popular culture.

'Oh, yes. The girls have a motel room booked at Candonin. More Norwegian. Helen wants him to stay, Ilsa isn't so sure. He may be crazy. An axe-murderer or serial killer or, worse, a boring man. Giggles. Marijuana is smoked, also by James, the Martian. He has money. He buys everyone hamburgers and a bottle of vodka. A party in their room, the three of them. He dances. He's athletic. Like a professional ballet person. He juggles. He juggles a variety of items, starting with fruit. He juggles a knife, fork and a spoon. He throws the knife and it sticks into the edge of a cupboard. This is a butter knife, mind. He does the trick again, juggling the knife, fork and spoon and flicking the knife so it sticks in the side of the cupboard again. Same place.

'He juggles Helen's cigarette lighter, cigarette packet and the car keys. They all begin to make jokes about Earthlings.

It becomes the theme of the night. Earthlings take oxygen for granted. Ilsa swears it is Helen who raises the question of Martian procreation and physiognomy. Helen agrees, it was she who fancied him first. He's quite beautiful, apparently. He has flecks of grey in his hair. Very clear eyes. Brown. Dark. It was light, funny and they all have no clothes on. James has sex with both girls, together.

'The girls are embarrassed to tell this part to the police and to me later. They make the point they did not have sex with each other, but both with him, at the same time, and it was a lot of fun. They are too drunk for orgasms, says Helen. Very nice, says Ilsa. Oh, wow, says Helen. They giggle, over the phone. They are maybe early twenties, these girls.'

Frank waved his hand in an appropriately European gesture.

'He has a strange back. He has strange skin on his back. He says it's where his wings were. Burn scars?'

Iris shrugged a yes.

Frank shrugged agreement. 'They sleep. The girls in the double bed where all the fun had been and James in the single bed also in the room. Each of the girls got up in the middle of the night to pee. All is well, if groggy. At dawn they were awakened by the smoke alarm. It's one of those small plastic ones which gives a piercing uninterrupted squeal. Ilsa wakes first. The room is full of smoke. Acrid smoke from burning plastic. James is fully clothed. He's feeding the fire. He's piled the cane chairs and the table against a cupboard in the kitchen. The furniture is well alight, the fire bending off the ceiling. Ilsa screams, wakes Helen. James is feeding the bedclothes from the single bed to the fire. He's singing something. Like a nursery rhyme. Ilsa grabs shorts and a top. The window in the kitchen pops, a rush of air and heat, everything gushes. Helen is in the bedsheet, they flee. Other guests are coming out of their rooms. The alarm continues.

'A road worker is already up, in his fluoro vest. Goes in, punches James, drags him out. People grab fire extinguishers. Too late. The fire is up into the roof cavity and spreads to the other rooms. James is in a state. He is upset. Perhaps incoherent. "I crashed. I crashed. I couldn't save them. It was a crash. Oh dear. Oh dear." This from other witnesses. Helen and Ilsa are hysterical. "I told you, crazy. Did I say, I said, crazy." '

'They still have not quite forgiven each other. They are resilient, though. Wrong Martian at the wrong time. The police have asked me to take a look at him at Biara tomorrow.' He contemplated his barely touched wine.

Iris said, 'I repeat my assessment. Check him for schizophrenia. Possibly triggered by the alcohol and drugs and whatever else he might have been on. He may have been acting out a psychotic episode – burning the voices in his head? Reliving the burns on his back, or the burns on his back are the result of a prior psychotic episode. You don't need me for this, Frank. You know this already. Anyone can do this, better than me.'

'Well, not better than you. He's not obviously dissociative. He's coherent in his delusion. All by the by. I need to know if he's a pyromaniac.'

Iris watched Frank studying her. She asked, 'Has this got anything to do with the school explosion?'

'It's unlikely.'

'Unlikely?'

'The police think it is possible for him to have travelled this far. They have reason to believe it might have been set up sometime Saturday night into Sunday.'

Iris's glass was empty. She felt numb, sluggish.

Frank stood. 'I think you're ready for this. I'd value your assessment.' He started over towards her.

Iris was up too. She scrambled the other way around the coffee table, keeping it between them. He stopped. He peered through the gloom at her. 'We want to know if this man could have blown up the school gymnasium or if we can cross him off the list.'

Iris was distracted by the roses. A single petal had detached. It lay, deep red on the white marble of the coffee table.

Frank said, 'My mistake, Iris. Rest might be best. Do you need some time off work?'

'No, I need to work.' She met his gaze. 'I was near an accident, Frank, but I was far enough away. It didn't hurt me.'

He studied her. Eventually said, 'Good night, Iris.'

'Thank you for coming, Frank. I do appreciate your concern.'

She waited until she heard the front door close before she collected the glasses and the fallen rose petal. She put the half bottle of very good shiraz on the counter for Mathew and put the note in the kitchen bin. He must not have heard about the school or he would have called. Unless he'd tried her mobile. That's how she'd get her purse. She'd call her mobile in the morning and have it sent to the practice. She retrieved the bottle of wine, took it upstairs, into the shower with her.

Chapter four

Iris woke. Her clock radio showed six-thirty, the news was all school explosion. Eleven dead. Mathew was not in bed although his side had been slept in. Iris felt heavy-headed. Her back was sore. She wondered if it was some kind of referred pain connected to the school explosion or her reaction to it. She found the empty wine bottle in the bathroom bin.

Mathew read the newspapers as he finished his morning smoothie. It had berries, coconut water, protein, yogurt whirred into a delicious violet. He was in his riding gear, blue and black lycra. On Monday he'd take enough suits, shirts, ties into the office so he could ride to work each day when he didn't have a trial on. He had fewer trials now, though. More strategy stuff. He was in pretty good nick for a sixty year old. Lean, muscular, tanned. His hair was dyed a convincing shade of black.

'Good morning,' she said as she went to the fridge to find her smoothie.

'Morning.' He studied her.

She smiled, reassuring. 'What time did you get in?'

'Elevenish. You were zonked.'

'Yes. Whoops.' She would have liked to have said "Frank started it", but this would only make matters worse.

'What have you done to your head?'

He pointed above his own left eyebrow.

Iris reached up to touch the plaster she'd put on. 'Banged into something. Clumsy me.'

'Anything to do with the wine bottle I found in the shower stall?'

Iris sat at the table, unsure about his smile. 'Perhaps. One glass became more than one.'

'Hard day?' He had already gone back to the newspaper. 'There's been an explosion at a school. Did you know?'

'Yes, I knew.' Iris didn't want to reach for the papers. She didn't want to read anything about the school.

'Did you know anyone involved?'

'I expect so,' she said. She saw the station officer signalling, arms up in the flash. She couldn't see his face. She said, 'Will you still be able to read newspapers when you're a judge?'

'What do you mean?'

'Well, you know they don't let juries near the media so they won't be tainted by the false stories.'

'We're hardly in the same category. But no, I'd probably steer away from anything I was presiding over.'

He examined her again. Added one plus one, and got three. 'You mustn't be upset by this. There's nothing you could have done. I'm glad you're out of it. You know that.'

'Yes,' she said, wan smile.

He stood, patted her on the shoulder. She tried to pat his hand but found herself rubbing the shoulder where his hand had been.

'I'd better be off before it gets too hot. Have a good day.'

'Yes. You too.'

Mathew clattered on the tiles in his cycling shoes. She watched him through the French doors, carrying his helmet and backpack around to his racing bike in the garage.

She should have told him about the school.

*

Iris crept into the practice, managing to avoid everyone except Mary. 'Patricia said you weren't coming in.'

'I'm not. I'm not here. Just writing up, Mary.' Iris put her finger to her lips.

Mary retrieved a handbag from a desk drawer and held it out to Iris. 'It came from the hospital.'

Iris shut herself in her office and got to work on Hannah's file. They'd made poor headway, although it had only been the second visit. Neither was compliant in the treatment, she noted.

Hannah resisted telling. Donna resisted giving up control of Hannah. Then, of course, the police had interrupted everything.

Until Iris could convince Hannah to talk about her life with 'the problem' she could not naturally externalise the problem in order to 'beat it'. Iris could see patterns, which wasn't the point. Hannah needed to see the patterns, want better ones she could believe in. An early step was to identify how not eating was a negative. Iris would explore the metaphors she'd read concerning useful approaches to anorexia. It erodes parts of life. It eats away friends and joyful experiences. Anorexia likes to divide families. It likes to isolate. Ed was a bad guy.

On the other hand, Hannah's eating disorder might not be 'the problem'. It might be the result of another problem. At first, Iris thought Hannah was trying to punish her mother, making her dance to Hannah's sickness, triumphing over the over-control or demanding attention from a busy working parent. However, Iris detected an enabler in Donna. Both, perhaps. The two had developed a loop. Hannah might be trying to please her mother. Donna's internal story: Look what I do for you. Hannah: Yes, mummy. Look how I need you. Look how I'm a child. Donna: Naughty, good girl. Be my child.

Further exploration of attachment theory might be useful. Insecurity of both. Hannah had physical health issues as well as her mental causes. Donna had fears for her child and of losing her child. Iris could help these two women. She was sure of it.

If they'd let her. If they came back. They may well decide that the storytelling was not for them. Iris still had trouble trying to sell it to people, even though she thought it could work for Hannah and Donna. Iris had lost patients already since stepping in for Dr Chew. She'd gained some too, especially those seeking help with post-traumatic stress disorder, police and firefighters loyally following her from her previous life to get counselling that had nothing to do with narrative therapy. Perhaps everything was to do with everything.

Next, Iris wrote notes regarding a client who was a retired athlete. He'd lost physical shape, developed a problem with prescription drugs, ones he'd used in competition to help him sleep before big games. He'd become addicted to the drugs, using them now to numb depression as he failed to cope with no longer being famous. In fact they were feeding his depression. Iris had recommended a discreet drug-treatment centre not offered by the practice, and was also working up ideas in which to enter into re-authoring conversations. Iris was confident he could be nudged back on track with his new life, if they could discover what direction he wanted to embark on.

When she heard the knock on the door, she ignored it. The door opened anyway.

'Iris. Thought I saw you sneak in.'

It was Gillian, a particularly loud clinical psych. Gillian had unwieldy red hair, meaty arms that were bare under a black kind of smock. She carried two coffee cups and pushed the door shut with her ample posterior. Her make-up appeared to have been put on by a four year old child who was behind in mastering his scissor skills.

'Brought you a cuppa. No milk. I never asked, but you look like a no-sugar, no-milk kind of gal.' Gillian liked to enter the lunch room saying things like, 'It's a madhouse out there. Absolute bedlam.' Gillian also liked to say, 'The problem isn't the problem. I'm the problem.' Iris thought she did it to annoy the other psychologists. Her specialty was public health, Iris recalled, especially dealing with the families of the mentally ill.

Gillian put one of the mugs down on Iris's desk. She peered at the plaster over Iris's left eyebrow. 'You have pissed off your god mightily, haven't you? Seriously.' Gillian could say exactly the wrong thing for a therapist to say, yet get it, therefore, entirely right.

'Yeah, well, his aim remains sloppy.'

'Him, eh. You sure you're not mindlessly repeating a dominant male-created cultural imperative, sweetie?'

Iris felt her smile strain now. 'I'm fine, Gillian. As I say, he missed again.' Iris held up the report she was working on. 'Well, thanks for the coffee.'

Gillian said, 'I saw Meredith Marsh for you yesterday.'

'Oh yes. Thank you.'

'Um, I wasn't trying to white-ant you. Trying to help with a holding pattern.'

'Thank you, I owe you one.'

'The thing is, she has set up another appointment. With me.'

'Oh.' Iris was shocked. While Iris had inherited Meredith from Dr Chew, she felt she'd been making small progress with her in addressing her shyness, especially in regards to how it affected her in her workplace. She would have thought Gillian was exactly what Meredith did not need.

'You're pissed. I can tell her no.'

'I'm surprised. Fine. Mary will send you the casenotes, I'm sure.'

'I'll make it up to you.'

'No need. Look, I'm really ...' Iris indicated the notes on her desk again.

'You've lost a patient, I'll give you one.'

'Gillian, there's really no need.'

'Me.'

'What?'

'Can I be your patient? Client. Whatever we're calling them, us, me this year.'

Iris blinked at her. 'But Gillian, it wouldn't be appropriate. We're in the same practice. Colleagues. It would be a dual relationship.'

Gillian let her 'hail fellow, well met' smile fade a moment to allow a little truth. 'I really need some help.'

'I'll refer you. Give me some time to come up with someone.'

'Okay. No worries. I'm sorry if I compromised you. I just didn't want a fluffy warm-fuzzy one is all and you seem ... anyway, onward and upward to infinity and beyond. Sorry about Meredith.'

Gillian hustled out, possibly mortified at the rebuff, if anything could mortify her. Iris pondered for a moment how much help Gillian might need.

*

Later Iris drove to Biara Prison to visit one of her more troubling clients.

Lisa and Kimberly had attended the practice during Iris's first week of replacing Dr Chew. Seven year old Kimberly was exhibiting troubling personality changes. A sudden return to bedwetting, trouble sleeping, reversal of good school results and disruptive behaviours in the schoolyard. Her regressions and the acting out could arise from many causes, so Iris sat on the couch with Lisa, asking questions while Kimberly emptied the toy box.

It transpired Kimberly's grandmother was sick and Lisa was spending extra time helping with her mother's care.

Iris thought she'd start there. 'Kimberly, tell me about your grandmother.'

'She's sick.' The child kept playing with the doll, pushing it into the rug.

'Do you help Mum look after your grandmother?'

'I stay home.'

'You often come with me. We take her dinner, don't we?'

'I stay home.' She was staring at the floor.

Lisa shook her head.

Iris began to think of ways she might approach the child's fears about her grandmother's sickness, perhaps ask what she most liked or disliked about visiting her grandmother.

The girl said, 'I help Daddy.'

'Good girl, Kimberly. Do you help him cook dinner?'

'I'm his nurse.'

'Are you your grandmother's nurse too?'

'They're not home. They're away. It's just us.' Kimberly was intent on the rag doll she'd lain on the floor.

Lisa said, 'Darling, you come most times. Only not when it's too late on a school night.'

Iris watched what Kimberly was doing with the doll, the way her finger was rubbing between the doll's legs. She felt a chill. She knew her next questions must be carefully done. She must not lead and she must not plant and she must not hurt innocent, loving relationships. She made sure her tone was light with no implication of blame.

'What do you help Daddy do?'

'It's a secret.'

'Do you have lots of secrets?'

'What are you doing?' asked Lisa.

'Are there secrets you can tell? That you can tell your mum?'

Lisa looked from Iris to Kimberly, concerned but not alarmed.

'No. Specially not.' Defiance again. Anger directed towards her mother.

Iris laid her hand on Lisa's arm. 'Has your mum been bad?'

'Daddy says she won't do it, so I have to.'

'Do what?'

Kimberly was struggling with the images in her head and promises she'd made. She wanted to tell, yet she was miserably compromised by counter-instructions and deep confusions.

'This is ridiculous,' said Lisa standing.

'I want to go home,' said Kimberly, also standing.

'You're putting disgusting ideas into her head,' shouted Lisa.

Kimberly howled, 'Something bad is going to happen. I said don't come.' She started to cry and her mother rushed to her.

'Mrs Fitzmorris, I'm sorry. I have certain doubts. They really need to be investigated. I have no option. I must inform ...'

'Stop it. We came here for your help. You're being crazy.'

Iris opened the door to the waiting room and called, 'Mary, do we have a GP here today?'

'You mustn't tell,' screamed Kimberly.

'Kimberly, what are you doing?' said Lisa in alarm.

Iris turned to see Lisa step back as Kimberly stood on the mat, wetting herself. She stared down at the spreading wet patch and the urine dribbling down her legs. 'You mustn't tell.'

Iris did tell. There was no choice. She was legally bound to notify authorities. Like all health people, her first duty was to protect the child. Above all else, protect the child.

Patricia convinced Lisa to have the health check, merely as a precaution. She assured Lisa it was probably nothing. The medical examination found evidence of sexual activity: bruising and thrush around Kimberly's genitals and her mouth. It set in train a series of procedures which included alerting Child Protection. They convinced Kimberly to give up her secret about cleaning Daddy's dingle till it squirted. The police became involved and Kimberly's father was charged and remanded to Biara Prison. His name was Rodney.

Lisa and Kimberly discharged Iris's services immediately. Clearly, Lisa felt betrayed by her. She continued to believe her family had been ambushed and was not yet ready to believe Rodney's guilt. Then Rodney engaged Iris. The logic of this continued to give Iris considerable pause.

*

The last visitors of the day were leaving the carpark when Iris arrived at Biara. A woman and two children in their Sunday best, handmade and over-washed, were getting into a faded Cortina. Two men with big beards climbed into a massive green Dodge. Prison carparks were strained, desolate places, hope overcome by the dry, dull glare of another hot afternoon.

Iris showed her card and was buzzed in. She sat, was moved forward, sat again.

Iris suspected Rodney's plan was to win her over somehow and somehow (Rodney was a long-term thinker) persuade her not to testify against him. After much discussion with Frank, amongst others, Iris's plan was to turn Rodney into a decent human being.

So far, Rodney had mostly refused to take responsibility for his actions. Iris had been trying to work with Rodney on breaking down the stories he told himself to justify his abuse of Kimberly. She had been attempting to get him to admit to himself that the sexual acts with his seven year old daughter were not reciprocal or appropriate. The behaviour was not justified or excusable, with awful consequences for his child.

'I looked after them. I looked after Kimberly and Lisa and Lisa's mum. Nothing was too good for them. You know that don't you.' This is a story male abusers tell themselves. The Father Christmas story.

'Lisa was being a bitch. Once her mum got sick, I'm cut off. "I'm looking after my mum so you can get stuffed." After all I've done.' This is the Wicked Witch story.

'Kimberly. She started, you know, kind of coming on to me. In a basic way she was flirting and wriggling.' Lolita.

'It wasn't even sex, per se. You know. Affection. We were both lonely. We both needed affection. A cuddle that went too far.' Denial. Projection.

Iris worked hard to establish empathy, not for Rodney, but on Rodney's part towards his child.

Iris could get Rodney to the threshold of accepting re-sponsibility for the awfulness of his actions, but at the doorway he'd slip away again, discover and practise new excuses for the next visit, as though it was merely an argument, one he hadn't quite mastered yet. The minimising, denying, justifying, blaming, deflecting, avoiding, false appeasing and negotiating seemed endless.

Iris was keyed through another door at Biara to the visitors room gate.

'Rodney Fitzmorris,' said Iris, showing her credentials again and a copy of an email the prison medical officer had organised.

The prison guard checked an authorisation list then telephoned. She came back carrying a clipboard. 'Bringing him over from Special Wing.'

Iris was surprised. Rodney had been within the general population.

'Are you aware of a prisoner awaiting psychiatric assessment?' she said. 'Picked up in Candonin?'

'The death-ray Martian.'

'Maybe. Death ray?'

'He's already set fire to a cell. Apparently, on his way down from Candonin, he set fire to the police van as well. I hear he death-rayed a whole motel complex in the desert. If you want to see him, he's locked in the Crisis Centre.'

'Oh, I don't have permission.'

She waved the clipboard at Iris. 'Yes you do. Says you're going to assess him in the next couple of days.'

'What? Who?'

'Dr Frank Silverberg and Iris Foster. Assessment of prisoner on remand.'

Son of a bitch, thought Iris. Frank had made assumptions. Iris was annoyed he'd read her so easily.

'Don't piss him off,' said the prison officer.

'What?'

'He'll zap you with his death ray.' A joke. She was joking.

*

Iris was shown into the visitor's room. It was empty but not yet cleaned. It smelled of male sweat and crisps. A birthday card lay on one of the tables.

The door was unlocked, Rodney shown in. He was in prison greens, about thirty, and soft around the face with dark curly hair.

'I've been sent to Special Wing.'

'Hello Rodney.'

'Some big bloke came up in the yard. I'm gonna get bashed.' He remained standing. 'I'm no paedophile and they got me in with the rock spiders. I'm a marked man in here.'

'It's to keep you safe.'

'You gotta get me out.'

'Not in my power.'

He sat down in the chair opposite Iris. He said, 'Lisa has dropped the charges.'

'She didn't charge you.'

'Kimberly. Kimberly was mistaken.'

'I thought we were working on that, mate. I thought we were taking responsibility.'

'But if she doesn't give evidence ...'

'It would hurt her, Rodney.'

'I'd make it up to her. See, I get the empathy. I'd see her right.'

'I would never support that.'

Rodney stood again.

Iris stood too, stepped back from her chair.

The guard inside the door took a step towards them. He was young and not so big.

Rodney said, 'How can there be charges if there's no witnesses?'

'There are. The police, Child Protection, the GP and me. We're all witnesses. You too, Rodney. You're the main witness to this.'

He banged the table.

The guard came all the way forward, 'Settle down, sport.'

'Fuckin Lisa shouldn't have taken her. You fuckin dykes got into their heads. They'll do me in here.'

'I know you're angry, Rodney, and I know you're scared, but let's think about Kimberly.'

'Can we think about me for a sec? How about that?' he

demanded. He glared at Iris, his fists bunching. 'You're supposed to be helping me!'

Iris edged back casually to put the table between them. The guard tapped Rodney's shoulder, stepping back before Rodney could turn. His feet were balanced. 'You are out of order. Lock-up time.'

Rodney glanced at him. Calmed, his head dropping. 'Right, right man. Sorry. Getting stitched up here.' He raised his hands showing surrender, compliant. Then he pointed at Iris. 'You put me in here. You get me out.' He allowed himself to be led towards the door.

The guard paused there, looking back to Iris.

She shook her head. No trouble. No report. No progress either.

*

Two guards led Iris to the Crisis Centre. She walked across an inner yard, ignoring a distant derisive catcall. It would be dinnertime soon, followed by the long night of prison. A gate was unlocked and relocked. A white door. A white corridor.

The Crisis Centre only had eight beds. It was a secure hospital-like ward which held potential self-harmers and successful self-harmers. Those who harmed others populated other parts of the prison and those particularly vulnerable to those men were held within another protective area. Iris passed a young man with bandages on his wrists. Someone was calling, plaintive, pained. One wall of the cells was open plexiglas, each with a closed-circuit camera. The toilets were visible with non-moving seats. Everything was fixed with rounded edges. Table, bed, toilet. Iris paused at a cell where a man in his thirties sat on his bunk growling to no one, 'Leave it. Leave it now. Leave it.' A schizophrenic not taking his medication, in need of a bed somewhere other than in a prison.

The statistics suggested one quarter of the prison population suffered from a diagnosed mental condition. This was besides those with personality disorders: the narcissists, borderlines and sociopaths. This was before they came to prison. Then you could add depression, anxiety and growing feelings of powerlessness. Followed by drug abuse and violence and enormous amounts of empty time.

Halfway down, they came to an Anglo-Indian. He was dressed in prison greens, his left arm bandaged.

He sat on his bunk with his feet on the floor of the cell. Iris detected the barest hint of rocking. He turned to her, when he sensed she wasn't moving on. He stood and bent slightly in a bow.

Iris stepped to the small round communication holes in the plexiglas. '

Hello,' said Iris, 'My name is Iris Foster. What's yours?'

'James. You can call me James.' His accent sounded Australian.

'Glad to meet you, James.'

'Really?'

'Do you know what day it is, James?'

'Let me see. A lot has happened in a short space of time. We travelled for a day. Some locking up and locking down. Is it Tuesday?'

'Yes.'

'Afternoon, nearly evening because I can smell food coming. I don't watch the news, I'm sorry, so current affairs won't be a useful topic. Can I choose astronomy for double points?'

'Have you been psychiatrically assessed before, James?'

'You remind me of an actress.'

'Oh.'

'Jodie Foster.'

'Why do I remind you of her?'

'You look like her. The hair, your face. Your figure. Jodie Foster.'

'My surname too?'

'What?'

'Foster. Iris Foster.'

'Oh, sorry.' He seemed momentarily uncomfortable, but recovered his grin. 'Hmm, that was probably the big clue.'

'She was in *Silence of the Lambs*, wasn't she?'

'Yes, she was.'

'Would you have a part in the film?'

'I'm not an actor.'

Well, he wasn't barking. Perhaps with elevated happiness

given his circumstances. Even charming. His thinking seemed ordered if slightly vague. It felt like he was playing games though. An ironic vibe.

'Do you hear voices, James?'

'Yes.'

'Oh.'

'I hear yours. I can hear murmuring. One of my neighbours is having a bad time. He's hearing voices, I suspect. Those two guards are talking world soccer.'

'Why do you light fires?'

He didn't answer. His shrug might have been apologetic.

'Tell me about fire, James.'

'It's not good. Terrible. Destructive things, fires. Heat.'

Iris felt James was reflexive about the fire, rote, expected replies, which were also disjointed. She watched his face, subtly contorting with an inner demon perhaps. He beat it down, and gave her his attention once more.

'What's your surname?' she asked.

'I don't have one. Are you angry with me, Iris?'

'Where are you from?'

'You won't answer my question.'

'I was asking.'

'Vee vill ask zee questions.'

'Where are you from?'

'Mars.'

Iris didn't say anything.

He smiled, embarrassed, 'I should answer differently. It always causes such problems.'

'You appear so human.'

'Yes. Everyone says that.' He stood quite still. His hands were clasped before him.

The Norwegian girls had described him as quite beautiful, Iris recalled. 'You know a lot about Earth. *The Silence of the Lambs*, for instance.'

'Yes. I've been here for a while. Jodie Foster was also in a film called *Contact*.'

'I haven't seen it.'

'Oh.'

'What's it about?'

'She discovers aliens.'

'Ha ha. Really?'

He grimaced.

'Do you really think you are a Martian, or is it a kind of joke?'

'No joke.'

'A little bit?'

'I understand you think it's weird.'

'Have you always been a Martian?'

'Yes.'

'Are there times, were there any times, when you wonder if the whole thing seems a bit "unreal", like a dream?

'Yes. Lots of the time. Do you ever feel like that?'

'You're educated.'

'What does educated mean, really?'

'Yes. You're right. I've heard you can throw knives, juggle.'

'Would you like me to show you? The juggling, I mean. Have you got items in your purse?'

'A lighter?'

'Oh.' He appeared shamefaced.

'Do you remember the girls in Candonin?'

'Where is that?'

'In the desert, I think.'

'Ahh.' It meant something to him.

'Do you remember you were brought here by policemen?'

'Yes, I was in the back.'

'There was a fire.'

'Yes.'

'Did you want to escape?'

'I had to get out.' James walked away from the glass, sitting again on the bunk.

'How was there a fire?'

'I crashed. I crashed, we crashed. They were shouting.'

Iris leaned closer to the communication holes to hear him properly. 'Do you remember the school, James?'

'I have to get back to them. Get them out.'

'At the school?'

'At the crash. There was a crash.'

'Did you hurt your arm in the crash?'

'Yes, there was fire.'

'Yet, you said you crashed a while ago. James, you told me you crashed some time ago.'

He considered his bandaged arm, blinked at it. He looked up at Iris, smiling. 'I get confused. It can be very confusing on your planet.'

'Yes, it can.'

Chapter five

Iris went straight to her home office. She and Mathew both had offices on the ground floor. Mathew's was moderately spartan. Huge desk. Wall of law books. A rug, a single reading chair under the window. Iris joked that Mathew's home office was modelled on the Third Reich. Space as power. Mathew didn't like the joke. He called her office 'the junk shop'.

Iris's office was cluttered. It had been her workplace at one point. Clients had been able to come around the side of the house, entering directly through the French doors. There was a comfortable couch, other lounge chairs. She still used the wooden filing cabinets to hold the few files she was working on from the practice.

Her office was full of relics. A large painting of a bushfire was on one wall, painted by a child. A battered brass fire-extinguisher sat in a corner, a gift on Iris's departure from the fire service. Iris still had pictures done by Rosemarie. They charted her life from barely recognisable faces and stick figures all the way to a couple of paintings from Rosemarie's high school art class. They were all framed, scattered about the walls and cabinets. There was a stethoscope and a microscope in a wooden box, both once owned by her father. A couple of his history books were in the bookcase.

It was the butterflies, however, which dominated. Framed display cases filled the walls. A smaller frame held a purple Lycaeides melissa, another a sole red-banded jezebel. Twenty blue morphos were arranged in a deep wooden frame. Another contained a spiral arrangement of different sized monarchs.

Ulysses swallowtails were everywhere, the blue and the green, also the darker Mexican ones with black dots. Once the family discovered Iris's fascination with butterflies, it became a default gift. The office had never been restful. It positively pulsed with detail and colour.

Iris opened her laptop to her file on Francesca Garbello. It was time to write a letter acknowledging the breakthrough of the recent visit. Francesca had been raped. Her husband was at work, her children inside the house. Francesca was unloading shopping from the car, which was in the garage. She hadn't closed the garage doors yet. He grabbed her from behind, pushing her face down on the back seat of the family car.

In spite of physical injuries, Francesca tried to keep the rape a secret. Her husband, Carlo, noticed certain of the symptoms, and assumed he had done something to upset her. When he attempted lovemaking, Francesca broke down and told of the assault.

The identification of post-traumatic stress in war veterans in the 70s led to the discovery of many of the same symptoms in rape victims. Indeed, the trauma, loss of power, assault on identity and benevolent world unity were common. Sleep problems, self-blame, anxiety, depression, bipolar, substance abuse and flashbacks were found to be common features in a number of soldiers and many rape victims.

Studies showed that in the first seventy-two hours after a rape, distress was acute. Ninety-four per cent of victims exhibited PTSD symptoms at two weeks, falling to sixty-four per cent at one month, and fifty per cent at three months. Fifty per cent of rape victims can self-heal after three months. For a variety of interlocking reasons, as in unaffected soldiers, these people are resilient enough to mend unassisted. However, the other half-need help. Trauma shatters the sense of self. It breaks the sense of personal autonomy, safety and justice. It also breaches attachments to family and society. Relationships suffer. Social support was essential for recovery.

Francesca, at her husband's insistence, had gone to Dr Chew a year before for cognitive behavioural therapy. Dr Chew began therapy at first with Francesca, subsequently with Francesca and Carlo. Dr Chew's files revealed she had been particularly sensitive to the cultural factors which might aid or inhibit Francesca's recovery. Whilst not a virgin when she married Carlo, Francesca had been with few partners; she counted fidelity as a central tenet of marriage, as did Carlo. Francesca felt she was now dirty, used goods. Her husband would never forgive her for her (unwilling) infidelity. Carlo felt he had not been a man, failed to protect his family. They were both filled with anger because they had not identified or exacted revenge on the rapist who seemed to have escaped completely. Certain of these attitudes were societal ideals, others were bound by gender stories. Dr Chew had unpicked some of these.

She had also explored their family and relationship concepts based on their heritage as traditional Italian Roman Catholics. God's justice was respected and they were persuaded to talk to a priest about these matters. However, the potential 'shame' from wider family was so heavily feared they had decided not to tell their respective families, even though both Dr Chew and later Iris continued discussions concerning which members of their families would understand their pain, would want to help them. Long term, eventually, it might be important to have other family members bear witness to their trauma.

Narratives of self-blame were also evident. Dr Chew was clearly focusing on these with Francesca and Carlo. Of course, Carlo had to go to work. He could not stay at home all the time. Yes, maybe Francesca might have closed the garage door before getting out of the car, which she now did (albeit in a different car). They'd sold the other car, moved houses. She did have to go shopping. She might have gone to the police and therefore obtained DNA evidence. This evidence may or may not have caught the culprit. Many people do not report rape. Francesca felt it would be like being assaulted again, by doctors, or by having her shame paraded to the world. It was also natural for Francesca to want to try to wash the dirt from her body, to want to crawl away – not to die, to recover.

Dr Chew had worked with them both concerning the negative self-narrative around Francesca's perceived failure to fight back. She had fought. She had protected her children through her actions of compliance in a situation beyond her control. She continued to fight back, in recovering, in remaining strong for her husband and children.

In their new life, they phoned each other a couple of times a day. Francesca was no longer hypervigilant or numbed. Her drinking was down to one glass of wine with dinner. She no longer experienced flashbacks of the assault, except when she and Carlo attempted intercourse. The specific stimuli surrounding imminent penetration caused Francesca panic attacks in which she couldn't breathe and felt imagined pain. Iris was helping them with their lovemaking. It was time to highlight how far they had come in a therapeutic letter.

> *Dear Francesca and Carlo,*
>
> *I am writing this letter to congratulate you both on the amazing journey you've shared with me. My intention here is to celebrate with you how far you have both come and to remind you about how strong and loving you are. I hope you might be able to refer to this letter in the future, should the snake start to try to sneak back into your lives from time to time (as we agreed, mainly when you are tired or feeling insecure).*

*

Iris heard Mathew come in around six, but she kept working on the letter. She wanted to bring in the phrase 'feed the love, starve the fear'. She also wanted to highlight Carlo's patience in his wife's recovery as a sign of their ongoing commitment to each other.

She might finish before she got ready for the dinner. It was an important law society do. Round tables of husbands and wives in black tie, ball gowns. It was a fundraiser for multiple sclerosis, also a see-and-be-seen affair. Networking. Weaving. Mathew Foster, charming, judicial.

The practice of law, of course, was boring. It was clerical, fernickety, time-consuming. It was an occupation of margins, of reducing risk, of exploiting increments. Except when one of them had a high-profile court case, although they were not supposed to share, especially at such events.

A couple of wives were friends outside the office and they compared children's tales that soon became too specific, too prolonged and too self-referential. Many of the men in the office went cycling together, which was a difficult conversation to join. Two of the lawyer's partners were interesting. Jacinta's husband, Thomas, was in education at the university, often provocative. Roland's wife, June, was an arts administrator, always very witty about visiting actors and drunk artists.

At six thirty, Mathew appeared at Iris's office door, already dressed in his tuxedo.

'Oh,' said Iris peering at him past the glare of her desk lamp. 'I'll get ready. I thought we were leaving at seven thirty.' She stood.

'I thought I'd go in early for drinks.'

'Right. Well, all right. Shall I meet you at the do?'

'You hate these things.'

'I said I would. It's important.' Iris went to him, touched his arm. He was wearing the cologne Iris had bought him last Christmas, lavender and sandalwood mixed with his own body smell.

'You have a lot on your plate. You can sit this one out. All good. Free pass.' He patted her on the shoulder, kissed her cheek, before turning away.

Iris said, 'Mathew, I'm fine to go. I can catch up with June on which plays to see this summer. I'll meet you there.'

'Don't.'

'What?'

He sighed. 'Strategically ... Conservatively speaking, it's important they see me as ...'

'Married?'

'Well, that they see me, for a start.' He'd taken the bait, didn't like her flippancy, even though it was a defence against hurt. 'It sounds childish, jealous, and it's not. They'll want you. They'll want to talk to you about this high school gymnasium business. Your theories. Your contacts.'

It was time to come clean. To tell Mathew she'd been there, at the school, when it blew up. When the station officer was erased.

Iris said, 'And it should be about you.'

He searched her face for intent.

'I mean it. Strategically, you need to be front and centre.' Iris smiled, intending encouragement.

A car horn, taxi or friend, beeped outside, on cue.

Iris grimaced.

'I want you to understand. It's ...'

'Nothing personal?'

He grimaced.

Iris said, 'I'm sorry, I do understand, Mathew. You're right. It will probably go better without me, but I am hurt.'

He scrutinised her. He wasn't a bad man. He came back, his hand gently clasped the back of her head and he kissed her quickly on the lips. Her right hand held his hip.

'Thank you,' he said. 'I'll make it up to you.'

The cologne was called Passion. It was *by* Elizabeth Taylor not for her, she'd explained, when she'd given it to him.

*

Iris changed into her gym gear, pounded out twenty minutes on the running machine in the gym room while she watched the news.

The school explosion led the bulletin, and cascaded into related stories. Most of the visuals were from mobile phones, repeating portions of the explosion, recorded from a variety of angles. A news camera was behind the fire appliances. It caught the digital flash of white before the camera went blank. General interviews with the police followed. Confirming it was not a gas explosion. There were no suspects yet. Experts were asked about terrorists. Old stories about American school massacres were repackaged. The Arson Squad was not revealing details of what they'd found under the gymnasium. There was an interview with the Fire and Rescue Service commissioner, with an overlay of women, grieving. They might be firefighters' wives, although the service usually shielded the families from the media. Rounding out the gymnasium explosion special was a civil liberties story about the confiscation of the students' phones, the subsequent scouring of student computers and Facebook accounts for clues.

In other news, bushfires were doused. The fires had been discovered early. Iris thought the pattern fitted a fire recidivist at work. Iris missed the old tag of firebug, but conceded it lacked enough censure. Overseas, people continued to kill each other, to topple governments, rape children, blow up women shopping in markets, murder young people at concerts.

She went to the fridge for water. The salads were dark or limp. She threw them in the bin. She couldn't face a Lean Cuisine. She pulled out a container of carbonara sauce, found frozen fettuccine. She put water on to boil.

She thought she would ring Rosemarie, although the time difference might make it too late on a weeknight, too interrupting and strained while Rosemarie sat at a pub or library raising her eyebrows at whoever she was with, while her mother made small talk.

She rang Frank's mobile. He didn't pick up. Moments after she rang off she could hear her own mobile ringing in her handbag.

Frank.

'At dinner. I missed your call.'

'Sorry.'

'Well? Is he our man?'

'How did he hurt his arm?'

'The motel fire, I believe. Apparently, they were onto him pretty quickly in the divvy van and in his prison cell.'

'How does he get matches?'

'As far as I can tell, he picks pockets. Pending more police reports.'

'Has he been tested for drugs, alcohol-induced psychosis?'

'Laboratory tests are being processed. He seems sharp, focused.'

'Yes. And non-aggressive, apart from the firelighting.'

'Yes.'

'Have the police examined his belongings?'

'I'm sure they will, Iris, if they are not already. They are checking for his fingerprints, as is police procedure. You're stalling.'

'I don't know.'

'What?'

'I don't know if he's faking. He is disorganised in his thinking. He may have a psychosis or he may be faking it. He's smart, educated – winning. Soft. Very troubled.'

'Could he have done the school?'

'I don't know.'

'Hmm. All right. Anyway, a bed has come up at Fieldhaven. I'm going to have him moved to a secure room in Park Wing. I'll put him on a neuroleptic, see if he responds, once toxicology comes back and I know if there's anything else in his system.'

'I'm not sure he's schizophrenic.'

'I can find that out, given time.'

'Don't drug him.'

Frank didn't say anything.

The swimming pool light came on. The pool shimmered blue in a breeze. Iris noticed her reflection on the window: Iris holding the phone.

Frank finally said, 'So you are going to take another crack at him?'

'Yes.'

More silence.

'So do you want to talk about the school yet?'

'The flashbacks of Georgina and the fire at my old practice have returned. I'm also getting flashes of the station officer. I was looking at him when ... He was trying to order the pumpers to back up when he was ... vaporised. Although I closed my eyes, I see two fire appliances burning. It was on the news.'

'How awful, Iris. Shall we meet?'

'No.'

'Any other symptoms of distress?'

'Just the usual. On a scale of anxiety pain of one to ten, I'm down at a three.'

'Ah, lower than the rest of us.'

'Hmmm. Except the rest of you are all self-medicated.'

'Do you need something to sleep? I think you were on Triazolam ... after the fire at your practice.'

'No. I want to work.'

'We probably need to discuss whether that's a good idea.

Whether this is a new problem.'

    'It's not a problem. When it was, I took time off. Now it's not.'

    'Are you sleeping?'

    'Yes.'

    'Tell me, Iris. Do you blame yourself for this school fire?'

    'How could I possibly ...?'

    'Exactly. Good. The first fire wasn't your fault either.'

    'Goodnight, Frank. Don't put him on anything.'

Chapter six

In the morning, Iris rang Mathew before she left for the practice.

'Good morning.'

'Morning, Mathew.'

'I'm sorry, I should have left a message. I stayed until stumps. Came back to the office and dossed on the stretcher in the sick room.'

'I supposed. It went well?'

'So hard to tell. Everyone important is still my friend or so it seems.' He paused, or was reading something at the other end. 'Everyone asked after you.'

'Good. Maybe next time.'

'Yes. Okay, well, onwards and upwards, once more into the breach.'

Iris rang Mary at the practice. 'I'll be out at Fieldhaven this morning, Mary, assessing a patient for the police.'

'Dr Hampton is trying to get in.'

Paul Hampton was a veterinary surgeon with drinking problems, one of the first patients to come to her at the practice who was not a Dr Chew leftover. He was a difficult narcissist and one of the patients she liked least.

'I thought I had today clear. Can you put him off?'

'I have. He's been trying since yesterday.'

'Okay. Afternoon.'

*

Park Wing was a maximum-security complex within the Fieldhaven psychiatric facility. Although Fieldhaven's remit was to assess, treat, rehabilitate and resocialise the mentally ill, most of the patients in Park Wing were referred by the courts or prison system. Its thirty beds were in high rotation. No one could park in Park for very long. It was the pointy end of mental health care where the failures were locked up after they had erupted into crisis with often catastrophic results to the patient or those nearest to them.

The only reason James had a place was because of the high priority the police placed on him as a suspect in the school bombing. Whether James was the school bomber or not, he was dangerous. His compulsive firelighting made monitoring in a safe cell vital. He needed to be isolated from other prisoners who had access to cigarette lighting items. By all accounts, he probably should not be given knives either.

Iris elected to see him in a secure interview room. He was escorted by a psych nurse into the room where Iris sat at a fixed table.

He brightened when he saw her.

'Jodie Foster.'

'No.'

'It was a joke, Iris Foster. Not a mad thing.' He grinned, slightly apologetic.

The psych nurse handcuffed him to an eyelet set in the table. He was compliant. Said, 'Thanks, Brad.'

Brad retreated to the corner of the room, but stayed standing.

'Yet, here you are, James.'

She indicated the room. His handcuffs.

He seemed pained, not so much at the predicament, but at her lack of tact.

Iris said, 'Why do you think that is, James? Why do you suppose people think you are mad?'

'I thought it was still under investigation. Dr Silverberg and you and the psychiatrists here. You're trying to work that out, aren't you?'

'Do you think people are taken randomly off the streets?'

'I'm not sure. It's possible. An awful lot of sick people are walking the streets, mumbling on buses. It's a conspiracy theory worth exploring. At least worth a TV series. I'll share the writing credits with you, Iris.'

'Can you think of nothing which might have led to your current ... predicament?'

'Ah. Yes. The fires.'

'Yes?'

He allowed himself to remember the fires, to look at them again. His lips moved as though he were praying or searching for words. He blinked rapidly, shook his head, to finally look up at Iris, as though by surprise. 'Maybe Earth people do this to all the Martians they find.'

'Tell me about being a Martian, James.'

'Tell me about being a human, Iris.'

'Sure. I live on Earth. You might call me an Earthling. My planet has large amounts of water. We humans live on land. There are fish in the sea and birds in the air and lots of plants which produce oxygen. Humans breathe oxygen with our lungs. We have gravity. We walk on two legs. We have opposable thumbs, which means we can hold things. Important for juggling, I'd imagine.'

'Not really. Not as important as you might think.'

'For picking pockets?'

'Again, not like you'd think. These two fingers are longer and together.' He waggled his free hand. 'That's more misdirection.'

'Can you see Earth from Mars?'

'Yes. We have telescopes, antennas. We can watch your television.'

'How convenient.'

'Well, a poisoned chalice, surely.'

Iris smiled.

He laughed.

Iris brought herself back to task. 'Why haven't we seen you?'

'We live underground, Iris.'

Iris scowled.

'It's bloody hot, Iris. The red planet.'

'It's not red.'

'Ha. Good. No, it looks red because of the iron. It's not very hot. It's very cold because we are further away from the sun than you. Did you know Mars only gets forty-three per cent of the sunlight Earth gets?'

'I didn't know. I imagine I could google it though.'

He was disappointed in her again. Perhaps for not playing. 'I'm sure you could.'

'So, why do you live underground?'

'Well, it's cold, but mostly because the atmosphere is thinning. We get pounded by asteroids, the surface water has gone, the dust storms are pretty bad. A great place for an adventure holiday.'

Iris made notes. She suspected they could bat around Mars facts all day. Of more importance was the coherence of his fantasy buttressed by these external facts. It appeared well practised. Maybe he'd been making his way with this act for quite some time – a good gypsy trick. A bit of juggling. A tale told. A pocket picked.

'You can put down that the surface slowly became too harsh so we gradually moved underground over centuries long ago.'

'Before we developed telescopes or launched space probes.'

'If you want to be Earth-centric. Such a backward people.'

Iris smiled, but didn't lose momentum. 'Yet you like us, don't you?'

James blinked, slightly off balance.

'You like talking to me.'

'Yes, very much Iris.' He batted his eyelashes, overdoing dainty.

'Those girls you met in Candonin. You liked them. They liked you.' Iris watched him carefully as she spoke. 'They were young, attractive women by all accounts.'

'Yes. And fun. They wanted fun. Fun is good, don't you think, Iris Foster with the sad smile?'

'Fun is good. What is bad?'

'Sugar is good. I like sugar. Yum.'

'Actually, sugar is bad for the human body. Rots the teeth. Adds the calories. White death.'

'Refined sugar.'

'Is fire good or bad?'

He paused but this time he didn't let himself imagine the fire, whatever the fire was to him. Instead he grappled with her question, considered it seriously. He stared up at her, then away, still thinking on it. 'I think fire is neither good nor bad. It has no conscience, you see. It goes where the food is, and it eats. It warms. It cooks and it devours. It does not discriminate. Like a plant, lichen – it merely spreads. It simply is, like the wind, like the sun. It's simply a chemical reaction, of course.'

Iris stopped taking notes. She looked into James's brown eyes. He looked back, engaging and still impenetrable – with possibly sufficient scientific knowledge to have done the things at the school.

'We have volcanoes on Mars but no fire because there's no fuel or oxygen.'

'Is that why you light fires on Earth?'

'I don't.'

'You don't remember lighting fires.'

'I don't. I hate fire.'

'You hate fire. Really. Why light them?'

'I'm tired now.'

'I have more questions.'

'I'm tired now.' He stood, turning to the psych nurse. 'Can I go back to my cell? Maybe my sugar levels are low. Ha.' He raised his shackled hand to wave goodbye. It was free. The handcuff remained chained to the desk.

'Hey,' said Brad, stepping forward.

'No trouble, Brad.' James waited for him, his hands folded in front of his stomach.

Brad touched him on the shoulder and James turned obediently towards the door.

Iris said, 'Can I come back later?'

Brad opened the door. James was about to go through.

'I'd like to ask you more questions about Mars.'

'I'd like that, Iris. I like watching you try to figure me out.'

*

'Here she is,' said Paul Hampton rather loudly as Iris passed through the upstairs waiting room. Iris's phone was buzzing in her handbag.

'Give me five minutes please, Mary,' Iris said, 'then send him in.'

She unlocked her door, switched on the lights. The tranquil sea painting loomed.

'Frank,' Iris said to her mobile as she went to the filing cabinet to pull out Paul's file.

'I hear you had another session with our alien this morning.'

'Yes.'

'I have the police clamouring, Iris. It's why I'm clamouring in turn.'

'I haven't written anything up yet, Frank. I'm going back later.'

'Thumbnail? No something, no pack drill.'

'I don't think he's schizophrenic.'

'Not even prodromal? What if he's making dislocated sense of early auditory and visual hallucinatory experiences?'

'I wouldn't put him on Seroquel quite yet.'

'Well, it would be a way to settle him down, find out who he really is. But the Feds also want him clean.'

'The Feds?'

'Yes, we're tag teaming. They went in after you this morning. I'm going in to have a chat after.'

'The Feds?'

'Iris, they are exploring the idea of a terrorist cell. They don't think he could have acted alone. I'm far from convinced he's not schizophrenic by the by, but that can wait. We're assessing, not mending right now. Anything?'

'His delusion is well practised, he has a clear awareness others are sceptical about it. He knows others think he's mad saying he's a Martian, and is quite okay about it. Even tolerant. He's very bright – intelligent, quick, educated. He's perceptive too, about others. Off the record, Frank ...'

'It all is.'

'He's normal in his social, intellectual and linguistic functions. If you imagine he's saying "I'm from Minnesota" instead of Mars. So, if the delusion is really a delusion or identity, that identity is well integrated. If.'

'So, as you said before, organised enough to do the school.'

'Yes. He has a thing for fire.'

'Well isn't this why I came to you?'

'More than compulsion. He thinks about fire. He personifies fire. He has a relationship with fire.'

'Oh.'

'I'm going to try a different tack this evening.'

'Is he a pyromaniac?'

'Is anyone?'

Actual pyromaniacs were rare. There were many reasons for lighting fires; pure compulsion was offered in the *Diagnostic and Statistical Manual of Mental Disorders* only if all other motives and psychological factors were ruled out.

'Iris, we don't need another psychiatrist. We need your expertise. We need you to do your thing.'

'I'm still feeling my way with him.'

'Thanks. You sound well.'

'Sleeping like a baby.' Iris buttoned off before Frank could press further.

Iris buzzed Paul Hampton in, tried to switch gears.

'So, you've been in the news, Iris.'

Paul stood in front of her desk, leaning forward slightly at the waist, peering at Iris who sat behind her desk. His cologne didn't disguise a strong smell of disinfectant.

'Yes, lots of adventures.'

'Are you hurt?' He said it oddly, as he did with many things involving feelings.

'I'm quite all right, Paul. Thank you for asking.'

He nodded, dismissed it, sat in the middle of the couch, both arms stretched out along the back. He wore a striped Country Road–style shirt, jeans and good boots, the horse breeder on a Saturday. Thirty-two years old, his body was starting to soften from the good paddock. His face was full, too pale to be the horse breeder.

'Well, enough about you. Let's talk about me.'

Iris smiled. She suspected it was not irony, but the truth. 'Let's do that. It's what you pay for.'

'Exactly.' His eyes went cold.

'So, Mary tells me you needed this extra session because you have an emergency.'

'Why were you so late?'

'I'm sorry, Paul. I have a number of patients.'

This seemed to make the narcissist in him angry. He paused, flicking through cards he might use before finally saying, 'Mary tells me you've been out at Fieldhaven talking to a suspect in the school fire.'

'She shouldn't have shared confidential information.'

'She's not very bright.'

'That's not fair, Paul.'

'Fair?' He waved the word away. 'Bigger fish to fry than my emergency.'

Iris sighed. 'I'm sorry Paul. I really am. I'm all yours now. You're the biggest fish I'm frying.'

He scanned her for a number of seconds before he found the joke and gave her a snort.

'I fell off the wagon.'

'Oh.'

'On the weekend. I could feel it building.'

'You didn't call me?'

'I gave in to it.' Paul was an alcoholic, not so much a constant drinker, rather an abstainer who occasionally binged.

'Your wife? The kids?'

'They were away for the weekend. Her mother's.'

'So, are you able to control your desire to drink, when she and the kids are around?'

'Well ... it is ... no, it's irrelevant. I can go away too. Say I have a conference. Say I have to see a man about a horse.' He snorted, checked she'd understood his joke. 'She wouldn't know if her arse was on fire, as you know.'

Iris had met Paul's wife only once when she attended a counselling session. She was quiet, eager to please her husband, proud of him and her children. She was compliant, outwardly, adoring of Paul's everything. The only problem she had was during Paul's dark moods when they all tiptoed around him. She was surprised to hear of Paul's drinking problem.

'Is this fair, Paul? She loves you.'

'Of course she does.' He missed a beat, came up with, 'I can be very lovable, Iris.'

'You're absolutely sure you can't give AA another try?'

'We've been over this.' He was angry. Very angry. He sat forward on the couch. 'I don't believe in a higher power. I don't believe in a higher power than me. It's a stupid fairy story for idiots. I don't believe in sitting around talking to morons.' He caught himself. He leaned back on the chair, his arms back out. 'Present company excepted, of course.'

'Of course.'

'You shouldn't make me angry, Iris. There's no need. You are bright, I know, so you don't need to badger me by returning to old ground. Let's move on.'

Iris suspected Paul would be happy talking to morons, just not happy having to listen to them.

She said, 'Bright people can have a problem with alcohol. If you found the right person ...'

'I have. It's you. You have to try harder.'

'Time out, Paul.'

'What? No, I didn't ...'

Iris raised her finger, like a schoolteacher, pointing it at him.

He sat up straight, clutched his knees together.

It was Iris who needed the time. She'd established rules of her own when Paul became too rude or manipulative. She was not going to enter into an abusive relationship with him. She suspected narcissistic personality disorder. He would not let her test. It was not her job to judge him in that way. His narcissism was part of his make-up and she must ignore it or work with it, exactly as she'd ignore the swearing of a Tourette's sufferer.

'Are you all right, Iris?'

'Yes, Paul. Thank you.'

'I was not trying to offend you.'

'Good. Very well. When did you feel like you wanted a drink?'

'Most of the time, but it built to a level a few weeks ago.'

'Yes?'

'Yes.'

'We talked about identifying a trigger ...'

He shook his head. Then he thought of something that made him smirk. He met her gaze. 'It's like sex, Iris. You have sex. It's good. It's good even when it's not great. You know what I mean.'

Iris didn't say anything. She waited.

'If you don't know what I mean, well, some things become clear. Let me tell you. After you have sex, your desire for more sex slowly builds. A pretty woman triggers a thought. Breasts pushing at the fabric of a t-shirt. A woman gets up on the bus. Another crosses her legs in the office. A commercial. The weather girl. Anything, everything, becomes a trigger because the desire has built ... the pressure on the walls of the dam. I really want a great big ... drink.'

Paul had trouble with jokes, both in hearing and telling them. He was often inappropriate. Iris also suspected transference. He was over-keen on her past celebrity. He tried to flirt in an overt, distasteful way. On the other hand, Iris also wondered if his narcissism merely called for an admiring listener, like a kind of ear prostitute. Sit, listen, tell me how amazing I am and I'll pay $120 per hour.

'I only told you because you asked. I thought the sex metaphor a good one. It describes the many triggers and the none. The anticipation, too. Surely as a narrative therapist, you'd like a good metaphor.'

'Do you have support mechanisms, Paul? At work?'

'Yes. As I've told you, as should be in your notes, I'm on a committee for the local veterinary association. My staff are loyal, obedient. My wife would do anything ...'

'All the same, as we've talked about, veterinary physicians have a high rate of depression. Suicide risk. There are studies ...'

'Of averages. Of weak people. Boohoo. The dog is whimpering. Oh my, I could save the cat but this lady can't pay, we have to put it down. Oh dear, I have to work long hours to save the horses. It's the job, Iris. We save animals. We reduce suffering. We are paid good money to do it. I've told you before why I think we're four times more likely to top ourselves – generation X and Y are spoilt children who think the world is their mummy. We have access to drugs which can easily end it and we know how to use them. The world is their mummy. Get over it.' He stopped, red-faced. He wagged his finger at her, suddenly smiling with no humour in his eyes. 'You got another rise out of me. Did you do it on purpose?'

'That was all you.'

Paul was pissed.

'Are those the views you express to the veterinary association?'

'Good lord, no. Wise counsel. Colleagues all. To answer your question, yet again. Your real question, which is probably what made me angry, actually. You keep asking me about my work. I don't feel stress from it. It pleases me. I am not depressed. I don't suffer from depression. Except at your continued stupidity.'

'So why are you here?'

'What?'

'You don't have any problems, Paul. Why see me?'

He sat blinking at her. He smiled his humourless smile.

He was hiding something again. Iris couldn't decide whether he'd fixed on her; was attempting to woo her in a massively contradictory way, or whether he did have something way down deep that part of him knew needed helping. It was as if Paul's first language was not English, he was always translating before he spoke or showed his emotions.

'As I've said from the beginning, the drinking.'

'Which you don't want to analyse, you don't want to stop.'

'I'm willing to listen to arguments that I should. Which don't involve fairytales or gods. So far you've been less than convincing, Iris.' He paused. Found a phrase. Added, 'Is there a money-back clause?'

He smiled again, smug. Was this a game he kept winning by blocking her? Was it, you can't help me, no one can help me? Was this a game about his superiority? You can't help me. I'm too complex.

'Was your dad pretty tough on you?'

'Now you're going to earn your money. I'm in for a tough time now.'

'Which is the same word I said to you. So he was?'

Paul thought. Finally said, 'Yes.'

Iris waited.

'All right, yes. He was tough, when he was home. Hard but fair.'

'Where was he, when he wasn't around?'

'I've told you this. He was a fly-in fly-out worker before they were all called FIFOs. Mining.'

'Did he drink?'

'Average.'

Iris waited.

Paul didn't go on.

Iris was getting close. No more smirks.

'The bedwetting ...'

'I knew it would get back to this.'

'Why?

'I should never have told you. You're obsessive about it.'

Iris hadn't mentioned it, this or last visit.

'It bothers you?'

'Of course not. Children do. My children did. You learn bladder control and you don't. Normal.'

'You told me you still wet the bed sometimes when you were of school age.'

'You're going to use it against me at every opportunity, aren't you? Page one of whatever textbook you read and never got past. I don't wet my bed now. I'm not here about bedwetting.'

'I'm sorry, Paul. I don't mean it as criticism. Seeing if a pattern emerges, is all.'

'Which you can't do.'

'I was going to ask if the bedwetting was worse when your dad was home.'

'Of course it wasn't.'

'Because?'

'He would have beaten me. Don't you listen to anything we talk about here? You haven't written many notes today. I'm not surprised. I don't think you'll be back on television giving many interviews about the correlation between wetting the bed at ten years old and binge drinking.'

Ten. He hadn't said he was ten. That was late.

'Can I write this? The bedwetting was worse when your father was away.'

'Are you having a bad day, Iris? Why do you keep trying to provoke me?'

Iris thought about this. 'Yes, you might be right, Paul. I have had a bad couple of days. I do have trouble sleeping. If those things have made me less than generous in this session, I apologise. I mean it. You could be right.'

He tilted his head slightly to the side as he studied her. It must be how he analysed a sick animal in his practice, thought Iris.

'You were nearly blown up, Mary said.'

'Yes.'

'Why were you there?'

'The police asked me for advice.'

He tilted his head the other way, studying her again. Iris realised it was a dog he reminded her of, a dog trying to understand a human.

She asked, 'Was your mother tough?'

'What?'

'Your dad was tough on you boys, what about your mother?'

'No. Wrong track.'

'You used the word "mummy" in a sentence before. I think you said the new generation of veterinarians think the world is their mummy, which is the usual sense of it, but then you said, "Well the world is their mummy. Get over it." What did you mean?'

He missed a beat, said, 'You're an idiot. A moron. I can't deal with you today. I'm completely wasting my time, aren't I?'

He stood, turned to scan the couch, perhaps to check for anything he might have left behind, then glared at her again. She remained sitting behind the desk, meeting his gaze. He shook his head as he walked out.

Iris glanced at the clock on the desk and saw it was fifteen minutes early. It felt like a small victory. Not only because he'd left fifteen minutes early. She circled the word 'mother' on her notes.

*

Mary looked up from her desk when Iris came out of her office. 'Rodney Fitzmorris has put in a call from the prison. He wants to see you.'

'Okay.' Iris did not feel like seeing Rodney again so soon after seeing Paul Hampton. In fact, she had a sudden desire to visit the butterflies.

'Gillian asked when you were next expected in.'

'Oh, yes. Um, probably something about Meredith Marsh.' Iris wanted the butterflies. 'Get me her mobile number, would you, Mary?'

'Patricia wants to see you.'

'No problem. On my way,' lied Iris.

She drove to the zoo playing a Brandenburg concerto. She wasn't even sure which one. Mathew introduced her to classical music and it had grown on her over the years, especially in the car. It helped create a bubble. She also liked to play classical music in her home office, composing the narrative letters and patient reports. It eased part of her, yet did not interfere with the writing. She rang Biara but couldn't get the duty psychologist. Iris left word to suggest Rodney Fitzmorris might need support intervention. Interview, possibly observation. He was not coping well in remand.

It was a weekday, the zoo relatively quiet. Retirees, mums with toddlers. The dim smell of animals and the yeastier one of their compost filled the hot, still air. She wore a hat, straw yet stylish. She wore a sky-blue blouse, bare-armed. Iris realised she must have wanted the butterfly enclosure this morning before she left home. Her top was a good butterfly-attracting colour. She stopped at the otters, watched them tumble under water. A squirrel galloped up a palm tree. A lolly wrapper floated past, in a sudden wind gust.

She entered the outer hatch, looking up to make sure no butterflies had made their way out before going through the other door into the humid rainforest inside. Monarchs were feeding on the orange hexagonal feeding tables. She watched closely as the proboscis unwound to dab at the sweetness, its wings flexing gently as if breathing.

Iris stood up, letting her eyes find whatever took their fancy. The warm, soothing air held scattered flutterings. The butterflies didn't so much fly as totter in the air, like random zephyr autumn leaves. The orange and the black and a splash of blue winked in real sunlight filtered through a panel in the roof.

Iris raised her arms, closed her eyes. She could smell real flowers, sickly sweet, beginning their decay the instant they opened. There were bananas somewhere too. She listened to her skin. One landed, tickling. She examined her arm. A common grass yellow sat quivering. She scanned the front of her blouse to see another sunning on her.

The butterfly house was not a place to think. It was the

opposite. It was a place where Iris allowed herself not to think. Simply to be. Mindfulness, it was called, but she liked to think of it as mindless, mind empty. Iris was a warm, floating flower. She allowed her sensations to rule, set to feel minute calibrations.

'Look, Grandma. The lady has butterflies on her.'

'Don't touch, darling. Look but don't touch.'

'I'll break them,' said the girl, dutiful.

Rosemarie had liked the butterfly enclosure when she was little. The animals were ticked off, as they tramped every avenue, but the butterflies were treated with appropriate awe. They were too delicate, too tame to be believed.

Chapter seven

As Iris was getting out of her car at the maximum security Park Wing in Fieldhaven, she noticed a man leaning on the bonnet of a yellow ute. He waved to her as he heaved himself up and limped towards her.

He wore jeans, boots and a business shirt that strained around his gut, tucked in under a firey's belt buckle. His chunky watch was clearly capable of calculating planetary orbits and sea depths. 'Gidday, Doc. I was hoping to run into you.'

'I'm not a doctor,' she said by reflex.

'Yes you are. It's what we call all you medicos. Saves time. I've got a couple of questions for you, and a few I'd like you to ask him.' He pointed towards the entrance.

The entrance was glassed, the building red brick with a red tin roof. The security started further in.

'They wouldn't let me in.' He raised his eyebrows, continuing to invite a complicity.

Iris recalled him from the hospital. 'The fire investigator,' she said.

He seemed hurt. 'Chuck. I'm working the school fire.' He stopped in front of her. His face was red, tanned, wind-chapped. His eyes were slightly weepy, which could have been from exposure to smoke and carcinogens – occupational hazard. His smile worked hard at reassurance.

'I don't understand, Mr ...'

'Call me Chuck. I hear you're already interrogating a suspect. What do you reckon?'

'Mr ...'

'Charles Koch.' Now he was pissed off, which was how Iris felt too. He reached into the back pocket of his jeans, pulling out his wallet to flip open at his fire service identification.

'I don't doubt you, Mr Koch. I'm not working for the fire service.'

'Yeah, sure. You're visiting because of your personal interest in Martians. I get it. There are things in the MO that might be useful to both of us, wouldn't you say?'

Iris thought she could smell whisky.

'I was under the stage at the school. I saw the set-up. I saw the zeds.'

'Zeds?'

'Reason I call him Zorro. He likes to splash accelerant around in the shape of a zed. He leaves a couple of them. How much do you know about arson investigation?'

Iris shrugged. She knew quite a lot, she supposed.

'Well, the thing about fire is most people think it destroys evidence. Fires are even set to hide another crime. But after the fire's been through, evidence can be found. Evidence of breaking and entering. Evidence of the ignition point. There are burn patterns, charring which is deeper or has tracked differently to the natural path of a fire. He leaves the zeds, amongst other things. I first noticed it in a deliberately lit bushfire a few years ago. No walls, fewer constraints, so bushfires follow the fuel and are driven by wind. I mean this one was heading up a valley towards the houses, which is what he intended I think, but that's another matter. Anyway, he set this one in a bit of a clearing so it was of quite low intensity where it started. He picked a good hot, windy day.'

As he talked, Charles Koch kept edging forward; Iris kept edging back to maintain her personal space. She now found herself backed to her car, loomed over, by the investigator. 'Mr Koch ...'

'Chuck. Oh, right. I'm starting at the wrong end. Here's what I got from the school. The zeds. The device he set up to start the fire.'

'Chuck, I'm not investigating the friggin fire. I'm interviewing a suspect.'

'You don't want to know some salient facts?'

'I'm working for a psych department, as a favour, not for the fire service.'

'You don't want to know the facts, either.'

Either?

Chuck went on. 'I stumbled across this ghost in the bushfire. I've been stumbling across him for years.'

Iris stood with her back to her car. The metal was hot.

Chuck continued, 'We found the can of Passiona.'

'What?'

'Way back at the first bushfire – I went up to the top of the ridge where the fire was licking at the houses, before the fireys got it out and I took a bo peep. You know why?'

'Because firelighters like to watch.'

'Yeah. I found a good parking spot where you could look down on the front of the houses. I found tyre tracks and a Passiona can. No prints, which is a bummer, but pretty interesting in itself.'

'Chuck, I have to go in.'

'Wanna know what we found under the stage?'

'A can of soft drink?'

'Exactly. They think it was kids. I found what I found.'

'A can of Passiona?'

'You have to put it together with the other things. In the other fires, which I haven't explained yet, the backpackers, the old people's home, there's this unexplained alloy melt – well, it was never properly analysed. It could have been the Passiona can. It's part of his signature.' His voice was rising, getting thinner with his desperation.

Iris considered his civvies and the ute, which certainly wasn't service issue. 'This meeting, this discussion we're having now ... is it official?'

'I understand you've had a couple of your own run-ins with the fire service.'

'I need to get back to work, Chuck.' Iris broke for the entrance to the psych ward.

Chuck tried to follow but his leg must have slowed him. He called after her, 'Doc, my man understands the science of fire. He understands fire investigation. He's smart. Smarter than nearly everyone. Doc!'

Iris made it inside, closing the glass door on Chuck Koch's thin complaint of a voice.

*

James was in the interview room when Iris arrived, attended by a different psych nurse, but unmanacled. He stood up on the other side of the table with his delighted grin. 'Welcome, Iris Foster.' He opened his arms as if for a hug.

Iris sat on the door side of the table.

'You won't hug?'

'Maybe another time.' Iris opened her bag, took out a notepad and pen, listening to James retaking his seat. She considered her pen, whether it might be taken from her, used as a weapon. Finally, composed again, she looked up.

James was still beaming. 'What a lovely blouse. You should wear more bright colours.'

'Why did you pick that chair, James?'

'Is it the power chair? Is it where you like to sit, Iris? We can swap.'

'You're playing games with me, already?'

'You weren't here when we arrived. I wanted to see you come into the room. It's the natural chair to take, facing the door, facing visitors. Was it ... inappropriate?'

Iris considered him. He smiled again, in unlikely innocent happiness. She said, 'I did the same when I first came in.'

'But your training suggests you should never put yourself between a client and the door.'

Iris studied him. No triumph. Matter-of-fact.

'It's why most psychiatrists have two doors,' he said. 'One for the patient, I mean client, and one for the shrink, I mean counsellor. Everyone can retreat. The room becomes neutral ground, a bit like the building in Korea. Did it upset you when I was here first? That you didn't get to be the one sitting and greeting. Because it put me in control. Do you like to be in control, Iris Foster?'

'Are you riffing Hannibal Lecter, or are you just very talkative today?'

'I'm happy to see you. I want to talk. You make it easy to share. What's your secret? It must make it easier for you in your line of work.'

'Have they given you something?'

'Probably. I feel buoyant.'

'Buoyant?'

'Positively bobbing – like a toy duck in a bath full of kids.' He went sad. Drifted. Blinked. Suddenly said, 'We don't have children on Mars.'

Iris wanted to reach for her notepad but instead feigned only mild interest. She didn't want to frighten him off.

'If you don't have children on Mars, how do you procreate?'

'It never takes you Earthlings long to get to sex, does it?'

Iris found herself wondering if James used sex or his attractiveness to get what he wanted, another trick like his juggling and his sweet banter.

'Sorry, Iris. Did I put you off your line of questioning?'

Provocative, flirting? Or was he tossing sand in her eyes?

'Children on Mars, James?'

'We reproduce asexually *and* sexually. We are made up of two organisms. In terms of what can be seen by the naked eye, we disperse through diaspores containing algal and fungal cells, whereas at a microscopic level it's vegetative sexual reproduction. This is at a kind of foetal phase in our life cycle, to put it in Earth terms.'

'I'm sorry, James, I don't remember much biology.'

'You didn't pay attention in class.'

'Too busy chasing the boys.'

'No you weren't.'

'Would you unpack your answer for me, about children on Mars?'

'We don't have children. We most resemble lichen.'

'The thing growing on rocks.'

'We're not a thing. We do grow on rocks.'

'Don't you get wind-blasted, frozen?'

'Yes and no. We are a hardy race. We live mostly in the cracks in our early life. If we are tough enough, we survive to migrate underground.'

'Underground.'

'Of course, Iris. Are you crazy? Nothing can live on the surface when the storms are blowing. We have built processes by which we can store oxygen, collect and create water, warmth, and enhanced sunlight without the punishing UV. These are all Earth terms, of course, massive simplifications.'

'For the dullard of the class.'

'Not you, Iris. I bet you sat up the front, near my desk.'

Iris desperately wanted to write notes. She regretted not putting her recorder on. He had knocked her off balance from the start.

'How does lichen build things?'

'We are lichen in our cell structure and in our procreation. We grow.'

'Into human form?'

'No.' He gestured to his own body. 'No, this is a form I found after the crash.'

Iris risked some quick notes. Key words. Crash. Teacher? Kids.

'So, why aren't there children ... in your Martian life cycle?'

Iris watched him closely during the question. Still the barest flicker on children?

'Well, the term has no meaning. It's not a stage. You spread outside on the planet surface. You become aware, like any animal, your instinct ultimately sends you into crevices. If you find your way underground, you sit and absorb, no one feeds you or offers affection. You listen and you grow until you take adult form, if you wish. We're kind of like lizards – but I don't want you to pigeonhole us, ha ha. Maybe very dry, scaly frogs. We have four legs, very dainty fingers.' He wriggled his fingers at her.

'So no school.'

'No defined period called school. We're always learning. Whatever interests. Lifelong learning.'

'Do you experience love?'

'No,' he said quickly, then reconsidered. 'We are a fraternity. No. We're asexual at this stage. Collegial. We work together. We know our survival depends on it. We are like ants, socially, without a queen.'

It was well practised, thought Iris, the construction was not random. There was a purpose. She would come back to this again later. Frank had asked her to test for pyromania. Many of the profile questions Iris did use were not of great use in this instance. They were socially focused. She could hardly ask James if he was unemployed or did badly at school, while his answer continued to be I'm Martian.

'Tell me about the crash, James.'

James's voice changed. It became almost childlike. 'I don't want to.'

'Why?'

'It distresses me.'

'Was it bad?'

His eyes were beseeching. Yes.

'You weren't alone on board, were you?'

He shook his head. 'I don't want to think about it.'

'We will need to talk about it, eventually James.'

'Why?'

Iris said it. 'So you can get well.'

'Well from what? From being what I am.'

'You don't want to get out of here?'

'Of course,' he said without enthusiasm.

Iris realised he probably didn't. He was clothed, fed, possibly safe from himself, safe from hurting others.

'Do you think it is wrong to kill?'

He thought. He faced it. He said, 'Yes,' like he knew it personally. 'Why I never would, never have.'

Iris did not believe him.

'I'm not getting out of here. I'm their Lee Harvey Oswald.'

'What do you mean?'

'The patsy for the school explosion.'

Iris suppressed a gasp. She said evenly, 'What do you know about it?'

'Quite a lot.'

'Tell me about it.'

'Gas cylinders under the Barnard Christian College gymnasium, with a timer made from an old urn. A flammable liquid spread on the floor as an accelerant. Blocked doors.'

'Do you mind if I write this down?'

'By all means. Everyone knows it already.'

'What do you mean?'

'The detectives. They were questioning me about the explosion.'

'And you remembered ...'

'What they questioned me about. They asked enough questions to suggest why you're all so keen on me. People tell you a lot when they interrogate you, if you listen.'

'Did you blow up the gymnasium, James?'

He said, 'I don't think so. I hope not.' No grin.

'Only you don't remember.'

'No.'

'Have you ever worked at the school?'

'I'm from Mars.'

'This body, the form you are in. It's very beautiful.'

'You're not so bad yourself.'

'I would have thought with the crash it would be damaged?'

'I took it, after the crash.'

'How?'

'I believe it's our spores. We can enter the crevices of an ailing human where we grow, wear the body.' He moved his arms, rather elegantly. In spite of the willowy nature of his stature, he gave the impression of strength and athleticism.

'Do they – the ailing human – remain inside still, after you've taken over?'

'No. Gone.'

'Not even memories coming from the body's past, like a residue you can't explain?'

He folded his arms for the first time. Thought. 'I do know things, don't I?'

'Anything? Feelings?'

'I think, deep inside, he's very sad. Lonely. Very, very sad.' James sat looking into the empty corner of the room. A tear came. He blinked, refocused on her.

Iris said, 'Do you want me to help you with that?'

'Yes. And I'll help you with your sadness in return.' He wasn't joking, then suddenly he was. 'This is all we have time for today, Iris. Jordan, can you show Iris back to her room?'

*

'Gillian.'

'Yes?'

'It's Iris. Iris Foster. From the practice. Is it too late to drop in for a chat?'

'When you called, I thought you might be a client. Scared the shit out of me, lovey,' said Gillian as she opened the front door of her duplex. She was in tracksuit pants and a Bali t-shirt.

Three kids were sitting on a couch playing with a variety of electronic devices while watching a singing contest on the television.

'Come out the back. Iris, this is Karen, Trenton and Rebecca.'

Iris said, 'Hi Karen, Trenton and Rebecca.'

'Hey,' said someone.

'Hi,' said another.

'You wanna drink?' asked Gillian in the kitchen. A bottle was open on the kitchen table.

Iris said, 'Yes, sure.'

'I hate those late-night phone calls, especially if I've had a couple of wines and shouldn't drive, let alone talk someone down.'

'I'm sorry I came by so late, without warning, too.'

'I didn't mean you.'

'This school bombing keeps hoovering up my spare time,' explained Iris.

'When was the last time you used a vacuum cleaner?'

'Well not me, obviously, darling. My Filipino maid. She does it badly unless I direct her. I have to supervise the other servants of course. Lazy, all of them. The whippings can be gruelling. You have no idea.'

'Sorry.' Gillian led her out the back to a table and chairs on the patio. She lit a mosquito coil. A scuffed old dog came out of the darkness, pushing its head up under Gillian's hand.

Iris sipped her wine. The night was warm. The scent from the coil was nearly pleasant.

'I am seeing Meredith Marsh, your shy client, next week. Any tips?'

Iris said, 'Let's talk about you.'

'No foreplay?'

'Very well. Nice old dog. How old is it?'

'Ha ha. My children's ages are nine, eleven and thirteen. I reckon it's still thirty degrees. Boy, it's hot.'

'It sure is warm,' said Iris.

'What happened to dual relationships?'

'I'm not seeing you as a colleague. I'm not seeing you as a patient. I've dropped in after work. I'm not treating you. Just talking. Only wine will change hands.'

'That's right. Your husband is a lawyer.' Gillian finished her drink, glanced over at Iris's barely touched glass and poured herself another, finishing the bottle. She looked from the empty bottle to Iris. 'I'm having trouble coping. I drink too much.'

'Are you a single parent?'

'Yes.'

'That makes things harder.'

'Not necessarily. It is just a matter of fact. The kids are great. I'd be lost without them.'

'It makes it difficult to find time to switch off, I imagine.'

'Do you have kids?'

'Yes, a daughter. She's away at university.'

'It's not the kids. It's the patients. I'm feeling jaded. Tired of them. Burnt-out.'

'Tell me about it.'

'I am telling you about it. Joke. So, what do you do?'

Iris studied Gillian, rejecting the obvious glib answers. She thought about the truth, but offered something halfway between. 'I struggle too. And I'm struggling with narrative therapy. I suspect I'm not patient enough.'

Gillian seemed disappointed.

Iris said, 'I try to stay focused on each patient and their needs. I remind myself of the successes.'

Gillian got up and went inside.

Iris peered into the dimness of the backyard. The lawn needed mowing. She made out bikes, chewed dog toys, patches of dead grass at the edges of the patio light.

Gillian returned with a new bottle of wine. 'A good vintage, this one. At least four months old, I'd say.' She topped up Iris's glass, then her own.

Iris said, 'Can you give me an example of what puts you over the edge?'

Gillian said, 'My main problem is one particular patient. Well, she's not really a patient anymore. I've had her for ages. Over fifteen years, I reckon, from when I worked for the Department of Community Health. Those were the days.'

Iris nodded but didn't say anything.

'What happened was this. Her husband was bipolar. Lots of problems as well as drinking, not taking his meds, refusing injections. Same old same old. Three kids. Yeah, just like me. I know. Don't go there. Anyway, this one night. Barbara was out with the kids. It had gotten bad: I think Barbara took the kids for a walk, a long walk up to the school, around the oval. I'm pretty sure they were in their pyjamas, hoping it'd blow over in a bit. When they came home he'd locked them out. He was a big man. He used to scare me. You know the eye-blaze angry schizophrenics can get. So they went round the back. They can see into the kitchen through the windows onto the back veranda. Enough windows for everyone to see. Barbara's calling to him, "Ernie, let us in." He's sitting at the table. He stands, he's got the carving knife. While Barbara and the kids are watching, he cuts his throat.'

'Oh Gillian.'

'Yeah, well. Fuck, eh. Cops, welfare, ambulances. Investigations. Anyway, she was my client as part of Mental Health. Once Ernie died, she was supposed to be removed from our case list. No service. Bastards. Anyway, so I kept seeing her and the kids, off the books, you know. Over the years, whatever job I was doing or whoever I worked for, I kept in touch. She's this amazing survivor woman. She tried to tough it out from the start. Focus on the kids, take on board how her husband's illness wasn't her fault. She's a battler. But her kids. A mess. Before you know it, well not before you know it, there was years of work, getting them into support. Before you know it, her oldest son has committed suicide, her daughter has schizophrenia too – nature/nurture, who gives a shit, right? Now the youngest has overdosed. A fatal.'

'Gillian!'

'Yeah, about six months ago. Another story in the naked

city. I didn't see it coming. I mean we knew about the drugs but I couldn't stop it. She couldn't do anything. I couldn't do anything for those kids. Nothing I could come up with. Various departments, caseworkers, so many people over the years. I can't even make any sense to her about her life, about the awful events of her life, the vicious torture of it. I mean you can't even begin to make a happy narrative of it. You know, "At least the milk comes." "At least you've still got both legs." She doesn't crack, not really. She's like made of emotional titanium. Is that the strongest metal? Every night. She comes home from work, she starts drinking and at a certain point she starts weeping until it's time for bed. Depression, yes. I can't help her. She doesn't want drugs apart from the alcohol. During the day, at work, she's fine. Cups of tea. Busy. She copes. Her daughter is living with her, taking her meds. Every night, she drinks, she cries. From the start I haven't made one bit of difference. Not saved her kids or helped her pain. Fifteen years of useless fucking talk.'

'Not useless, I'm sure.'

'Sure, are you?'

Iris said, 'We can't cure everyone.'

'Who said? Do you believe that?'

'I think we aren't an infinite number of psychologists with an infinite number of hours.'

'Glib bullshit. I fix people. That's why I got into this. To fix people.'

'That's an incredibly high standard to set yourself.'

'You should talk. You're a machine.'

'Not. Okay, well, she keeps coming back to you, doesn't she?'

'A bad habit.'

'You must offer her something. Maybe something she can hold onto. A constant in her life. Maybe you're the one person who understands. Really understands all of it, in detail, from the beginning. She wouldn't have to re-explain with you. You know what she's been through. What she's going through. You're her witness.'

Gillian looked dubious, but not resistant.

'You're in her corner. Over all these years. Maybe in the end we all need at least one sympathetic ear. A shoulder. Maybe it's enough. Maybe that's all she's got. You're all she's got. Can you imagine if she didn't have you?'

'All right.'

'All right?'

'Well, it makes sense. It seems to me it might be a useful way of thinking about it, cognitively speaking. We'll see if it makes any difference to my inner workings.' Gillian examined her empty glass. 'My non-figurative glass is definitely completely empty. Another?'

'I'm good.'

'Don't you judge me!'

Iris was taken aback. Then Gillian guffawed.

Iris said, 'You set tests.'

'Yes. Trust issues.'

'Some of them are traps.'

Gillian grinned. 'You keep passing the tests.'

Iris said, 'If you want another drink go ahead. I'm not sharing my Quaaludes.'

'Those were the days. Marijuana didn't cause psychosis, sex didn't kill. It only broke your heart.' Gillian sighed. 'Why do I only remember my failures?'

'The sex or the dope?'

'Sex with dopes.'

'We remember our failures because it's how we're programmed. Survival for hundreds of thousands of years has depended on remembering pain, death, the mistakes. Our wiring privileges pain.'

'We have to sleep at night, surely, without drugging ourselves.'

Iris stood. 'Really? Who told you that?'

Gillian grimaced.

Iris said, 'It's been a long few days since I was nearly blown up.'

'Do you want to talk about it? I owe you a shoulder.'

Iris smiled, shook her head.

Gillian said, 'I'm not only loud and gauche. I can do gent till and sub till.'

'It's nothing to do with you. Truth is, I don't think I can take counselling from a woman. I'm not being sexist. Mother issues. Please, don't start. I'm too old to be cured of my mother.'

Chapter eight

Only the burglar light was on. The rest of the house was dark. Iris noticed that the gardener had been, leaving the smell of fresh mowed lawn in the warm summer night. She looked up to the sky, wondering whether Mars was visible, if James knew where to point amongst the litter of stars. She heard a car and turned to the street where a Mercedes four-wheel drive was parked across the driveway. The veranda security light came on, illuminating Iris where stood.

The passenger door opened, triggering the interior light in the Mercedes. It was Mathew and June, Roland Hyland's wife. She gave a wave. Mathew closed the passenger door and came down the driveway.

'Hello darling,' he said, tiredly.

'Was that June Hyland?'

'Yes, she gave me a lift home from the city.' He went to unlock the front door. 'Another long day.'

'Yes.' She followed him in.

Mathew said, 'We made a huge breakthrough, so had dinner in the city. It was too late to ride home – not after the wine.' Mathew went through the lounge and into his study with his briefcase.

Iris followed to his study door.

She said, 'June was at dinner?'

'Good lord, no.' He was emptying papers from the briefcase, laying the stack on the desk, his back to her. 'She came by to pick up Roly. She works in the city at the Arts building. Roly was working on so she dropped me off. They live down along the river. You know that.'

'Yes, I suppose I do. Yes.'

Mathew came towards her but kept on past to the kitchen. 'We've had a breakthrough on the Nullabin Peninsula. The local people have agreed.'

Iris followed him, leaving her own work bag outside her office door.

'All hands to the pump before they change their minds, or a greenie group digs up the contrary family members. The younger ones are a bit put out. Leave cancelled. Flights to and from, lots of paperwork before anyone changes their mind. We've got state-government backing. In fact the premier has taken a special interest. Jobs, jobs, jobs.' Mathew went through to the toilet in the laundry.

Iris opened the fridge to discover the same lack of food as the previous night. She took out some mineral water, sliced a lime.

Mathew came from the laundry, smelling of the lavender soap they kept by the back door.

'This is big, even for us. I'll have to fly up in the morning. Wave the flag, make sure no one trips over their shoelaces.' He put on the kettle, took out cups. 'Tea?'

'How early?'

'First thing.'

'Would you like mindless television and biscuits?'

'I can't. I have papers. A stack.'

'How about an early night and mindless sex?'

He stopped making the tea, blinked at her.

She smiled, to push up the joke, remove any trace of pleading.

He sounded regretful. 'Oh, I can't, darling. I've simply got too much to get done.' He came to rest his hand on her shoulder. 'When I get back, let's make time for ourselves, stay in, give each other a good seeing to?'

She smiled again.

He kissed her, rather chastely, on the lips, patted her shoulder, once, then two more times, before turning back to the tea. 'Rosemarie called,' he said. 'In the afternoon.'

'Oh.'

'She's doing very well. She's eager for her exam results. She's not back until Christmas, she said. She's moving into a house, out of the college. I was a bit concerned but it sounds like two other students – girls from the residential college. There's this fellow, Brodey. Not a promising name, Brodey. His name came up a few times. I managed to establish Brodey isn't moving in with them. Just the girls for now. A place within walking distance from the university. Has she mentioned Brodey to you?'

He jiggled his tea bag, squeezing out the excess moisture with a teaspoon before depositing it in the kitchen bin.

Iris said, 'I haven't managed to catch her.'

'She sounds on top of the world, full of plans for the break. I'll report back on her new digs when I'm over next on business.' Mathew took his cup of tea to his study, all but whistling.

The tea he had made her steamed on the bench. Iris surveyed the spotless kitchen. The cleaner must have come today too.

*

Iris took her cup of tea and a packet of chocolate biscuits into her home office. She gazed at her butterfly displays for a moment, recalling her peaceful morning in the enclosure at the zoo. She opened her laptop to check her emails. There was an invitation to the funeral for the firefighters who'd perished at the school. On Monday, a state funeral with full honours. They must have hastened through the forensics, Iris supposed.

Patricia had scheduled an appointment with her. Iris pressed accept. She next went through the office emails from Mary. Iris had two clients the next day. Howard Philips was having trouble in his relationship with his wife, Anna. Iris, Howard and Anna were exploring Howard's pornography consumption as the prime suspect. The other client, Jacqui, was seeking to rebuild her relationship with her philandering partner. He seemed to want to save the relationship, and the philandering. It appeared sex and infidelity would be the theme tomorrow.

Iris had sampled pornography sites as part of her preparation for Howard. It was very easy to google examples once key words and phrases were learned. After the embarrassing problems with virus infections on her computer, Iris found a few relatively safe sites.

What Iris discovered was quite surprising. She did find

nasty sites of hurt and humiliation, of drunk girls being abused, of wives being shared, of cheating men and women secretly recorded, yet she also found many dramatised fantasies played by attractive, endowed models. The scenarios appeared consensual, equal in terms of gender, issues of the financial exploitation aside.

Iris found sad videos from Russia, and exquisite, haunting dramas from Japan. Sexual organs were pixilated in the Japanese genre, the dramas unfolding over a longer time with large sections devoted to allure and relationship building, turning them into erotic tales of sex, sometimes even lyrical rather than anatomical or gymnastic or gynaecological.

Iris found lesbian sex, married-couple sex, and porn with humour. She uncovered sites devoted to the woman's pers-pective in which young, firm men complied with a woman's wishes with tenderness arriving in a variety of uniforms, including firefighters. Iris had to admit, amongst the wide range of choices, flavours, and preferences, she had found porn she liked. Yet she could never quite shake the dark presence of child pornography. Many windows hinted towards that evil. It was a shadow presence normalised too easily, if not constantly attacked.

Iris also wondered about some of the sexual positions she witnessed. Was a particular position pleasurable or merely photogenic, for want of a better word? Did this account for the predominance of completely hairless genitalia? Large cocks were popular, of course. Long cocks seemed to have advantages for filming angles of penetration. It seemed more important for a male porn actor to be able to perform sex vigorously for a long time without climaxing. For female stars, breasts were the big thing, enhancement was obvious. Like any academic, Iris had surveyed the literature, finding a small portion arousing, although she soon tired of the repetition.

Iris's sexual history, before she met Mathew, was fairly average, she supposed. Early fumblings and experiments giving way to longer relationships and serial monogamy. However, it was not until Mathew that Iris had felt the strong physical as well as emotional desire for loving. He was gallant, dashing, handsome, quick-witted and self-contained. He craved admiration and deserved it. Ten years older than Iris, she could look up to him and did. The sex was great. Desire charged them. They raced each other off, in cars, in the country, in rooms. They spent whole days naked, lounging, recoupling.

They'd met in court, Iris a police witness of dubious legal standing, Mathew the Department of Public Prosecutions tyro still. There were further consultancies on witness transcripts, profiling techniques, assessments of witness statements, trips in the country where Mathew's relatives had dairy farms, lunches at the big city house where politics was discussed while tennis was played on the grass court in the grounds. Then Rosemarie and marriage and another chapter to life, concurrent chapters. Parallel? Divergent?

How does a relationship become stale? Reach stalemate? Stale mate? There had been no massive, clear breach, no incident or signal of collapse. Instead it was death by a thousand kindnesses, the tiny compromises and adjustments making a relationship pleasant and smooth. Pin pricks. Or callouses perhaps. Iris was as complicit in the long, slow silencing of desire and sharing. Things moved to Saturday nights only and then to Sunday mornings, and ... Mathew and Iris accommodated each other in all things. They parallel played. What Iris missed most was the affection.

She roused herself. She was still sitting in her home office. Her laptop was running screensaver shapes. The biscuit packet was empty. Iris decided to have a bath. She might paint her toes. She would not think. When she went to say goodnight to Mathew she found his office door closed.

*

Iris added bergamot oil to the filling bath. She went to Mathew's built-in robes, pulled out his suitcase and put it on the bed. It was always pre-packed to cover four days away, his usual business trip. She opened it, pulling out his socks and his underwear. She replaced them in their drawers, zipped up the suitcase and put it back where she'd found it.

Frank felt Iris compartmentalised. He felt this was a valuable defence mechanism in which she locked down certain unpleasant things while getting on with other things. He felt her compartmentalisation was not fulfilling its function. She had too many bombs ticking away in locked rooms. Or to use a ship image, too many watertight compartments were filling with water for the safety of the ship. Frank left no metaphor unlaunched. She was personally strong and professionally successful, but she might want to integrate it all one day. Compartmentalisation was not good if you didn't know where you'd hidden the life rafts.

Iris went to the medicine cabinet. The small plastic bottle was near the back. She shook it, hearing a rattle. She had not finished the course of Triazolam she'd taken as she recovered from the fire at her private practice.

She took the pills with water, then lowered herself into the stinging, orange-scented heat of the bathwater. She looked down the length of her still-firm body, to her feet. She had beautiful feet. They were small and perfectly formed. Although her feet were usually hidden in closed shoes, she painted them lurid colours. They were a deep red at the moment. She thought she might redo them purple. Her toes were pretty. They'd all said that. All her lovers, even, especially, Mathew. Iris's toes wriggled in the warm water at the other end of the bath like little dancing flames. Maybe she should have said yes to a couple of the fireys. She giggled. Were the sedatives kicking in too soon? Iris recalled having wine. Whoops.

Iris, the jack of all psychological trades, had started in post-traumatic stress, counselling civilian victims of crime. She did some work for the police. She'd done some months as a narrative therapist, then more counselling with victims of domestic abuse. Her first contact with the fire service had been as part of the human relations department, attempting to explore PTSD within the fire service. Iris saw herself with big tizzed hair, shoulder pads, pumps, possibly a lime green top in the 1980s. Young, naïve Iris, empowered with American armed forces data and a military PTSD checklist questionnaire, marching into a fire station with the temporary acquiescence of the platoon station officer.

She remembered the reactions of the young, lean, mostly men; their lazy grins growing, their confident eyes turning wary.

'A pilot study.'

Arms folded. Ranks closed. Nobody suffering from post-traumatic stress here. No one's shooting at us. They refused to fill out the symptom-related forms that the girl with the clipboard brought round.

But they were suffering. Now we have statistics, of course. Around fifteen to eighteen per cent of firefighters suffer symptoms of post-traumatic stress. Which was more than soldiers. More than police. The only ones higher were the paramedics driving ambulances. It's a stressful job. It is often life-threatening. Injury from toxic or superheated gasses, risk of over-exertion, and heat stress form higher percentages in firefighter hazard lists. Buildings can collapse. Fire traps and kills. Yet their job description also involves dealing with the dead and injured. Burnt flesh has a certain smell, as do bodily fluids voiding from a car crash victim. They cut screaming people from car wrecks. They retrieve burnt pets. They enter burning rooms stepping on children's toys, see the cracked baby bottle on the road as they approach the roll-over on the country bend. Firefighters are well trained, incredibly brave people. They are fit and strong and they suffer from post-traumatic stress disorder the same as everyone else. People don't get used to it. Repeated exposure to trauma increases the likelihood of developing PTSD. No one gets used to it.

They can receive help, they can recover. It's now called critical stress debriefing, but back then it was called harassing the men or picking at the scab. Youngish Iris, hair cut shorter, wearing more sensible shoes, managed to get out to fires. The truth be told, she fell in love.

She was immediately excited by the urgency of the work. The calm way the fireys deployed hoses, advanced through walls of flames through toxic smoke. She was caught with the calm, concentrated way they stepped into their over trousers, boots ready, the zipping of the yellow fire tunics, the checking of breathing apparatus; the casual way they chose the various breaking and hooking tools from their kits. The firefighters worked together with easy trust. They seemed unfussed, almost amused as they dodged falling material or brought people out of houses and buildings.

Iris was bewitched. Inveigled. The flames mesmerised and transported her. The heat was immense, an almost solid thing that took her shoulders, shook the breath from her. The crackle, pop and shatter of consumed material. The shimmer of yellows, blues, greens, fluttering reds. The roar and scream as the fire found whatever it liked, raced, grabbed and danced around the burning fuel with a glee. It fell back from the water applied to it but found ways to pounce again with renewed potency. Fire had a personality as well as a terrifying, attractive power. It was feline, wild, a phantom panther. It transfixed her. It made her feet tingle, her knees feel weak.

The firefighters who skittered, advanced, retreated, became attendant rather than conquering even as they subdued the beast, hosed down the black, steaming house bones, pulled down the smoking walls as the fire investigators arrived to slither in like parasites feeding on the dead buildings. Iris didn't stay for them. She went with the firefighters.

Individuals, sensing her excitement, occasionally tried it on. 'So you like a bit of fire, do you, Iris?' 'The rush doesn't have to end at work, you know.' 'I could use some help with my hose.' They used tired lines, those boys, but they were magnificent, very sexy young men with the aroma of earned sweat and adrenalin. Iris sensed from the beginning, to sleep with one of them would be to lose all of them. It was a male world and to become a girlfriend, or worse, a screw, was to be consigned to a utility. She worked hard to give as good as she got, fighting to become, if not one of the boys, at least not one of the girls.

Fast-forward to the boss's office. Assistant Commissioner Deb Bennett was the head of Human Resources and Training.

'We are not going to pursue PTSD at this stage.'

'Ma'am, you can't be serious.'

'We have new work for you, Iris.'

'We have sick men, Assistant Commissioner. We've got men who aren't sleeping, nightmares, flashbacks. We've got men who have big weight gain, drinking to excess. Anger, through the roof, affecting their work. Poor concentration. Look at their home lives. Divorce rates.'

'Yes, it's a tough job, not for everyone,' Bennett interrupted, glaring to make clear the extra threat.

Iris tried to recall more statistics.

The AC took her silence as acquiescence. She rewarded Iris with a confidence. 'This comes from the top. If PTSD gets hold, it'll be the new RSI. We'll be so busy compensating and watching the numbers skyrocket, we won't have anyone left to fight fires.'

'Money's hard to come by but we can always grow more firefighters.'

Bennett hardened. 'You're a bright, motivated self-starter.' She pushed a file towards her. 'I want you to go to a place called Quantico, in Virginia, attend the workshops they are running. Interviewing has always been a strength. I want you to start boning up on arson profiling. I want you to start working for the service instead of against it.'

Chapter nine

Iris woke up in bed. It was light. She felt blurred, dull. Thirsty. She was naked. She'd been in the bath. Mathew was gone. The sound of a distant car door slamming had woken her. Mathew's taxi?

Iris drank water and coffee while she dressed. Grey skirt, enclosed shoes, an apricot blouse. She got a glass of orange juice but left it sitting while she did her face. She recalled grapefruit juice and Triazolam did not mix. She wasn't sure about other juices. She went to one of her jewellery boxes and chose the white opal chandelier earrings she'd found on a country trip.

She bought more coffee, and a bacon and egg burger on her way out to Fieldhaven. She played an Amy Winehouse CD Rosemarie had left in the glovebox, skipping 'Rehab' to play 'Wake Up Alone' on repeat. She'd squeeze in a session with James before seeing her patients at the clinic.

The front desk staff were reluctant to let her in until she reminded them of the importance of the case, the time component.

'He's showering,' they told her at the nurses station in the locked ward. One of the male psych nurses pointed to a bank of small television screens where high angle views of each cell were displayed. James was in the top quarter of his screen, naked in the shower. His body was beautifully proportioned, long-limbed and muscular without bulk. His chest seemed hairless. Iris saw a clump of dark hair under an armpit, the hair on his crotch and balls, water-slicked and dark.

'Ah, you probably shouldn't be watching that,' said the nurse.

Iris turned to see him smirk, like he'd caught her.

Iris looked back to the screen, as James swivelled under the shower to reveal two symmetrical burn marks on his back. The shrivelled, shiny skin was like melted plastic. Yet, as James moved under the shower water, Iris saw the beauty in it, like the markings on a butterfly wings.

'They're burns,' said the psych nurse. 'He's got another one on his arm you can't see on the monitor.'

'They do look like folded wings, don't they?'

'What?'

'I'll go out here, shall I?' said Iris heading for a hard chair in the corridor outside the nurses station.

Frank found her five minutes later.

'What are you doing here?' she said.

'I sometimes work here. Remember?' He was angry with her. 'Let's talk.' He gestured down the corridor.

Iris followed him. He wore baggy trousers, a loose business shirt without a tie, a thinning sports coat covered in dog hair.

'Your phone is off,' he said without turning.

'You're up early,' said Iris brightly, as they paused for a door to be unlocked.

'Mathew telephoned.'

'My Mathew?'

They went outside to the large grassed area with the picnic tables. Deep ashtrays, too heavy to lift, were plentiful. Three separate fences ran between them and the carpark. The first was constructed of wire mesh, the gaps too small for even a toehold. The next fence was topped with barbed wire, the third with a large round plastic cylinder, again to prevent climbing. There had been escapes from Fieldhaven, usually with fatal consequences to the escapee, but none from this recreational yard.

Frank sat on a bench on one side of a picnic table in the shade of the building they'd come from. Iris sat opposite.

'He said he pulled you out of the bath, unconscious at midnight.'

'Ah, my guardian angel. Him I mean. I try to be asleep by midnight Frank, in bed not in the bath. No razor blade, if that's what you're thinking. I'm sorry he rang you.'

'Your eyes are a bit rheumy.'

'Roomy?'

'Misted. Blurry. He's worried about you.'

'He's worried about the mess I might make.'

Frank studied her, troubled.

'I'm fine. Another big day. I took two spare sleeping pills before my bath. I recall reviewing my life. I must have drifted off. Best night's sleep in ages.'

'Mathew said you kept demanding sex. Quite aggressively.'

'Did he? Nice of him to share it with you. Did he give in to my demands?'

'I'm going to take you off the Martian case.'

'I've barely started.'

'The Feds want to ship him off to a medium security prison, so they can interview him more fully. He's not blathering.'

'He's sick.'

'Not your problem.'

'He has obvious evidence of trauma. He's stuck on reworking the event. He's constructed ...'

'Those are matters to be dealt with over years, Iris, and by a psychiatrist. The job at hand was to assess his competence – which I have done. And for you to give an opinion on his firelighting.'

'Which I am nearly ready to do. He's got a science background by the way. He may have been a teacher.'

'Interesting. I'll pass it along to the police.'

'Oh come on, Frank. Are you going to punish me because I fell asleep in the bath because of the drugs you prescribed me? Or because I stole my husband's socks and undies?'

'You what?'

'Mathew is off up north for the weekend, another weekend. I went into his suitcase, took out his socks and underpants. He likes his underwear. He likes the feel of expensive stuff against his skin.'

'Why did you do it?'

'I don't know. I'm being naughty – acting out.' Iris slowed herself. 'I have been feeling flat since the school thing but I am working my way through things. Working with this patient is helping, as I'm sure you anticipated it would. I can help you, the police and him. I am actually good at this.'

'Iris, you're not a psychiatrist. The recidivist firelighting, a brief profile for the police.'

'Okay. One more visit then I'll file my report.'

'No more tranquillisers. I prescribed them under a different set of conditions.'

'Aye aye sir.'

'You need to come see me. For a proper session. No more of this bullshit trying to throw sand in my eyes.'

'Yes.'

'One visit followed rapidly by the report.'

'Deal.'

*

Iris was shown into the interview room where she found James sitting on the other side of the table. He stood up, delighted to see her, his arms wide for a welcome hug. 'Iris.'

'James.'

'No hug?'

'No hugging, no.'

'I thought on your planet this was a harmless greeting.'

Iris said to Brad, who was standing in his usual place by the door, 'I don't want to interview him in here. Is there another room?'

'You can have this side of the table.'

'No, not here.'

'I'll find out,' said Brad. 'Um, I'll have to take him with me.'

'Fine by me.'

'Are you angry with me?' asked James.

'Yes.'

'What have I done?'

'I don't know but it must have been very bad.'

He blinked meekly as Brad took him gently by the arm.

*

The psych nurses, a doctor and a shift supervisor negotiated against Iris. It was finally a phone call to Frank that got them into a secure day room. The flooring was scuffed grey linoleum. The battered couches were purple, the chairs orange, the security boxed television off. Half the room was empty, though, which suited Iris. She wanted to be able to move around, also to deny

James his control-shifting games.

Brad and James walked into the bright room. James opened his arms to the space, turning a complete three-sixty degrees before looking at Iris.

'Have a seat, James.'

'Do you mind if I stand? I've been a bit cramped lately.'

'How did you get the burns on your back?'

He blinked a couple of times before he said, 'Maybe they are my wings, my Martian wings.'

'You never said you could fly.'

'You never asked.'

'Weak answer. That's what you told the Norwegian girls. You've practised it. Did your wings burn off in the crash?'

He spun away in a kind of pirouette and walked to a large window overlooking the grassed area.

Iris followed. 'Can you tell me about the crash, James?'

'Can we go out there?' He pointed to the grass. A patch was bright with sunlight at the end of the building shadows.

'How about the other side of the fence?'

He turned, beaming, then saw she was only joking. He was suddenly crestfallen, then almost instantly modulated it into a performance of crestfallen. He must be able to charm people to do all kinds of things he wanted. 'Nice earrings,' he said.

'Thank you.'

'You like delicate earrings. Fancy, old.'

'Australian antiques. I like looking for them in second-hand shops in the country. There's a myth though. The bargains are long gone. I don't care. I like the dusty glass cabinets, the smell of country dust.'

He was watching her.

Iris said, 'Dr Silverberg doesn't think you're schizophrenic.'

'Glad to hear it.'

'Why would he say that?'

'Lack the symptoms, I suppose. No little voices.'

'Yes there are. There are voices at your crash. I know you hear them.'

'You're getting tiresome now, Iris. One track. Like Dr Silverberg working his way through the *DSM-Four* questions.'

'Where have you had those tests before, James? Australia?'

'He makes me sneeze. He's got a dog hasn't he?'

'Yes. A labrador.'

'I'm allergic to dogs, so I sneeze. You know what kind of dog he has, so you're more than colleagues, I suppose.'

'When I left you yesterday, you told me you were sad and lonely. I said I could help you with that.'

'I'm not sad.' He put his arms out, performing slow high steps like a minuet from a medieval court. Was acting in his background? The theatre? He was avoiding.

'Why did you say you were?'

'I lied. I thought you were sad. You have this smile that's forced, a tight smile of the lips but your eyes don't join in. Mostly. Just occasionally you forget your troubles and you smile for real. I said I was sad too because I thought it would make you feel better.'

'Crap.'

'To which part? Do you want to dance?'

'You dance. Show me.' Iris stepped back to prop against the back of a couch.

James stepped into the clearer part of the room to dance. He did a couple of ballroom steps with an invisible partner before segueing into tango. He was rusty, although Iris supposed it must be harder without actual music.

Iris clapped and he bowed. Even his bow was elegant with a hint of self-mockery.

Iris said, 'Dr Silverberg says I throw sand in his eyes so he can't see my problems.'

'He treats you?' James was astonished.

'He's my psychiatrist as well as a colleague and a friend. It's how I know about his dog.'

James stood still, leaning ever so slightly towards her, listening.

Iris went on, 'You dazzle. You point bright lights, toss fairy dust. With one hand you distract and leave them ... smiling, while you ...'

'Dance away,' he said, not dancing away.

'Or throw a knife?'

'No knives,' he said showing her his palms.

'What if you're not a Martian?'

'What if I am?'

'I think you picked up bits from *Starman* and *K-PAX*, and whatever other alien-on-Earth films you've seen and added snippets of science about Mars.'

'Because you can't imagine such wonder.'

'Wonder? It's kind of banal. It's only half a step more complicated than thinking you're Jesus or Hitler or Elvis.'

'Now you're just being mean, Iris. You look like you've had a bad night. Your eyes appear hollow, a little weepy. Are you having trouble concentrating? What are you taking?'

'You know quite a bit about psychiatric matters, James.'

'Martians trapped on Earth learn about psychiatric matters, Iris.'

'Yes, well the Earth isn't kind to Martians. If you want to get back to Mars, don't you need to think about the crash? Don't you need to maybe find the spacecraft, repair it so you can get back?'

'I'm marooned.' He stared out the window again.

'Because you did something wrong.'

He didn't answer.

'Do you have consequences on Mars, James?'

He didn't answer.

'Is there right and wrong? Are there bad things on Mars which hurt other Martians?'

'Of course there are.'

'Did you do something wrong that caused the crash?'

'I can't remember.'

'You don't want to remember.'

He twisted to her. 'Okay, maybe I don't want to remember. What's wrong with that?'

'You've done something or experienced something your mind can't deal with. It has locked the event away, not to be remembered or confronted. It's so frightening, your mind can't even think about it. Junk psych says confront it. Me, I'm not so sure. If you can successfully lock it away, leave it gone. I have the same arguments with Frank.'

'What does Frank think you're locking away?'

'It doesn't matter.'

'Oh really, but it matters that I do?'

'Mostly my mother hated me. It's not a biggie. I think I mostly deal with it. We all have less than optimal things which are part of what made us. Your secret, your trauma – is stopping you. Part of you is trying to deal with it. Another part is trying to not deal with it. So, there's this made-up thing, this complex construction of an alternative story – explaining both things. It's a third thing so the warring parts of your mind can coexist. It's the ordinary madness that sustains you, keeps your whole self from completely imploding. Here's the thing: if you are really a happy little Martian, why do you light fires? Why do you do these destructive, self-destructive fires?'

'Thunderbolts. Gamma rays. I fire gamma rays.' He was subdued.

Iris advanced on him. 'This is my last visit. Work with me.'

'No.'

'Here's what's going to happen. The police will question you, not getting very far because of your Martian defence. You'll be in prison, no longer watched very closely and you will get a cigarette lighter from another inmate. Maybe he gives it to you, most likely you will steal it, possibly during a violence done to you. Prison is not a good place for Martians either. Maybe an inmate will trade you lighter fluid or petrol. They might give it to you just for the fun of it and you will set yourself alight in a locked prison cell. You will die in immense pain.'

Iris was less than a metre from him.

He looked into her eyes. 'Good.' He smiled, a nasty, twisted sneer. His eyes blinked rapidly and started to roll back, and close. He bent at the knees, sliding down the wall under the window.

Iris grabbed him by a shoulder. 'James, why? Why would it be good? What did you do?'

James was gone. He sat against the wall on his haunches, his arms around his legs, his stare far away. He wasn't smiling now. He wasn't crying. He didn't seem to be thinking anything. He didn't seem to be anywhere.

*

Iris found a metred carpark a block from the practice. She thought she might be able to write Frank's report on James before seeing her patients. Outside the practice, she stopped to prop her work satchel on a brick fence, rummaging inside until she found the files for the day's patients. She must have put them in the night before when she reviewed, although she couldn't remember. Frank was right. Going back on the sedatives was a bad idea. She'd pushed James too far, too fast. Now he was no help to the investigation, although probably he never was.

Helen shouted from behind the downstairs reception, 'Iris! Stop.'

Iris turned, not two steps up, to see her reaching for a telephone. Other office women behind her actually stood to look over the reception counter. 'She's here.'

'I have clients, Helen.'

Patricia came from her own office. 'I need to see you, now. Immediately.'

Patricia wore a bright dress, white with lots of orangey ochre dots.

She came up the steps and took Iris's elbow, pulling her, somewhat gently, down the stairs towards her office.

Iris said, 'Patricia, can we do this later? I have clients to prepare for.'

'Your phone is off.'

'Yes, I was interviewing. At Fieldhaven.'

Patricia led Iris into her office, closed the door. The indigenous themes were here too. African artefacts. Mayan spherical calendars. Aboriginal paintings. When Patricia trekked she never came back empty-handed.

'Rodney Fitzmorris.'

'Biara Prison, yes.'

Patricia held Iris's left shoulder, firmly, almost tenderly. 'He took his own life last night.'

'Oh.'

Patricia's earrings were green boomerangs. A deep green not necessarily occurring anywhere in Australia, unless on a frog. Iris wanted to voice a protest about the earrings. She couldn't put her finger on it, yet there was something politically incorrect about them.

'You visited him yesterday?'

'I'd have to check my notes.'

'He put in three calls to you.'

'I wasn't picking up.'

Iris regarded Patricia, suddenly appreciating the implications.

'I think I called an "at risk" watch on him.'

'You think you did.'

'I'd have to think about it.'

'Notes.'

'I'd have to look.'

'You didn't diarise everything?'

'I hope so, but things have been on the fly lately.'

Patricia sat, grave.

'They're sure it was suicide?' asked Iris. 'He'd been outed as a paedophile a day or so ago. He thought he was in for a bashing.'

'Locked cell. It looks like he choked on his towel. A coronial inquest will be held, as you know.'

'Yes.'

'You will need to prepare. Your contact. Any actions you took or didn't take. Conversations.'

'Yes, I know the drill.'

'He was a human being, Iris.'

'Yes, Patricia. I know. I was trying to treat him.'

'Do you need to see Frank? Do you have family members you trust who can give you support?' Patricia was no longer pretending. She was box-ticking for an imaginary Occupational Health and Safety audit.

'Yes. Yes, of course.'

'Take next week.'

'I don't need a week, Patricia. I can prepare for an inquest in a few hours.'

'Take the week. I want you to consider your place here. If it's what you really want. I know this might seem like bad timing, but I can't get hold of you, here or via telephone or email. I have concerns about Dr Chew's patients.'

'I have a fullish calendar.'

'Not many of them are Irene's anymore. The narrative therapy presents as particularly perfunctory in many instances.'

'How ...?'

'I was forced to look through the patient files with Mary. When I couldn't get you to participate in audits or reply to my meeting requests. Or telephone calls.'

'Not so confidential.'

'You know they are not. This is a practice. Our practice. We see ourselves as a team. I appreciate the timing is appalling.'

'Bad things do coalesce around me, don't they? Bit of a lightning rod.'

'Yes.'

'So, suspended?'

'Leave.'

'Your office, or the practice, or take some?' Iris couldn't help it.

'I've moved today's patients. As soon as I heard about Rodney Fitzmorris. I thought you'd be too upset to work today.'

Chapter ten

Iris drove to the Emergency Services complex. She'd never actually worked in the new building, having gone into private practice before they moved, but she had visited regularly, especially during a contract to advise on firefighter recruiting.

She found a parking spot outside and searched her purse for change.

Rodney Fitzmorris. What should she have done differently? She certainly should have sent him to prison. Might she have been more encouraging? About what? Perhaps she shouldn't have taken him on. He might have done better with a male psychologist or social worker who was not so determined to change him, merely to get him through his jail term. Of course he would attempt to change her mind, mitigate the testimony, exaggerate the recovery, overturn the charges.

James. She should not have pushed James. That was criminal. It was unhelpful, to James, to Frank and the police investigation. Iris was obdurately refusing to face her own issues while pushing James into his. In whose name? By whose ego? Her tunnel vision made her a highly effective fool.

Georgina. Damn. Georgina burning in the upstairs window.

Iris went to the parking metre, started feeding in coins, getting rid of her small change first.

Iris had been angry with her. Georgina had been embezzling Iris for all of the five years she'd been working for her. An accountant uncovered Georgina's 'extra tax', which had grown after the first year to twenty-five per cent of profits, on top of her wage. Iris didn't need the money, but found the betrayal immense. They'd shared confidences, Georgina anyway. Iris confronted her that morning, which was difficult, because Georgina, from the start, reminded Iris of her mother. Iris had trouble with older women; red flags, roadblocks, blind spots. Gravel on the shoulder. During the confrontation Georgina stressed the primacy of her needs. I've told you about my sick mother. You know my son is having trouble getting work. You know he's got a child. By the time she'd added her car repairs and a new carpet, Iris chose to leave the office. Angry.

It was conceivable, thought Iris, only now considering it, Georgina might have lit the fire which engulfed the office, the office records, Georgina, and Bradley Williams. It was unlikely, but had a twisted logical possibility. She might have been covering her tracks, about to leave when Williams arrived with his shotgun.

As Frank and many others kept insisting, a psychologist cannot continually analyse everyone they know. It's an undergraduate's annoying trick, the continual categorisation of friends and colleagues. It's poisonous to relationships. It is also mostly beside the point. Georgina might have cultivated a self-image of superior need, the crutch entitling her to redistribute another's unfairly gotten gains to the more deserving. The meanness of spirit, the mild chip on the shoulder, the tendency to whinge about personal problems, were not criminal offences. Iris suspected Georgina had regarded her practice as quackery, her prominence no more than successful deception. Georgina was a tough cookie. Even if recommended for treatment, she would never have gone. Iris was not even sure she would have reported Georgina to the police, although she should have. She was sure she was about to fire her. Terminate her. Sack her.

Iris might have allowed Georgina to rip her off. This could have been Iris's fault, but she did not cause Georgina. On the other hand, Iris felt she did cause Bradley Williams.

Iris performed many contracts for government departments after she left the Fire and Rescue Service to enter private practice. She profiled firelighters for the police, fire services and for legal teams. She testified, often amidst press as the Fire Lady. She was, ironically, finally able to treat firefighters for post-traumatic stress disorder.

It was around the time Rosemarie went from primary school to high school. The patient visits were lowering the tone of the house, according to Mathew and also, rather mysteriously, the planning folk from the shire council. Iris hired Georgina, secretary, bookkeeper and office manager extraordinaire, and moved into a modest office on the second floor of a small suburban shopping complex. Downstairs was a chemist, a video store, a vegetable market and hairdressers. At the rear, external stairs led to an outside walkway and four offices on the second floor. There was an accountant, a denture builder, a somewhat shady importer, and Iris. *Iris Foster, Psychologist* it said on the outer door. Inside, there were a couple of chairs, Georgina's desk, a persistently failing fish tank and lots of files. Iris's office beyond was far from chic. There was a couch and two very comfy chairs. Iris's desk was against the wall. If she stood, she could look out of security mesh onto an intersection with two petrol stations and a cake decorator.

The firefighters and fire service, who were her main customers, clearly preferred the lack of femininity, the absence of charm. She guessed it felt vaguely like a temporary crib room. When Iris worked for lawyers including Mathew or the DPP, she met them at their better appointed digs in the city.

At the time one of Iris's new clients was the community cousin of Fire and Rescue, the Volunteer Fire Brigades. Their problem was that a couple of the volunteer firefighters were starting the fires they fought. Many men and women volunteered to protect their own properties and their neighbours', especially in country areas where distance and fuel loads increased the vulnerability to fire. The Volunteer Fire Brigades were noted for their structured training and camaraderie as well as community respect.

Worldwide investigations, however, began to show a dangerous subgroup of volunteers, the Exciters and the Groupies. Firefighting can be exciting. Being around people including the police and professional firefighters is also gratifying, as Iris well knew. What better place to view fire than at the battlefront. So, when home life was slow and emotionally unrewarding, a small percentage of volunteers lit the fires themselves. Occasionally, the fire got out of hand, was not so easily quelled and property was destroyed, people died.

Iris adapted a composite of the Minnesota Multiphasic Personality Inventory, Raymond Cattell's 16 Personality Factors and the Keirsey Temperament Sorter questionnaires, adding questions of her own. As in everything she did, however, she also used her own instincts in interviews to weed out the most obvious firelighters in the volunteer ranks.

Bradley Williams was twenty-three years old, single, employed as a forklift driver, had not finished high school, suffered from low self-esteem. He was firmly in the zone of the profile. He was also depressed, lonely. The volunteer fire service provided one of the few affirmations in his life. It meant activity and comradeship. It was his life. He also exhibited a mild personality disorder, a low-level persecution complex, which by itself should not have ruled him out of serving. The personal interview, after the questionnaire, drew Bradley to Iris's attention. The questions in the questionnaire upset him. 'What's all the questions about how often I go to the toilet? I mean we all think about it, when we go, but what's wrong with that? What are they meant to find out?' 'What's the right magazine to read? If I say stick magazines, I'm a perve. It's normal. Isn't it? I'm not answering questions about my sex life. It's an invasion. It's all an invasion.' 'Anger. It's another question about anger. It's natural?' Iris had trouble reassuring him. She had trouble getting him to move on from the questionnaire and into the live interview. 'I know you, you're the woman who loves fires, hates men. You're going to fuck with me, aren't you?'

Ironically, Iris didn't target him for removal from his brigade. She believed Bradley when he insisted, swore, he'd never lit a fire since being a volunteer. He had, of course, when he was a child. She encouraged him to get help with his depression, to do things about his image of himself. Her report suggested Bradley Williams needed to be monitored but not ousted. If given treatment and special supervision he might well remain a very good, particularly devoted firefighter. He certainly believed strongly in his responsibilities to his fellow volunteers and the esteem from his community. It could have been seen as win-win.

The Volunteer Fire Brigade played it safe, however, terminating his services.

Bradley must have come to Iris's office while Iris was at the petrol station getting the coffee. It was later found that Bradley Williams was armed with his farmer father's shotgun, stolen the day before. According to the fire investigators, he must have locked Georgina in Iris's office before setting fire to the place. He must have bought petrol in the can found in the charred debris. A falling beam probably knocked him out before he perished. No shots were fired.

Iris watched the fire from the carpark below the offices. The fire spread with particular speed. The ceiling panels were especially volatile, made of a plastic compound outlawed years before. It burned as a yellow flame tinged with blue. It was estimated ignition until flashover was no more than three minutes. It was a fast fire. A conflagration. Three minutes would not have passed quickly for those inside. Not for Georgina as she appeared at the security grilled window; trapped, feeling the heat coming, breathing the toxic fumes from burning office furniture. Iris saw her hair catch alight.

A man was talking to her. He looked vaguely familiar.

'The green button, Mrs Foster.'

'Ross?'

It was a chief superintendent Iris had once worked with. He pointed to the parking metre in front of Iris.

Iris turned and pushed the green button where she'd loaded enough coins for seven hours parking. The coins fell heavily.

'Welcome back,' said the chief superintendent.

Iris put the parking ticket on her dash, then went straight up to the Fire Investigation and Analysis Unit offices. The messy desks were mostly empty. A young man was listening on a landline at the back. He glanced at her briefly, so she gave a wave. Iris saw the operations room was open. The man on the phone was writing with one hand, holding the phone to his ear with the other.

Tables had been pushed together in the centre of the operations room to form an island covered with file boxes, manila folders and hard drives. Pin-up boards and whiteboards covered the walls. They were papered and scrawled with the information, lines of inquiry. There were headings like CAUSE, INCENDIARY DEVICE, MOTIVE. Lists of guesses and facts were printed in a variety of marker colours underneath. Question marks, circlings, underlinings, arrows crisscrossed, the product of officers writing as they talked, an investigation in progress. On one board were photographs of the burnt-out appliances, the closer one charred and melted in parts; the further one bent and torn. A mud map marking body positions was taped on. So were aerial photographs of the school grounds, of the crater, parched grass, torn bitumen where the gymnasium had been. There were photographs of the piles of bricks. Close-ups of the burn patterns on the bricks.

Iris went closer to read a report. The incendiary was DIETHYL ETHER, confirmed by lab reports. Someone had written the word SOURCE? Two detectives' names were attached.

On another board was a list of interview subject headings clustered around motive. Iris read through the list: SCHOOL STUDENTS, TEACHERS/WORKERS, NUTTERS, TERRORIST GROUPS, EXTORTION, OTHER, with names of police officers next to each.

Some boards were assigned to the different contributing investigators: coronial investigators, Arson Squad, the Fire Investigations and Analysis Unit, local detectives, federal. There were names, mobile numbers, internal extension numbers, tasks to do written next to these headings. It was a breakdown of tasks and lines of communication for a rapidly assembled multi-agency taskforce. Superintendent Richards was high on the tree.

On another board there was a picture of James with Frank's name, his mobile number attached. Comments were appended on James as a suspect. Unlikely, they suggested. AWAITING REPORT – IRIS FOSTER.

On another board was the word ZORRO. Koch, his phone number written under. A smiley face had been drawn in blue.

Iris moved to a large board of drawings and photographs. They'd been rebuilding the fire scene, piece by piece, adding speculations to the evidence. She studied photographs from underneath the stage. There was an urn with burnt-out thermostat, close-ups of the charring and ignition area. There were photographs of the zed burn pattern Charles Koch talked of. More photographs showed sections of PVC pipe leading to a sealed area under the sprung wooden court. A drawing that seemed partly speculative joined the photographs so the point of origin appeared to be the urn. Zed patterns led towards the PVC. They'd drawn the pipes leading under the floor where they'd drawn packs marked DE – SECONDARY LOAD. Someone had written GYMNASTIC MATS??? A dotted line led to a photograph of the truck on the oval, under which was scrawled SECONDARY ELECTRONIC IGNITION SOURCE. There were a series of photographs of a release pin in the truck passenger door. A mobile telephone. A list of potential electronic ignition devices likely to have ignited the ether.

'What are you doing in here?'

Iris turned to see the young detective who had been conducting the interview with the schoolboy in the school gymnasium. He was in shirt and tie, his arm in a sling.

'I was looking for Charles Koch,' said Iris pointing to the Zorro board. She focused on the phone number.

'Why?'

'He has some information I want to follow up with him.'

'In what capacity are you here?'

'Capacity?'

'Who are you working for... I'm sorry, Superintendent Richards introduced you as someone with useful questions, but didn't give a name.'

'Iris Foster. I'm completing a report on James...' Iris pointed towards the relevant board. 'For Doctor Silverberg.'

'My name is Detective Stuart Pavlovic, Mrs Foster. You most definitely can't be in here.' He held his good arm out towards the door.

Iris headed out. 'What happened to your arm?'

'A flying brick.'

'Where is everybody?'

'A briefing with the Arson Squad downstairs. We're trying to collate witness statements.' He went into the incident room where he gathered four or five files. He flicked the doorjamb, shut the door to the room, locking it.

'The truck,' said Iris.

Pavlovic regarded her.

Iris said, 'I don't understand the logic of the truck.'

Pavlovic still said nothing.

'Why two different ignition points? The urn and the device on the truck? Why not use the mobile directly, if it was to be used?'

'I'm not really at liberty to share our work, Mrs Foster. Such permission would have to come from someone in authority. Superintendent Richards or above. Do you have a theory or are you only curious?'

'It's relevant to my discussions with James ... the suspect.'

He put the manila files on a desk, pulled out a drawer. 'Do you mind if I record this?' He pulled a small cassette recorder from the drawer. His unslung arm was sinewy, his shoulders broad. Iris wondered what sport he played.

'You'll get my report, Detective, when I deliver it to Doctor Silverberg and he sends it down the line. As you suggest, chain of command.'

'You're here. Impressions. Grist for the mill. A thousand thousand details. Police work.' He was pissed off she'd broken into their case room. He pushed the record button.

Iris leaned towards the recorder. 'If the offender was going to back the truck up to the doors, once all the students were in, so they couldn't get out, when the fire took hold ...'

'Who told you this?'

'I'm surmising from information I've gathered.'

'From the Martian?'

'No,' said Iris.

Pavlovic nodded, but didn't follow up.

Iris went on, 'Well, James couldn't have done it, surely. He was nine hundred kilometres away when it would have been time for him to back up the truck.'

'Unless he lost his courage. Unless he had a nervous breakdown halfway through, ran away.'

'I see.'

'You don't think he did it?'

'I don't think so.'

'What are you going to say in your report?'

'I can't brief you. My report isn't complete.'

'We're spitballing.'

'Throwing the tea bag at the ceiling to see if it will stick?'

He didn't smile. He was smart but not a joker.

Iris considered the recorder, which he continued to hold casually in her direction. She said, 'He has a science background, I think. He's impulsive. I don't imagine he's patient enough for the school. The Martian is empathetic too. He's a compulsive firelighter who probably shouldn't be released into the community or put in prison.'

'Quite a profile.'

'I could offer more, if I knew more.' She glanced back at the locked incident room.

'Not my call, lady.' It sounded like an insult.

'Is Charles Koch down at the briefing?'

Pavlovic shook his head, put the recorder back in the drawer, picked up his files.

The fire investigator at the back desk called out, 'Works out of Southern Metropolitan usually, but he's not at work. Suspended.'

Before Iris could ask why, Pavlovic interrupted. 'Could I have your mobile number please? In case I need to follow up on anything?'

Iris fished in her bag, found a card.

The detective held out the files towards the corridor. 'You can't be here, Mrs Foster.'

Iris headed out. She heard Pavlovic say, 'Pugsley, what the fuck you letting people into the incident room for?'

She heard Pugsley say, 'She works here, doesn't she?'

Chapter eleven

Iris telephoned Charles Koch.

'Huh?' was his inelegant reply. She could hear seagulls.

'It's Iris Foster.'

'Who?'

'The Fire Lady. I want to ask you about the case. Compare notes. Like you suggested.'

'Good. Come to my boat. It's at the back of Tradewinds Marina in the Lochland Cut.'

'I don't think so,' said Iris, suddenly wary. 'How about somewhere ... closer to the city?'

They arranged to meet at a pub on the river near the port.

Iris couldn't see him when she arrived so she ordered food. The crowd was mostly blue-collar, still in fluoro vests, with a scattering of office workers. It was one pm on a Friday. She found a table outside. Occasionally a car or cyclist passed between her and the water. Boats headed upriver with the same frequency. A large concrete traffic bridge spanned above. Trains wiped back and forwards hypnotically on another bridge further downriver. It was summer; the sea breeze wasn't in yet.

'Sorry, the traffic was crazy.'

Iris blinked back into the present to see the puffing redness of Chuck Koch.

'What are you drinking?'

She looked down to see she had eaten most of a mixed seafood plate. Prawn tails lay amidst untouched chips. Her wine glass was empty.

'A sauvignon blanc, I suspect.'

Koch went away.

Iris took a chip, stirred a glob of mayonnaise. Two more trains crossed in the middle of the distant bridge.

The drinkers at the adjoining table were gone, leaving a packet of cigarettes and green disposable lighter amongst their finished lunch. Iris leaned over and took the lighter, holding it up towards the sun. It was a quarter full. She thumbed the flint and turned the tiny yellow flame, noticed her greasy fingerprints on her empty wine glass.

Koch came back carrying her wine, a glass of scotch and a pint of beer. He was dressed in jeans, boots and a purple-striped shirt, which might be his best. He'd tucked it in to his belt with the big firefighter buckle. The shirt strained over his belly. Tiny beads of sweat collected on his balding head. He ran his hand back over his forehead and down the back of his neck, casually clearing the sweat. 'So you like Zorro for this?'

'I'm open to all theories, Mr Koch, if you're willing to share them.'

'And you'll help me with the profile?'

'Yes.'

'Call me Chuck. Have you finished with these?' He pointed to the chips.

'Yes.'

He pulled the plate over, started on the cold chips.

Iris asked, 'What do you think his plan was, at the school?'

'He was waiting for the students to go in, for the main doors to be closed. He was going to back the truck up all the way to the doors so they wouldn't be able to open them. All the other exits were already chained or glued. They are trapped when the fire starts, panic, screaming in the smoke and growing heat. Possibly he was hoping for a crowd outside including the fire service, gathered close for the coup de grâce, boom.'

'So what went wrong?'

'I'm guessing those two kids who went down under the stage must have upset things. Made the urn spark too soon. Then the kid put out the accelerant trails before they could reach the motherload, whatever that was.'

'Diethyl ether.'

'Really? Fuck. No wonder it vaporised everything. Fuck. Excuse my language.'

'I'll cope.'

'It's kind of weird stuff to pick. Amazing the sparks didn't set it all off. It must have been sealed pretty good.'

'You didn't know about the ether?'

'The science boys must be keeping it to themselves. How did you know?'

'Have you been suspended, Chuck?'

He banged the table, not very forcefully. He sipped his scotch, looking at her. 'Strange earrings.'

'Antiques. Opal.' She waited.

'I punched a bloke.'

'A fellow worker?'

He constructed a bravado smile. 'Some of the boys give me shit. Hopalong. Festus or Chester, you know. The deputy or whatever from Gunsmoke with the limp. Missa Dylan, Missa Dylan. So, enough is enough.'

'Is that the only reason they gave?'

He glared. 'So I still got to do an interview to get to work with you, huh?'

'Not at all. Let's compare notes. I'm not allowed in the room either.'

'I'll tell you a story.'

'I wish you wouldn't.'

'You're a psychiatrist, you love this shit.'

She didn't bother correcting him. Was he flirting with her? The wine tasted like cold mineral water with barely a hint of grape. It was perfect.

Chuck took a gulp of his beer. He seemed surprised to find a gut, loosened his belt a notch. He glanced up at her, embarrassed. 'I wasn't always a fire investigator. I used to be a firey. Part of a platoon. It's good work with fine men, men you can count on.'

She nodded. She found them fine men and women too.

'Yeah, you know. The Fire Lady. Well, this day, the one I'm talking about, to explain a few things, this day, it was winter. It hadn't rained but it was cold. So there were fires. You know, summer is bushfire season, winter is house-fire season. Candles, open fires, heaters next to curtains. Faulty electric blankets. It was a busy day.

'We got back to the station, already feeling the weight. Eight at night, we haven't eaten. Steaks were on the barbecue out the back when the call came in. A dosshouse near the harbour. Shit.

'You got to hate old building fires. You can't see anything from the outside, can't attack the fire from out there either. May not even be any rear access. Wooden beams, not steel. Not many windows or ventilation, which, you know, is good or bad depending on where you are, where the fire's at, which fire genius you're talking to.

'Sure enough, we're fighting to get the pump close. Cars are parked in the street, which isn't wide. We have an art gallery on one side with the staff running in and out trying to save the artworks. On the other, it's art supplies, so you don't want that stuff to go up. There's a pub across the street with patrons offering drinks, advice, applause. The cops are trying to clear things, including a bunch of deros from the building. Two appliances are already there. A clusterfuck.

'Jock's running out two lengths of forty-mil hose. I connect the mate end into the delivery. The pumpy, it was Marco, is finding the hydrant. I can see him and some cops with axes attacking a car parked over the fire-hydrant cover. We're sent up the stairs to try and suppress the source of the fire from inside. A couple of crews are already in there, primary search and another hose. We don our masks and BA. My peripheral vision is already gone. Jock barks, "Water on. Line one." Helmet on. Jock has the branch and I back him up on the hose, a metre back, feeling it getting heavier as it fills with water.

'There's an old lobby. Water is dripping from the ceiling sprinklers, but they're not going now, either out of water or busted from their first work-out. Twenty or so fire alarms are squealing and squawking up and down the building. No crackles yet. No smoke, but I see the glow of fire up the stairs, ready to get it on.

'The lights are out, the electricity isolated by the SO. Getting toasted by live wires lying in all the water is not good. Blue and red flashes come in windows and the doorway from our appliances and the police. Soon someone will set up lights, arc them in through windows, maybe.

'The second floor is deserted. There's smoke up near the ceiling but the corridor is pretty clear. We pass the other crew on the third floor, where the fire is. Heavy dark smoke on the ceiling, getting thicker and lower. They are gas-cooling the thermal layer at the ceiling, trying to take the heat down, slow down any flashover. Half the floor at that end is flame.

'We keep going up. The flames are yellow and new up on the fourth floor down the D-end, powerful and hot. The fire has found or made a hole in the roof, is gorging on air. It's roaring up here. Windows are exploding. Wood is too. I can hear metal screeching and groaning. It's a corrugated tin roof I guess. It's at the point where you no longer care about restricting oxygen to the fire, because you have to ventilate. Clear the smoke, attack the fire directly.

'I realise the noise is not metal. I hear voices. We hit the doors, one at a time working our way towards the fire. Serious heat. Our tunics are good from two hundred to a thousand degrees, but the masks are fogging. Jock's hitting it, but our water is vapourising even though he's got it on full jet. I hit the next door, it pops but I can't get it open. I can hear coughing. Someone is slumped on the other side of the door. I try to push the door. I reach around and feel a person. They tap my arm. I push the door. I get them out. Jock turns to look. I can see because his helmet torch flares in the smoke. It's a young chap, dressed in a shirt and collar, coughing. You know there's a lot of bad shit in the smoke. Not just carbon monoxide and carbon dioxide. Plastics. Paints. I'm trying to get him up by his arms. The guy's coughing, calling. I can't make it out. I get him to the stairs, where smoke is coming up as well as down. There's a firey there now feeding Jock's line.

'"The others," the young guy bawling in my ear.

'"What others?"

'"In the room. The room."

'Fuck. I hand him over, run back to Jock.

'The floor is looking bad. A piece of ceiling halfway down has fallen in a big chunk, now the flames are above and below. Jock pours water at it. "Time to go," he yells.

'"There's more. In the last room we were in."

'Silence. We both know. Shit. I'm not even sure where the room is anymore. The neutral plane is almost at floor level – full smoke. We have spot fires breaking out, dancing angels in the smoke. We have floor subsidence under the roof fall.

'"One look," I tell him.

'I feel my way up along the left wall, patting each closed door until I reach an opening. Jock is at my shoulder. I'm in. I feel bodies, legs in the middle of the floor. Another person under the window. Flames are starting to lick in through the open doorway. They've opened the window to breathe and now the fire wants some too. Jock's painting the door jamb, beating the fire back. I stand, knowing my back is to the door. I grab the bloke's ankles, drag him backwards and out. I can't really see Jock, only the flash of his luminescent stripes. I can't see his hose line. I get this bloke up on my shoulders. My knees are strong. I'm a bull. I keep the wall to my right shoulder.

'I hand this one over to a crew at the stairs. They're screaming, "Pull back. Retreat. Pull back." My radio hasn't been working all job. I call, "Roger." I'm getting short of breath.

'An alarm is still going. How? It's me. It's my air. I'm down to sixty bar. I can't believe it. The cylinder can't have been full. Then I remember my consumption is bound to be way up. I'm running. I'm hauling bodies. Which is when I should have pulled the pin. That was the time. Abandon ship. No air. You can't save everyone, right?'

Iris nodded. It is true. Is this the point of Chuck's story? The reason he's telling her? What is his burden? What does he need her to know?

'I didn't do the smart thing. I wasn't finished. I bumped my way back along the wall again. I passed Jock, who was pulling out. He couldn't get enough water in. Deep in a fire, it's like being under water. The eddies of smoke, drifting yellow flame, licking orange. It's all in slow motion. The noises are distant too. Like all you can hear is your breathing and your boots on the floor, everything is slow and floating.

'A chunk of the floor is completely gone. I have to skirt a big hole. I hit the open door, fall into the room as bricks and metal crash down in the corridor. It's a lot of weight. Something has given up the ghost.

'I close the door. Hope the fire goes somewhere else first. It likes the least resistance. It goes where it's easiest. I find the man near the window, fuck me, there's another one under him. I know I am sucking last breaths from my oxygen cylinder. This is when I find I've lost my hooligan – my prying, levering tool. So, I'm patting myself down, seeing what tools I might have on me because I know there's steel mesh on all the windows. The front corner of the ceiling starts to glow pink.

'I've still got the hook knife. I don't know how it stayed tied on or how I didn't trip over it. I can make out the lock with my helmet torch. I get the hook knife, dig it under the window, bend. I dig it into the mesh, twist, keep hacking and twisting at it until the whole thing comes away. The window is also locked halfway down. It's a sash. So I get my hook knife and try to smash the wood. It won't break. I hate wood.

'There's a wooden cabinet, like a bedside table under the sill. I throw it at the window. Right through, like Hercules. I lean my head out. I rip my mask off, get a mouthful of air, but smoke cuts into the back of my throat like steel wool, my eyes water.

'There's no fire-escape outside this room. I can see the metal steps going down under the fire, but none outside the window I'm at. Firefighters are down in the alley, but I can't see hoses, let alone pumps. It's all dead-man zone down in the alley, the building's sure to collapse on you. I set off my PDA. It's loud, but they don't seem to hear it.

'I take off my useless BA, throw it at one of the firefighters, four floors below. Of course, I don't hit him. But it gets his attention. My PDA is still blaring. I take my helmet off, I wave it. I'm still not sure he sees me. I wave my arms. The stripes on the end are really noticeable, especially to other firefighters. The fire is in the room now. It's coming down from the ceiling onto the wardrobe. The door is glowing. It's starting to shimmy across the ceiling towards the window. Air is a motherfucking double-edged sword.

'Outside I see the boys running up the lane with ladders. I

wave the helmet again, until I know they are setting up under. Fuck me, they had to reposition the ladder twice, but I hand out the first old guy and realise it is going to take time for them to half-carry, half-pass him down the ladder. That's when I get the idea of the mattresses. I grab the mattresses off each bed, put them behind us, like an extra turtle wall. I lift the last guy up to the window to get air. I have to lean out myself cos I'm nauseous, about to faint. I pass over this guy. My mattress is on fire. The firefighter is carrying him down and I try to get out the window. Halfway out I'm stuck. My tunic, or something on the tunic, is catching. I'm on my back now, half out the window, hanging on to the top of the ladder with one hand. The flames are actually coming out the window and over me. I shake off my right glove, unzip my tunic and slide out backwards. I'm falling. I'm heading headfirst down from four floors up. My left hand grabs the ladder and I spin but my hand slips so I throw out my leg. It slides between rungs of the ladder and I bend it, like a hook. Pop. Fucked knee, but I'm hanging on the ladder, my leg folded under so I can grab another rung under with my hands. I know my leg is fucked up, but all I care about is the fresh air. Cold, sweet air is whooshing into my lungs like cider on a hot day.

'You've probably seen the shot of me handing out the old blokes and falling out of the window.'

'Yes, I have,' said Iris.

'A news crew.'

'That was you.'

'Famous.'

'Quite a hero.'

'Pah,' he snarled.

'Jock?'

'Was as much a hero. Took it better than me too.'

'I don't understand, Chuck. Jock made it out?'

'Yeah. When they said abandon ship, he did. No reason to feel guilty either. He did a bit, though.' Chuck looked from his empty beer glass to his empty whisky glass.

Iris said, 'Do you want another?'

'Another beer.' He named the type, let her go to get him one.

The pub was emptying of the lunch crowd. Younger people were filtering in, dressed in shorts and t-shirts, tattoos twirling up their arms.

If Iris had heard Chuck's story at the practice, she might start to fashion this incident. She'd audit it, look for the patterns. What it said about the chapter of his life as a firefighter. He was a brave man. A hero. Did he miss it? He certainly remembered it. In very specific detail. Why was Charles Koch so obviously suffering all this time later from depression, anger, the many signs of things gone wrong rather than right?

Iris returned with a pint for Chuck, a Diet Coke for herself.

'Cheers,' he said.

'So, big story, Chuck.'

'Yeah, it was the day I fucked up my knee, so I'm out of the job. As talkback radio suggested, the men we saved were hardly any prize catch. Life's a bitch. That was fifteen years ago. I became a fire investigator, I find the cause of fires. Many are accidental, some are lit by this sneaky boots I call Zorro. Now he's done the school, nothing surer. Up-to-date, you reckon?'

Iris saw a lot of resentment and anger in Chuck, hostility towards authority.

He studied the sky. Maybe he'd smelled the first hints of the sea breeze as it flicked around them with a mix of salty ocean and diesel fumes from the harbour.

'What do you want from me, Charles?'

'I was a great firefighter.'

'Clearly.'

'I'm a good fire investigator too. I'm not a joke.'

'Yes. I understand.' Iris smiled.

'At last. Now, how about a profile of my baddie?'

Iris grimaced. Her next explanation was not what Charles was looking for. 'The trouble with profiles is they are brilliant – after. After you've caught the person.'

'You caught the dickhead in the housing estate. Told the police how to trap him.'

'One of the few from the textbook. Unemployed, under twenty-three with a fire-lighting pattern within two kilometres of where he lived. Absent father. I know we identified him, watched him until he lit his next fire, Charles. What no one talks about is how two other young men in the estate were also watched. They also fitted the profile. One was a gentle dope head, the other was studying university units online.'

'You narrowed it down.'

'The profile also has a huge statistical problem. It's based on interviews with convicted recidivist firelighters – the ones who'd been caught. Maybe the older, female, educated, high self-esteem ones don't get found. Or are smart enough not to share.'

Charles appeared confused. Said, 'We catch girls who light fires.'

'Yes, although they tend to do it for revenge rather than profit. Self-harm too. They burn their own things, of sentimental value. Anyway, I'm telling you about the limits. As you know, fires do start by accident. Half of those that are deliberately lit are for financial gain, which includes hiding other crimes.'

'Did you miss the bit of my story where I told you I've worked as a fire investigator for fifteen years?'

'I'm sorry.'

'Is it your Martian?'

Iris took in the pub clientele, delaying more discussion until a waitress moved on from clearing the table behind.

Chuck sipped his beer watching her.

Iris said, 'I don't think the Martian did it.'

'Because?'

'The school is highly organised, the Martian is not. It also looks to me like the school suspect is pretty patient.'

'Very. He cases the joint, has to spend time setting it up without being noticed. He likes to use ignition devices that look like an accident when investigated. I think he builds them himself. Steals an item from the place, tricks up the electrics to create short circuits that can look like an accident. He turns off the water supply or disables the sprinkler system, again so it looks like it might be lack of maintenance. He blocks escape ways with stuff that might naturally be stacked incorrectly or places a skip bin in the wrong place. He did these same things at the school, only we got there early enough to see his handiwork.

The superglue hadn't been burnt up. The truck wasn't in place. We still have the truck, intact.'

Iris said, 'The choosing and planning might be part of the pleasure. If he signs his work he's proud of it. Forget the Martian. These other buildings, how does he choose them, do you think?'

'I'm not sure. They are bigger each time. Places with people in them.'

'You said a backpackers and an old people's home?'

'Yep.'

'So old people, schoolkids. Is he targeting the weak in other ways? He's not sentimental. Why did he choose a school? This school? Pathological firelighters still use their own logic. What's his pattern? What's the connection between all these buildings?'

Charles nodded. 'Yep, that's good. What else?'

'Go back. Go back before the bushfire where you found him. Unless this person came from elsewhere, he probably started experimenting with fire when he was young. You might find a good list of candidates in juvenile firelighters.'

'Good plan. I like it.'

'Where you found the drink can at the first bushfire. It was at a vantage point. He wanted to watch.'

'They all do. I also think he likes to see up close. Smell the smoke. He likes the idea of people dying, screaming. Why he didn't blow the ether at the school as his first option.'

'Which means he might have been interviewed.'

'One oh one. Already looking.'

'I mean look for earlier crimes, the ones you haven't found yet. Get the witness names to similar crimes, see if there's a match. He's very bold.'

Chuck drained his beer.

Iris stood.

'You want to get something to eat?' said Charles.

Iris saw his neediness. 'I have things to do.'

He looked at her plate. 'I mean later.'

'If I think of anything else, I'll let you know.'

Chapter twelve

When Iris got home she collected the week's newspapers from the recycling bin where Mathew or Sandra, the cleaning woman, must have put them. Now Iris was no longer resisting the investigation she was hungry for information.

She made coffee, read chronologically. Details were slim. Emotion was high. A photographic essay of the school oval showed bits and pieces of abandoned student material. Schoolbooks, a pair of reading glasses, a shoe. It was like a domestic copy of the international war zone pictures, no less poignant for the lack of blood or obvious carnage.

During the week, the fire service had allowed the police to release the names of the fallen firefighters and police. One of the firefighters was a woman. The oldest man was the bomb-disposal expert, a forty-six year old police officer. The previous day's paper printed photographs of them, their name and a brief biography, which included marital status, family details, hobbies or sports. They were mostly young, handsome people. Most of them were married. Both pumps had come from the same station, so the firefighters were friends, their partners and children friends too.

Iris found herself studying the face of the station officer. It was his figure Iris could still see, often and unbidden, frozen in the flash. He was thirty-four. His wife's name was Nancy. There were three children, all girls. Louise fourteen, Shellen twelve and Kristabel nine. He coached them at netball. He did carpentry. He was in Rotary. A life story in two paragraphs.

Iris tried to focus on information concerning the investigation, looking for the forensic trails, but the police were being cagey on this detail. Police confirm bomb was not fertiliser based. Police rule out gas leak at school explosion. Police reveal locks tampered with at gymnasium. Police confirm ignition device found at Barnard's. The taskforce was only confirming or denying, not volunteering information in an ongoing investigation.

By day three, the police were ruling out the schoolchildren. Kids unlikely, says Fire Lady. Iris wondered who the police source had been. The terrorist threat was a popular one. The list included returned Muslim fighters, bikie gangs, illegal boat people and a variety of anti-government backyard right-wing groups, all of whom were currently being interviewed. A portion of the groups, particularly the Muslim community and the bikies, were most vocal in denying involvement. 'We don't blow up kiddies,' says bikie sergeant-at-arms. James was mentioned on day three. Man held at Fieldhaven undergoing psychiatric assessments. Fieldhaven pyromaniac grilled on School Explosion.

Iris found an article in the business section of one of the papers mentioning Mathew's company, the negotiations with the Nullabin people and the mining company. Then she saw an article in the arts section. June Hyland was at a major arts launch, attending an opera in a mine cut, ballet on the rugged, red cliffs. What a coincidence that June should be in the same mining town as Mathew this weekend.

Iris decided she'd run. It was still hot outside, so she headed to the bedroom to change for a run on the machine. She checked her phone for messages. There was one from Frank. Gillian had called a couple of times and left a text, which Iris didn't read. There was a missed call from Superintendent Richards. Mathew had called too, probably when he discovered his socks and jocks were missing.

Iris tried Mathew, but was switched to his answer service. 'Hi Mathew. I got your call.' Her mind went blank a moment before she said, 'Bloody hot down here. Hope you're in air conditioning. Hurry home.'

Iris changed into her running gear, hearing the door chimes as she was heading to the gym room. She regarded her running shorts and daggy t-shirt, but headed down to the front door unspruced.

Gillian stood smiling, her three children in dishevelled school clothes rubbernecking on the front veranda.

'Holy shit,' said the boy, looking up at the house.

Gillian bellowed, 'Trenton, stop bloody swearing.'

The girls gaped at Iris.

Gillian said, 'We won't stay long. Popped in for a cuppa and a chinwag on our way home.'

'Oh,' said Iris, not yet letting go of the door.

'Sorry, came out wrong. An afternoon appara tiff and a quick confab, darling.'

'Seeing as you are now speaking my language, how could I refuse?' Iris stepped back.

Gillian turned to her kids, ordering, 'Do not touch anything.'

'Come through everyone,' said Iris leading them towards the kitchen.

'Look at the staircase,' said the older girl.

'How many rooms are here?' asked the younger one.

Iris said, 'I'm not sure.' She grew embarrassed as she considered this. 'Downstairs we have lounge and dining and kitchen and our offices and a laundry and bathroom. Upstairs, mostly bedrooms and lounges, ours and Rosemarie's, and a gym. More bathrooms.'

'Look at the pool!' yelled the boy. They'd reached the back. 'Like in *The Sopranos*.'

'I've got soft drinks. Not sure about any nibblies for you kids. We're a bit out of practice.' Iris didn't want Gillian to see how bare her fridge was. 'Biscuits!' Iris found chocolate biscuits in the cupboard, cool drink in the drinks fridge.

'Are you rich?' asked the youngest.

'No,' said Iris.

'Can we go outside?' asked the oldest girl.

'Yes, of course,' said Iris.

'Don't touch anything,' repeated Gillian.

Gillian's kids took their sugar looty outside to roam around the gardens.

'It is a very large swimming pool,' said Gillian.

'Yes. A bit of a chore really, since Rosemarie left. She had parties in and around it during high school. Came with the house.'

'I heard about Rodney,' said Gillian.

'Oh,' said Iris. 'Drink?'

'Does the Pope shit in the woods?'

'That would probably be a no, Gillian.'

'Could the bear be Catholic?'

'It's entirely possible. This way.' Iris led her to the wine fridge.

Gillian said, 'This is a seriously big house, Iris.'

'It came with the pool. Is white all right or would you prefer red?'

'Wine is good.'

Iris poured. 'How is Barbara?'

'She's good. You were right. I started looking at her differently.'

Iris handed her a glass of wine.

Gillian went on, 'I'm seeing her as a friend who wants to see me, not as a problem I can't fix.'

Iris examined Gillian but she was looking into her wine glass. 'And her daughter?'

'We've got the right mix, I think, of meds and living adjustments. They're both still working through Trent's death. Anyway, I'm not here about that.'

Iris led Gillian up the hall to her office.

'Oh, my dear god. This is the office in my heaven.'

'Well, it's starting to turn into a knick-knack graveyard.' Iris gestured towards the couch.

'Butterflies, huh?'

'Yes. Once the family found out I liked them, they became the Christmas present of choice. Birthdays, Mother's Day. I'm delighted by the way. Can't have too many butterflies.' Iris sat. 'How can I help, Gillian?'

'I've telephoned Biara.'

'Oh?'

'I know you're busy. I thought I'd help with the coroner's report.'

'I don't need any help.'

'Yeah, right. None of my clients are sick. You look like shit.'

Iris sipped her wine. It was a chardonnay, she decided. She hadn't taken in the label when she'd chosen it.

Iris looked up to see Gillian watching her.

She thought of throwing her out. She was an annoying person who talked like a shearer, however a shearer talked. Now she'd become a kind of Chinese albatross, or whatever it was that never left until the debt was repaid.

Iris said, 'I took some old Triazolam last night to help me sleep. On top of yesterday's wine, they kind of knocked me about.'

Gillian was still staring.

'I am fine, Gillian. I'm already feeling stronger. I'm tough.'

'I'm not your mother.'

'Thank god for small mercies.'

'Ouch.'

'For a start you'd also be six feet under.'

'What I mean is, I'm simply trying to help, not take anything.'

Iris said, 'Those blue butterflies are morphos, everyone's favourite. From South America. We went through a period, at Rosemarie's instigation, where killing butterflies so they could be put in a glass frame for one human's pleasure was very wrong and selfish. I think it was Mathew ... of course it was Mathew, pointed out that butterflies only live for a very short time in the wild so we were only culling a few who would die anyway and it was all right again, as a gift, to preserve them forever. It was an answer we could all live with. Not the butterflies.'

'Rosemarie's your daughter?'

'Yes.'

Gillian explored the room as though trying to find her.

'Away at uni. I don't want to do this.'

'I wasn't trying. God, Iris. No. All I've done is made calls to the prison to chase up any paperwork. I thought I could save you a bit of time. I've requested copies. Your visits are all listed on their files. They also registered three calls you made the day before, one of them got through to suggest Rodney be put on suicide watch.'

'Yes. I remember now. I wanted him listed "at risk" because I thought he might be in for a bashing.'

'It looks like your telephone message got through to the

medical office. It was noted on Rodney's file. There was a change of shift and the psych on duty was called away before he could complete handover. As you know, they're always understaffed. A violent offender hit another violent offender over the head with a spaghetti maker in the kitchen, and an ice addict who was in the middle of a psychotic episode didn't choose a convenient time to act out. The loudest emergencies won. They didn't get back to the secure cell until ... He slipped through the cracks.' Gillian sighed. There were always cracks. Chasms. 'Anyway, I wanted to drop by to let you know you didn't slip up. Far from it. You did everything you possibly could. If you were feeling ...'

'No.'

'A paper trail exists which backs you up, which is legally important, you know.'

Iris shrugged.

'Do you feel you let him down?'

'No.'

'Good. Tough case to take on, by the way.'

'If he'd had someone else ... who knows.'

Gillian's hand was on her shoulder. Iris let it stay, let the warmth come through her t-shirt.

Iris said, 'You said you fix people, Gillian. I'm not sure I do. I seem to be better at catching them and breaking them.'

'I know that's not true.'

Iris was pretty sure Gillian didn't know this at all. She was trying to be supportive. Her hand felt good on her shoulder.

*

Gillian left soon after, having extracted Iris's notes concerning conversations with Rodney so Gillian could write up the bones of a report for the coroner to mollify Patricia. Iris promised to take it easy during her brief suspension from the practice, which was a lie. She had told the kids she wasn't rich, which she supposed was another lie.

She decided after her second glass of wine she would not exercise on the running machine. She stayed in her office writing her report for Frank and the police Arson Squad regarding James. She reiterated her belief he was suffering from a trauma that he was compulsively reworking by lighting fires.

He had constructed, she felt, an alternative personality in order to evade an unknown but specific heinous act. She was aware this conclusion fell outside her remit and perhaps expertise, but used it to support her observations about James in relation to the degree of planning obviously required to construct the gymnasium bomb. Put more simply, the projected personality of the school bomber and the assessed personality of James were not a very good match.

Iris did not send the report. She found herself imagining a possible scenario. What if James did get the ether? She did not know how. Someone had. What if, in his psychosis, he imagined the ether as fuel? What if the gymnasium was to be his rocket ship? What if he was going to save these kids, take them home to Mars? Might he be able to plan these two parallel procedures? They were not mutually exclusive. What if, as Detective Pavlovic suggested, he'd found a brief oasis of clarity once everything was set to go and, in the horror of this realisation, he broke down again, or further regressed and fled – only to become compulsive again twenty hours and nine hundred kilometres away? Was there anything in what Iris knew of James's personality, symptoms and profile that proved he could not have committed the crime? Was she certain?

Iris didn't feel sleepy. She felt too restless for the junk on television. She poured herself another glass of wine, the sedative of choice for many, and picked over her pile of dead writer books. She picked up Janet Malcolm's *The Silent Woman: Sylvia Plath and Ted Hughes*. She'd bought *Virginia Woolf and Neuropsychiatry*, but knew she wouldn't read it. She'd been reading a wonderful biography of Virginia Woolf by Woolf's nephew. She'd been intrigued about references to sexual molestation when Woolf was a child and her evident bipolar. Then Iris had read *To the Lighthouse*, and she didn't want Woolf picked apart like a faulty clock. Explanations can reduce rather than deepen our understanding.

Long after joining the fire service, after all the court cases, profiles and press stuff, after working for the police, meeting and marrying Mathew, having Rosemarie, Iris returned to the fire service and became known as the Fire Lady. It was a media thing. A newspaper thing the television news took up. In spite of the fact she worked in police cells and courtrooms now, they used old photographs, archived video clips, those news people, of the times at the beginning when young Iris attended the fires. There was a famous shot of her with her hand on an exhausted fireman's shoulder in burnt-out bush, another of her silhouetted against a wall of flame as a house erupted. Worst of all was a closer shot of her face, orange tinged watching a fire with an expression of ecstasy.

Iris put her empty wine glass in the dishwasher. She switched off the kitchen light and the lounge light, then went to her office to turn that light out. She noticed dust on her father's microscope and wiped it away with her hand. She drifted to look at a butterfly in its frame, found herself focusing on her own reflection in the glass. She studied the face there: part blue morpho, part Iris Foster; two dry, pinned things in a frame.

Chapter thirteen

Iris dressed in an olive-green skirt, a white blouse, black high-heeled sandals. She didn't put on any make-up or earrings, but she chose the antique pendant with the vague hieroglyphics etched into the breloque. It felt cold on her skin. Iris thought she'd drive. It was Friday night, the streets were busy, full of taxis and threatening cars. Iris considered a drive in the hills, discounting it as too far, possibly too forlorn, so her whim sent her towards the beach. The coast road was busy, the carparks along the ocean full. Young people were wandering, office workers staggered. Iris passed a pub on the corner with huge windows on the second floor. She considered going up to be jostled and unserved, to edge her way to the glass and look out on a dark moonless ocean. She wound down the passenger window so she could smell the salt, hear the crash of surf. Cars beeped behind her, long angry horns forcing her to drive on.

Iris parked in the staff carpark behind Park Wing. High, strong lights made the three fences look grey, the no-man's land a shadowless yellowy green. Moths swirled and circled way up like tiny seagulls.

Iris buzzed at the outer door. The attendant, in his fifties and dressed in a psychiatric nurse's blue windcheater, peered at her through the glass in the door. It was after midnight. He talked through an intercom. 'Can I help you?'

Iris said, 'Iris Foster. I've been assessing James. No surname. For Dr Silverberg.'

'The Martian.'

'Yes, the Martian.'

'Just a minute.'

He went behind the dimly lit reception counter, read the schedules.

Iris looked across to the other buildings of Fieldhaven. They were barely lit, the rooms and dormitories for voluntary patients were dark, only corridors lit, only skeleton night-staff cars in the carparks. A security van drove slowly up along the vacant nursing school at the top of the rise.

'He's been moved,' came the voice through the intercom.

'Oh,' said Iris. 'Has he been sent back to Biara?'

'No. Across to Grange Wing.' He pointed behind Iris, across the road to another secure ward.

'Thank you,' said Iris. 'Oh, can you do me a favour? Let them know I'm coming over?' She gave a sad, tired smile.

He nodded, returning a similar smile.

Grange also held involuntary patients, but it was not maximum security. Fewer locks, no CCTV, only one high security fence. The patients here were disturbed but had committed no crimes. They were often experiencing episodes, or due for diagnosis, or off their meds. In spite of the security, its purpose was assessment and treatment. It was a hospital.

At night, most patients were sedated. The night duty staff held a watching brief, mostly paperwork to fulfil, and care of a number of wards. The night duty nurse waited at the outer door.

'I'm Iris Foster. I've been assessing James – the Martian – for Dr Silverberg and the state court.' Iris flashed her ID.

'It's very late.' The nurse was Indian, in her mid-thirties, plump in her uniform like a pudding.

'I'm overdue with the report. I wanted to check my conclusions.'

The nurse stepped back, allowing Iris to enter. 'He's not talking. He's not doing any tricks either. Apparently he used to do magic tricks over at Park.'

'Yes, a juggler and a knife thrower. A pickpocket and escapologist. I think he's a pretty good dancer too.'

'Yes. On his file.'

'Have they got him on anything?'

The nurse went into a nurse's station. Another woman

worked at a computer in the office behind. The nurse checked the whiteboard inside the nurse's station. It listed thirty names, their medications, some with adjoining asterisks indicating danger, either for the patient or the staff.

'No. He's not very responsive. Complies with physical manipulation and firm requests. Not communicative. Looks like you've wasted a trip.'

'Not at all. I'm on my way home,' lied Iris. 'Listen, I couldn't go and sit with him? He's not dangerous, I can write up my report, be done. They're quite anxious about it with this taskforce, the school bombing.'

'They said that's what he is here for. Hardly seems possible. You never can tell.'

'I'll make my last observations about his state and write up my notes. No more than an hour, we'll be done.'

'Do you think he did it?'

Iris gave the barest roll of her eyes, a secret shared.

'I can't let you in, Dr Foster. Not without authorisation.'

'They didn't send my paperwork over with him? I had blanket authorisation at Park. It should be with his paperwork.'

The nurse sighed, glanced vaguely at the back office, not keen to wade through days of emails, doctors' reports, police transfers, visitor lists and the like.

Iris said, 'Well, you could call Park. They'll have me down on the visitors log for the last few days. Be easy for them to look it up.' Iris gave her a conspiratorial smile at bureaucracy circumvented in the interests of common sense. She glanced towards the door. 'I'll come back in the morning. The taskforce are clamouring, I thought I could beat the weekend.'

'I'll call them.'

'Thank you. You're a lifesaver.'

Iris opened her bag and took out her notepad. Clearly she must have formulated the possibility of seeing James because she had everything she needed.

The nurse came back, mollified by her call to the maximum-security ward. She unlocked the door to the ward to reveal six individual locked rooms, each with a small viewing window. The lights were out in all the rooms, Iris noted, as the nurse led her through to another ward, where she unlocked another door.

'Why do they think it is him?'

'He lights fires. A bit compulsive. So they're looking at everyone.'

'I heard it is terrorists. You know, against girls being educated. This happens in a lot of countries, I can tell you.'

'I hope it's not true, but you never know, do you?'

'There are a lot of crazy people in the world who aren't in here.'

Iris could tell she said this quite a lot. 'Yes, with all kinds of definitions of crazy. Although we're more strict about it in here, aren't we?' They shared a laugh.

The nurse led her to James's room. She flicked an exterior switch that dimly illuminated the room. It was at quarter power, for sleeping and observation. He lay on his side under a sheet, his eyes closed.

The nurse unlocked the door. She whispered, 'Do you want an attendant? We've got one on duty, three more on call for all the wards.'

'He's never shown any sign of violence. You have panic buttons in these rooms, don't you?'

'Yes, there are ...' Second thoughts were starting to sneak in.

Iris held out her hand, 'Thank you ...'

'Julie.'

'Thank you, Julie. You're a lifesaver.' They shook hands. 'You'll leave the door unlocked, won't you? I can come back out here, wave to you when I'm done.' Iris pointed to a camera mounted in the hall to cover the doors to the rooms. Iris inspected her watch. 'I will be done at 1.30.' Iris stepped into James's room and closed the door.

She sat in the plastic chair by the wall to look at James.

He opened his eyes, blinking.

'Hello James. It's Iris Foster.'

He closed his eyes again.

Sensing Julie at the viewing window, Iris took the notebook and a pen out of her bag before putting it down on the floor next to her chair. She said, 'You're looking well rested. I hope you've recovered from ... our session the other day. I'm sorry. I crash or crash through. It caused you to crash too. And all this is about the nature of your crash. The spaceship. The nature of the spaceship. The metaphor of the spaceship. Dream therapy and dream reading suggests we share certain symbolism so we can analyse our subconscious thoughts through decoding the symbols. Anima, animus. Fire is often passion but context is all. It is warm, but it also devours. As you told me. No symbolism required. Context, see. What is the fire doing? What is it saying in the story of the dream? The dreamer is the one who knows. The pop psychology dream reader can suggest interpretations but only the dreamer can know if it fits. What if the dream is about an actual fire? Surely all snakes are not sex. Or even sin. Sometimes someone is quite reasonably afraid of snakes.' Why did I bring up snakes?

As Iris spoke, she scanned the room. She spied the panic button by the door. She noted the empty desk under the window. She saw the empty viewing window. She looked at the plastic smoke detector, the automatic sprinkler. It was the kind with red alcohol liquid sensitive to heat. The sprinkler blade was recessed, covered in a special mesh, to prevent it being used as a tying off point for any suicide attempts.

'I think narrative has become fetishised. I think it's as capable of silencing complicated conclusions as of discovering truths. Do you think Phil Spector did it? Or is he locked up because of his manifest oddness? What about Pistorius? Did he mean to kill her? Or is his feetlessness what really gets to us; what makes us so sure he snapped; couldn't cope with such a beautiful girlfriend? I'm old enough to remember Azaria Chamberlain. Excuse me. I've been reading the newspapers. They disturb me; they have dark fairy stories underneath, our tribal fear of the dark and danger – whatever it is outside the campfire light.'

James lay on his side, his eyes staring unfocused. He may not have even been listening.

Iris went on, 'I'm talking about whether what I want to do is wrong. I think I know what's wrong with you. At least where to look to find out. I think, when we get to the other side of this event, it will be towards a better condition. I hope. Maybe this playful, funny, intuitive, light, inquisitive self is a preferred one. Who am I to say you have to grow up? I have come across all kinds of things. I can imagine ... well, to lock it away forever, never remember, would be a fair decision. Only it's not locked away, is it James?'

Iris leaned forward in her chair.

James didn't move, but his eyes remained open.

'I'm trying to explain, but my mind isn't very clear. I think of it like an injury. Like a car accident or war or skiing. Let's go with skiing. You take a fall, or hit a tree and your leg is shattered. It has to be taken off because you will get septicaemia or all kinds of blood loss and infections that will kill you. So, without your consent, they cut the leg off – to save the rest of you. But ... and my little story moves beyond that – you're at the point where we can give you a prosthetic. We can get you walking again. Not as good as before. Maybe as good as before. Different, because of the accident. The crash. The prosthetic, the solution, the physiotherapy and uncomfortable fittings, sweat; retraining your body is worth the new things you will be able to do. Not as good as before the skiing accident, sure, but better than only one leg.

'That's my metaphor. That's my story for this. You have rights about taking on a false leg. You have the right to refuse to learn to walk again. You don't have rights about losing the leg. The code amongst doctors forces them to decide that. Well, so here is where I am, I guess. If you did try to blow up the school, if you did burn those old people and those backpackers and who knows what else, then not remembering those things ... well. I cannot imagine. I cannot imagine that far.' Iris stopped speaking. She dribbled to a halt, sighed.

James lay on the bed looking across the room at Iris. She was sure he was listening.

'I don't think you are, but if you are this bad person, I am going to find you. I'm here for another crack, without your permission. Your leg is shattered. Whatever happens, I will not abandon you, even if you are the bad man, hiding. I'm here for the long haul, one way or the other. We leave no man behind. My promise.' Iris pulled her chair closer to him. 'So, we're going to conduct an experiment.'

James's eyes came up to meet hers.

'I'm proposing a dangerous type of therapy, like aversion therapy, where you might confront your fear, and by confronting it learn it is not insurmountable. Sounds a bit like Shakespeare, doesn't it? By opposing, end it.'

Iris touched her pendant nestled at the base of her neck.

'You've commented on my jewellery. You like jewellery. Nice, old things. Here's another Australian antique. Silver, eighteen-nineties. I think you'll like it. Old.' Iris took the pendant, pulled the chain over her hair, held it out towards James.

He still lay on the bed, his head on the pillow, but his eyes focused on the dangling silver object Iris held out to him, slightly below his eye level.

She kept speaking, in a calm voice. 'I can never quite decide whether it looks like a book or an empty sack. Maybe it mostly looks like a purse, a long, skinny purse. See the shape at the top. Look at these marks on it. Do you think they are actual writing? Or is it fake writing? Etched marks? Can you see it?'

Iris let the pendant swing slightly at the end of the chain.

'I can see writing, Iris. It looks like writing.'

Iris let out a long breath. 'I think it is. Do you think it says anything? Can you see?'

'Is there writing on the back? Look closely. It says, "Look at me. Look at me." You look tired Iris. Relax.' His voice was low and constant like Iris's, as though he were matching her slightly monotonous pace. 'Relax your neck while you read the writing. That's good. Relax. The pendant is floating, floating in the air. "Look at me," it says.'

Iris said, 'Look at me. Are you reading it?' Her voice sounded distant to her.

James said, 'It says, "Read me. Read me." Imagine it is your breathing. Imagine you are calm and at peace. Breathing with each swing, each swing of the pendant. Imagine you are resting, Iris. Resting and happy and asleep. You want sleep. Sleeping peacefully. Finally at peace. No worries. Peace.'

Iris heard James sigh. Or was it her own sigh.

James sat up on the bed. He wore boxer shorts and a white t-shirt. He took the pendant from her. 'It's very pretty, Iris. Like you. I like your old jewellery, the way you've left it tarnished with a hundred years of dust and human sweat in the crevices.' James reached past Iris, came back with her handbag. He said, 'I might borrow your car. Do you mind? Can I borrow your car?'

Iris said, 'Yes.'

'It might be time to go.' He froze, looking in the handbag. He sat on the bed looking deep into the opening. He reached in slowly, pulling out the green plastic cigarette lighter Iris had taken from the table at the pub that afternoon.

Iris sat, immobile. She couldn't stop him. She didn't want to stop him. She watched him.

'No,' he whispered. 'No, no.' He closed his hand into a fist around the lighter. He was looking somewhere far from the room where he sat.

'What do you see?' said Iris.

'The bedroom.'

'Whose bedroom?'

'Mine. Ours.'

'What's happening?'

'They're leaving.'

'Who?'

'No.' James lay down on his side on the bed. He raised his legs up. He sang something, low. It sounded like a nursery rhyme, but in another language. He stopped singing. Said, 'Sleeping.' He put his thumb in his mouth. He still held the lighter in the other hand.

'What happens now?'

'I light the fire.'

'Do it,' said Iris.

James sat up again, opened his hand to reveal the lighter. He searched about him, saw Iris's pad in her lap. He took it, tore pages out of it, layering them in a tiny pyre on the bed. He pulled up the sheet, fashioned it loosely around the paper.

Iris sat, unmoving, watching James prepare his fire.

James lit the paper. It caught quickly, the sheet started to smoke. It took up the flame. James watched his fire, intent.

'What do you see?'

'Fire.'

'Where?'

'My house.'

He froze again, as though listening.

'What is happening?'

'No. Got to get them out? Oh no. I have to get them out.'

'Who?'

'The kids.'

'What kids?'

'My kids. I have to get them out.'

'You said they've left?'

'They're here. They're shouting.'

'Go to them.'

'I can't.'

'Go to them.'

'Fire. Fire everywhere.'

Iris stood, bumped past James where he sat on the bed next to the circle of burning sheet, grabbed the pillow, and smothered it. She leaned on the pillow over the fire, grinding down on it, not wanting to release the smoke from under.

James remained sitting on the bed. 'I have to get them out.'

'What do you do?'

'I go to the door.'

'Do it.'

James stood, walked.

'What do you see?'

'Fire everywhere.'

'Where are your children?'

'Downstairs, screaming.'

James fell to his knees.

Iris, still leaning into the pillow, said, 'What's happening?'

'Something fell on me. It's burning.'

James stood, twisting around.

Iris said, 'What?'

'She's screaming?'

'Who?'

'Nisa.'

'Who's Nisa?'

'My wife. I have to get them. I have to save them. I have to get them. They're burning.' James's body began to shake. He gave an anguished cry.

Iris let go of the pillow and went to him. 'It's all right.'

'They died.' He drew out the words like a fragile bird cry.

'Shh. James, you are not there.' Iris knelt next to him. 'That was in the past. It is gone. You are here, with me now.' She hugged him around his shoulders, pulling his shuddering body to her. 'It's all right now. Shh. Shhh. We will fix this. We will heal you.'

'They burned. I burned them,' he whispered.

'You're safe. Let's go back. Before the fire. Why did you light it?'

'No. Please.' He begged.

James was crying.

'It's okay. Shh. Enough now. We've done enough for today.' She kissed his wet, salty cheeks. He smelt of hospital soap and of fresh male sweat, kind of animally and leathery, like horses and wheat. A chaff smell. How did he smell like flour? Iris had her hands in his hair. 'Shh. Shh,' she was saying or was he saying, 'Shh. Shh.' His hands were on her hips. He held her hips while she held his head. She tasted his tears. 'It's okay now. It's all right. We'll talk about the fire. We can talk about it now,' she whispered. Why was she whispering? Or were these thoughts, unspoken words?

Her hands found their way inside his t-shirt. He was wet. His shoulders were wet with hot sweat, her hands were rubbing down his sides. She found his scars, the tessellated pocks on his back, smooth yet rippled. Her fingertips played with the dips and ridges of the burn scars. 'Poor boy. It's okay now. Poor boy.'

His hands were at her breasts, on the outside of her blouse. His fingers were plucking at her nipples. No!

Iris pushed him away. She skittered up to stand by the bed. An alarm sounded, outside of her. Above.

He knelt before her, head bowed. 'I'm sorry, I ...'

'I'm sorry. This is unforgiveable. James, I'm so sorry. Are you okay?' Iris reached out and touched the soft dark hair on his bent head, a reverse act of contrition.

'Do you remember the fire?'

'Yes,' he said. His head was still bowed.

The fire alarm continued to whine. Iris saw a movement at the viewing window. She saw Julie, the night nurse's dark face, eyes wide.

Iris considered the charred bedding. She looked down to see the top of her blouse unbuttoned, bra showing. She could hear an alarm. Not a fire alarm.

James stood, dazed.

Iris spoke quickly, as she searched the room for her pendant and the cigarette lighter. 'I took advantage of you, James, and I will be punished. I will come back. You've faced this awful thing in your past, but we have to talk about it again. Okay?'

Iris went to James as the door opened and two orderlies came in. She touched him on his arm, on the bicep. She said, 'You hid this memory from yourself because it is awful. But you are strong enough to deal with it. Do you understand?'

James said nothing. He stood in the room looking towards the bed.

Iris said, 'James? Can you hear me?'

Julie said, 'I think you need to come with me.'

Iris said, 'James?'

One of the orderlies held up the blackened pillow. 'There's been a fire.'

*

'He confronted the traumatic event which triggered his psychosis. He needs to be watched.' Iris continued to argue for James's welfare in spite of the orderlies taking him away, in spite of being escorted herself to the ward office near the front door.

'How did the fire start?' asked the ward supervisor.

'Where is he?'

'We've moved him.'

'Has he been put on suicide watch?'

'We will.'

'It needs to be done now.'

The supervisor nodded to a male nurse who headed off.

Julie hovered in the doorway. She had remained silent so far concerning what she'd seen or not seen through the viewing window whenever she'd arrived. Julie was conflicted, aware she'd bent the rules perhaps in allowing Iris unfettered, unaccompanied access to a patient after hours without direct authorisation.

'How did the fire start?' repeated the supervisor.

Iris had her own battles. Full disclosure, right now, would not help anyone, least of all James. 'I was writing notes. I'm completing an assessment for Dr Frank Silverberg, who I believe is reporting to the School Bombing Federal Taskforce. I thought James was asleep. He managed to get a cigarette lighter out of my handbag. I panicked, but then I managed to get the pillow and smother the flames. Completely my fault. I shouldn't have left it in my handbag. I was tired.'

'You know we lost a patient to a fire last year? Set fire to his mattress.'

'As I say, completely my fault.'

The supervisor turned to Julie.

Iris said, 'After I got the fire out, we struggled, well more grappled. He tried to get to the ashes. I stopped him. It wasn't violent. He was upset.'

The supervisor paused. She looked to Julie again.

Julie was fitting the pieces of what she had seen with what she now knew.

Iris said, 'The fire compulsion is strong. Something for Dr Silverberg, I suppose.'

'He's on his way. I need you both to write this up. While it's fresh.'

'Yes. All right,' said Julie, refusing to look at Iris. Her jaw was loosening. She thought maybe this could have been what happened. She might have jumped to the wrong conclusion. She would have to think about it while she wrote. She still might go either way, although one way would clearly have greater consequences than the other way.

*

Frank found Iris in a small crib room in Grange Wing around three am.

'You look like shit,' she said.

'I'm old. I need my eight hours sleep. You look strangely radiant, which is a worry.' He didn't sit, instead went to the sink and started the kettle. It whirred, hissed in the background.

'Why are you here, Iris?'

'I couldn't sleep,' she said brightly.

He examined a coffee mug in the dish rack before teaspooning instant coffee. His coat was covered in dog hair as usual. Frank's hair was wild, full of cowlicks, tufts, thickets. He'd rushed in, without a shower. He was used to this, of course. Part of the gig as a government psychiatrist. Always an emergency.

'Have they got him on special watch?' she asked.

'He is subdued but alert. Calm. No obvious distress.' He went to the fridge, sniffed a carton of milk. He flinched, leaving it in the fridge, and returned to the bubbling kettle.

'That stuff will rot your guts, Frank.'

'I have developed a taste for it. My gut craves the special blend of caffeine and soap.' He topped up his mug of black coffee with a little water from the tap before coming to sit. 'What happened?'

'I came in for one last assessment.'

'Bullshit. You had all you needed.'

'I had doubts.'

'Bullshit. You've worked the slowest I've ever seen.'

'Yeah, well, maybe you shouldn't have dragged in a damaged person to do your police work.'

'You seemed well. You promised me you were okay.'

Iris said nothing.

Frank said, 'So you're acting out. Is that it? You're punishing me.'

'Hmm. It's worth thinking about.'

'Naughty daddy.'

'Don't.'

'Okay, so ...' He sipped his coffee, wrinkling his face at the acrid taste he needed. His eyes remained down, contemplating the coffee. He was trying to get his brain up to full speed.

'I crossed the line. Way over.'

He raised his eyes to hers, but gave nothing. He listened, withholding judgement. Only listening. His glasses were covered with the thinnest film of dust on the lenses.

'I must have formulated the idea before I left home because

I chose this pendant.' She pulled it out from her blouse. 'I did have my doubts. Not big. What if his Martian persona were merely one character creation? What if there was a twisted, calculating bomber too? What if? So, I talked my way in here, I hypnotised him.'

Iris stopped, waited for Frank to speak. He didn't.

'Not one of my ... safest ideas. I wanted to confront his trauma. Which I did.' Iris couldn't help the triumph sneaking into her voice, in spite of everything. 'So, I tried to hypnotise him, which I'm not sure I did. I think he hypnotised me.' Iris laughed. 'Blowback? He took a cigarette lighter from my purse and he lit a fire on the bed. Yes, I let him, kind of. Maybe he hypnotised me, maybe I hypnotised myself, or maybe it was a kind of ... swoon of possibility – I was present while he acted out his compulsive behaviour, I observed and asked questions.'

Frank seemed about to say something, but waited again.

'I believe he started a fire in his house, his family burned to death. The name of his wife is Nisa. I think we should be able to check. It doesn't sound common. Also he sang a song in an Asian language. Not Chinese or Vietnamese.'

Frank nodded.

'We were intimate, Frank. Physically.'

Frank still didn't say anything. He scanned her face, examined each pupil. He finally said, 'How intimate?'

'I put the fire out. He was crying. I hugged him. It started as a hug. I kissed him. I stroked his back.' Iris recalled the strange feel of James's back, the odd, hard smoothness of the scars.

Frank said, 'But you didn't have sex?'

'I was comforting him and I got lost in it. I took comfort.'

'Did you have sex with the patient, Iris? Manual, oral, penetrative. Did you?'

'No. Nearly, but no. Frank, it wasn't the sex. It was the intimacy. My patient, powerless, sick, in need, and I took advantage of that vulnerability and trust. I forced to him confront his trauma and I have not followed up, not talked through the ramifications. What's wrong with me, Frank?'

Frank reached across the table, took Iris's hands in his own big mitts. They were warm from holding the coffee mug.

'I'm glad you told me, Iris. I love you, mate, you know, don't you?'

'Yes.' He did, she guessed. 'Am I having a breakdown?'

'Well, that's a funny word.'

'Break, broke. Down. Up.'

'People can wear out, Iris. Need – a break from. Would you consider having a proper rest somewhere?'

'Here?'

'Good gracious no. Not a public hospital, nothing like here. You know, somewhere like Xavier, in the rolling greenery of the hills with rock stars and politicians. Resting, recuperating with groovy dieticians and personal trainers and very subtle cognitive therapists.'

'I must be sick. You're talking to me too gently. I'll go home and think about it.'

'Iris, the light bulb has got to want to change.'

'But we need the eggs.' Old psychiatrist jokes.

Frank finally let go of Iris's hands to pat his suit pocket. 'I'm going to go find a script pad. Try a mild sedative.' He leaned back against the fridge. 'I will let the police know about what you've found from James. I will have him examined and organise follow up. In terms of the contact, I think it was wrong, but I'm not sure how it's going to play out. Counter transference, I'd guess. Clearly you can't have any further professional contact with him. I should have seen. The school explosion may have triggered a relapse, set back your recovery. Or just be a whole new thing. I should not have put you onto this case so soon after ...'

Iris could tell Frank didn't want to finish it so she did. 'Georgina and Williams dying in the fire at my office.'

Frank blinked at her. Simply said, 'Interesting.' He stood, shuffled, said, 'I'll write you that script. You know we'll get through this, don't you?'

'Yes. I'm strong, Frank. Stupid, irresponsible, deeply disturbed – but strong.'

He leaned down and kissed her on the top of the head. It sent a warm glow through her.

Iris got up, washed Frank's mug, put away the coffee. She

suddenly remembered James sitting up in the bed and the voice he'd used to say he would borrow her car. It had been quite cynical. It was not like boyish James or Martian James. Was the hypnosis a performance too? Was the family tragedy another cover, the sexual advance too, another bit of glitter to distract?

Chapter fourteen

Iris woke in her own bed to sunshine. Mathew was away. Frank had allowed her to drive herself home. She hadn't filled out his sedative prescription. She wasn't going to. The front doorbell chimed again. She looked to the clock. It was ten fifteen on Saturday.

Iris put on a robe, went downstairs. The doorbell chimed again as she reached the bottom steps. Impatient, she thought. Where's the fire? She opened the front door to Detective Stuart Pavlovic.

Pavlovic wore a striped shirt, dark trousers, black leather shoes. He carried a small soft leather bag, too effeminate for a cop. He was looking towards the garage when she opened the door. He swung back, noting the robe. 'Oh, sorry. I woke you.'

Iris shrugged.

'I've been sent to ask you some questions.'

'Come in.' Iris led him towards the lounge. 'Let me help you with your inquiries.'

'Thank you.'

'Do you want coffee?' asked Iris.

He nodded.

'Okay. Come through to the kitchen. Do you know how these pod coffee makers work?'

'Yes, of course.'

'Very well. Could I have a green one? You can pick your own colour. I'll get dressed.'

Iris went upstairs. She recalled the last thing she'd done before bed was to put all her clothes, including the skirt, into the washing machine. She supposed she had destroyed evidence. She'd thrown away the clothes she'd worn the day of the school explosion. Was it really so easy to put disconcerting events behind her?

She put on shorts and a t-shirt, went into the bathroom. She decided not to subject the detective to more of her morning face. Her eyes were puffy. She dusted the wrinkles, chose a subtle pinkish lipstick, Chanel.

He stood at the back windows, sipping his coffee and gazing into the garden. It was magnificent in the morning, a tangled forest dappling sunshine onto the grass and limestone surrounding the huge swimming pool. The jacaranda still held the last of its flowers.

Iris said, 'Your bandage has gone.'

He held up his arm, flexed it gingerly. 'It was in the way.'

Iris found her coffee on the counter.

'You don't have any milk,' he said.

'Sorry.'

'I don't need milk.' He went to the kitchen table, sat at the other end.

'You're not going to comment on the house?'

'Nice house.'

'Everybody comments on the house.'

'There's all kinds of houses.'

Iris thought he pretended to be unimpressed. He didn't want to show any inferiority. Maybe he even resented the house. Iris used to. 'Well, enough pleasantries, Detective. What?'

'A few things, Mrs Foster.' He took a pocket sound recorder from his man bag, placed it on the table. He took out his mobile, a small notebook, fished for a pen.

Iris took her coffee and sat at the table within range of the recorder. She said, 'How is the investigation going?'

He looked at her sharply. 'It's an operational matter.'

'I can help more, if I know things.'

'Let's deal with the incidents at Fieldhaven last night first.'

'I am working on the case.'

'As far as I know Mrs Foster, you have been helping Dr Silverberg. You used to work for the Fire and Rescue Service.

You have also done contract work and consultancy for a number of departments, including the police.'

Iris noted the recorder, raising an eyebrow at the detective.

'It's all in your file, Mrs Foster.'

'Well, if it's in my file.'

'I'm working for people, Mrs Foster. They like transcripts.'

'To add to the file. You're not on the terrorists.'

He shook his head.

'Or the bikies.'

He sat back watching her. He didn't answer.

'You're on the Martian.'

He paused ever so slightly before saying, 'I was on the schoolkids.'

'Until it played out. Now you're miscellaneous.'

He nearly smiled. 'Yes. Miscellaneous loose ends. Speaking of which, any problem with me asking a couple of questions for the record?'

He had a healthy ego, this man. He believed in himself. He knew who he was, where he fitted into the world. Maybe he wasn't a type A personality, but a healthy B, happy to work within the team. He'd make a good firey, thought Iris.

'Fire away, Detective.'

'The suspect at Fieldhaven, the Martian ...'

'James. He calls himself James.'

'He apparently disclosed an incident to you.'

'Yes. While I was assessing him, he appeared to re-experience a particular traumatic event which I believe forms part of his psychosis. A fire in his house. I believe his two children and possibly his wife died in the house fire. The wife's name is Nisa. I'm not sure where it occurred. Asia. He speaks an Asian language. Not Chinese or Japanese or Vietnamese. Oh, and I think those burn wounds on his back were part of the same incident, so hospital records and some police investigation should be available.'

The detective took notes.

Iris added, 'I went back partly to test your theory, Detective.'

'My theory!'

'Yes. Whether he had a breakdown after he'd set the school bomb.'

'And ...'

'I don't think the school bomb is in his life. Only this family fire.'

'An odd way to put it. Not very conclusive.'

'I live in a world of guesses.'

'What do you guess about our school bomber?'

'I think he likes the numbers, the fuss. He keeps score. He likes the attention. And he likes getting away with it. Because he likes getting away with it, he doesn't get too close. He liked preparing. He is content to imagine the pain. He rigs things so as to cause suffering. He likes hurting.'

'Who are you working with on this?'

'Your taskforce, I assume, through Frank.'

'You have a lot of information, even considering you might have seen a couple of our files in the incident room. Your profile is way ahead of the curve.'

'Theories.'

'Why were you in the incident room again?'

'I was looking for one of your team members. I didn't realise the room was off limits, Detective Pavlovic. I'm sorry about that. The breach has clearly put me offside with you.'

'Who were you looking for again?'

'A fire investigator.'

'Why?'

'I possessed information he'd asked for.'

'Was it Charles Koch?'

Iris considered the recorder again. An interrogation trick is to have a suspect go over the same story a number of times to see if it tallies with itself. Interrogations were now called interviews, of course. Just the facts, no prejudice. 'Yes. I think if you check back on your previous recording of our conversation outside the room, you'll find I said so.'

'So you're working with him on his Zorro theory, huh?'

'I've given him a few ideas, yes. Shouldn't I have?'

'Did you know he is looking up old cases?'

'Good for him. It is a sensible line of inquiry, don't you think?'

'The taskforce are aware of his movements. They've sanctioned his involvement.'

'They.'

'Yes?'

'You said they, rather than we. Odd choice. Does it mean you don't feel part of the team, or do you disagree with their decision regarding Chuck's access?'

'The school doesn't fit the Zorro pattern Chuck put forward.'

'I'm keeping an open mind,' said Iris.

'Me too,' he retorted. 'Do you think Chuck could have done this?'

'The school!'

'Yeah. Keeping an open mind, could Charles Koch have set this up?'

'Why?'

'To confirm his ideas. To be a hero again. He misses the limelight. His plan was to stop it, only it went wrong. Like the security guard in Atlanta.'

'Richard Jewell?'

'Yeah. Sad, lonely fake hero looking for affirmation.'

'Richard Jewell was innocent. He was sad and lonely but he was a hero. It was the media who suggested he did it, because his personality and background didn't fit their idea of a hero. A classic case of bad profiling and it victimised a man who should have been applauded for doing his job.'

'It does happen. You tossed people out of the volunteer fire brigade on those grounds.'

Iris grimaced. He was annoying, the detective. She quite liked him.

'So, is Kochie a hero or the other?'

'Yes, I've read his file. So, he was a hero once. Does he miss it?'

'Yes he does.' Iris lifted her empty cup. 'Do you want another coffee?'

'No, three's my limit for the morning.'

Iris went to the coffee maker, chose a Rosabaya. She said, 'You're married. Your wife suggested the coffee limit. You've got kids. You play sport. You went to a Catholic boys school and university. You admire your father enormously. He never went to university. He's very proud of you.'

Pavlovic studied her. 'I'll have a glass of water. Correct. Every single one. Nice party trick. Or I'm very shallow. So, why won't you answer about Koch?'

'It feels disloyal. And I don't trust you.'

'You shouldn't trust me. I'm investigating the murder of eleven people and the attempted murder of over a thousand. I'm not asking you to lend me money.'

'Give me more information.'

'This isn't a negotiation.'

'Yes it is. I did my party trick to impress you so you might entertain the idea I could be valuable to the investigation.'

'I know you can be valuable. I saw your work at the school with the boy who put out the fire, remember. Pegged him, cleared him in a minute. I'm impressed. A fan.'

'You are reading my file.'

'I've started, yes. It's more than one file.'

'Chuck's really a suspect?'

'Everyone is a suspect until the case is solved. Poor policing is when you concentrate on only one suspect, consequently work the evidence to fit.'

Iris brought her coffee back, indicated the recorder. 'Off the record.'

He buttoned it off. He got up, went to the cupboard, found a glass, went to the tap and got his water. He was used to being in other people's houses. He knew where they put things.

'Sorry,' said Iris, meaning the water. 'Like a number of heroes, he is angry his life didn't turn out better, after his heroism.' Iris thought about Charles. 'The world didn't reward him. In fact the event hurt him, both physically and mentally. His co-workers tease him because of his injury, and I'm sure he's crotchety. Well more than grumpy. Was he dismissed for punching a colleague?'

'Sick leave, but yes.'

'Is this the first time?'

'No.'

'Drinking?'

'Yes.'

'Has he been sent to counselling?'

'Yes. He doesn't cooperate.'

'He's angry that he's not been listened to over many years concerning Zorro.'

'Could he bring Zorro into being? He has the technical knowledge.'

'He does. In spades.' Iris considered Charles in this new light. 'He's no longer married, is he?'

'Not for years. Lives on a boat, apparently.'

'So he doesn't have an alibi?'

'No. Now he's put himself next to the Fire Lady. A pretty good way of getting the strokes, keep an eye on things, on the inside of the investigation.'

'Just keeping an open mind, are you?'

'I'm not saying he did it. I'm saying is he a possible?'

Iris thought about it before answering. 'I don't think so. I don't think he's got the chutzpa to fly so close to the inside, to the heat, while doing it. He's not secretive. He's not compartmentalised or ... you're looking for the personality type who makes a good spy. I don't think Charles fits. He's a puncher. We're looking for a sneaky waiter who spits in your food before he brings it to you, smiling.'

Pavlovic seemed to weigh the image before he said, 'Do you want to step out for a cigarette? Don't mind me.'

'I don't smoke.'

'So when you were seeing James, in the hospital room, after midnight, why did you have a lighter in your bag?'

'You never can tell when you might want to offer a light.'

'This fire, the one in the hospital room ...'

'Yes. I was distracted and he got the cigarette lighter from my handbag.'

'What were you distracted by?'

'Notes. Things I was doing during the assessment. Perhaps I was more tired than I realised. He's a very clever pickpocket. He can also get out of handcuffs.'

'Was he in handcuffs?'

'Of course not.'

'You wrestled with him?'

Iris felt herself blink before she said, 'Yes.'

'Was this before or after he set the fire?'

'After I put it out.'

'How long did you wrestle?'

'He tried to get past me. I blocked him. Less than ten seconds I'd say. I let him light the fire so I could see what he did.' She smiled.

Pavlovic blinked. Twice. His lips tightened ever so slightly.

She added, 'I will probably lose my job and my accreditation if you tell anyone.'

'Do you always get away with shit like this?'

'Detective, I never get away with shit. Ever. It always comes back. Will you tell me what you've got so I can help?'

Pavlovic studied her again before he finally said, 'They stole the ether from a company called LabSup. They did it all by phone and paper. Deliver here. Pick it up here. Drop it here. Invoices and requisition forms. They knew what, how and even what kind of voices to use. They got stuff delivered. We have the paper trail but no human presence.' He took the time to study her before adding, 'We are about to announce a raid on a lockup where forensics tell us he stuffed the containers into gymnastic mats.'

'The gymnastic mats were delivered to the school in the same way?'

'While the head of the sports program was on leave, so no one could contradict the order. The physical education staff simply pointed to a wall where they were stacked.'

'Do you have any CCTV footage of the weekend?'

Pavlovic sat filtering through what he would and would not reveal to her. He finally said, 'We have a dog walker, over a couple of weeks. We think he's casing the place. Disguised.'

'A man?'

'Disguised.'

'The truck?'

'Stolen from the school weeks before. Landscapers had been working on a wall. When it reappeared, it was familiar.'

Iris said, 'No wonder they're concentrating on terrorist cells. It's almost military. Absolutely meticulous. I told Charles that profiling the school could almost be more important than profiling the bomber. Finding a motive for this school.'

'Yes.'

Clearly they were pursuing that line. Iris recalled James was allergic to dogs, or he'd said so.

Pavlovic closed his notebook, put away his tape recorder. 'Anything else you think of, or anything I can ask as it arises. Or thoughts on Koch.'

Iris said, 'You aren't miscellaneous. You're investigating leads which are not connected with terrorism or organised crime.'

He shrugged.

'The crazies.'

He nearly smiled.

Iris showed him out. As they reached the front door, he said, 'Nice house.'

She laughed. Said, 'It's a bitch to clean. Or so I'm told.'

Chapter fifteen

Iris showered, changed into jeans and runners. She thought she might take the day off completely, in a way following Frank's instructions. Clear the mind, unsedated. She would shop, garden, iron clothes, cook. She'd make sushi, which she always found calming. However, after she'd put a load of washing into the machine, she found herself ringing Charles Koch.

'Huh?'

'Chuck, it's Iris. Where are you?'

'On my boat.'

'Can I come see you?'

'Here?'

'Yes, of course. I've had a visit from Detective Pavlovic. I may have more things to share.'

Charles gave his address, behind a marina, an hour down the coast. Iris drove along the old coast road, where new apartments had sprouted amongst the ageing industrial areas. The suburbs of smaller and smaller blocks formed an uninterrupted tapestry, all the way to what was once a coastal seaside retreat, now a city of retired people and their service providers.

Iris played Vivaldi. She thought about James. He had burned his own children. His mind unable to cope, yet striving to defend itself from the unthinkable, created a complex fantasy which allowed him to approach the incident, to come at but not face it. There are no children on Mars, no families. If he can get back to the spaceship he can save his fellow crew. It was a wrapping, not a solution. Unlike pus around a thorn, it did not lead to expelling the foreign body. James was trapped in replaying the incident in its disguised form, trapped in a loop because he could never bring them back. His children, possibly his wife, were dead.

Iris followed her GPS, turning down before the Lochland Cut, driving between three-storey villas to the marina, where concrete jetties moored yachts and cabin cruisers with unimaginative names like *Livin Da Dream*, *Calm Seas* and *Nirvana*. She followed the main road to the end of the marina where a smaller track ran across the edge of the canal and around the back past abandoned boat trailers and an ancient beached dredger.

Iris parked near a torn wire fence at the entrance of a boat repair business. She smelt raw kerosene, diesel smoke, rotting seaweed. She looked into the boat repair, at the yachts in dry dock. A worker moved a mast on a forklift in the distance. She spied Chuck's yellow ute a little way up inside the fence.

The ute was parked between a tiny yacht and a small power-boat, both up in wooden cradles, dry and high. A power cord and a hose led up to the powerboat.

Iris called, 'Hello.'

Charles came from behind the cabin, called down to her. 'You found it, huh?' He wore torn pants, a firefighter t-shirt.

'Looks like your directions were good.'

'Come on up.' He pointed to a wooden ramp constructed along the side. Chuck stood at the back of his boat, admiring the mishmash of stored and disassembled yachts as if it were a regatta in full sail. He swung around to Iris as she stepped onto the deck as though surprised. He gazed out again, inviting her to share what he saw.

Iris said, 'Detective Pavlovic says you're back in the room, off suspension.'

Chuck gave a shy smile. 'Yeah. I took some of your ideas to them.'

'Oh?'

'I wasn't going to get access to old cases from here. The wi-fi is a bit patchy.' He pointed towards the marina. 'I get it from the *Majestic*. Not always in port. Once they heard you were working with me, they took Zorro more seriously. Maybe I'm just the errand boy.' He pointed to a director's chair. 'You want a beer?'

'Water if you have any.' Iris sat, watched Charles limp down into the cluttered cabin. She had meant to ask Detective Pavlovic if the dog walker limped.

Iris closed her eyes a moment to listen to the growl of the forklift and the intermittent throb of boats re-entering the marina. She could hear seagulls, someone hammering on metal. Iris squinted at the interior of Chuck's cabin, making out plastic storage boxes, clothes, and takeaway food wrappers. A laptop sat open on a table next to a pizza box with an empty whisky bottle. Iris realised she was searching for evidence of electronics, plastic piping, maybe big cylinders marked STOLEN ETHER.

Charles came back up to the deck with a bottle of water and a manila file. 'The tap water is drinkable, not very cold.' He handed her the bottle, sat in the other director's chair next to a plastic storage box with an ashtray and an open can of beer in a stubby holder on the lid. He fished about in a cavity along the side of the boat, came up with a cap, which he held out to her. 'The sun's got a bit of bite to it.'

The cap said Pro Dive. Iris put it on. 'Aye aye, captain.'

He squinted at her, looking for the niggle. 'I'm doing the boat up. It's going slower than I thought.'

'How have you gone with past cases?'

'Jesus. You only put me onto it yesterday!'

'Yesterday?' Iris thought about the many things that had happened since she last saw Chuck in the pub near the port. When she tuned back in he was watching her with an expectant smile.

'What?' she said.

'I got some hits on the Passiona.'

'Where?'

'I ran a check. They've got like a keywords software. They're entering old cases. Taskforce has analysts and go-fors and computer nerds. It's still slow, but this is what's already popped up.' He patted the manila file on his lap.

'Can I see?'

'I'm telling you.'

'I might be able to see – patterns.'

'Will you let me lay it out?' Charles was not giving up the file.

'Sure.'

'So, firstly we got a pattern. Early December. The school and two years before, the old people's home in Riverside and four years ago the backpackers was also in December. I plug December into their software search, we come up with another old people's home in between the backpackers and the Riverside fire. They put it out, which gives us a list of inventory including unexplained faulty alarms and ... a Passiona can.'

'Any fingerprints?'

'Being run. We ran Decembers going way back, even smaller fires.'

'When he was learning.'

'Like you said. Seeing what he likes, practising. There's a couple of house fires. The computers are grinding away right now.'

'Are you working in a team on this now, Chuck?'

'I've got my own remit. Take things as I see them. Bounce stuff off you.'

She asked, 'Have you met with Detective Pavlovic?'

'Who?'

'Young detective. Stuart Pavlovic. He was at the school, interviewing the boy from under the stage.'

Chuck shook his head, impatient. He'd grabbed up the manila folder.

'What?' asked Iris.

'I think we got something else. From earlier still.'

'What?'

'I don't know if you remember, about fifteen years ago a nasty shithead was setting fires to young couples. The newspapers called him the Lover's Lane Pyro.'

'Yes. It was before I got into profiling.'

'Yeah, I was still a firey. We used to call him Springsteen because of the song. You know. Dah dah ... got a bad desire, oh oh oh, I'm on fire.'

Iris vaguely recalled the incidents. Couples on blankets and in parked cars were splashed with petrol then set alight.

Chuck said, 'Well, we got a hit on cool drink cans, one of

them already looks like it's a Passiona can.'

'This is back fifteen years ago.'

'Yes.'

'Are the cans in an evidence box still?'

'We're looking. If they are we'll do another fingerprint run with current technology. There's more. Free set of steak knives. The year before Springsteen, I found another spree by maybe the same baddy.'

Chuck watched Iris's growing excitement, enjoying himself. 'Several deros were burned, and the summer before that … December again, a homeless man got burned. The computer is smart when it's told where to look.'

Iris said, 'Further back, it would have been animals, burned animals, also disappeared pets.'

'Not sure they'd be on file.'

'Merely thinking aloud. Chuck, any witness statements surrounding these various events, especially the Lover's Lane, Springsteen case?'

'Should be, we'd have to go find it. The computer spits out matches to lists. There's no detail unless you go back. The physical evidence is warehoused or destroyed.'

'I'd like to see the evidence. I'd like to read the witness statements.'

'You're asking for a big pile of paper.'

'He might have been careless when he was starting out. He might have been caught watching, given a statement to the police but been let go, so I might find him in the paperwork.'

'Like the Nightclub Rapist?'

'Yes,' said Iris in surprise. A series of rapes had been committed by a man who pretended to befriend girls leaving nightclubs. His physical description and the particular things he'd said to the girls reminded Iris of a firelighter she interviewed years before. The combination of his cognitive behaviour problems, anger issues with women, as well as his ability to turn on a rough charm caused Iris to contact the police to suggest they look at him for the rapes. Iris said, 'Of course, the arson wasn't displaced sexual desire – the sexual crimes and the fire crimes were not causally related, rather, they occurred together in the same offender. His anger and poor problem-solving evinced more than one manifestation.' Iris stopped speaking. She was quoting herself, from the trial.

Chuck smiled, a little besotted, thought Iris with sudden alarm. She asked, 'Do you like dogs, Chuck?'

'I don't mind them, you know, not enough room for a pet on board.'

'What's the name of your boat?'

'*Justine.*'

'*Justine?*'

'A mythical woman who is fair. Meaning just, rather than pretty.'

'Very poetic.'

'The name came with the boat. I've made the rest up.'

'Have you been living here since the end of your marriage?'

Charles scowled at her, squeezing his fist. It was still a red-button topic for him.

'Marriage is hard, Chuck. Do you have kids?'

'Yes. They've moved. They call. They send Father's Day cards. We see each other but it's a fucking poisoned well, isn't it?'

'Your wife made them take sides.'

'I keep forgetting. You're a counsellor.'

'I have a group of firefighters and others who meet once a fortnight. I don't even go very often myself anymore. They run things. A policewoman. An insurance guy who pulled people from a car wreck. They compare experiences.'

'I took the end of my career pretty hard. I hit the bottle. Instead of helping, my wife pissed off and took the kids and the house and the friends too. It happens, or haven't you read that study yet.'

'I'm sorry.'

'I thought we were working together.'

'Okay. I won't share my problems, you won't share yours. Back to work.'

Chuck finished his beer. He pulled the can from the stubby holder, crushed it before dropping it into a big white container with other empties.

'I'm sorry, Chuck.'

He went into the cabin again to a small fridge. 'How's your water?'

'I can't hold it like I used to.'

'What?'

'It's good, Chuck.'

He came back with a fresh beer.

Iris said, 'Have you heard about the ether paper trail?'

'What paper trail?' He was still grumpy with her.

'Apparently, the school bomber, Zorro, got the diethyl ether to a workshop, from the workshop to the school via order forms, delivery people and invoices using computers and phones. All sight unseen.'

'I didn't know.'

'He plans meticulously, is highly organised and is pretty smart.'

'He'd have a workshop.'

'A workshop. Why?'

'To prepare stuff. Choose his ignition points. Mostly he tricks up stuff in situ. He rigs up the fault with a selected item, say a toaster or washing machine or urn, so it appears to be the most probable ignition point of an accidental short circuit. It is never a pristine laboratory where we work. If you're searching for causes in a completely burnt-out building, with melted metal, burn patterns under a fallen roof, hacked up doors from the firefighters, all swimming in ashy water, most investigators would go for it. Most fires are accidental.'

'So, he's worked at all those places? He has time, according to you, to turn off the water supply, disable the fire alarms, and block escapes.'

'Well, half the stuff can be done very easily and quickly if you know what you're doing.'

'Is there any way the school could have been a copycat crime, made to look like Zorro?'

'How? I'm the only one who knew about Zorro, except Zorro. Copy what?'

'Have you told other firefighters about your theories?'

He took a gulp of beer. 'It's not a fireman.'

'Firefighters have been known to start fires, for ...'

'I know. Wanting to be wanted. No way a firey is going to burn people. No way. Not a chance.'

*

As she walked back to the car, she thought through the many firefighters she had known. She could not imagine even the most broken doing something as calculated and vicious as this. On the other hand, this person was capable of hiding. He, and Iris felt it was a he, had been hiding for fifteen years at least. Was he hiding inside the fire service?

Iris imagined a boy, possibly a young teen, having trouble with his own emerging sexuality. So he spied on it. Punished it. He was struggling with his urges and their expression. Contrary to her own pronouncements, the crimes of fifteen years ago did appear to have a sexual dimension, conflicted with attempts at sublimation.

She didn't think it was Charles Koch. She would be happy if it was not. She liked his wounded self-confidence. Mind you, his life was in the toilet, to use a phrase he might. His physical health would have to be in the orange zone. A candidate for a heart attack or stroke if the liver didn't get him. He did not see it that way. His personal narrative trumped reality. Chuck lived on a boat on wild seas while he chased down a criminal he'd been after for years. He was not a washed-up fireman living in a parking lot, he was the Lone Ranger.

Iris pulled off the coast road and drove down to the beach, parking near the ferry jetty where they took daytrippers to the bird sanctuary on an island five hundred metres from shore. She got out of the car, following the path through sand dunes down to the sheltered beach. The island was close. Kayakers and snorkellers floated in the water. She could see people on the island disturbing the sea birds, sending them up and cawing. It was a sanctuary only at night perhaps. A yacht sailed south beyond a break beyond the island.

Iris took off her shoes to feel the sand. She wriggled her bright red toes in the cold water, imagining them as darting fish. She remembered her mother, the particular day when they'd driven to the beach. Bathers, buckets, hats, towels and chatter. They were excited, Iris and her four year old sister, Charlotte, and even her mother, Elsie. Iris could not remember what she'd said wrong that day. She rarely could. Everything warm and happy would suddenly snap cold and silent. As they'd pulled into the parking lot at the beach, Iris had sensed the freeze.

Iris's hand was on the back car door, when her mother turned, 'Not you. You can't come.'

'Why, Mummy?'

'You've been bad.'

Charlotte spun around in the front seat to stare at Iris with fearful expectancy.

'What have I done?'

'You don't love me.'

'Yes, I do.'

'Charlotte loves me. She's my good girl.'

'I'm good.'

'You only want your father.'

'I love you too. A lot.'

'No, you only love him.'

'I love both of you. Charlotte too.'

'Charlotte and I are going to have a lovely swim together. You stay here, you bad girl.'

Iris began to cry. She saw her sister watching her with wary fascination, her mother with a mean triumph.

She stopped crying soon after they left. She watched the people who came and went in the carpark. There were people with dogs. There were young men with surfboards, leaving. There were young women in bikinis or long billowy shirts. There were families, tumbling litters of boys and girls and mothers carrying babies and fathers laughing. Only Iris couldn't hear the laughter. She couldn't hear anything even though the back window of the car was wound down. She sat in the back of the car, sweating in the rising heat, imagining what was being said, putting together who was who in the coming and going carpark high above the ocean.

She lay on the back seat, watching seagulls in the blue sky and she invented stories. It was good, this hot bubble she lived in. She stared at her feet up on the hand rest of the passenger door. She was in a boat, she drifted on the sea. Near an island.

Iris read books. Iris loved books, like her father. She went on a book adventure in the back of the car, exploring the island and bringing peace and prosperity to the dark naked people who lived there.

By the time they returned from the beach, hot, red and sticky with sand and drying salt, Iris was changed. She'd found some strength against her mother's tantrums. She discovered the foundations of defence against the irrational hatred.

*

Iris shopped on the way home. The bright light in the aisles, perky colours of packaging, soundtrack of music and intermittent store speaker codes comforted her. Iris did not have a list. She was free-floating, following the whims of remembered recipes. It was not very efficient, as she was forced to constantly abandon her trolley to go back through the aisles looking for recalled ingredients.

Iris made a cup of ginger tea while she packed away the shopping. She would make sushi after doing an hour of gardening. She'd use half the salmon for sashimi to have with it. She checked in the fridge, found a tube of wasabi.

Iris went to her home office and opened her laptop. She sent the report on James to Frank without making any additions. Irrespective of her findings about the nature of his trauma and her shocking behaviour, her initial report still stood. He was not the school bomber. She started to imagine him as a fifteen year old riding through the night to a fogged car in a misty forest.

Iris changed back into her shorts and t-shirt. She hung out her whites, smelling the summer air of dry grass and chlorine. She put on a load of coloureds, put on her sunhat and headed for the garage. She caught the scent of the jasmine, faintly sweet, almost sickly, by the side fence.

Mathew's workshop door was open. Iris looked in at his myriad steel tools, the dusty assortment of model airplanes, the helicopter he'd used to delight Rosemarie and himself. There were unused golf clubs, broken tennis racquets, bike parts and an old valve radio he must have inherited from someone. Men were boys, their whole lives, boys still. Her father had possessed a similarly mysterious shed, forbidden and enticing. Iris shut the door, going to her own gardening bench at the back of the garage. Mathew's black Audi was parked next to Iris's Honda. Iris felt the sudden desire to take her pruning shears to the side of it, to make a screech of paint peeling from metal.

She headed to the backyard where the jacaranda and the fir tree provided broken shade. Iris started on the bougainvillea, where its new sprouts were attempting to break out from the wall. It was already heavy with rusty orange blooms.

Iris found herself thinking about her mother again and almost immediately saw her father, smiling. Smiling with love, with sadness, with apology but mostly with pride. Nicholas glowed at her achievements, in toileting properly, in learning to walk and talk. He showered her with admiration. At some point, even before Iris could comprehend her own independent mind, her mother conceived of her as a rival. She withheld affection, chided with little reason.

When Iris started school, Elsie began her acts of physical sabotage. Iris would find her homework gone, or water spilled on it or it was given to Charlotte to chew and mangle. Iris tried to appeal to her father for help. 'Dad, my picture for Mrs Antonio! It's got food spilled on it.' Elsie calling, 'Well, you shouldn't leave it on the bench. I have food to cook.' 'It wasn't,' said seven year old Iris. 'Are you sure you didn't put it there?' he asked, home from the hospital, in a crumpled shirt, twisted tie.

Iris recognised her father's growing panic. Nicholas understood the war but was incapable or unwilling to intercede. He would chide Iris on Elsie's behalf. He might even punish her at Elsie's urging. Iris was denied outings, toys, school excursions. Her father would then find secret ways to compensate her, a piece of chocolate or a new book hidden under her pillow. Late at night, Iris listened to her mother's screams about lovelessness and ingratitude, his weak appeasing.

Grown Iris pruning in the garden tried to imagine the picture she'd have drawn as a child, based on her current understandings of child psychology. How big would the house be? Would a path wind up to the door? She would have drawn her father and herself on one side with the tree and the rainbow, her mother on the other. How big would she have drawn her mother? She imagined the drawing of her father with a smiling face, her mother with no mouth.

Elsie did not have a psychiatric disorder. She would not have qualified for any category listed in the *DSM-Four* psychiatric handbook. Adult Iris developed theories about her mother's personality, her uncommon beauty, her poor rural upbringing, Elsie's tough mother, violent father. How ill-equipped she was for life with a doctor. Whatever Iris's attempt to reconstruct the formation of Elsie's social and physical DNA, it always amounted to the same conclusion. Her mother was just plain mean. She was a cow, in the parlance of Elsie's hometown. She was hard, selfish, determined to keep those around her down at her level.

Nicholas was not the first man to fail to consider the later consequences of marrying a gorgeous spitfire. Iris's father had been weak but also intelligent and giving. He became an anaesthetist at the prompting of his wife because that's where the money was, yet he still insisted on working in a public hospital. He was interested in the arts, particularly in reading history. His hobbies were of the mind. And Iris knew he adored her. She certainly adored him. Iris supposed her father saved her. He saved her from her mother, from her becoming her mother. The two of them made Iris something else of course.

Iris was only sixteen when her father died. Firefighters cut him out of his car, which had gone off the freeway into a bridge stanchion late at night. He had been on his way home from eighteen hours at the hospital. He'd had a heart attack. Iris imagined the firefighters talking to Nicholas as they worked to free him, giving him a joke, asking about his loved ones, giving secret sad looks as they passed each other equipment to extricate the dying doctor. A romantic story of course, constructed, for he was probably dead before the car even left the road. Elsie broke the news in the morning. 'Your father's dead. You broke his heart.' Iris did not believe her until she telephoned his hospital to confirm it for herself.

Iris did not break down. She grieved quickly. She studied. Iris's father clearly knew Iris would need protecting. He bequeathed Iris a large sum to be used for her education. Elsie went berserk. Not figuratively. She became deranged, physically out of control.

She took to Iris's bedroom, tearing the room apart. It was like a scene from *Citizen Kane*. No doll unbroken. No dress untorn. No papers unripped. She broke a door off the cupboard, cracked the window glass. This event probably did qualify as a bona fide psychotic episode.

Iris became a boarder at a private school. Elsie sold the family home, moved down the coast, went a little hippie. She had several boyfriends. Charlotte and Iris kept in contact. Their relationship had always been difficult. They were never close but regarded each other with sympathy tinged with envy. Charlotte left school early, married young, moved east. Elsie followed her but never found or gave peace. When she died of cancer, Iris did not go to the funeral. She could admit it to Mathew, to Frank and to herself that knowing her mother was no longer on Earth filled her with enormous relief. Her shoulders were lightened. Dr Chew, I did not like my mother. Dr Chew would not be shocked. Narrative therapy accepted certain filial ties are the worst ones for our health.

Rosemarie, then three years old, would never have to meet her. Yet Elsie remained, it seemed, inside Iris and between Iris and her own daughter. Iris loved Rosemarie with an ache. She missed her enormously, yet she didn't seem capable of maintaining the narrow bridge between them.

Mathew, Mathew's whole family did it with such ease. Iris was careful to a degree that was fearful. This is who her mother made her, what she'd not been able to overcome with her husband or her daughter. Not all her fault, to be sure, but real. She loved in her own way. She was not able to change, no matter how often it was identified by Frank and others, no matter how many affirming, outreaching positive potential narratives were offered her. There was no counter-narrative she could transplant onto the person she'd been made into in her childhood. She was closed often to herself.

Iris saw movement through the French doors. Mathew? She waved but the figure had gone. She looked again. The sun was low, reflecting the trees back onto the glass. She took more prunings to the pile. She would clear them tomorrow. She put her shears, gloves and hat on the patio table and went in.

'Mathew?' she called.

Iris went into the kitchen, drank a glass of water, wandered upstairs. 'Mathew?' Was it Sunday? No, Saturday still.

She searched through their bedroom, the exercise room, the upstairs lounge, finally down to Rosemarie's end. Her study and her rumpus room were empty. Her bedroom smelled musty, covered with posters of bands whose names Iris couldn't recall. The lead singer with the dark hair and blackly made eyes. Johnny Depp as Edward Scissorhands. Butterfly stickers covered the ceiling where they had remained since Rosemarie had been small. None of them, least of all Rosemarie, wanted them removed. Some still glowed in the dark.

Iris thought she heard a door close. 'Mathew?'

She went downstairs. 'Mathew, is that you?'

Mathew's office was empty.

Iris opened the front door. She thought she'd locked it, but now wasn't so sure. The front gates were open. She went out to the garage, flicked the button for the gates. They swung closed, clanged pleasingly, signally, the end of the day.

The trees shimmered, darkly. The sea breeze was in. Iris could smell smoke. A neighbour was barbecuing something plummy.

Chapter sixteen

Iris slept late. Another restless night. She recalled feeling hot. She remembered dreaming, images she couldn't quite recapture. She'd stayed off the alcohol before bed so maybe that was it. The word menopause flashed into her mind. What if her troubles had been masked or enhanced by pre-menopause as well as the wine, the overtiredness? Would that be a comfort or cause for further angst? Or completely beside the point?

'I need butterflies,' she said to the ceiling. 'I need to stop talking to myself.'

The zoo teemed with all manner of human creatures. It was Sunday. The monkeys got antsy on Sundays and school holidays. The baboons liked to disgust by throwing their poo, spitting. The lions would try to spray.

Iris bought a coffee, stood watching the otters. It was warm already and they were gliding miraculously under the cool water.

She switched on her phone, saw lots of missed calls, cued texts. She ignored them, dialled Rosemarie.

'Mum.'

'Hello, darling. How are you?'

'I was going to call you later.'

'I've saved you sixpence.'

'Brodey and I are shopping.'

'Sounds like he's house-trained. Brodey?'

'I've told you about Brodey. Or Dad. Didn't he tell you? Anyway we're doing the grocery shopping.'

'I did the same yesterday. I made sushi. I used the special roller pad. You used to love helping with sushi.'

'Yeah, well it's easier to buy them made here.'

'How's uni?'

'Waiting for results. You know.'

'I was thinking about our walks to school.'

'Oh.'

Iris ignored Rosemarie's tone. She said, 'Remember how it used to be my job to tell stories on the way to school and your job to tell me about your day on the way home?'

'Kind of. I remember you telling me about it. You had to pry it out of me and at some magic point I became articulate and impossible to shut up.'

She was including Brodey now, Iris supposed.

'I also remember playing I Spy, very early on. This wasn't in the car. It was on a walk to school.'

'No, butter. Not margarine.' They were still shopping.

'I spy with my little eye, something beginning with S.'

'Hmm.'

'I tried and tried. Stones. Stop sign. Sign. Street. I went through every S word in the entire dictionary, everything that could possibly be seen or passed by on the way to school, including some pretty esoteric words like sister and sunshine and story. Finally, I gave up, which, as I recall, was pretty uncool with you if I didn't keep trying. And the word was ...'

'Cement.'

'Yes. Cement. I didn't have the heart to ...'

'Tell me until later. I became a bit obsessed about the S sound.'

'Yes. You were around ten years old. Ceiling. Centipede.'

'Cereal. Centre. Celestial.'

'I'm not sure whether celestial was one of your ten year old words, although you were pretty precocious.'

'A smart only child. Ha ha. Mum, I pretty much have to go.'

'Oh, I thought I'd call. No problem. See how you're going.'

'Yes. I'll call you later. Oh, but there's a thing after.'

'Yes. Love you.'

'Yes. You too. I'll call. Which does start with a c, rather than salute.' She said it with the Italian accent. Witty girl. 'Bye mum.'

'Bye.'

Iris stared at her phone as though it were a young child's hand. She felt a little weak at the knees, a little like tears, but happy too. And sad. Melancholy. Why has melancholy got a ch that is not a chhh sound? Rosemarie became a bit obsessed in high school about the many inconsistencies of spelling and sounding in the English language. If it's an s sound write s and not ce. Silent letters infuriated her. Gh and ps and particularly the silent s such as in Grosvenor Street.

'French!' she declared one day at the dinner table. 'The bloody French ran everything and they've made all the words unpronounceable.'

'It was the language of diplomacy,' said Mathew.

'Autobahn,' said Iris. They shook their heads at her, moved on before Iris could explain about words constantly being added from all over. Schadenfreude. Viennese Freud words.

'I've seen a documentary,' Mathew explained. 'The history of English or the story of English. It was spoken by only a couple of suburbs of London.'

Iris grinned at the memory. She headed to the native bird section as she dialled Mathew. The blue wrens weren't very blue. She stood searching for them in the fake undergrowth.

'Iris. Good morning.'

'How's it going?'

'Oh, you know. Lots of roundtable reading of documents. Lots of long dinners. Field trips of very hot tramping over red rocks with the Nullabin.' When Iris didn't reply, he asked, 'Is everything all right?'

'Yes. I'm at the zoo.'

'Oh, I thought you hated it on weekends.'

'It's nice today. I've been talking to Rosemarie.'

'Excellent. How is she?'

'Good. She was shopping. With Brodey.'

'Yes. Met at a rally or student gathering. The sciences. Something sciencey.'

Neither of them spoke. Iris filled the space. 'Do you want to get a dog?'

'Certainly,' he said rather quickly. 'Yes, let's both think about a breed. Nothing small and yappy, I hope.'

Iris laughed. Asked, 'Shall I cook when you get back?'

'Yes. Perfect.'

'When are you back?'

'Should be tomorrow the way we're going.'

Iris took a breath, said, 'I miss you, darling.'

After another slight pause, Mathew said, 'Good. I'll see you soon.'

Was someone else listening in? He could have been talking at breakfast, surrounded by Chinese and Nullabini. There might well be no arts bureaucrats there, he might not have been in his motel room still at ten o'clock on a Saturday morning. He might have been still peeved over his missing socks. There could be all number of reasons for his guarded, determined brightness on the phone.

Iris saw finches. Many finches, drab, camouflaged. Camouflage was undoubtedly a dastardly French word, like bureau. Unspellable.

Iris headed for the butterfly enclosure. She checked the messages. Missed calls from Gillian, Patricia, Frank, Detective Pavlovic. Her gang. Pavlovic and Frank had left a number of messages. She'd check them later. She'd been hoping for news from Chuck. A development in the teenage theory. She'd call them all in the afternoon. She composed a text message for Frank.

I am not having a breakdown. I am having a recovery :) x

Iris paused before pressing send because a monarch landed on her telephone screen. It was a darker orange than the garden variety. She examined the markings on the wings, like veins branching out to the black perimeter. Lighter dots like desert painting. Iris blew gently, watching its wings vibrate, its long dark antenna quivering in her breeze.

It was warm in the butterfly house, humid. In the summer, the glass portion was dismantled because the temperatures outside were sufficient. Small sprays behind the special plants kept things humid. Water trickled in a channel alongside the path leading from entrance to exit. They'd created a tropical rainforest inside a tent.

Two girls and a boy came to Iris almost immediately. 'Look.' The children gazed in awe. Iris knew a number of butterflies must have landed on her yellow blouse.

'Are they yellow?' asked Iris. There were common grass yellows tumbling about up near the net roof canopy.

'Black,' said the girl in the pink t-shirt.

'Are their wings closed?' asked Iris, turning slowly.

'Yes.'

'Aha. They are my favourite. They're called the Ulysses swallowtail. When they fly you can see a beautiful blue colour and I love the shapes of their wings. Like a bird's.'

The girl examined Iris with suspicion, downgrading her as a generic form of teacher or zoo worker, therefore slightly less interesting than she had first thought.

The boy said, 'They won't land on me.'

Iris said, 'You have to be very still. It's the colours they're attracted to.' She pointed towards the coloured discs on the white feeding tables set throughout the false forest of the enclosure.

'Like a flower,' said the less suspicious girl.

Then Iris smelt smoke: plastic, acrid.

The children were looking up above Iris's head.

Iris whirled around to see flames. Half of the enclosure was made of a fine netting that allowed air to pass but reduced temperature and wind. It was now covered in a yellow shimmer of flame like the sun setting in the ocean. The edges dripped melting net, goops of bluer flame falling into the entrance end of the butterfly house. Iris heard a dull roar like water down a distant fall, also crackles, pops, children's calls of fear.

'We need to get out.' Iris turned away from the fire, towards the other exit at the solid end of the butterfly enclosure. The back section was constructed of wooden walls protecting the butterflies from the weather. Iris recalled from previous visits how it was warmer here, the temperature controlled to tropical heats of thirty degrees with higher humidity.

A man in a baseball cap banged on a side door that led to the incubation room. The sign said STAFF ONLY. People, mostly mothers and children, were at the exit, piled there, stacking into each other. Why weren't they leaving?

Iris looked back again to the fire. The heat was already

intense, pushing at her. It looked like a wall of yellow liquid, descending as well as spreading above. A wave of yellow turning to red and orange. The molten drips from the material started smaller fires below. The wood of a feeding container and the wood of the building structure were bursting into bluer flames, dotted around the ground. A plastic electrical outlet exploded in a sizzle of green and white sparks. Plants were frying, searing, sagging, collapsing in black heaps. One burst into momentary flame like a flare.

The butterflies were gone. Instead of the garden of blooming orange, yellow and blue drifting, fluttering flowers, there was only dry heat. Iris supposed the occasional sparkle and flash was a butterfly burning, cindered in an instant. She inspected the ground, finding a scatter of them. Autumn. They were still. Dead from the heat before the flames would reach them. One quarter of the butterfly house was on fire, orange now, not yellow.

One entrance was completely engulfed, the other seemed closed, a pile of people gathered there. Someone screamed, a cry of despair. The man in the baseball cap smashed a bollard against the wooden wall on the side of the incubation room. The wall was smoking.

Iris looked to the pond. A man-made stream fed a fake pond in the middle of the fake rainforest. Iris shouted to the children who hovered at the back of the blocked entrance. 'The pond. Get in the water.' She held her hand out.

They looked at her, looked at each other, looked at the walls of the enclosure, thinking of their parents beyond.

Iris stepped towards the fire, then off the path and down into the water. She lowered herself into the water, dipping herself to neck height before sitting up, turning to the children. She yelled, 'Get into the water!'

The boy came first, the two girls ran after. They came down into the half metre of water, and Iris splashed them. The fire felt near, the heat harsh. Iris squinted up to see the plastic net roof and walls were nearly gone. She could see sky past the smoke. She wasn't sure there were still flames above.

Then came the explosion like her recurring nightmare,

like one of her flashbacks. It seemed distant, hollow, a truck backfiring without echo. Iris turned towards the fire to see a cylindrical object flying towards her, like a black torpedo in the air with yellow flame coming from the back. It swerved and fell with a metallic clunk into a pole, bending it. Then came another explosion, a deeper whump, white, complete with a hot blast of air. Metal sprayed, flying, falling fast. Iris recoiled from it, crouching her back to shield the children, turning with the blast of hot air, a piercing tickle in her shoulder.

It was quieter, suddenly, a freeze in time like at the school, as though the physical world complied for an instant with the emotions of the humans, physics and stress taking a rest beat. Iris heard the crying and the alarms. She breathed in the faint noxious smell of all kinds of burnt things, plastic, rubber, plants, gas, meat. Iris finally opened her eyes. One of the girls was whimpering. Iris put her arms around all three.

'It's okay,' she said.

And it was. The fire had gone. The huge wave of flame was nowhere. The fire had evaporated. She heard alarms. Someone moaned in pain up near the exit. She became aware of waves of wailing coming from outside of the butterfly enclosure. She imagined a hundred parents standing outside, crying for their children in the gutted zoo enclosure. Iris stood, nearly tripped over the three kids still cowering in the plastic walled pond. Her shoulder hurt. She'd been cut. Water dripped, discoloured with blood. The cries outside were surreal, a mix of fear and keening, altogether inhuman.

She focused on the edge of the pond, looking for a safe way through the burnt material. Zookeepers with fire extinguishers and hoses began to come through the missing end of the butterfly house, through the smoke like a patrol in a Vietnam War film.

Iris held out her hand to the kids. She got them standing. 'We've been in an accident, team. We didn't get hurt. It missed us. How lucky were we? What a story we've got to tell. Did you feel the whoosh like a wind?'

They stared. Shock. They weren't talking yet. Good idea.

Iris saw more advancing zookeepers in their green zoo shirts. One figure wore a yellow fire tunic, not yet zipped. Other staff were coming into the burnt forest now too. Some carried first-aid kits. Others wore emergency team vests. They were tentative, frightened as though they might step on mines. They weren't professionals. They fed hippos, mucked out lion poo. They didn't want to find cindered corpses or screaming, half-melted children.

The exit opened, the people there tumbled out into the arms of other men in yellow fire tunics. Iris helped her three kids out of the pond. 'Are your parents here?' asked Iris.

'Granma,' said the boy.

'Good. She will be so happy to see you kids. What a story you've got to tell, hey? Imagine what the kids at school will say.'

'We were in the fire,' said the distrustful girl in awe. Her long blonde hair had frizzed slightly in the heat.

Iris passed them up, one at a time, to the zoo workers. She took an offered arm, pulled herself out of the pond.

The person called, 'Wound here. Bleeding.' He put one arm above his head, called again, 'Hurt person here.'

Iris swivelled to search behind, imagining someone hurt, but turning sent a stabbing sensation into her shoulder. Iris gagged. She bent, which made her shoulder hurt more. She vomited, felt hands lowering her to kneel.

'Stay still,' a woman's voice said.

'Let's get you to first aid.'

They took Iris to one of their own veterinary units housed within the zoo. It was out of the smoke, well stocked, sterile. The more badly injured were placed in the first ambulances. A gas cylinder had exploded. They were taking names, addresses, contacts. Iris had lost an earring and her phone but had apparently kept hold of her purse this time. No one had died. The wailing Iris had heard was the monkeys. The gibbons, rightly terrified by the fire, gave cries of warning and fear, which set off other apes. Iris's hair was singed at the tips. She couldn't help rubbing at the melted ends in spite of the gingery burnt hair smell she kept releasing.

As Iris was loaded into an ambulance she looked back down the hill to the butterfly enclosure. A third of the building had gone. A fire appliance was parked nearby, its hoses no longer charged. Iris could make out news crews and the familiar uniforms of the Arson Squad, fire investigators and police. Forensics in their booties and overalls were fanning out over the ruins. Standing at the perimeter in their bulletproof, black uniforms were members of a tactical response group. They carried semiautomatic weapons.

*

Iris borrowed a phone to call Mathew from the hospital. He wasn't answering. He would not have recognised the number, Iris supposed. They gave her a local, removed the metal with large tweezers, stitched. She was bandaged, given a tetanus shot. She monitored her own emotions for signs of trauma but felt remarkably calm. Maybe she was getting used to this. Or was it simply too soon? She did not believe in the God story to explain the universe, but if there was one, she was prepared to agree with Gillian; he/she was indeed pissed at her. Hubris seemed the most likely cause. Icarus's wings were melted. None of the gods were particularly fond of self-worshipping humans.

They'd given her a pair tracksuit pants from lost property or in stock for such occasions and a green hospital top worn by surgery nurses. Her clothes had been ruined in the fire, water and medical treatment, but were also being held now as part of the new arson investigation.

Iris was not allowed to leave, even though she was out of bed. She couldn't lie on her back, nor sit back against the chair in the hospital room. She'd need to go pick up her car again. At least this time she'd kept her keys.

She turned to a knock at the open hospital room door to see a uniformed policewoman accompanying Detective Pavlovic. He was wearing the same dark pants as the day before but a striped business shirt with thin red alongside the thicker blue.

'How are you, Mrs Foster?'

'Detective Pavlovic.'

'This is a police officer.'

'So I see,' said Iris. 'And she has no name.'

'We're interviewing witnesses to the fire at the zoo.' He spoke over the policewoman before she could answer. Pavlovic surveyed the room. He put his tape recorder on the hospital server table, rolled it towards Iris before sitting up on the end of the bed.

Iris said, 'Iris Foster. Witness. Not a lot useful to tell really. I was in the butterfly enclosure at the zoo where there was a fire. I don't know how it started. I think an exit was blocked. Some children and I took shelter in the water. I suppose we should be checked for meningococcal. There were explosions, possibly a kind of rocket was fired in at us. Then a bigger explosion which put the fire out. Have there been other attacks? Are we at war with someone? I was inside the maelstrom so I don't have much overview. All I know. Is everyone all right?'

Pavlovic said, 'No deaths. No serious injuries. A big show. Should we have expected other attacks?' He peered, studying her as though she were the darkness outside the cave.

Iris considered the policewoman again, found herself searching the floor for meaning.

Pavlovic said, 'The fire investigators have already made early reports. The rocket was probably an LPG cylinder. It didn't explode – the intake nozzle detached so it flew. The bigger explosion was from oxygen cylinders stolen from the veterinary surgery at the zoo.'

'The fire was deliberate,' said Iris, her mind whirring suddenly.

'Absolutely. One of the golf buggies the zookeepers zip around on was parked up against the exit door. We figure they used it to get the gas cylinders and later to block the entrance.'

Iris stood. 'Have you found a Passiona can?'

Pavlovic said, 'Not yet. Or any zeds. Where should we look?'

'I don't know. Around where the gas cylinders were put, possibly.' Iris racked her brains to think of anything odd. Was someone following her she should have noticed? She had not been paying attention.

Pavlovic said, 'The thing is, the zoo has lots of security cameras. Walkways, enclosures, the two surgeries. Day and night, they need to see who's where and what the animals are doing and what crazy person wants to hug a polar bear. We're looking at it now. We're going to see the whole thing – like an episode of *Big Brother*.'

'Good. Can I have a look too?' Iris searched for her handbag.

'Anything you want to tell us, now, before it comes out in the video footage?'

'What do you mean?'

'Anything you got up to at the zoo or last night you want to share? Experiments and all?'

'Last night?'

'Yes.'

The policewoman was listening intently. Very intently.

'Detective Pavlovic, why would I try to burn myself to death?'

'I'm not a psychiatrist.'

Iris didn't say anything. She re-ran the conversations of the previous day. When the detective said he was looking at her file, she had assumed it was ascertaining her strengths.

He said, 'I think working out why people do things is over-rated. Sure, motive is worth looking at, but mostly I go over physical evidence. I don't believe in coincidence. Fires happen around you, Mrs Foster. You're a common denominator. Like Chuck's zeds and Coke cans.'

'Passiona.'

'Sorry. Does the brand have any significance?'

'I am sure it does. Detective, if this is not a coincidence, then I have been targeted. Which would go to motive. Why did Zorro or the terrorists or whoever try to kill Iris Foster?'

'My superiors are asking the same question. Where were you on the weekend of the school bombing, Mrs Foster?'

'Do I need a lawyer?'

'I've been asking you a variety of witness and consultation questions in this interview, Mrs Foster. If at any point you feel you need to protect your interests, I would advise you to have a lawyer present. Certainly, if we take you to the station, I would apprise you of your rights. You don't have to answer any questions and any answers might be used as evidence against you. On the other hand, you could keep helping us with our inquiries, especially if you're innocent and caring. Isn't that right, Officer Johnston?'

'Yes, Detective Pavlovic. Those are Mrs Foster's rights.'

She did have a name. This was an interrogation.

'I'd have to look at my diary, Detective.'

'It appears your husband was away that weekend.'

Iris tried to think. She couldn't remember.

'I understand your husband is away at the moment.'

'Yes. He's ... yes.'

'Is there anyone who can account for your whereabouts last night, Mrs Foster?'

'Why are you asking me about last night?'

He watched her, making one of his calculations, weighing up the risks of giving her information against what he might gain.

'Last night, the Martian escaped from a non-secure ward at Fieldhaven.'

'My god. Why wasn't I told?'

'Your phone was off. Where is your telephone, Mrs Foster?'

'I seem to have lost it again.'

'We have it, actually. Recovered from near a pond in the butterfly house.' He watched her as though she might crack.

'Good. I'd like it back if it still works. Are you saying James did this, this fire?'

'Open mind.'

'How did he ...'

'Still piecing it together. We do know that as a consequence of a fire in his secure room and the reports from you and Dr Silverberg, he was moved to an even less secure ward. Fewer staff, less security, no cameras. He might have picked the lock on that room. He might have been able to break into the drugs cabinet. He might know medicine and needles. He might have sedated both night staff and taken their keys. I'd suggest it is more likely someone else did the sedating and let him out. James the Martian left via a route which evaded the well-placed CCTV cameras in the grounds.'

'It doesn't make any sense to me.'

'Sense? I can make all kinds of sense. You're Zorro, he's your patsy. He's Zorro, you're his partner. You broke him out and went to the zoo and he thought he'd get rid of you, to shut you up, close the loop. You broke him out and started the fire to throw us off the scent while he escaped. He broke himself out and came after you because you're blackmailing him. There are lots of ways of making sense of this. It is only a matter of time before more evidence comes to light. Mrs Foster, I could arrest you ...'

'For what?'

'AVO could get us by for now.'

'An apprehended violence order?'

'Lighting fires is violent. We have other terrorist provisions too. How about you agree to come to the station, while we gather more facts – clear these things up?'

Iris did need a lawyer but her mind leapt to Mathew, not for the fact he was a lawyer, nor that she knew dozens, but because this could be fatal to his aspirations for the bench. Her thoughts on her husband were particularly complicated and contrary at present, so she built a quick wall around the issue of lawyers. She stood, grabbing her handbag. 'Of course I will help you, Detective. I've been trying to. I am innocent by the way. I need to help you prove it. You can be my champion.'

Pavlovic smirked even though he was shaking his head in a pretty good rendition of disbelief. 'Excellent.' He opened his hand towards the policewoman. 'We have a car.'

As Iris stepped towards the door, he said, 'I don't suppose you'd tell me where the rest of the diethyl ether is?'

'The rest?' said Iris.

He studied her for some seconds before retrieving the recorder from the table. He didn't turn it off.

Chapter seventeen

Johnston drove, Pavlovic in the back with Iris. He tried a couple of times to chat, the recorder sitting casually on his lap.

'Did you see anyone suspicious at the zoo?'

She shook her head.

'Why were you at the zoo?'

'I wanted to see the butterflies.'

'The butterflies? Why?'

'I like butterflies.'

He didn't believe her. It did not sound plausible. Iris did not doubt she had been targeted.

Zorro? If not Zorro, who else? Even if James was Zorro, he had no reason to kill her. Indeed, he could have killed her when she had been hypnotised. He could have killed her before, during or after the bed fire. He had safely established his own madness and in a strange way his own sanity. He might have been released. He didn't have to escape.

Iris said, 'Do you think the offender of the school fire might be spooked to see or hear I'm working on the case and try to take me off the board?'

Pavlovic considered before conceding, 'Possible, I guess.'

'Well, could you please add it to your list of theories? Do you know where Charles Koch is?'

'I don't think it's him.'

'I don't either. If Zorro came after me, could Chuck be in danger? He's poking around, might have raised a red flag.'

'Yes. Fair enough.' Pavlovic used his mobile. 'Charles Koch, the arson investigator. Yes. Yes. We might need to put a car at his boat. Might be a target. Yes. It is her suggestion. Bringing her.'

An exploratory nudge of media were outside the police station.

Iris said, 'Don't handcuff me.'

Pavlovic said, 'I wasn't going to.'

'Look at these clothes the hospital gave me. I look like a recaptured fugitive, not a consultant. Which is what I am doing, what I will be doing, after I'm cleared. I'm not even helping you with your inquiries, Stuart. I'm consulting, whether you think so or not.' Iris tried to keep pleading from her voice.

Pavlovic blinked at her. Finally he said, 'No parade. Let's go in the gates, Lorraine.'

Officer Lorraine Johnston turned into the alleyway beside police HQ, buzzed them through an automatic sliding metal gate into the underground carpark.

Pavlovic took Iris up in the lift.

Iris said, 'So you have incident rooms at Fire and Rescue Command, and interview rooms here?'

He shrugged.

Iris said, 'It's getting bigger all the time, isn't it?'

Pavlovic didn't answer.

A uniformed officer was waiting when the lift arrived. Pavlovic said, 'Room four.' The floor was busy with detectives, uniforms and civilians with identity tags, all moving with urgent purpose.

The uniform led Iris to a small interview room. Affixed to the single table was a microphone. A camera was mounted above a mirror, which filled the wall by the door.

Iris said, 'Could I have coffee and some water?'

'I'll see,' he said, a young man with big shoulders. But he stayed where he was by the door.

Iris went to the mirror, saw again how she looked in second-hand hospital garb. At least she'd managed to redo her make-up at the hospital. She should ask them if her earring had been found. That's not an incendiary device, it's my antique.

The door opened, a man and woman entered. He was Chinese. They were both in their fifties, dressed for comfortable professional work. She wore dark slacks, a dark grey summer jacket over a pale blue, fine-knit t-shirt. He wore light chinos, a blue striped shirt not tucked into his pants.

The man said in an Australian accent to the policeman, 'Could Mrs Foster have the water and coffee please?'

The woman said, 'Mrs Foster, my name is Clara and this is John.' They remained standing at the door. Clara said, 'We're here to carry out a couple of psychological tests.'

'Really?'

'We're helping with assessments, screenings ...'

'You're forensic psychologists.'

'Yes,' said John with another smile touched with embarrassment.

'Seconded to the federal taskforce,' added Clara.

Iris said, 'Well folks, I must say I have been on the other side of this process quite a few times.'

'You can give us marks at the end,' said Clara, rather too lightly. She indicated where Iris should sit, facing the mirror, then sat next to her before bringing out a folder.

John took a chair, put it near the wall, so he was out of Iris's direct line of sight, but could watch her face, mostly in profile.

Clara said, 'Are you familiar with the Rorschach test?'

'Yes.'

'Have you done it or used it often?'

'A few times at uni, I think. I am probably familiar enough with the test to skew valid findings.' Iris tried turn to Clara, but she'd taken her chair back, so Iris concentrated on Chinese John and the mirror as she spoke. Perhaps he was younger than fifty, although his eyes were lined. They'd been working long hours, Iris assumed, possibly since the explosion at Barnard's.

John said, 'I might ask other questions afterwards to fill things out. I hear you had a close call at the zoo?'

'Is this part of the test?'

'Well, breaking the ice I suppose. I do hope you're okay.'

'I had a small piece of metal taken out of my back. I'm not in shock though, if that matters. They gave me a local anaesthetic, so I'm not on anything. I'll need Panadol soon I'm sure.'

John took extra time to make notes about Iris's responses.

Iris finally said, 'I'm sure shock will kick in later, right now my dominant feeling is embarrassment. I've been brought here dressed like a refugee.' Iris indicated her hospital apparel.

John gave a polite smile.

Iris said, 'Or is this a standard interrogation technique? Humiliate. Take away dignity. Decentre core values.'

It didn't get a laugh.

Clara leaned forward, opened up the file to the first inkblot image.

Iris recalled there were ten cards in total. She said, 'I don't want to turn them around. I know how it works. This looks like two seahorses. They're not talking.'

John took out a notebook, jotted something. Iris could hear Clara scribbling in her file.

Iris said, 'Wow, got you going right off the bat.'

Clara said, 'The next one?'

Iris said, 'Two Cossacks dancing. Together. Their knees are bent. They're clapping hands in the middle.'

Iris flipped to the next image. Said, 'Two women. See their boobs. They are lifting up a basket.'

She regarded the next. 'A woolly mammoth. See his trunk. I think he's smiling. He's a bit of a scallywag. Not an adult woolly mammoth.'

'A butterfly.' Iris flicked over the cards at her own pace, ignoring the frantic scribbling around her. She mostly tried to tell them the truth of what she saw. 'I have to give you some background about this one. I know it's the sex card or one of the sex inkblots and I'm pretty sure I did not see female genitalia here until I was told, so now I can't help seeing a woman's pudenda. I'm afraid I can't go back to my Rorschach virginity on this one. It's the shading along here where the labia would be curled. Which would make the angel standing on top a kind of wonderful metaphor for either her clitoris, or is it an orgasm?' Iris glanced to catch John smiling, as he wrote something in his notebook.

Iris turned to the next one. She recalled this as the mother card. She said, 'Two girls dancing. So much fun. Their ponytails are bobbing.' Iris started to turn the page, but stopped, went back. 'I fibbed. What I first saw was a girl looking in the mirror.

She's not happy with what she sees.'

Iris went to the next page. 'This card is colour. I'm not sure where to look. I see a trophy maybe. Hang on, I also see two panthers climbing up a boat. Those are the sails. The panthers are sailing the boat. I've seen the film *Pi*, which might be suggestive of influence.'

Iris dealt the next. 'Two swans. It's a ballet.' Iris didn't say what she'd really seen. She turned the page. What Iris had first seen were two witches fighting as they stood in flames. It surprised and frightened her.

'And this ink spot?' prompted Clara.

'Caterpillars, chrysalis and those might be butterflies, already born. They won't be gone long those poor little critters down at the zoo – rebirth, regeneration.' Iris turned to John, 'So Doc, what's the prognosis?'

John smiled but checked to Clara. She must have signalled because he said, 'What is in the ladies' basket, do you suppose?'

'Washing. They were bringing in the washing.'

'Would you mind turning back to that one?'

Iris found it. 'Will I have to keep going until I guess the right answers?'

'Some people see blood in those red splotches.'

'Oh, I didn't. I didn't really notice the red. Clothes, still on the line? Did you want blood?'

'Card number seven. I realise you are familiar with the popular responses and categories. Why did you feel you needed to lie?'

'I'm in a hostile environment. I felt the first response might weaken my position further. Oh, she has self-image issues! Oh, she has an unreconciled duality. Maybe we need to explore her relationship with her mother. My professional instinct suggested I not raise these as possibilities.'

'Yet you corrected it. You didn't stay with the lie.'

'I am innocent, so I thought I shouldn't hide anything. Let the chips fall where they may. Having parent problems is not yet a prosecutable offence ... in police stations anyway.'

'You saw lots of butterflies.'

'Doesn't everyone?'

'Yes, but you saw butterflies where participants see other things and no butterflies where many people do.'

Iris didn't answer immediately. It was not a matter of right or wrong answers, even if there were common clusters of what people saw. Context and other information were more important. The whole picture. The story constructed about it. The time taken to decipher or process or mediate. 'I like butterflies. I saw lots get fried,' she offered.

John thought about it. Clara kept scribbling, the scratching behind Iris like rats in the ceiling.

'Card nine,' John said, as though reading her mind. 'What upset you about card nine?'

'None of your business,' said Iris with a disarming smile.

'So you lied about the second last card?'

'I didn't lie. I saw lots of different pictures in the card. I chose which one to tell you.'

'Do you often do that?'

'Modify my response in relation to who I am talking to? Yes, like anyone over three years old.'

'Have you ever been in trouble with the law?'

'I used to work for them. I thought I was working with them now.'

'I'm sorry, Mrs Foster. You're quite right. And, for what it is worth, you are showing an appropriate amount of anger about this process, yet you're still trying to cooperate to a degree, I think. I'm sure Clara's notes will be far more comprehensive, however I would have expected a greater degree of … hyper-vigilance. Seeing what you've been through today … over the last year, this week.' He looked at her with particular attention.

Iris said, 'Hmm. Agreed. Not what you'd expect.'

'Do you ever feel like you're watching yourself do things?'

'Yes, sometimes, I do feel slightly detached.'

'Ever fall asleep and wake up elsewhere?'

'No,' said Iris. Where was he going now?

'Ever have time seem to jump, like fast forward or bits are missing?'

'No. Well, I wouldn't know, would I?'

'Sorry?'

'Well, it would be missing, wouldn't it?'

'So no blackouts.'

'Not as I am aware.'

John looked to Clara again.

Clara shuffled her chair forward. 'What do you think of the government, Mrs Foster?'

'They're crap. I voted for the other mob. I vote. I don't blow up.'

'Do you ever get depressed?'

'About the government. Yes.'

'About life.'

'Yes. I do.'

'Occasionally does life feel like it's all too much?'

'No, never.' Iris met Clara's gaze.

Clara said, 'Thanks, Mrs Foster. Thank you for your cooperation.'

John stood. 'We have to report to people.'

'Yes,' said Iris.

'Yes,' said John.

Iris said to Clara, 'I don't suppose I can get ... presentable clothes?'

Clara said, 'We will ask.'

They didn't bring her any clothes but an older constable bought her a collection of runners to pick from. Iris imagined him rifling through his colleagues' sports lockers. She was escorted to a nearby toilet by a different policewoman when she asked. They finally brought her a bottle of water, lukewarm machine coffee, a sandwich in a wrapper. It appeared to be grated cheese and carrot with lettuce on white bread. Iris wasn't hungry. She asked for more coffee and Panadol. She asked again for clothes. She also asked for Frank. They said they'd see.

Two detectives whom Iris did not recognise came in with Detective Pavlovic.

'How are you getting on, Mrs Foster?'

'As you can see, Detective Pavlovic, I'm dressed for a marathon. And, if you'd like your spleen removed, I can scrub up. Be a pleasure.'

He actually smiled. 'This is Detective Scanlon and Detective

Minchin. Federal police agency.' They were in their forties. Scanlon was thin, dark-haired, Minchin portly, bald. Their suits were wrinkled, their ties probably unfashionable when they were purchased.

'Thanks for helping us, Mrs Foster. Can I call you Iris?'

Iris nodded. Scanlon was going to be her friend.

'I'd like to pick your brain about the school.'

'Pick away.'

'Downstairs, under the stage ... that's a pretty elaborate set-up, don't you think?'

'Um, yes. By all accounts. I've seen photographs.'

'Where?' asked Minchin gruffly.

'At the Department of Fire and Emergency Services incident room.'

'What were you doing in that room?'

'I was looking for the arson investigator, Charles Koch. He'd asked for feedback on a theory he's formulated concerning a possible suspect nicknamed Zorro, so named after the distinctive burn patterns he had found at a number of suspicious fires. He found similar zed-shaped accelerant spill patterns under the stage at Barnard's. Koch also told me of a particular kind of soft-drink can at the school which also matched the modus operandi of a serial firelighter he had detected.'

Scanlon said, 'Relax, Iris. We're not in court.'

'Oh,' said Iris, looking at the microphone, then to the mirror. 'This is where you ask, "What kind of soft drink, Mrs Foster?" and you Detective Pavlovic, you should possibly say, "Hearsay," and then Detective Scanlon might offer, "Reported conversation to an expert witness, Your Honour."'

'You think this is a joke?' said Minchin, reddening. The bad cop.

'It's humorous in the silly sense because of a kind of circularity and repetition. For that reason, I want to make it clear I have held many conversations with Detective Pavlovic, for instance, and Charles Koch and others about the crime scene and other crime scenes and I have seen evidence relating to the crime. So, there are things I have been told and things I have surmised ... I was never under the stage, Detective Scanlon. I have formed an image of the important elements of what was down there. I have a pretty good schematic picture of the whole thing including how the truck worked. I also have a pretty strong image of a fireman being vaporised which I'd like to forget one day.'

'You sound pretty callous to me,' said Minchin.

'For a woman?'

Scanlon waved his hand in front of his partner, either in a gesture of rescue or calming. He said, 'Want to lay out what you've got?'

Minchin wasn't so sure. Iris noticed Pavlovic stiffen before folding his arms to feign boredom.

Iris leaned towards the microphone, said, 'I repeat, I've had a variety of sources in obtaining this information. Most of the conclusions are not mine, they have been shared with me.' Iris took a sip from the cold coffee. Her bottle of water was empty. 'You can tell me how I'm doing.'

The detectives did not.

'He or they steal diethyl ether, a chemical I still know nothing about. They do this by telephone and order forms. Apparently you can. And courier companies. They have it delivered to a temporary storage space. No one sees anyone.' Iris kept watching their faces, looking for the tells of confirmation. 'Gym mats are also delivered. The diethyl ether is put in the gym mat covers and is delivered to the school gymnasium.

'Oh, he's already made it in a week in which the person most likely to question this odd delivery is away. Again, no one is sighted. It's another delivery company. Some time on the weekend immediately prior to the bombing, he arrives – with a number of materials. Quite a bit I imagine. There's the urn and pipes to attach to the gym mats, flammable liquid to spread on the floor, chains and glue. Witnesses?'

Iris scanned their eyes. Got nothing.

Scanlon said, 'You're telling the story, Iris.'

'The truck! A week or so before this, he steals a landscaper's truck one night from the school. So when it reappears, no one really sees it as odd. Was the gym open over the weekend, for sport or anything?'

They were uniformly closed, which gave away the answer.

'It wasn't open. Okay. He does it Saturday. Another workman or workers unloading stuff. Do you have CCTV footage? I would love to see it.'

They paused. They were tempted. Pavlovic stepped up, said, 'Not now, Mrs Foster.'

'He goes in and shifts the gym mats.' Iris thought back to the stage in the school. 'It comes apart at the front. I'm guessing he could make a bigger opening to get the gym mats down. To stuff them in under the gymnasium's wooden floor. Even if we're dealing with more than one person, it would have taken time.

'He doesn't mind. He's methodical. He loves the precision of doing it. It's part of his pleasure. His foreplay. This, then this. This urn will lead to this burn pattern. This line will erupt at this temperature. This glue will prevent this door. This chain will not be noticed. Everything he does over the weekend is giving him a charge of pleasure. He's building the physical bomb, imagining how each part of it will deliver its grief. It's a sculpture. He plans and prepares over a long time. He loves the anticipation. His pleasure is in working it out as well as carrying it out. He's not impulsive. Maybe he's anal like Detective Pavlovic.'

No smiles.

Iris gulped the last of the cold coffee. Yes, she silently agreed with herself, this is how Zorro works.

Iris said, 'You know, it's not two. No way. This fellow works alone. It's his – all of it. It's one person, definitely. He signs it. Charles is right. If Charles is also right about the other crimes, it is worth considering his other claim. This fire got out of hand. Zorro got the mix wrong or the timing. And not just because the young lovers stumbled on the fire.'

Iris checked their reactions for confirmation or affirmation but this was not the room.

'The school,' said Minchin. He had a boil on the side of his neck where his collar rubbed.

'He waits. His plan is for ten past eight or whatever, when all the kids are in and the assembly is running. He's set the timer on the urn to start sparking like a malfunction, he's going to back the truck up to the front doors to block them. Like he did at the zoo, possibly. I find it strange he should try to disguise the urn malfunction though. He had the truck. I think he followed his usual way of doing things even if not essential. Sticks to the rite. Maybe he's superstitious. He's fastidious. I suppose if the truck was where it was supposed to be it would have been blown up with everything else and no one's the wiser. His plan got changed. I think it got changed by the kids under the stage. I don't think they just came across the fire. I think they knocked something or started it early. Maybe.'

'The assembly started late.' It was Pavlovic, searching for a reaction to his information, still probing at her.

Iris said, 'Really? Ha. The unforseen.'

'The headmistress missed her flight from a weekend conference. The deputy delayed while he got her talking points emailed and printed. The kids were milling outside when the fire started.'

'He would have been livid. Fuming. He's beside himself, nearby. He sees the students running out of the gym, or he hears the sirens from the approaching fire appliances. He's off. Dumb luck, he's thinking. How can you plan for ... no, he's livid. Not sanguine. He can't abide this. It's not over, is it?' Iris whirled to Pavlovic. 'You said you still have ether unaccounted for. Was it at the zoo?'

Pavlovic blanched. The two detectives spun to him, aghast. A banging noise came from the mirror. He shouldn't have told her.

She said, 'Do I have it? Was it at the zoo?'

'You tell us,' said Minchin leaning forward.

The door opened and Iris watched a senior policeman whisper to Pavlovic.

Iris called, 'I have more!'

Scanlon said, 'He'll hear. Don't worry. Is there diethyl at the zoo? We haven't found it.'

Iris thought.

Minchin said, 'Where would he put it?'

'Can I see the CCTV footage please?'

'We'll ask.'

'I didn't know I was going to the zoo until I went. A whim I shared with no one. He's followed me and improvised. He has no time to get the ether, unless he's driving around with it. It's big, isn't it? All those gym mats and ... it's in big containers. It's not a gel? I'm sorry I don't know my explosives.'

'It's big,' said Minchin, deadpan again.

Iris glared at the mirror. 'I don't think it is at the zoo. Ninety percent sure.' She refocused to those in the room. They did not believe her. They did not believe her because they conceived another alternative.

'What time did James the Martian escape from Fieldhaven?'

Closed. Not telling.

'Would he have time to stash the ether at the zoo? How would he get it in unnoticed? How would I? I suppose in any number of ways, if you consider the school. Under hay. In a water tanker I suppose. Do they have them? Anyway, this only works if I am in collusion. If I was working with Zorro and the plan was to blow up parts of the zoo ... and I went to the zoo to set it off and it went wrong.'

Bingo. Their lips were set but their eyes were bulging to not give anything away. Not a victim; Iris was a failed bomber.

'Why?' said Iris.

They didn't answer. No one answers because you're mad. If you're mad, logic is not a problem to be respected. You did it because you decided to or your voices told you. That's the only motive they needed, madness.

Iris said, 'It's not at the zoo.'

*

They left the room. A constable with red hair and pimples brought Iris her cup of coffee in a takeaway container, this one hot. There was a biscuit in sealed plastic, dark brown with a peanut on top. Iris ate it, sipped the coffee. He brought her Panadol, a cup of water, took away her rubbish.

She considered James again. She tried to cast him in the role of Zorro, imagining him performing each of the procedures necessary to create the school bomb. He certainly possessed the breaking and entering skills. He knew the science. It was plausible that in his Martian psychosis he believed he was building a new spaceship, the ether his fuel supply. Perhaps he thought he would meet his new spaceship out in the desert where he claimed his old one had crashed. These things were possible. And yet ...

When Iris requested the toilet again the woman constable took her a different way, around the corridors. They passed a glass-walled office where officers gathered round a television set.

The constable said, 'Just a minute.' She went into an office, leaving Iris at the corridor window.

Iris saw Hill Church on a television screen through the window. Police and detectives were watching the news. The old church sat atop the highest ground of the city. Bouquets of flowers were piled at its iron gates. They ran an interview with a grieving wife who cried proudly. Two children and a man who would have been her father stood behind her, his arm resolute around her shoulder. They showed photographs of the dead when they were alive, smiling, their names superimposed, dissolving from soft-edged photograph to photograph. A media tribute. They returned to a wide shot of the church, seen from above, supered the details of the public funeral which had been scheduled for Monday. Tomorrow. Monday, already.

The next story featured the zoo, using a lot of helicopter shots of the burnt-out shell that had once been the butterfly enclosure. Dazed victims sat around on the grass. Two appliances stood by, a respectful distance from the extinguished fire. Ambulances were being loaded. Iris strained to see the television set past the police in the room. There were a lot of trucks. Cattle and circus trucks. They were evacuating the animals from the zoo.

Iris became aware of people nearby. The psychologist John and the psychologist Clara's faces came into focus. They were standing in another office inside the television room watching Iris through the window, gauging her reactions to the television material. It was another test.

Chapter eighteen

They brought her some new detectives. Scanlon and Minchin had peeled off. One was a woman of about Iris's age. She was tall. Not quite an amazon. He was older, very straight. He sat straight, he stood straight. Iris watched him plant his feet, at ease. They were soldiers in spite of their nicely cut suits. Iris had lost the capacity to remember names.

'Could you let Detective Pavlovic know I remember what I was doing last Monday morning? I had an early morning counselling session with a girl suffering from anorexia. Her mother was present, as were other witnesses. Superintendent Richards sent a police sergeant to get me. I was picked up and taken to the school after the first fire started.'

They were having none of it, of course, because now they thought Iris worked with a partner or gang. Iris could be in two places at once because of her accomplice or accomplices. Once they were on this track there could be no alibis – only networks.

Iris said to the soldier, 'Have you got my telephone?'

He blinked. They did.

'You'll see I haven't been communicating with anyone.'

The amazon said, 'Where is your laptop?' She had a country accent, from the east coast.

Iris said, 'At home, locked in the top drawer of my desk.'

'It's not.'

'I sent a report to Frank. Um, yesterday evening. I would have locked it away. It has confidential files. People's secrets.'

'No.'

'You've been to my house? In my locked desk?'

The soldier said, 'Everyone you've ever emailed. Every call you've ever made. We will find it all. We will know. Do you have other telephones?'

'One is already too much for me.'

'Are you saying no?' he said.

'Yes, it means no. One phone.'

Amazon said, 'You are very close to a man who is about to become a Supreme Court judge.'

'Yes, I've managed to position myself well.' Iris she felt a cold shudder pass through her, making her shoulder ache where the metal had struck her. She felt like she'd passed through Alice's portal, only the land she'd entered was of *Bourne Identity* or *Mission Impossible*. Her potential lives were multiplying and layering too quickly for Iris to even imagine. 'He's my husband. Of many years.'

'This could completely jeopardise his promotion.'

Iris stood. 'Stop this now! Stop it. I did not do this. You have no right, no possible lawful reason to intimidate me or blackmail me as if I'm the third fucking wife of the fucking village mayor in Afghanistan. I am not part of a cell. I am not part of a conspiracy. I am a psychologist who used to work for the fire service. I'm a narrative therapist. Not a good one, I grant. I consult for the cops. And you people. I'm an Australian citizen. Get me a lawyer and get the fuck out of here.'

The soldier went steely, said, 'We need you to answer our questions.'

Iris sat down hard, hurting her shoulder on the back of the chair. She gasped, trying not to show them.

'It's our job to protect this country,' said the Amazon.

'I have a right to silence.'

'We have the power to hold you for quite some time, if we think we need to.'

Iris folded her arms, looking to the mirror. She thought she appeared particularly small and puny sitting before the army folk. She always considered herself to be bigger than she actually was.

The door opened and Pavlovic stepped in, saying, 'Iris, it's okay.' He'd changed his shirt, this one black with tiny silver stripes.

Iris said, 'Stuart, you're a prick.'

'Shall we take a short break?' Pavlovic asked the army questioners. They exchanged information, silently. An order from beyond the looking glass. The Amazon gave Iris one last look promising future combat possibly in the nearest laneway.

Iris glared at Pavlovic. 'They've been in my house.'

Pavlovic said, 'Of course we've been in your house. Firstly we checked to see if he was there. Then we gathered evidence. We've left a uniformed officer to watch over things.'

'Now I'm a terrorist?'

'I'm the maître de, Iris, not the chef.'

'In that shirt you're more like the Greek waiter.'

'Are you trying to insult me with a racist put-down?'

Iris said, 'I shouldn't have singled out the Greeks. They have enough problems.'

'My father came from Croatia where the sticks and stones were real.' Pavlovic came forward from beside the door, sat in one of the interrogator's chairs. 'Everyone we interview gets put past the different investigations. Everyone wants a turn at you.'

'Like a pack rape.'

He looked wounded but not very. 'You're pissed at me.'

She didn't answer.

He said, 'This thing, it's like a machine. It has moving parts which interlock when it works, although mostly they don't fit very well. Each moving part is also made of lots of other parts. You were a small part of the machine but you have moved to the middle of it and now I'm a bit connected to you, maybe all the way to the end or maybe for just a while. So, I thought we should work together ... better.'

'Is that an apology?'

'It's how I make sense of the big cases. And this is the biggest thing I've ever been part of. The psychs say you're very perceptive and sane. Coherent and ordered thinking. Which is bad news really if you've done this – you won't evade the consequences. They say you use minor rebellion, humour and ground shifting to control situations. You like to take control. You think you're superior.'

'They got the last one wrong. Do they think I'm a bomber?'

He paused for the longest time before he finally conceded, 'No, they don't.'

'You still do.'

'We've seen the CCTV footage at the zoo. The consensus is you didn't know he was there.'

'You've seen him?'

'Your car is clean.'

'You have my car!'

'We've checked your phone. You made two calls at the zoo, received none. They were to your husband and your daughter. The intelligence officers,' he indicated the empty seat behind him, 'say suicide bombers say goodbye to their loved ones before they ...'

'So even if I didn't say this is my last goodbye, any declaration of love could be seen as a veiled goodbye.'

'Apparently.'

'You did psychology at uni.'

'Yes. Undergraduate. Not in your league, I know.'

'A double major.'

He nodded.

She said, 'Psych and ... business?'

'I did psych and forensics.'

'Ha. You always wanted to do this, didn't you?'

'Yes. You?'

'I didn't want to become the Fire Lady. But it's all I'm good at.'

'Do you only do things you excel at?'

'I didn't say excel. I'm an average gardener, promising cook, under-appreciated wife, poor mother, terrible sister, selfish citizen. I'm not good at most of the things I do.' Iris realised she felt tired, maudlin. Sympathy would probably completely undo her.

Pavlovic was watching.

Iris said, 'The funeral is tomorrow.'

'Yes.'

'I'd like to go.'

'We'll see. Yes, probably.'

'I'd like to go home.'

'I don't think so. If he's after you, you wouldn't be safe. We can't find James. We can't identify Zorro.'

'I'm locked up?'

'Protective custody.'

'It's a bet each way, isn't it? You still don't think I'm innocent.'

He didn't answer her question. Instead he asked, 'Why do you keep pushing to see the CCTV footage?'

'I want to see if I recognise him. I want to observe his body language; you can tell things, as you know. He tried to kill me. Maybe it's personal. Maybe I know him.'

Pavlovic stood. 'Okay. Not great footage. It's all pretty wide and high, where they put CCTV cameras. It's not like ... they zoom in.'

Iris followed him. A policewoman lurked in the corridor. Iris recognised her. 'Hello Lorraine Johnston. High rotation.'

Johnston replied, 'Yes,' with the hint of a smile.

Iris said, 'Can I see Dr Silverberg?'

'I'll ask. It won't be soon. He's pretty busy explaining and reappraising. James the Martian fooled everyone, but it's on Silverberg. In the end it was his call.'

Iris had fed Frank's report. Iris's actions complicated Frank's processes and his reporting. Frank was in the shit.

'He is adamant you are not Zorro.'

Iris met Pavlovic's gaze. He was studying her again.

Iris said, 'I have one fan.'

'You have more than one. Superintendent Richards is anxious to get you back to work.' Pavlovic led them into a post-production suite of multiple television screens and computers. A young man in a blue t-shirt sat at the console. Detective Scanlon and Chinese John stood at the back.

The young man said, 'I've done an edit on them both. I've followed him back from the surgery to pick him up here. So, this is my guesstimate – not for court. Watch both screens.'

He pushed buttons, Iris saw herself enter the zoo. Her yellow blouse managed to stand out in the faintly blue low-resolution wide shots. She lined up to buy coffee, just another office worker at lunch, meandering and dreaming.

The other screen showed a service gate somewhere else in the zoo. Green-clad keepers came to a utility, taking bags. An office worker went out.

Iris bought her coffee, went to the otters. She stood for some time before she telephoned. She was only in the corner of the shot. It was hard to make out the phone.

'This is him, I think,' said the media man.

A man in a coat and wide-brimmed hat marched in through the gateway, hunched over, his head twisted away from the camera. He passed through quickly, as a worker went the other way.

'I've re-run the street, can't see anyone like this scoping it out.'

Pavlovic said, 'It's enough time to walk from the front entrance of the zoo to here. They don't have cameras outside. We've interviewed the worker who passed him. Didn't remember anything and yes, he could have pushed through the security gate before it closed after him.'

'Here,' said the young man.

The camera angle switched to a different view, a different camera. A zookeeper emerged from the rear of a shed, dressed in green, wearing a wide-brimmed hat with fly netting draped over. Close-ups would not have helped, as his face was hidden.

Iris said, 'It doesn't look like James.'

'Why?'

'Looks fatter. He's heavier on his feet.'

'He could be wearing street clothes under his zookeeper stuff? We think he wears disguises.'

He moved with purpose. She checked her screen. She'd drifted to the birds, was on the phone again.

The other monitor showed a series of shots from various cameras, merely glimpses of the worker seen past trees or the edge of buildings. He was rarely centred in the frame. He'd been found later, his journey built from all the camera views. The screen cut to an interior shot. A hospital room.

Iris said, 'This is the zoo surgery?'

'Yes. They have cameras inside. Sometimes the patients wake

up and bite so they have to assess when it's safe to go back in.'

The zoo worker ensured the surgery was empty before picking up an oxygen cylinder from near an empty surgery table, leaving with it.

'He's very confident. Knows what he's looking for.'

He returned, disconnected another cylinder, left.

Iris walked towards the butterfly enclosure. She could see the three children she'd met, already at the entrance door. They were talking with their grandmother.

'Here.'

A golf cart drove slowly down the back lanes behind the animal cages passing curious monkeys then the empty swings at the top of an orang-utan enclosure.

'He's working very fast,' said Iris.

Scanlon said, 'Yes. We don't think he entirely made this up on the spot.'

Iris was at the entrance of the butterfly enclosure, taking her time on entering. She passed the children who still negotiated with their grandmother.

The golf cart was parked near a shed. He came back to it carrying a huge cylinder.

'He's strong,' said Iris.

'The LPG.'

The children entered the butterfly enclosure.

The golf cart disappeared behind the enclosure, didn't re-emerge. The man with the baseball cap entered the enclosure.

Iris said, 'He was inside, trying to break open a side door during the fire.'

'Yes, he's being interviewed.'

'Here comes the fire.'

It was hard to see, in the beginning. A gaseous gossamer rising up above the back of the entrance wall like a heat shimmer.

'Here, he parks the buggy. You can see the edge of it.'

A white square jutted from the other end of the enclosure. The fire gave off dark smoke. The yellow flame spread slowly like spilled olive oil. You could see people run up to it and away, gesticulating.

'Here he goes.' They were back at the rear gate. A worker

leaving, still in his work clothes, still in his hat and fly net.

'He didn't stay,' said Iris.

'He's getting away,' said Scanlon.

Iris said, 'He's not staying to enjoy his show.' She turned to John who she'd decided was a federal profiler of some kind. 'We were thinking he enjoys the ... results of his work.'

John said, 'That fits.'

They returned to the screen.

The fire continued to spread. The silent vision was haunting, unreal. The fire spread up over one third of the roof like moss growing, like a tide coming in. It consumed the plastic netting, lapped at the wooden section.

Someone came up to a far wall and sprayed a fire extinguisher. Someone else waved a hose. At the other end zookeepers were pulling at the golf buggy. A white puff of smoke. The LPG cylinder rose up above the roof before falling into the enclosure, a hint of flame behind. The firefighting staff fell back. A whoosh of white, which the cameras or recording material couldn't handle, filled the screen for a couple of seconds. When they came back to the wide shot a third of the building was gone, the edge of the rest was smoking. The man with the extinguisher climbed up off the grass.

Iris said, 'The fire just stopped.'

'It was snuffed out. The easy fuel load was about gone, the explosion starved the fire of oxygen for enough time to kill it. The rest doesn't have enough heat to combust the heavier fuel.'

Charles Koch leaned on the doorjamb as if it were a saloon doorway and he'd just ridden into town. He was in jeans and boots, his fireman's belt buckle gleaming over a purple Rivers shirt. 'How ya doin', Doc?'

'Pretty good, Sheriff.'

Pavlovic said, 'I thought you were working out of the Fire and Rescue op centre.'

'I heard you were interrogating the doc.'

'She's not a doctor,' said Scanlon.

Chuck sneered at Scanlon like he was a dried dog turd, then turned back to Pavlovic. 'Maybe you should stop investigating your investigators so's we can catch this scumbag for you.'

Pavlovic said nothing.

Chuck said, 'Yeah, I still got one or two friends.' He grinned at Iris. 'The few I haven't taken a swing at.' Charles was happy, invigorated to be inside a big operation. Or he'd had a few glasses of scotch during the afternoon.

Iris said, 'I didn't know he was there. I didn't know I was going to the butterflies until I went. Which means he's been watching me. He got his stuff, was ready by the time I got to the butterfly enclosure.'

'What'd he use?' said Charles.

Pavlovic calculated before sharing.

Iris said, 'Two oxygen cylinders and an LPG cylinder.'

'He knew where everything was and how to get it,' said Scanlon. 'Mapped out before he went in. This is a man who plans, he's very methodical and cool. Attracts no attention.'

'Any signatures?' asked Chuck.

Pavlovic shook his head.

Iris said, 'He didn't stay around. There were children, families, about twenty people. He lit the fire, jammed the exit, left without seeing the show.'

Charles grinned at Iris. 'We must be getting close.'

Iris asked the media tech, 'Is he the same man who was at the school?'

He looked to Scanlon, not Pavlovic.

Pavlovic said, 'We're working the zoo right now.'

Scanlon said, 'Show her.' He asked John, 'Have you seen this?'

The psychologist shook his head.

'Tell me more body language stuff.'

Iris noticed an identification card in a plastic folder suspended from the media tech's neck. He was a detective too. He changed thumb drives, opened different files. He hit play, and up came a high angle wide shot of the school gymnasium and the grass beyond. He said, 'We have two angles. This is the only one showing the truck.'

It was an open-backed truck with METRO LANDSCAPING painted on the side. Shovels and limestone blocks were visible in the back. When the truck did a U-turn on the bitumen they all strained to see through the front windscreen, getting only dim reflections. The truck parked near a side door, leaving only a corner of the rear tray visible.

Chuck said, 'He broke in the side door. Jimmied the lock. It's in the reports. Then he chained and padlocked it.'

Hands came into the back of the truck, occasionally a hat. Rolls of reticulation hose were removed.

'He works mostly the other side of the truck, so he's hidden by the gym wall.' The tech fast-forwarded the tape, pressed play again. 'Except here.'

The man was up on the truck. He wore an orange visibility vest, a wide-brimmed hat. He straightened and waved off screen before picking up a large silver object.

'The urn,' said Charles.

Iris said, 'So who is he waving at?'

Scanlon, 'We haven't found anyone.'

John said, 'Us. He's waving at us. You can barely see it, it's a finger flutter.' He did the gesture, slightly effeminate, an ironic wave.

The man disappeared, the truck came forward, then veered out to the grass side of the gymnasium, no longer visible to the CCTV camera.

Chuck said, 'He knows where the blind spots are.'

'Yeah. He knows. You can see a bit of the truck from the camera near the home economics rooms, but not worth any detail. Here he comes.'

The man appeared again, coming back around the corner of the gym. He carried a broom, his head down.

Iris said, 'You are right. He likes playing dress-ups. He likes props.'

John said, 'You wear a high-visibility vest, you become invisible. The props are the things people notice.'

Chuck said, 'Have you got him coming out?'

Pavlovic said, 'We can go into that later.'

Charles said, 'Why?'

Pavlovic said, 'The timing of his egress might be crucial to the ongoing investigation.'

Iris thought this to be about an alibi, hers or James or whoever. They weren't sharing the time Zorro came out.

Scanlon said, 'Keep us in the loop.' He pushed past Chuck who had to step out of the tiny media room to allow him to go.

John said to Iris, 'He's a cool customer. He's done this before. I still think he's ex-military if not current.'

'But why me?'

No one answered.

John followed the federal detective out.

Iris said, 'Someone said something about a dog walker on the weekend before.'

'On a couple of weekends.' The tech checked with Pavlovic who nodded.

Charles limped into the room, eased himself back onto a desk at the back.

The tech fast-forwarded. 'It was set on a four-week turn-around, erasing the first week with the fifth week's recording. Luck for us. Bear in mind they're not recording twenty-five frames a second and they're saving in low-res.' People were kicking footballs, dogs walked, balls flew, all in a slightly jerky motion. It was the same angle as the previous shot. The tech went to another file, clicked on that.

A man in a dark coat and a floppy cricket hat. Sunglasses. He had a dog on a leash, a golden retriever. He walked into shot leading the dog. The retriever limped. The man regarded the camera. He was a long way away.

'Does he have a fake beard?' said Iris.

Pavlovic said, 'A scarf. We've got an enhancement. Pixilation noise so useless.'

Iris said, 'It's a similar coat to the one worn going into the zoo.'

'Yes.'

The man pulled the leash, dragged the limping dog out of shot.

A new shot came on. The same camera but in different light. It was later. The timer running at the bottom of screen showed 1713.

'This is the week before.'

A woman with long blonde hair walked into shot leading a poodle. She wore the same coat, with a beanie and big sunglasses.

209

She walked like a man trying to walk like a woman. She went to the side of the gymnasium, disappeared near the side door. She re-emerged, walked away moments later.

'Checking out the lock,' said Chuck.

'Same man. Different dog,' said Iris.

Pavlovic said, 'Dog hairs in the truck too. Lots of animal hairs on the truck seat. Looks like he scoped out the place walking his dogs.'

Chuck said, 'Only the outside. I've been thinking about what you said at my boat, Doc. He knows where everything is. He comes prepared, sure, but he also knows the layout and precise technical elements.' Chuck asked, 'Was a fire preparedness inspection carried out on the school gymnasium any time in the months before this?'

Pavlovic interrupted. 'Thanks, Adam,' he said to the media detective, and, 'Let's go get a coffee,' to Charles and Iris.

Chapter nineteen

Pavlovic led them along another corridor.

Chuck said, 'This place is hard to get into, by the way.'

'Harder to get out of.'

'Soldiers.'

'Until we find the missing gas.'

'How much is missing?'

'From the calculations of the boffins, about half of what was stolen.' Pavlovic led them back into a detectives room. The desks were messy, some still occupied even after eleven on a Sunday night.

Chuck talked about the gas while Pavlovic dragged chairs over to his desk. 'Diethyl ether is a strange choice. It can be used as starting fluid. Eighty-five to ninety-six cetane. Low flashpoint. Highly volatile. Not your regular bomb choice. Too bulky. Too unstable. As I've said, why it got away from him.'

Pavlovic said, 'Ether, it's an anaesthetic.'

Chuck said, 'Not anymore. Too flammable. It's used in laboratories though as a solvent. It can be mixed with other pharmaceuticals. Knockout drops and recreational drug use too.'

'So, Chuck, what else you brought us?'

Charles said, 'I've asked for more back files. The old people's home last year, the backpackers the year before, there's three house fires the year before I'm looking at especially one where the husband, wife and four kids were all killed. Security screens on all the windows and doors. Keys melt, but these keys might have been missing, which would be a fit for Zorro. Anyway, I want to find out if any building inspections were carried out on those properties.'

Iris said, 'And the school.'

'I think it's how he gets the precise layout. It's not a firey, Doc, but you were close. He goes in as a fire safety inspector. Goes over where the water outlets are, what alarm systems are used, access points, probably disables some of the smoke detectors. Takes photos, does drawings, notes entrances, checks shift movements. He'd even be able to select the appliance he wants to trick up as the accidental ignition point.'

'Scanlon. Yeah.' Pavlovic spoke into his mobile. 'The building inspection done at the school gym. Yes. Yes, can we get descriptions of the inspector?' He listened, raising his eyebrows to Chuck and Iris. 'Yeah, well back we go. I think the head of the sports department too. If this is our man, he knew when the coach was going on holidays. It might be the only time he doesn't wear a disguise. Oh, and we need to fast-track witness statements in at least two old cases Charles Koch is working. Can we get clerical help? Yes. Yes.'

Iris said, 'Charles, can you thumbnail the earlier cases? Chronologically.'

'I'm still getting more stuff in from police files, I reckon the deros were probably over a few years, not just December. Pretty sketchy reports, it's enough to look like a spree. Most of them were sleeping or passed out. Accelerant was poured over them and set alight. They wake up screaming, on fire and mostly they put it out. No one died. The ones in hospital were interviewed, not very thoroughly.' He shot a glance to Pavlovic.

Pavlovic nodded. 'Deros.' It was not an endorsement. Simply an acknowledgment of past priorities. Possibly present ones too.

'I've also got a teenage kid seen leaving one by a couple who came to the old man's rescue. I've got reports of two soft-drink cans. One's identified as Fanta, the other isn't identified. Smelled of petrol.'

Pavlovic, 'Retest for prints?'

'Weren't kept. Minor assaults. The following year Springsteen starts and no more deros are lit up.'

Iris asked, 'Were they in parks, like the vagrants?'

'Yes. Lover's Lane–type places. Where you'd park your car, deserted, private.'

'Any on the coast?' asked Pavlovic.

'No. I'll check again, mostly the hills.'

Iris said, 'He's still a teenager. He can't drive. It's close to where he lives.'

Pavlovic made a note.

'So, first these two are on a blanket near a creek, maybe under another blanket because the reports suggests in flagrante delicious-io. First thing they know their blanket is on fire. Petrol. No can found. Most might not be reported, of course.'

'Why?' asked Iris.

'Some lovers shouldn't be loving, either full stop or with whomever they're loving with,' replied Pavlovic.

Charles smirked then said, 'I'm going to have to go get my notes if you want more detail, Doc. I think the next one was in a car. Door suddenly open, petrol tossed in. Doesn't light. The lover chases the kid. Thinks he's young although it's a gravel parking bay overlooking the city so it's dark, surrounded by bush.' Chuck took more time to think things through.

Pavlovic took more notes.

Chuck said, 'I think young Zorro leaves cars alone for a while. Picnic blankets, couples sitting on benches. Always dark.'

Iris said, 'Are they always lovers?'

'Yep. Distracted when he sneaks up. He changes to lighter fluid halfway through the spree. Lights faster, I guess. Sprayed from the lighter can. Burns aren't as deep, mind you.'

Iris. 'Does he spray both or only one of the couple?'

Charles thought for a while. 'I'd have to check, but I think both are burned. Most of the times. I'll check it. By this time the police had stepped up their patrols, were taking the names of teenagers they found out and about. Sniffing them for petrol fumes.'

'You've got the names?'

'Should have in about ...' he indicated his watch theatrically, 'in about eight or nine hours.' Charles's legs were stretched out in front of him like he was on a lounge talking about the football scores.

Pavlovic said, 'The funeral is tomorrow, so I might have to chase them up.' He made another note.

They went quiet as they contemplated the funeral.

Finally Pavlovic said, 'So, the Lover's Lane Pyro?'

'Is now in the newspapers and the police are stepping up. They nab a couple of burglars and a firebug. He goes back to cars using lighter fluid. He burns two more couples. He waits until they're ... more than petting. They're getting right into it. Some very bad burns. Then the big one. You probably remember.'

Pavlovic nodded.

Iris said, 'Remind me.'

'She's a hairdresser who still lives at home. Very pretty. Twenty-two. He's an apprentice carpenter and a promising footy player of the same age. They've been going out since year eleven. They're engaged, I think. It's a Subaru station wagon. They're in the back. He pours petrol all over the back and over the top and lights it. They're trapped inside. The fire is fast. Big. It attracts a police car. They both die screaming, according to the cops who can't get close. The car exploded. Fuel tank. Sounds familiar when I put it like that.'

'It stopped,' said Pavlovic. 'I remember. Springsteen stopped after them.'

'I pick up his trail later.' Charles glanced at Iris, added, 'interestingly in the hills again.'

Pavlovic leaned forward. 'Have you mapped these?'

'Give me a fuckin break. The Doc and I only started on this line a couple of days ago. And I was on a bloody suspension.'

'I'm not dissing you, Chuck. This is brilliant. It's a question.'

'You blokes are the ones dragging your bloody heels. Give me the fuckin files.' Chuck glared.

Pavlovic shuffled some papers on his desk. 'Do you mind if I put these things on a map?'

'I can't stop you.'

'No you can't. Why would you want to? We're both trying to catch this bastard.'

Iris interjected, 'It's the summer he changed. For some reason. He matured. Possibly in age too. He started planning more. I think he liked the trapping.'

They both stared at her. They didn't follow.

'Lots of firelighters like watching fire. Most are kids, don't forget. They love to see a building kindle then glow as the fire slowly takes hold, before eating everything. Compulsive, recidivist firelighters – the firebugs love to see it take off in the bush, from this tiny flame they lit to tear away as a wall of flame suddenly beyond anyone's control. Immense and powerful. See the people flee, watch the firefighters run around like ants trying stop the thing they've unleashed. Most of them aren't seeking to cause death. Certainly not in any direct way. It's been called a coward's crime because even those killers who use fire as a weapon, light it and walk away and don't see the consequences. Fire is not face-to-face. It's impersonal.'

'You like fire, don't you?' said Pavlovic darkly.

'Which is beside the point. It is elemental. Like lightning striking near you. Like trying to stand against waves at the beach. It is how others see it which is important, Detective. What I'm getting to is Zorro uses it, as Chuck once said, to hurt and kill. Sure he likes fire, he particularly wants to trap. He wants to control the fire so it hurts and kills at a pace and order he imagines. This is now, now he's the adult butterfly.

'When he was a caterpillar, I think he went looking for the homeless because they were easy and burnt them for a thrill. I suspect he'd burnt animals before. He stepped up, like his pupa stage. His Lover's Lane summer was about his sexuality, his urges or his confusions. It might have been adolescent, I suspect, something larger is being worked out. I know a lot about Zorro doesn't fit the profile but I'd bet he comes from a broken or dysfunctional home. He has sexual issues. I'd be surprised if he wasn't known to the police or child protection during this time.'

'Why'd he stop?' Chuck asked.

'I don't know. Something happened or maybe was resolved. Maybe he was sent to prison. Juvenile detention is worth checking against the other names. Maybe he moved away and never did stop.'

'Like Malaysia,' said Pavlovic.

They both gaped at him.

'We think we've got a solid lead in Malaysia by the way.'

Iris said, 'Are we all sharing, Detective, or is this still one-way?'

'Yeah, you're not passing the ball much,' added Chuck.

Pavlovic stood, really cranky for the first time, 'People! Do you have any idea how big this is? How many departments are involved? Massive amounts of information are being sifted, interviews run down, old stuff like we're getting for you, Chuck? There are chains of command where I live. Then the fucking Martian escapes. Now the zoo! It's getting pretty reactive all around. As essential as I think your line of investigation is, every time I'm here or with you Iris, I'm not in about five other rooms all moving ahead as fast on as many other lines of inquiry.'

Iris said, 'Yeah, Iris, stop being so selfish.'

He stood glaring at her.

Iris said, 'Point taken. I'm sorry. We're tired. We're stressed. I'm hungry.'

He sat again. 'They don't usually share fingerprints, so we finally nudged the Foreign Minister in on the negotiating. We have a house fire, children killed. James Jules, an Australian citizen who married an Indian Malaysian. By accounts he's Anglo–West Indian, which all fits.'

Charles said, 'Time frame?'

'Five or six years ago. Definitive paperwork is winding through channels.'

'December?'

'Don't know yet.'

Charles pointed to Pavlovic's notepad. 'So the first question to the school people is, "Was the fire safety inspector a bit Indian looking?"'

Iris said, 'So jail in Malaysia?'

'I don't know yet. If it is the same man, we have to assume he wasn't jailed. He came home, started again. He is very good at getting out of locked places.'

Iris checked to see if he was having a dig at her, but Pavlovic was busy thinking.

Chuck too seemed to be running time lines.

Pavlovic asked, 'Anything else he told you in the interviews we can use? I am assuming his escape and the targeting of you is related.'

Iris said, 'He is in pain. He has suffered trauma. He killed his wife and children, which accounts for his retreat into the Martian delusion. A dissociative identity disorder. I believe he has been reworking this trauma in the construction of his spaceship crash – he wants to go back to save his family from the fire. Which is in my report.' Iris still struggled to see James as Zorro, but went with the hypothesis. 'It was a different breakdown which caused him to light the fire and attempt suicide in his house in Malaysia. I would have liked to have worked with him further.'

Charles said, 'Yeah. I'd like to work with him. With a pair of plyers and an oxyacetylene kit.'

Pavlovic nodded.

Iris said, 'You should talk to Silverberg about his conclusions.'

'Yes,' said Pavlovic, closed once more. His telephone beeped, he glanced at the screen. 'Good. We've got your clothes for you, Mrs Foster, and some of your toiletries. There's a shower and a cot adjoining the commissioner's office which you can use tonight.'

'Can I have my phone back?'

'We haven't exactly told anyone where you are. In spite of Chuck's mates filling him in. We have also not released the names of those in the butterfly enclosure or if anyone was injured. They were running with a gas cylinder malfunction, but the cover story fizzled when the zoo started evacuating the animals.'

'So I can't have my phone?'

'Who do you want to call?'

'My husband. I think he can be trusted.'

Pavlovic pointed to the phone on the desk where he was sitting. 'Dial nine to get an outside line. I'll get a constable to show you up to the top floor. Chuck, how about we find a map to pin these crimes up. Mrs Foster, Iris, thanks for your help.' Pavlovic had his hand out.

Iris shook it.

'On ya, Doc,' said Charles with a big wink. 'With a bit of luck we'll have him locked up by the time you get up in the morning.'

'Don't take any of their shit, Charles.'

He laughed as he followed Pavlovic out.

Iris went to the desk, lifted the phone. She supposed the line was being monitored. She supposed Pavlovic still didn't quite trust her. Iris cleared her mind so she could remember Mathew's mobile number without the aid of her mobile telephone's memory.

It rang for some time. When Mathew finally answered, his voice sounded groggy. 'Mathew Foster.'

'It's me.'

'Good god, Iris. I've been sick with worry.'

'I'm fine. A piece of metal caught my shoulder.'

'I saw the news coverage. It must have just been after you called me.'

'Yes.' Iris couldn't hear breathing in the background. 'I can't say a lot because they're holding me for my own protection.'

'It wasn't an accident?'

'It might even be the mad school bomber.'

Silence, as he processed the enormity, thought through the implications.

Iris said, 'I wanted to warn you.'

'Me?'

Ha. I want to warn you about June. She's a bit flighty and she's starting to really stack it onto her hips. I thought you liked skinny things. 'As part of the investigation they are looking at possible terrorism.'

'Yes.'

'Some army intelligence officers felt I wasn't cooperating so they tried to threaten me by threatening you. They made half-hearted threats regarding your seeking the bench.'

'In what way? I can't see any ...' He went silent again.

'They were trying to see if I was implicated and sought pressure points.'

'That's ridiculous.' He sounded certain, which made Iris's heart jerk.

'I think we've all moved on now.'

'Do you need a lawyer?'

'No. I'm working with them. And sorry, it's all happening very quickly and now I'm consulting on this because it's all blowing up around me. Ha. I know I promised I wouldn't but ...'

'Yes.'

'I hope you'll forgive me.'

The barest pause. Nearly not one. 'Of course.'

'I wanted to let you know I'm all right.'

'Thank god, darling.'

'And to let you know about the army people.'

'Can't hurt me.'

'I love you. I wish you were here with me.'

'I'll be back tomorrow. I'll get the first flight I can.'

Say you love me. Say you love me, even if you don't mean it.

'I love you, darling,' he said. 'See you soon.'

'Bye.'

Iris felt teary. She saw an older policewoman hovering in the doorway. The policewoman gave a sympathetic grimace. She followed the policewoman, wondering idly how they could misconstrue her conversation with Mathew, looking for terrorist codes in the marital ones.

In the lift the policewoman said, 'You're having a big week.'

'Tell me about it.'

They went up, Iris feeling her tiredness grow incrementally with the passing floors, like extra gravity.

'You probably don't remember me. I did court duty when you testified on the warehouse arsonists. On the heritage warehouses.'

'Oh, hi,' said Iris. She didn't recognise her. It had been years ago.

The doors opened to quieter hallways. Offices were closed, frosted-glass doors unlit from behind.

The policewoman led her past the dark-wooded door belonging to the commissioner's suite to a smaller grey door beyond. Inside Iris found an ensuite, a small single bed with neat piles of Iris's clothes on top.

'Thank you,' said Iris.

'Hope you get this creep.'

'Me too. Thanks.' Iris gave her a warm smile.

She latched the door, explored the toilet bag they'd brought from her house. She supposed they'd conducted a search at the same time. Iris wondered about her laptop and whether it was with any of the investigative streams. She suddenly remembered thinking someone was in the house late on Saturday.

The shower was not very hot. Iris supposed the heating system must be a distance away. She washed the grit and the hospital smells. Her shoulder didn't really hurt much. She supposed a clean cut, neat stitches. A small interesting scar.

She remembered the feel of James's back, a flash of memory, followed by a hot flush of shame. Iris washed her face. If James was Zorro, he had completely taken her in. He might have been playing her from the beginning, even following Iris before the school. He must have, to know about the butterflies. He had tricked her, then was about to have intercourse with her. It would have been a multiple victory, using the Fire Lady sexually then to engineer his escape. He had attempted to dispose of her when he'd finished with her. Humiliate your enemies before killing them. Iris scrubbed herself roughly. She worked her hair, scratched at her scalp. Iris was not so clever. A puny, wrinkled old fool.

'Well, fuck him,' she said into the tepid water.

Iris rinsed off the soap, turned off the shower only to realise there were no towels. It made her laugh. It pleased her how the world could still be normal, the tiny things slipping through. She dried herself using the tracksuit pants and smock she'd been dressed in for most of the day. She could feel a cool slick of water still on her skin.

Zorro was overreaching, jumping things up exponentially with the school. He'd used a chemical that was beyond his control. Was he angry with her? Is that why he'd tried to kill her at the zoo? Was the triumph of making a fool of her so short-lived? Or had revealing his real identity through naming his children been another mistake, another piece of overconfidence, to be corrected? He'd failed at his target with the school. The firefighters would not have been enough. He'd failed at the zoo. Would his ego implode?

No. He had ether left. He'd do ... the church. He'd rework his plan so the failure at the school became a feint that lured even more to the funeral. All those firefighters. Televised. How could an angry Zorro live up to his own image of himself, without trying for the church? As if he had planned the trap all along. As if destiny delivered the best option to him.

Chapter twenty

Iris poked her head out the door. The policewoman sat in a chair in the corridor, still guarding perhaps.

Iris said, 'Can you contact Detective Stuart Pavlovic? Or Scanlon or Richards?'

'What's wrong?'

'I think he's going to try for the church.'

The policewoman opened an office, turning on the light. It could have been an office in any government department. It was not policey at all. She dialled on the landline. 'Detective Pavlovic. Senior Constable Fergerson. It's ... um the Fire Lady. She thinks it's the church.' She handed the phone to Iris.

'The church has been swept,' said Pavlovic.

'Lately?'

'We have thought of this. Uniforms have been posted to watch the place. And Parliament, the zoo, every school in the state by the way.'

'I think it's the church service. I think he'll make a try for it.'

'We'll check it out again.'

Iris turned to see Senior Constable Ferguson holding out the damp green smock towards her. Iris realised she was standing in nothing but her bra and panties. 'Oh, I haven't dressed yet.'

Iris returned to the anteroom, dressing for work not sleep. They'd brought her a dark skirt, a sombre blouse. She did her face quickly.

She walked past the policewoman who was back in her seat.

'You're not supposed to leave.'

'Are you kidding? I want to see what they find.'

'I haven't any instructions.'

Iris stepped into the lift. She said, 'Well, come on. Let's get some. Where's Pavlovic?'

The policewoman stepped in. She said, 'He was in the taskforce office when I got him.' She pressed the lift button, they descended. She said, 'You will get me into trouble.'

'The only place to be, Senior Constable. I don't suppose there are any food dispensers on any of these floors?'

They found them in the room of detectives desks where Pavlovic had brought Iris earlier. Pavlovic and Charles were leaning towards a police radio scanner. Detective Scanlon and Minchin listened in at nearby desks.

Iris ate a muesli bar.

'Can't raise him. You?'

Another voice came through. 'Constable Ryan, report your position please. Ryan.'

There was no response.

'Who is Ryan?' asked Iris.

Charles said, 'Guard duty at the church.'

Pavlovic scowled his displeasure at Senior Constable Ferguson for bringing Iris but refocused on the radio.

'We can't get the lights.'

'Clarify can't get lights, Officer,' said a voice of authority from on the radio line. It sounded like Superintendent Richards.

'GC220, reporting. We're in the front door of the church. We're flicking the light switches. Nothing. Can't see anyone.'

'All right. Back out and return to your car, Constable.'

'Ah, I can partly comply, sir. But, um, Dave, Constable Bradley has gone round the back.'

'Get him out. Withdraw now. Both of you out and back, GC220. Wait for backup, do you understand?'

'Sir.' The officer must have kept his finger on his intercom because they could hear him yelling, 'Dave, we have to get out of here. Dave!' They heard an indistinct reply. The responding officer said, 'Constable Duncan, report of an electrical van round the back sir. Are they fixing the power?'

Charles bawled at the scanner, 'Do not touch the van. Do not touch the van.'

Scanlon pushed past them at a run.

Richards was already on it. He said, 'Son, withdraw. The van could be booby trapped. Back out now.'

'Withdrawing sir.'

Charles said, 'See you at the church,' as he pushed past Iris.

'I don't think that's a good idea, Chuck,' said Pavlovic.

'I don't work for you, Stewie. I work for Fire and Emergency and the police Arson Squad. I'm not going to spectate this.'

Iris said, 'Let's go. It's five minutes from here.'

'You stay here,' ordered Pavlovic. He said to Minchin, 'Chuck is right. We are better near the scene in case we have pertinent ...'

'No one is more pertinent than me. I gave you the church.'

'Anybody could have done that. This could be a power failure, a cop helping to fix it.'

'I can help. I know this man.'

'Which still bothers me.' He said to Ferguson. 'Keep her here. If she tries anything, shoot her.'

'I'm not armed.'

'Use your initiative.'

He strode off with Minchin in tow.

Bradley had returned on the scanner. 'Sir, we can hear sirens. Police and fire engines I think.'

'All good son. Are your blues flashing on top?'

'Roger sir.'

'Good. Now the bomb squad are scrambling. Do you understand? No one is to enter the building before them. Do you understand? No matter how far they outrank you.'

Iris said, 'I need to speak to Superintendent Richards.'

'He's a bit busy.'

'Senior Constable, you don't want to be the person who Superintendent Richards discovers prevented me from attending the scene. Let me see, whose orders were you following? Oh, a detective's. If Superintendent Richards orders I stay, I'll sit next to the radio ... and knit.'

Iris picked up a phone from the desk, held it towards her. 'Call Superintendent Richards' assistant's assistant. Tell him I need to go to the scene.'

Still she paused. She was good at following orders. She was

not a sergeant so she might be content to follow everyone's. She would not like to get into trouble.

Iris added, 'You said you saw me in court. You know I'm one of the good guys.'

*

Ferguson drove her to the scene. Iris had argued with Richards too. Her only card was the potential negotiation with James, should it be him, should he be captured at the scene. Otherwise she would have to stand back as an observer, behind the perimeter. She'd still be listening on a radio, but one a lot closer to the potential bomb.

She said, 'We girls should form our own squad. Like TRG, only for fires.'

'I'm not stupid, Mrs Foster.'

'What? What?'

'Detective Pavlovic wanted you watched. Superintendent Richards said the same thing. I have booked out a firearm. Please don't think I'm stupid.'

'No. Nor friendly. Got it.'

Ferguson drove in silence through the city streets that rippled with a variety of police, fire and ambulance vehicles. Iris had to admit she probably could contribute little. She wanted to be there. She wanted to see if he'd really target the church. If she had that right, then she was starting to know Zorro.

The church stood at the top of the hill. When it had been built two hundred years before, it would have been the highest building in the fledgling colony. The city had encroached and by-passed if not quite overwhelmed. City towers jutted the skyline. The major hospital of the city loomed adjacent, taller. A Catholic girls school spread into once church-owned land. Yet it kept its majesty and grace. Roses and bench seats dotted the ample grass grounds behind the wrought-iron fence. Which was where the perimeter had been set, where police, fire, rescue, assorted squads were gathered like a besieging army.

They parked a couple of blocks back where a cordon of street closure bollards and temporary fencing was erected. The media vans were coming in but only one crew had set up. 'Iris, Iris, is it the school bomber?' Iris kept walking. Her chaperone tried to shield her from the approaching camera on the shoulder of a t-shirted part-timer. Even the usually immaculate journalist looked dishevelled. Iris thought it might be around two am on a Sunday night. 'Is it true you were at the zoo?' Iris kept walking. 'Is this a serial bomber? Is the city under attack?'

Yes, thought Iris, heading up towards the packed cluster of vehicles winking blues, reds and orange lights up against the church walls. They found their way to the command post set up near the black van that usually ferried the bomb robot.

'Hey Doc.'

Iris turned to see a firefighter waving. He was in full kit so she couldn't see his face. She stopped, peered at his name tag. 'McDonald. Is that you, Jock, you old bastard?'

'Can't complain.'

'Bullshit, you're a great complainer.'

'Only to effect the change, Doc.'

It was an old joke from years before. Another firey came up behind Jock, pointed at her.

Iris waved.

'Let's get this thing, hey?' Jock said.

'Pants on fire,' said Iris. Another old joke. It had been uncool to say be safe.

Iris spun away, getting the flash of the station officer who'd died at the school. Only now he had a face, the face she'd seen in the newspaper, on the television. Now she knew he'd come from another city looking for the better family life for which the city had once been famous.

Two paramedics carried a stretcher from the church. Iris supposed it was the missing officer who'd been guarding the church. The paramedics trotted, a policeman in helmet and bulletproof vest running backwards behind them, covering their retreat with a rifle aimed everywhere at nothing. Arc lights were set around the perimeter giving the grass the glow of a sports ground. Long shadows made crazy shapes as the paramedics neared an ambulance at the gates. A uniform tried to clear rescue vehicles and police cars to give it a path out. The fire services would not have allowed such a logjam on the fire-ground.

Iris heard someone reporting to Scanlon who stood in a

cluster of police. 'He's in a bad way. Head wound. Blunt trauma.' Pavlovic turned, almost a silhouette against the arc lights.

Iris veered towards the bomb-squad cluster of men, where she noticed Charles Koch. A hand grabbed Iris, making her gasp at the sudden sharp pain in her shoulderblade.

Pavlovic.

'Ow. My stitches.'

'What are you doing here?'

'Superintendent Richards countermanded your order.' Iris couldn't suppress her little triumph.

He glared at Ferguson, who confirmed the overrule.

When Iris started again towards Charles, Pavlovic pulled her back.

'What is it with you?'

'Search her,' he said to the policewoman.

Some nearby officers glanced at them but most found more of interest elsewhere. The stretcher was loaded in the ambulance. A marked police car backed out of the way. Up at the church a bomb disposal officer in full protective suit came down the steps. He gave a thumbs down. Iris watched him standing alone on the church steps, clearly listening to instructions on his radio. Two of his colleagues had died a week earlier in similar circumstances.

Iris was patted down. She'd left her handbag back at police headquarters. Iris said, 'What is she looking for?'

'Mobile phone. Television remote. Garage door opener. Any electronic device at all. A tiny torch. A battery. Anything electrical. Anything at all really. Chewing gum packet. Silver paper. A hair pin.'

It made sense. If Iris was working covertly with James she could conceivably be the trigger who chose the right time. She might have done it at the school, the truck another feint.

Senior Constable Ferguson found nothing. She didn't even have jewellery.

'Her shoes too.'

Iris clutched Pavlovic by the shoulder, lifted her foot to take the shoe off and present it to the policewoman. Pavlovic remained steady if not entirely happy to be used by Iris as her support while Ferguson checked the shoe. Iris took it back, put it on and repeated the procedure, still holding the detective's shoulder. Iris said, 'Stuart Pavlovic, I think you have trust issues.'

Pavlovic said, 'I always have an open mind, Mrs Foster. Your voice is higher. Your face is slightly flushed. Your pupils quite dilated. You're excited.'

Iris put her other shoe on, let go of Pavlovic's shoulder. 'Always glad to see you, Stuart.'

He glared.

'Yes I am. Always have been ... at the scene.' Shoes on, Iris continued on towards the bomb team.

She heard Pavlovic order, 'Watch her.'

Iris squeezed up at the back of the group controlling the robotic and human search. There were four monitors. A small camera was fixed to each man's helmet. The third monitor belonged to the robot.

One camera showed the crowd outside the main gates and the city behind. It was the man on the steps. He swivelled and re-entered the main doors of the church. Another screen showed a search inside the confessional. It was a big, mostly stone church with ornate wood panelling. Occasionally a lead-lined glass panel twinkled or shone.

'Don't lift anything. Don't move anything. Not even curtains.' Their team leader talked into a microphone. 'Watch for trip-wires.' A name written on masking tape had been stuck to the front of each monitor. 'Stevo, don't touch the van.'

'Not touching.'

Stevo's camera showed a white van around the back of the church. The ladder and a conduit cylinder on top gave it the appearance of a contractor's van in spite of a lack of signage. Stevo panned to the church, to an open doorway down worn, stone steps. Stevo moved towards it. The door was green. The robot, running on its mini tank tracks, went through the door, its affixed light flaring. Stevo scanned back to the van. Iris caught sight of a fire crew standing ten metres from the van, their hoses ready. They would have been praying if they believed, standing so far inside the blast zone.

Whoever controlled the robot must have been in their own van parked amongst the others, with their own monitor no doubt. The robot stopped at the top of more stone stairs. Iris watched the robot camera monitor intently.

'Sweep for a view,' said the team leader.

The robot swung slowly, pivoting, Iris guessed, on its tracks. A storeroom. It appeared neglected. Dust drifted in the robot's torch beam. There were stacks of chairs, old wooden ones, like you'd see on ships. A shelf held dirty glass canisters.

'Hold,' said the leader. 'Zoom.'

The camera zoomed in to a roll of black pipe. It stood upright, like a hoop, leaning against broken wooden panels, the kind used to announce hymn numbers and readings.

'Chuck?'

'It looks like the same piping used at the school.'

'Everybody slow down. We have possible contact. Stevo, hold there!'

Stevo had moved to the back of the van. The windows were covered in cardboard. He was trying to peer through a gap between the cardboard and the window frame.

'Tweak your light.'

Stevo focused his helmet light to reveal one large silver forty-four gallon drum with a red sticker on it and smaller silver and orange tins beyond.

'Chuck, talk to me.'

'It looks bad. It could be the diethyl.'

The bomb disposal team leader made a decision. 'Withdraw. All men, withdraw. Stevo, come back in. Mark. Percy, out of the church. We have contact. Withdraw.' Then he called, 'Have I got a chemist here yet?'

'Travelling,' yelled someone.

A commander peeled away from the group around the monitors, started giving orders. 'Get those fireys out of there. It could be hot. Tell the hospital to go to code orange. That's code orange. Everybody out. Have we got snipers in those buildings?' A ripple of murmuring was his only reply. 'Talk to me, people. Is TRG here yet?'

'Travelling, sir.'

The robot camera continued to pan around the basement. It found a wheelchair, then an electric cord plugged into an ancient power socket. The robot camera zoomed into scorch marks on the wall above the socket. It tilted down to an electric jug, also scorched. The robot moved forward on the landing, elevated, panned over to a face. The camera zoomed out. It was James. He was lying on the basement floor, dressed in the loose blue pants and windcheater top of a psychiatric nurse.

'We have someone down,' the team leader noted.

Iris lifted her eyes from the monitors to watch the three fully kitted bomb disposal men walking back towards them. They walked slowly. They could only walk slowly in all the protective gear, as if they were walking on a planet with heavy gravity.

The team leader called, 'Commander, we have a man down in the church cellar.'

'Commander Davies. They want you at the monitor,' someone repeated.

Iris stared at the monitor. James appeared dead.

Chuck said, 'It looks like he's electrocuted himself halfway through setting up the bomb.' He glanced to see who was listening, caught sight of Iris. He winked with a grin.

Davies came back, Pavlovic with him. Pavlovic said, 'Can you zoom in to his face?'

Davies yelled, 'Where the fuck is my goddamn TRG crew?'

'It's James,' said Iris. 'It is the man we were interviewing at Fieldhaven in connection with the gymnasium bombing.'

The commander noted Iris for the first time.

Pavlovic ignored her, studied the screen. 'It's James the Martian. Possibly James Jules. Fingerprints coming.'

'He's alive,' said the bomb disposal team leader.

Iris stepped forward. Everyone leaned towards the monitor. Iris couldn't see. The leader said, 'See the dust on the floor. He's breathing.'

'Shit,' said Davies.

'Pan left. I'm looking for a remote control devices on the ground or wires on his person.'

'Would he commit suicide?' Commander Davies was asking Iris.

She said, 'Yes. Zorro would. So would James.'

'What?'

'Yes. He could be under a delusion he's going to launch himself back to Mars.'

'He probably will with all that diethyl ether.' Chuck.

Davies said, 'Can you get your robot down the stairs?'

'Easily.'

'I want to turn him over.'

'We can do that. Take Fred down the steps.' Apparently the robot had a name.

'How long until the hospital is evacuated?'

A uniformed sergeant got onto a handheld, listened.

'Look for trip-wires too,' said Pavlovic.

The officer on the handheld called back, 'Another half-hour. They calculate one more load of patients.'

Iris peered past the police and rescue vehicles to the hospital building no more than three hundred metres from the church. They would have started their evacuation protocols as soon as the police discovered the church was unguarded.

'Okay, we wait. Hold your robot for the minute. Maybe in half an hour my fucking TRG team will have finished their muffins and be able to join us.'

'They were rostered on tomorrow, sir,' said a functionary voice in the crowd. 'They were told to get sleep.'

'Okay, let's double-check all these buildings around here. Let's clear out these non-essential personnel, can we? Let's do another sweep of the surrounding laneways and streets for secondaries.' He swung back to Iris. 'If he's awake, do you think a negotiator could talk him out?'

Iris considered. James could be talked down. Zorro, she wasn't so sure about. He'd want to go out big rather than with a whimper. His ego couldn't stand to lose. On the other hand, if James was in charming James mode or in Martian mode they might be able to talk him down.

'You don't know,' said Davies.

'Not with sufficient certainty to be useful, sir.'

'All right. Very good. Useful. Thank you.'

'I'd be willing to try.'

'Of course not. No. No need at all.' He went back to planning how to take James.

Iris had probably signed James's death warrant. If he moved, they'd shoot to kill.

Davies bawled, 'This is not a television set. Can I have some room?'

The cars and the trucks began to move, unclogging from the rear to fall back to safer positions further down the hill. The redeployment took the full half-hour required to finish evacuating the hospital.

Only after everyone had cleared did Fred the robot begin the painstaking, meticulous viewing and lifting of James. They found no remote control. The truck with the remaining diethyl ether had not been hooked up to any detonation device. James was not conscious. Although he'd managed to electrocute himself, he was still alive. If he'd been left much longer, according to doctors, he would not have survived. Iris's alert probably saved his life.

Chapter twenty-one

Iris heard about these things through channels as did the other police, support staff, firefighters and rescue workers two blocks back from the church, and later from Charles, who stayed at the front. It was like being outside a full football ground, only hearing about the close result after the event, not with a bang but an unexpected sigh of relief.

Ironically, the nearest high-security hospital room was across the road from the church. James the Mad Bomber, like other patients, however, was not allowed back in until the church site had been judged secure. The drums of ether were sprayed down with foam then packed into trucks supervised by a fire services chemist before being driven away by the army.

Discussions were held about the funeral. The church had been swept, the missing ether accounted for, the bomber in custody. The funeral went ahead only one hour after the scheduled start with a grim note of victory, a tone of justice. The standing down of the active emergency services and transformation into pomp and respect was a testament to training and organisation but also to its multifunction within society. So said the commissioner speaking at the service.

The city street leading up to the church filled with grateful people, families with awestruck children, police officers in full uniform, fire appliances from the Volunteer Fire Brigades, those men and women in full turnout gear. Each of the armed services was represented. The SAS sent their own honour guard. The precautionary snipers spread through surrounding buildings were not part of the ceremony.

Iris attended with Mathew. She had intended to approach the wives to offer counselling or at least put them in touch with the appropriate PTS procedures, but she lacked the will, also the sense of purpose she'd once felt when trying to set up those things within the fire service twenty years before. As Chuck rightly said, these things were common now, especially for the families of the fallen. After the public church service the wives and children were to be taken up to a firefighters' memorial in the park on the other side of the city for a partners and kids picnic. Firefighters' families only.

Iris and Mathew nodded to people they knew, not stopping to talk. Mathew said little in the service. He had appeared in a dark suit at the end of the aisle and they made way for him. He sat with her during the service, looked compassionate yet restrained. Iris thought he'd make a good judge. Possibly a better judge than a lawyer. He'd developed gravitas. He didn't need to display his intelligence or his energy. It was a given. Mathew took her elbow, steering her out of the church grounds, now verdant in sunshine under clear blue sky. The fire appliances were still parked, the firefighters, volunteers, police, ambos and soldiers milling now in sombre groups of serving men and women. Mathew manoeuvred Iris to a laneway and an illegally parked BMW.

'Benjamin's. I came straight from the office. I need to sign a few things, if that's all right?'

Iris shrugged a yes, suddenly feeling exhausted. She checked her face in the mirror on the back of the sun visor. She'd borrowed extra make-up from Senior Constable Ferguson, friends again after the capture of James the Mad Bomber.

Mathew drove down the laneway and out into the busy city street beyond.

'I think they did a good job, for the ceremony, don't you?'

'Yes. It was good. It was ... fitting and ...' She struggled for adequate words.

'Not too much pomp, a lot of respect ... and sadness.'

'When a fireman dies, it's never a shock or even a surprise, even though it's not common. It's always a possibility. But this, this wasn't them doing their job. It was murder. Evil.'

Mathew pulled into the driveway of Lee Steere, Court, Lefroy, Shenton & Foster, Partners at Law, called variously 'the practice' or 'chambers' or 'the office' by Mathew. It was not particularly far from the church. The security grill started winding up.

Mathew said, 'Will you come up?'

'I'll stay down here.'

'We'll be getting a taxi. This is Benjamin's car.'

'Oh, yes, of course.'

'Come up. You haven't been in for some time.'

Iris felt Mathew was putting her through a further ordeal. The promenade to the car. Making her go into his office. She'd like to be in a butterfly house.

'Mathew,' called a very pretty thing at the front desk. 'Oh, Mrs Foster. Hello.'

Iris knew her face but not her name.

Mathew actually took her arm, hooked it in his own, led her through glass doors and down the carpeted corridor past more frosted-glass walls. People looked up. Diligent young men and women in power suits hunkered over files.

'Mrs Foster, hello,' said someone.

'Iris,' said Benjamin.

They paused.

'Thank you for the car, Ben.'

'It was a loan. I hope I haven't given it away,' he said with a grin. He was a senior partner, thin with killer eyes. He shaved his head to hide his baldness, which made him look like Vladimir Putin.

Mathew handed him his keys.

Iris smiled.

'Awful business. We saw parts of it.' He pointed to a large television set in his outer office, now switched off.

Mathew said, 'I'm going to sign those special conditions then take the rest of the day, mate.'

It sounded odd hearing Mathew say the word 'mate'.

They were confronted by Roland Hyland. He stood solicitous outside another office. He was a pear of a man who made his suit look like a bag full of yogurt. He was June's husband.

'Iris, how are you? Terrible events.'

Personal or public, Iris wondered. 'Terrible, Roland.' They called him Roly. Sometimes Landland. Iris did not say, so, Roly, how was your wife's weekend? This would be the time. Is this why Mathew was parading her? Testing? Besting?

Roland squeezed her shoulder as they passed, making Iris wince.

Mathew's office lay behind an outer chamber with green leather couches, a personal secretary's desk. An enormous piece of Aboriginal artwork hung above the couches.

'This is new,' said Iris.

'Yes, we're doing a thing with the university. Rotating some of their bequests.' He led her into his inner sanctum where they discovered Reggie laying out piles of paper.

The back wall was covered in law books. The large window showed a glimpse of river between two larger buildings.

'Just these last ones, Mathew.' Reggie wore a dark suit. He had been Mathew's secretary for fifteen years. 'Mrs Foster!' he said loudly, like the host at a party. He stepped forward, his hand extended.

'Reg,' she said. You look good.'

'I'm riding, like the boss.'

Mathew would take him to the bench if he could wangle it.

'The kids?' Iris couldn't remember their names although they'd attended christenings.

'Marvellous. And Rosemarie is doing well at university, I hear.'

'You probably hear more than I do.'

Reggie looked alarmed, as though he'd put his foot in it.

'She makes us so proud,' Iris added, to defuse.

Mathew said, 'These are going into Ben and Liz.'

Reggie rustled papers.

Iris noted Mathew's luggage in a corner, the barest hint of red dust along the edges. She retreated to the outer office to look at the artwork again. Dots and circles. Tracks leading to special places. This is how it had often been explained but of course they were considerably more, the red and white and shades of brown. They were a map yes, and also an imprint, the land imagined from above and within.

Of course, it was no coincidence Mathew hung art from the

Nullabin region at the time he was negotiating. Would he be accused of bias, or of hypocrisy?

Iris wanted to call Frank. She wanted to find out about James, the things she'd missed.

'Amazing, isn't it.' Mathew had joined her. 'I could get lost in it. Lost up north contemplating the horizon.' He called, 'Can you send the luggage home at about five-ish, Reggie?' He said to Iris, 'Let's go to lunch.'

Iris saw Reggie standing in the doorway between the two offices. 'Wonderful to see you, Mrs Foster.'

'You too, Reg.'

He suddenly came forward with his hand out again. When Iris shook it, he said, 'I knew you'd catch him. I knew you'd get the school bomber.'

'Reg has always had a crush on you,' said Mathew as they went down in the lift.

'The Fire Lady makes the streets safe once again,' said Iris flatly.

'Yes,' said Mathew, even more flatly.

They caught a taxi to Beaumont's.

'Beaumont's!' Iris said.

'Yes, I told them they must squeeze us in or I'd never speak to them again.'

'You did not.'

'Practically.'

Iris said, 'Was it hot, up north?'

'Like a whack in the head with a rusty shovel,' he said.

After she stopped smiling, Iris thought to ask, were you cold at night? She didn't. She didn't think she could carry it off without inflection.

There were more respectful greetings at Beaumont's. They were a local crowd who knew of them. They would know about the funeral. They were given a prime table near the window so they could see glimpses of water past the arse ends of the yachts. Most afternoons the ping of rigging proved comforting.

Iris thought she'd like to catch up with Charles, to see what else he'd found under the church. He'd returned to the cellar following the service.

'Would you like the fish, Iris?'

The waiter hovered. Wine was already on the table. A sauvignon blanc. Lots of French spelling for Rosemarie.

'Isn't it funny how the less grape you can taste and the more like icy water it is, the more we love a sauvignon blanc?'

A mildly red-button observation Mathew always refuted. He seemed about to launch into his very detailed breakdown of aroma, dryness and grape age, but changed his mind. He said instead, 'So, the zoo.'

'Yes. They think the man I have been assessing has followed me, possibly from before the school bomb.'

'The school?'

'Ah, yes. I was at the school when the gymnasium blew up.'

'Oh.'

Iris saw that Mathew must have heard this piece of news somewhere in his travels. 'It didn't seem the time to bring it up.' Iris watched him waiting for her. She couldn't read him this afternoon. 'He escaped from Fieldhaven, from the secure mental facility there. Tried to burn me and a lot of innocent bystanders in the butterfly enclosure. He was going to blow up the church probably during this morning's ceremony.'

'Seems barely credible in our small town.'

'He overreached.'

'But are you okay?'

'A characteristic of the denizens of our fair city, overreaching.'

'Are you okay?'

'I've got a cut on my shoulder, well more on the shoulder-blade. Stitches.' Iris smiled as she said it. Realised she was proud of a real physical wound. 'Be a bigger scar than the one on your knee.'

Mathew said, 'I get worried when you joke.'

Iris said, 'I get worried when you don't talk to me.'

He flinched. He admired his wine glass, did not lift it. Was this a public place? Here and at his office? Was he keeping her in public places so she wouldn't make a scene? So he could tell her something important, final. I've met someone else. He didn't say that. He said, 'Remember when we used to play poker?'

'Yes. No one would play with me.'

'You learned their secrets.'

'I learned their "tells".'

'They got all funny about it, started getting self-conscious about other things they might reveal.'

'It was only about their cards. And if they were timid or rash – I could only work it out if we played for a while.'

'Shame. I liked the poker games.'

'I liked the tennis. They fancied their chances with me as your partner in doubles.'

'Underestimated your speed at the net. The killer flea.'

Iris wondered where this was leading. Entirely too much nostalgia, past tense. She hoped there wasn't going to be a confession. She didn't need it, she decided. She could push the hypothetical event of June aside and if she could put it aside for long enough it would simply cease to have been. She decided she didn't want the mess, or the risk of wounds that might never heal. James never had been, but might have, and June had passed, it seemed; our tax returns have been completed, our books balanced.

Mathew said, 'I think the judiciary is one of the most important things one can do for society.'

One? He'd been talking.

Mathew must have seen her face, caught himself. He could see into her mind, she could never see into his. Maybe she should tell him this.

'I have many years of work left in me. I have the energy. The will. And I think I can make a real difference to society, Iris. Not merely make money, make a difference. It sounds like a cliché, I know.'

'It doesn't. Mathew, I believe you'd make a great judge.'

'Yes.'

Iris leaned forward, her chin in her hand.

'Are you with me or against me?' asked Mathew.

'Me? I'm with you.' Was this what he wanted? Or was she making it more difficult for him? She said, 'Would you like me to leave the Park Centre? Be more available for functions? Cook more, be more ...' Iris couldn't think of other domestic or wifely chores to add to her bag of offerings.

Mathew searched her face and Iris realised what she'd said sounded sarcastic.

'I think the Park Centre practice has left me anyway. I would like to put more into your push for judge.'

'No,' he said, and Iris's heart sank. 'No, I think you should work. You should do what you do. Anyway, it's hardly going to change my career, not really. You catch the buggers, you don't light the fires. So, I realise I have been selfish and insecure. I wanted to be Batman, not Robin.'

'Mathew ...'

'No, I'm on a roll here, so overruled. Look, I know I work hard. If I become a judge, I will have to work even harder, at home too. I know I can dazzle and ... well, it's always been a relief to not have to burn quite so bright at home, to be loved by you and Rosemarie and know it's okay. But is it?'

A public display. At the church, the office, here. He was making public his marriage, whether in regret or in dedication or possibly as part of his job application.

Iris said, 'I'm for you.'

Her grilled fish, his crayfish arrived. They discussed Rosemarie and their favourite cities of Europe. His was Barcelona, hers was Venice. They were well-worn topics full of familiarity and rebinding.

*

Two of the butterfly collection frames were askew, otherwise there were few signs of a search at home. Her car sat impeccably pristine in the drive. The assured Mathew took it all in his stride. He was delighted she'd shopped. He noted her pruning in the garden. There was touching, he squeezed her unwounded shoulder, rested his hand on her hip.

They went to bed early. Mathew loved her in her favourite way, sucking her nipples as he used his fingers, devoting himself to her pleasure first. Groggy, she was about to open to him, when she grabbed him by the arm. 'My shoulder,' she said. Getting on top she performed an abandoned dance that increased her own pleasure watching his face until she felt his silent shudders, saw his smile go crooked. Mathew always came in private. Iris knew the words at lunch had not been easy for him. He manipulated words for a living, so distrusted them. She lay on top of him, hugged herself to his still lean body. She felt warm. She smelled his salty sweat, the faintest trace of his cologne. She let her tongue dart to his shoulder to taste him.

*

He woke her in the morning, already dressed in his bicycle gear.

'I have to go to work. You stay asleep.'

'See you tonight,' she said in a little girl voice.

'I'll phone.' He kissed her, left like a smug boyfriend who'd got to sleep over. It pleased her.

Iris recalled a restless night yet couldn't remember what she'd been dreaming.

She showered, dressed slowly. She put The Waifs on the bedroom iPod. She didn't want any news. She took her time doing her face, focusing on the detail and the minute tasks at hand. She chose a silver cable necklace, earrings with tiny opal droplets.

The police still hadn't returned her phone, so she used the downstairs phone to call Frank on his mobile but was diverted to message bank. She called Fieldhaven, who told her Frank was working from home.

Iris called Mary at the practice.

'Hi Mary, it's Iris Foster. Can I have Lisa Fitzmorris's address?'

'Iris! Aren't you still on sick leave?'

'Loose ends, Mary.'

'We saw the news about the bomber.'

'It should be on the files, Mary. The address. Under Rodney Fitzmorris too.'

'I'm nearly there. By the way, a couple of the patients are getting a bit pushy about seeing you.'

'Not yet, Mary. Like you said, sick leave.'

'Did he nearly kill you?'

'He missed.' He got the butterflies.

Mary finally gave her the address. Iris bought a bunch of white chrysanthemums on her way to a treeless suburb with two-storey block houses over triple garages. The grass was green, the driveways wide.

Iris pressed the bell next to the heavy front door.

Lisa opened the door. 'You.'

'Hi, Mrs Fitzmorris. I've come as soon as I could.'

Lisa stood blinking.

'I was sorry to hear about Rodney.'

'Were you?'

'Yes. He was trying.'

'You put him in prison.'

'We ... once the investigation began, you know that.'

'I don't know anything about any of that. I know we went to you for help. I know you put Rod in prison. I know he went to you for help. Now he's dead. I know that.'

'As I say, I wanted to tell you he was trying.'

'I've been reading about this. I know about you people planting fake memories.'

'No.'

'I know you made it up. I saw you put the idea into everyone's mind.'

'Mrs Fitzmorris.'

'Get out.'

'Lisa, do you need to see someone?'

'You must be joking.'

'Is Kimberly seeing anyone?'

'Not a chance.'

'She needs to.'

'Don't you tell me what she needs.'

'She really, really needs to see a counsellor to help her get past this.'

'Past her father's imprisonment and suicide, you mean.'

'Yes!'

'We don't have any rent. We're going to lose the house. You mess people then turn up to mess with us again?'

'I'm not suggesting me. Kimberly does need to be able to talk about this. It is absolutely vital she understands it wasn't her fault.'

'It wasn't. It is yours.' Lisa grabbed the flowers, using them to slap Iris's face.

They stung. Iris stepped back, her eyes smarting.

Lisa sneered. 'Don't think this will change anything. We're suing you.'

'Please, you must make sure Kimberly gets counselling.'

Lisa dropped the tattered flowers to the porch step, slamming the front door.

Iris felt her face, found no blood. She picked up the bouquet, leaving the scatter of white petals where they'd fallen.

*

Iris found a telephone outlet in a large shopping centre where she bought a temporary mobile with its own number, prepaid credit. They were called 'drop phones' by criminals, Iris recalled.

She called Mary again, got Gillian's mobile again. She rang Gillian, discovered she was at the practice. They arranged to meet around the corner amidst the business folk at the edge of the city.

'You are in disguise,' said Gillian as she plonked herself into the seat opposite Iris in the walled garden of the coffee shop.

'Disguise?'

'Out of your red leotard and flaming cape.'

'Pardon?'

'The Fire Lady.'

'Oh.'

'Heard that one, huh?'

'Never.'

Gillian wore jeans and a quite smart t-shirt with an orchid print on the front. 'You don't have to talk about it if you don't want to.'

The waitress took Gillian's order. Iris already had a pot of tea.

Iris said, 'How is Barbara, and her daughter?'

'Good. We're chipping away. Actually, you know, you do have to talk about it. Eventually. Are you going to see a counsellor about what you've been through?'

'Probably. I'm not sure. I'm trying to get to my psychiatrist.'

'Good.'

'I've been to see Lisa, Rodney Fitzmorris's wife.'

'Oh, I don't think that's a good idea.'

'Too late. Did you know she is suing?'

'Yes.'

'Can we – not contest it?'

'Of course the practice will contest. We did nothing wrong.

243

You did nothing wrong. What's this about?'

'If it goes ahead, she'll put her daughter on the stand.'

'It would be in camera. It would be handled.'

Iris said, 'Her mother is in complete denial.'

Gillian watched her coffee arrive.

Iris said, 'Her daughter needs treatment. Her recovery has to be the priority.'

'Yes. It is. Always. But not within our power, darling.'

'I had been drinking too much, not sleeping and possibly still suffering from PTSD from the fire at my practice. I came back to work too early. Was over-focused on the gymnasium investigation. For good measure, my husband and I were having problems.'

'You are making a very good case for the prosecution.'

Iris glared.

Gillian said, 'Yet, looking through your files and the notes accompanying every stage of uncovering the incest, the police charges and your process in Rodney's subsequent treatment in remand, your behaviour is above reproach. Some shorthand in the notes but it is all there, caring, diligent, procedurally correct.'

Iris smiled. Gillian was speaking impeccable psychologist. It was easy to forget she was good at her job, and a top-shelf advocate.

Gillian said, 'In fact, looking at the files and knowing all the shit that was going down in you and around you, it's amazing you functioned so well. You are a bloody machine.'

'I can compartmentalise.'

'Maybe some of the compartments might have lower walls or a spring clean.'

Iris sipped her tea. Gillian gulped her coffee.

Iris said, 'What can we do for Kimberly Fitzmorris?'

'Right. We could work up a few ideas about her treatment. A list of the best people who work with children, especially in abuse, would be a start. We need to let her mother vent. She needs to. She's still fighting her own guilt, her inner doubts about complicity. Her mother is sick, isn't she?'

'Damn. I forgot to ask about her mother.'

'Shame on you. Anyway, no one operates in a vacuum. It did

happen, Iris. You planted nothing. The words are Kimberly's. She has years of treatment ahead and her mother has to admit the truth before we can start.'

'Yes. I knew you'd understand, Gillian. I can pay for people.'

'Not necessary.'

'I want to.'

'Let me talk to Patricia and the practice lawyers. Can't have an apparent admission of guilt, as you know.'

Iris guffawed, bitterly.

'Lovey,' said Gillian, 'I didn't build any of this. I just know where some of the doors are.'

'Thank you.'

'Hey.'

'You're right. If anyone can find a way of making this happen quietly, actually happen, I've come to the right person.'

'Can my kids swim in your pool?' Her eyes were narrowed.

Iris said, 'How can I refuse. Your ten year old son watches *The Sopranos.*'

'We'll leave the machine guns and the horse's head at home, if you cooperate.'

'Deal.'

Iris got up, as did Gillian. They hugged.

'Ow,' said Iris, adding, when Gillian stepped back, 'a recent wound. It will heal.'

Chapter twenty-two

Iris drove to Frank's house, an old stone place high on the hill overlooking the harbour.

Frank's wife, Janine, opened the door. 'Iris!'

'Janine. How are you?'

'I'm wrapping. For Christmas.' Janine led Iris down their dark central hallway. The walls were entirely covered with generations of family photographs from around the world. The house smelt of old flowers and cabbage. 'I'll tell him you're here.'

'He's not expecting me.'

'Oh. Oh, well. Hmm. All right.'

'I'll go out the back, Janine. It's such a lovely day.'

'Yes dear.'

Iris passed a Christmas tree in the lounge room, wrapping paper, presents and ribbons on the gnarled kitchen table. Soup simmered. Light flooded in from the French doors that opened onto limestone steps down to their small backyard.

The jacaranda still bloomed but had shed flowers. The grass and huge weathered table were covered in purple, abuzz with foraging bees. Iris looked out over the railing at the river, bridges and cranes of the port beyond. The sky was immense.

Rufus, the dog, appeared from a cool place around the side, trotted to Iris, his tail wagging, head bending for a sniff and pat. The children named this one, a constantly moulting, fat golden retriever. Iris realised Rufus reminded her of Frank. Their previous dog had been an ugly Pekinese with bug eyes named Ziggy Freud. A rather obvious joke, Frank lamented. Rufus went away, came back with a rancid-looking bit of pulling rope.

''Fraid not, Rufus.'

'Might need to put in for a new one of those from Father Christmas, I think. Although they are only any good apparently if infused with slobber and gooz.' Frank eased himself down his back steps. He wore big orange shorts, slippers, an enormous t-shirt with the psychedelic design of a motorbike on the front.

'Gooz. What a good word.'

'You're looking at the t-shirt.'

'Where do you hide your hog?'

'Was a time when I rode wild and free. The kids never believed the war stories. They taunt me every chance they get. This one is nearly restful.'

He hugged her, holding her in the hug.

Iris suppressed a groan in spite of her sore shoulder.

When he released her, he scanned her eyes. 'You look well.'

'You sound surprised.'

'Not now I think about it.' He took the back of one of the chairs, tipped it forward so the jacaranda blossoms cleared, offered it to Iris. 'The bees only sting if you sit on them.' He went to the other side of the table, performing the same operation before sitting.

'I've tried to get through to you.'

'I'm sure. I'm sorry.'

'Busy.'

Frank sighed. He projected enormous pain. 'I was constrained, Iris.'

'It doesn't matter,' she said, not meaning it. 'Gooz.'

'I need to explain. You aren't answering your phone, by the way.'

'Oh. The police have it, or ASIO.'

'Ah. Okay, well ... when James Jules escaped from Fieldhaven ...'

'Have you been talking to him?'

'Yes.' He saw her eagerness, grimaced. 'When he escaped, questions were asked, fingers were ready to point. I'm sure I was a suspect. Why did I move him from Biara to Fieldhaven, and then why from Park to the less secure Grange Wing? And then move him again ... Where is the drug cabinet? Where was I when ...? They moved onto questions about you and your relationship with the patient.'

Iris waited.

'I invoked patient confidentiality, Iris. Which, as the Hollywood people found during the McCarthy trials, is tantamount to a confession. One of the consequences is the intense focus on you as a suspect.'

'Yes.'

Frank waited.

Iris said, 'It's all right, Frank.'

'We were both being isolated. They also needed me to give any views on where James might be and what he might do.'

'Me too.'

'Then you got the church.'

'Anyone could have done that. Rather obvious.'

'Afterwards, yes.' Frank grimaced again, looking down towards the harbour. Iris watched his mood lighten. 'A team of us have been interviewing him. I'm writing up the implications now. All kinds of things are coming out of this.'

Janine brought down two mugs of herbal tea, a battered hat for Frank. 'Don't tell him, but he's going thin on top.'

'Is this a calming tea or an energetic tea, Janine?' said Iris sniffing at it.

'I think it's good for your liver and bowels.'

'Which can never be a bad thing,' said Iris to comfortable laughter.

Janine headed straight back inside, used to the need for privacy of most of Frank's visitors.

Iris sipped the sweet bitterness. She detected raspberry.

Frank looked out into the water, possibly adding notes to himself about the case.

'So what did we miss, Frank? How did he fool us?'

Frank grimaced yet again. A convocation of grimaces? A scar of regret?

Iris said, 'You put me in the middle, Frank. To assess. You have to let me know where I went wrong.'

'What do you know about Dissociative Identity Disorder?'

'Split personalities. The Three Faces of Eve. Very rare. Contested. Distinct identities. James Jules is separate and distinct from James the Martian? Is that what you're saying?'

Frank beamed. 'We've found another.'

'Another personality?'

'Yes.'

'Makes sense. Is it a child?'

'Good point. There's evidence the psyche learns to defend itself during childhood trauma through this compartmentalising. It's a learned defence and these other personalities grow, taking over in different circumstances, almost like specialists. James the Victim is not James the Martian is not James Jules. We haven't found a child. Not yet. We've found an identity called Zeus.'

'Zeus.' Iris's head was spinning. Zeus. The zed of Zorro. She said, 'So, James does not know of Zeus's existence?'

'He does. Now.'

'Why now?'

'Well, we suspect the electrocution. Like an accidental ECT. He had residual drugs in his system, then the electric shock, he achieved new clarity once they revived him. There is also your ... final session with him might have incited a confrontation and confusion too. Which might be why he came after you at the zoo. Not as James Jules, though. It was Zeus, seeing you as a threat to Zeus but also a threat to James Jules as the primary identity and main custodian of the shared body. The Martian might have evolved out of the infanticide trauma, but we propose the Martian identity would have established itself earlier. It took over after the child killing because James Jules couldn't cope. Zeus, on the other hand, could regularly pop out to do his business, as he has been doing for some time. The core of both identities would have formed during middle childhood. Detective Pavlovic has a long list of potential crimes the identity who became Zeus may have perpetrated.'

Clever Detective Pavlovic. 'Does James know of these crimes?'

'More details emerge with more questions.'

'He's available for them? His ... um, physical body has no alibis?'

'Being checked. It accounts for why you and I saw no signs. Our patient wasn't privy to the information himself. He is not the person who committed those crimes. His acting out may well have been a cry for help concerning Zeus as well as his children. By the way, Zeus might have committed that crime, seeing the children as a threat to Zeus's freedoms. James Jules wakes up in the midst of it, an innocent bystander.'

'Is this another game?'

'To what purpose?'

'I'm mad, not bad. Put me in an institution, not prison. I'll look for a way to escape again.'

'Yes. We have many sessions ahead.'

'So if you haven't met Zeus, and if he doesn't remember Zeus, how ...?'

'He knows details, even though he's talking in the third person. Zeus did the school. The zoo. He got quite upset about the zoo. He kept asking if you were all right.'

Iris watched the dog stand, stretch in the shade of the tree. She said, 'James said he was allergic to dogs.'

'Yes. I make him sneeze.'

'The bomber, if it's Zeus, has dogs. Lots.'

Frank glanced at Rufus as though inviting input before he said, 'If the allergy is psychosomatic, it is reasonable to suggest one identity might be allergic while another is not. In fact, if the identities were playing off each other, if, say, the James identity suspected the Zeus identity, he might well have a reaction as a projection, a projection of protest. Massive speculation of course.' Frank was quite excited by it all.

He went on, 'I asked him if he'd known about Zeus and he said not until he woke in hospital. I asked if he remembered James the Martian. He does. He calls you Jodie Foster. You are sad but you make him happy. I asked if he remembered James Jules and he said, "Quite clearly. I know who I am." It's a breakthrough. It's almost sudden. I know you gave him a nudge with your hypnosis and I know I joked about the electric shock, yet we must acknowledge we have arrived at a special climax in relation to his inner crisis. His core identity, his biographic namesake, James Jules, has possibly risen up to try to quell Zeus now James the Martian has failed, possibly died. That battle was fought under the church. A massive metaphor, possibly irresistible to both Zeus and James Jules. He's still confused. Oh, and he said he intentionally grabbed the cord. He thought it the best way to save himself from Zeus.' Frank stopped talking. His smile had become a little delirious.

'You said Detective Pavlovic was present.'

'Yes. Detectives, other psychologists who have been on the case, military. It's a bit of a feeding frenzy, already. People are jumping on planes all around the world to get at James. Pavlovic is still asking questions about you, if that is what you want to know. He asked James if Jodie helped him, and he said yes. Pavlovic clarified, "With the school?" and he said no. Later Pavlovic asked why he used the bomb chemical he used. James explained the chemical properties. Pavlovic asked how James knew so much about the chemical. He was a laboratory technician! You were right about his science background. It all clicks into place, afterwards. Someone asked him why Zeus wanted to blow up the school. He said it seemed sexy, ripe for the taking. Oblivious and smug. He thought it suitably challenging. James does not like Zeus at all. He scares him. He described him as vicious and callous.

Frank regarded Iris, steepling his fingers. He entered lecture mode. 'James swears Zeus tried to kill him. I've been reading up on this. Subsidiary identities can fear they will be ended when the primary identity is "cured". Why it's essential they are offered integration back into a whole personality with all the memories of all the identities. This raises a central ethical question. Well, it's not really a question and it is perhaps legal rather than ethical. Should Zeus be allowed continued existence? Is Zeus sufficiently independent to be regarded as the legal entity to be charged with heinous crimes; and contingent on that, is James Jules innocent? It's one body. One jail cell, but ... the legal implications are mind-blowing. Excuse the pun.'

'Can I read your report?'

'No.'

'When can I see him?'

'I don't think that would be wise.'

'He's tried to kill me. Zeus will come out for me, Frank.'

'Detective Pavlovic still entertains the notion you might have push-pulled that combination of identities.'

'Have cameras on me, your whole panel watching. You can slow motion any sleight of hand.'

Frank considered it, assessing the leverage, the possibility of further discoveries.

'You owe me, Frank. You dragged me into this. Even though I wasn't ready. Even though it's … been tough.'

'You are massively compromised, Iris. You don't sleep with a patient. Ever.'

'I didn't sleep with him. I stopped, remember. I need to know, Frank. I need to know how I didn't see – the evil, the hate.'

'None of us see. We don't see until we see. Which is another reason to be objective. You've wanted to cure him all along, instead of studying him. You've been fighting not to see.'

'Closure. Give me closure. Have me supervised, three guards and chains – give me the closure … the closure I never got with my mother or my father.'

Frank watched her with mounting disappointment.

Iris saw Janine up at the kitchen window. They'd been talking loudly, perhaps shouting.

The dog's ears were down.

Iris looked back at Frank but didn't say anything.

Frank said, 'Let me ask.'

'Good.'

'Using your therapy, your fractured relationship with your parents as a bargaining chip, is not healthy, Iris.'

It was Iris's turn to grimace. She noticed the grey in his beard, the dark circles under his eyes. She realised he would no longer be her psychiatrist as she went around the table to hug him. 'Careful of my back.'

Chapter twenty-three

Chuck came through the locked door. He wore dark pants, a collared checked shirt with his official card hung around his neck. He'd shaved, had his hair cut. He swaggered in spite of his limp.

'Doc!' He waved his arm toward the door.

Iris grabbed a visitor badge and followed him.

'Back on the inside,' she said.

'Seconded still. The case goes on.'

They got into the lift. 'Red faces at Fire and Rescue?'

'I don't get to see those faces. They slink back into the shadows. No more jokey tags stuck on my stuff, but. Nice shit-eating email from the boss. I'm a commended person.'

'You're a goddamn warrior, Chuck.'

'Are you working on me?'

'Always. Once you become one of my projects, it's for life.'

Chuck grinned. 'I'd like that, Doc.' He seemed about to try to hug her. Everyone was hugging today. He got embarrassed, coughed, said, 'We could do worse than do a few more cases together.'

They went into the office where Pavlovic had met with them on Sunday night. The detectives were gone, their boxes of work already stacked on desks and the floor. On the wall was a streamlined case tree with new branches including the school gymnasium and the backpackers, the old people's home, the house where the four people died and the early Springsteen case sites. There was also a map of the city and hills marked with Zeus fire sites, a cluster in the hills, otherwise an almost direct line from there to the old people's home. The school fitted along that line. The zoo and the church were marked with different coloured pins off near the city.

Iris said, 'What does the line mean?'

'What are you doing here?' Stuart Pavlovic entered the room.

'I brought her up,' said Chuck.

'Why are you here?' he repeated.

'You're still working the case.'

'Of course we are. The case doesn't stop, even if we caught the right crim. Evidence. Court.'

Chuck said, 'Just cos the circus has left ...'

'You haven't answered my question, Mrs Foster. Do you have any official standing here?'

Iris said, 'I'm going to interview James.'

'Under whose authority?'

Iris said, 'Yours.'

Pavlovic blanched, scratching at an itch he'd developed on his ear. He sat on one of the desks. A lot of work had gone into his nonchalance.

Iris said, 'So, the line on the map?'

Charles said, 'We don't know yet. It's not random.'

'Have you found any descriptions of an Indian or Anglo-Indian questioned at those first fires, Charles?'

'Some Abos and a Chinese bloke. No other suntans.'

Iris ignored Chuck's casual racism. Now was not the time. She asked Pavlovic. 'Was the fire safety officer at the school?'

Pavlovic shook his head.

Charles said, 'We showed a photo. Nope. He is described as white, non-descript, a bit officious. They mostly remember a big bunch of keys and a red iPad he used to take notes and photos. Not Indian, not a woman.'

Pavlovic said, 'We're working the case.'

Charles said, 'Yes. We're not working James, we're not working you, Doc.' He glared at Pavlovic.

Pavlovic said to Charles, 'Our job is to corroborate the facts. Find any holes. Support the evidence.'

Iris said, 'Did you ask James about the map?'

Pavlovic studied her. He was computing, wondering, assessing.

Iris said, 'I heard you were on the team to talk with him, since the church.'

Pavlovic said, 'Have you got any guesses about what the map might mean?'

Iris studied it again. It traversed six or seven suburbs. 'You clearly don't think the zoo or the church are part of the pattern. No, no idea. It doesn't escalate as it moves in either direction. It's not chronological, so ... he's from the hills, grew up around there, for sure.' She asked Pavlovic: 'So he gave no clues about it?'

Pavlovic shook his head.

Iris turned to Charles. 'Zeus. You even got the zed right! All along, Charles.'

Charles smiled, grimly. 'Stuart asked him about the Passiona cans. He said, maybe he gets thirsty. He's a smart-arse, still playing with us.'

Iris sat on a chair, rolled it back a touch so she could look into Pavlovic's eyes. 'When you were interviewing James, did any of you meet Zeus? Did his personality pop out and take over?'

'No. It was all third-hand stuff. I couldn't get in with many questions.'

'Did anyone ask James if he felt he *is* Zeus?'

'No. If you ask me, he talked like he wasn't, but the psychs all seemed on the same page. Really charged up and burrowing in.'

Iris said, 'So no one asked the question: is Zeus another person?'

Pavlovic smiled. It was open and uncomplicated, a look Iris had not seen on his face before. 'They did not,' he said.

She asked, 'So, what do you think about all this Zeus stuff?'

Pavlovic included Charles. 'I think he knows stuff. Stuff about the case. I think there is another person. I think James was broken out of Fieldhaven.'

'Do you have evidence?'

'Toxicology has come back from the two staff who were put to sleep during the escape. The drug in their bodies is not from the hospital. They are animal tranquilisers.'

Chuck said, 'The wheelchair at the church is from the psych hospital. Why did he take it?

Iris said, 'Was James sedated too?'

Pavlovic said, 'Awaiting the toxicology test.'

Charles said, 'The forensic laboratory is working the scene under the church. Things don't add up. The cord James fried himself on had been tampered with. The piping to feed off the ether has no connectors. Not in the basement room or in the van. I can't figure how it was actually going to be set up. I can't see why he'd go to all that trouble if he's going to blow the thing anyway. No one would think it was an accident. Makes no sense. He's stark raving, of course.'

'I'll ask him,' said Iris.

The telephone rang. Charles picked it up. 'Koch.' He listened.

Iris said to Pavlovic again, 'I will ask him about a lot of this, if you'll support me. Get me into the room. I want to speak with him. I don't think he's Zeus.'

Koch was off the phone. He said, 'I got to go to Child Services. They've pulled the files for me from two thousand. See if James pops up. For what it's worth, I think James is Zorro. I mean Zeus. Anyway, we have lots of loose ends. There's always loose ends, always bits no one can explain, that even a cornered, confessing, fingerprinted crim can't answer. Why'd you smash the glass on the way out? Why'd you do a shit on the bed before you torched the house? They don't know. They don't even remember it happening. Anyway, if it were up to me, Doc, you're in the room. Break the prick.'

'Thank you Charles,' Iris said.

He lumbered out, his shoulders stooped, happy to be back working too hard.

Pavlovic got off the desk, grabbed another chair. He brought it forward in front of Iris, planted his feet and eyeballed her from less than a metre.

Iris glowered. 'Every big break on this case has come from me.'

'Did you have sex with him? In the room in the psychiatric hospital?'

'No. I did not. I thought about it, but I did not.'

'Did you let him light the fire?'

'Yes, but ...'

'Did you break him out?'

'No.'

'Did you assist with the fire at the zoo?'

'No.'

'Did you kill your secretary twelve months ago?'

'What?' Iris felt a wave a nausea. 'No.'

'You're not so sure. Did you kill your secretary?'

'You must have the reports.'

'I do. They don't add up.'

It was time, Iris realised. It had been on the edge, trying to come to, to break out of its compartment. It was time.

Pavlovic went on, 'She was embezzling you.'

'Yes.'

'Her son put in a complaint. Explained your possible motive.'

'I was having it out with her. Margret was her name.'

'You lured Bradley Williams. You knocked him out and you locked Margret in your office and you lit the fire and went for a coffee.'

'Except I didn't. I was having it out with her. She was being unreasonable. She was making demands. I left to get coffee, to cool down.'

'In that ten minutes, in that tiny window, that's when he came and that's when it all happened and you come back and it's already too late. All in that ten minutes. You expect anyone to believe that?'

'Yes.'

'You only had one coffee.'

'Really?'

'It's in one of the police reports. Young go-getter noticed you only had one coffee, even though you said, "I was getting us coffee."'

'Will you let me tell you?'

'Tell away.' He didn't sit back. He stayed leaning forward, looking into her eyes.

Iris took a breath. She could, she knew she could. 'The thing is, I think I noticed his truck. I stormed out. She'd been ripping me off for years. She'd been taking about twenty-five percent of my profits. That is a lot. When I asked her, she went on the attack. She had problems and I had everything. Anyway, I was really angry with her. Livid. I left, not sure where I was heading. I was about to cross the road and I remember thinking, Bradley Williams' truck. He owned a big, reddish, American utility. A Dodge? His own number plate, it all came up in the report I'd done, Pumper 1. A pumper is one of the fire appliances. It also suggests an inflated macho attitude, way too into it. Anyway, I was at the road, the image of his truck came into my mind. I crossed the road and ordered the coffee. I'd received a warning on him. He'd made a threat, about me, when they'd let him go. Do you know about his case?'

Pavlovic said, 'He was a candidate for firelighting. They were weeding them out of the volunteer brigade.'

'I suggested they keep him, but watch him. So...he was in the carpark and I could have phoned the police. Immediately. I could have phoned Margret too. Told her to lock the doors or get out. I was angry and not thinking clearly. Are you happy? I did contribute to what happened. I could have stopped it, maybe. I could have gone back in. I might have talked him down. I might have been more explicit with how I directed the volunteer service to deal with him. As it turns out, he was a firelighting risk! And a killer. I suffered a mini breakdown. I kept seeing Margret in the window. I didn't even call Fire and Rescue. I have been on sleeping pills. I have been trying not to think about his truck, seeing it in the parking lot and not taking a better action. I've been suffering from stress and imagined guilt and dissociation and also real guilt. Like a few of my patients, I've whispered to myself: I am not sick. And lo and behold, here I am, better, through time and other things, ready to face it. Pop. No, I haven't finished, Detective. Margret was a nasty woman. I think she reminded me of my mother. I believe I kept her on for that reason. I let her get away with it for that reason. I felt guilty about hating my mother. I continue to feel guilty because part of me likes that she is dead, both my mother and Margret. Awful, isn't it? What a despicable thing to understand about yourself. Someone you know is murdered and you're glad. We are not brought up to find that acceptable. But I didn't do it. I did not kill her. I am not responsible for her death. I am not a nice person. Or a particularly happy one. None of this makes me a killer.'

'You only bought one coffee.'

'Apparently.'

'How did he get knocked out?'

'I don't know.'

'If she knocked him out, why didn't she run out the front door, rather than back into your office?'

'I don't know.'

'What bothers me most is this same MO. The church, the zoo and maybe even the school are like the fire at your office. We have a fire where people die, we have a very obvious offender, the patsy who's either mad or dead, wrapped up in a bow, and we have you, standing nearby with a cup of coffee and a Mona Lisa smile.'

For a person who claimed to have such an open mind, Pavlovic proved to be dogged in his adherence to a single theory and a single suspect. Iris said, 'Put me in with James. I'll make another mistake and you will have your evidence. Bring the whole show.'

Chapter twenty-four

Which is how they did it. On a middle floor of the Royal Hospital – the very one that overlooked Hill Church where James had been electrocuted only days before – was yet another secure ward given over to violent patients and criminals of indeterminate mental state who needed medical procedures too complex for prison infirmaries.

Pavlovic had gathered a team. To augment the permanently fixed camera high on the wall of the hospital room, were two camera operators from police technical support. They set up one camera facing James, another facing an empty chair next to the bed. John, the Chinese federal psychologist, appeared bemused. The uniformed policeman standing next to the bed presented as experienced. He was armed with a pistol and taser. Frank Silverberg arrived, acknowledging everyone including, but with no special attention, Iris.

Iris said, 'I feel like I'm doing my final exams.'

No laughter.

'Half an hour,' said Iris. 'I want half an hour with absolutely no interruptions. No other voices apart from mine. No eye contact, apart from those camera people.'

'Demands?' said Frank with a quizzical eyebrow.

'Therapy as public sport, televised. You can be executive producer, Frank, maybe take care of casting.'

Frank gave his wounded face, but said, 'Iris has my confidence.'

John said, 'Half an hour.'

Everyone turned to Detective Pavlovic who merely gestured towards the door of the hospital room where James lay.

Iris went in.

James was strapped to a bed with leather belts across his chest and legs. He was hooked up to an ECG, a drip. His left hand was heavily bandaged, as was his foot. His right foot was manacled to the bed, although the manacle was softened by a cloth collar around his ankle.

His eyes were closed, his face pale, his dark complexion a little yellowed although his pallor might have been affected by the hospital lights.

Iris said, 'James. Hello. It's Iris.'

He opened his eyes. They were filmy. He'd been drugged. Iris should have asked what was in the drip.

She sat, ignoring the camera person at the wall, the people behind her. She dragged the chair forward so she was closer to James's face, then became distracted when the policeman moved forward too, his hand on his taser. Iris raised her hands to show him they were empty. She had been searched by her favourite policewoman before being allowed to enter the hospital.

Iris said to James, 'I told you I'd be back. I told you I was here for the long haul.'

He smiled.

'Can you hear me, James?'

'Yes, Iris.'

'More burns.'

'Don't cut it off.'

'What?'

'Don't amputate, even if it's good for me.'

'It was a metaphor. A bad metaphor.' Iris felt pleased. He sounded like James, tired, sedated yet still lucid.

'My foot is sore.'

'The electricity. It went in your hand and out your foot, apparently.'

'Which was the idea.'

Iris didn't pursue it. She said, 'I asked them to lower your pain relief a little, so I could talk to you.'

'Zeus. Everyone wants to talk about Zeus. I'm yesterday's man.'

'I don't want to talk about Zeus.'

'Yes you do.' He talked slowly, his face unanimated.

'I want to talk about you, James. I don't want to talk about him. Zeus. What a poncy name.'

James giggled. 'The father of the gods. Don't rile him.'

'Who am I talking to?'

'James.'

'From Earth?'

'Yes.' James giggled again.

'James Jules?'

'Yes.'

'What is your wife's name?'

James went quiet. He grimaced. 'Nisa. She ...' He sighed.

Iris said, 'It's all right James. I don't want you to have to think about that right now. Let's talk about other things. Tell me about yourself.'

'What?'

'I feel like I'm meeting you for the first time.'

'No, we ... did you kiss me?'

Iris felt a mild ripple behind her. 'Possibly. I hugged you. I was forced to leave. I'm sorry. I talked a lot with a Martian.'

'Yes. Yes. I remember.'

'What do you remember?'

'Bits. I lived rough. Couch-surfed. Roamed. Odd jobs. It was good, fun.' He drifted for a while. Iris let him. James said, 'I know it was a fantasy. I kind of knew all along but I couldn't stop doing it. The more I did it the more I felt bound to keep it up.'

'Where are you from?'

'All over.'

'Where were you born?'

'On the road. Queensland.'

'Where in Queensland?'

'In a circus.'

'I beg your pardon?'

'I was born in a circus.' He smiled the smile he used when he said he was from Mars. 'Truth is stranger than delusion. You don't have to believe me.'

Iris decided she'd come back to it later. 'What's your full name?'

'James Benjamin Jules.'

'JJ.'

'I don't like being called JJ.'

'Your parents?'

'My mother was a farm girl. My father was a horse rider, like a horse acrobat, in the circus, and knife thrower. It wasn't a big circus. My mother became the girl who stood very still while the knives missed her by as little as possible. She ... he ... well, those things happened, two attractive young people. She took me back to her farm, but I am black, which meant it didn't go well, apparently. She became hurt, bitter. We were forced to go back to the circus after a while because we ... had to go somewhere. My father wasn't there anymore.' James drifted off.

'You did tricks.' It made sense suddenly.

'Yes. Tough way to make a living, working the circus. Hot, dusty. No glamour at all. I don't want to talk about it.'

'We don't have to talk about the circus, James.'

James shouted, 'I don't want to talk about it.'

'Shh, shh. It's okay James. They tell me you're a laboratory technician?'

'I went to school. I was taken in. I went to school and university.'

'Where did you go to university?'

'I became a science teacher for a two years before leaving.'

'Why?'

'I like science.'

'Why did you leave?'

'Georgio and Lena died.'

'How?'

'Car accident. They were old. I was down south working in a school. I left Australia after the funeral. I went to Malaysia. Lots of parts of Asia. I searched for my father for a while. I got a job as a lab tech, in KL. I met Nisa.'

'How long were you in Asia?'

'Six or seven years, I suppose.'

'How often did you visit this city?'

'Once in a while. Not often.'

'Did you set up a fire at Barnard Christian College?'

'No.'

'No? You seem sure now. You weren't before.'

'I don't see why I would.'

'Where were you when it happened?'

'With the girls.'

'The girls were after. Where were you before the girls?'

He thought for some time. 'The desert. Hitchhiking. Walking sometimes.'

'Do you remember the fire at your house, in Malaysia?'

'Yes.'

'What happened?'

James was quiet.

Iris thought she might have to steer him away from it again. She knew she was pushing things too fast, hoped the random nature was led by James.

He said, 'I wanted to die.'

'When?'

'In my house.'

'Why?'

'I don't remember. Nisa came back to save me. I thought they were gone. I thought they'd left me. I was behaving badly. Sick. Like the Martian, but not the Martian. I wanted to die. I lit a fire downstairs, went up to Benny's cot. I lay in his cot, to sleep. Forever. They came back and they were the ones who burned, not me. I got out.' James began to moan, his moan breaking down into sobs.

Iris stood up, touched James's cheek.

The policeman made a sudden move and Iris saw the taser out of his holster. She glared, then returned to James.

Iris said, 'Shh, shh. It's awful, James. It is very bad, I know. We'll talk about this later. Your poor kids. You didn't mean to, did you?'

'No.'

Iris stroked his forehead. She returned to her chair, keeping her eyes down. She didn't want to see the crowd at the door, along the back wall of the hospital room. She sat on her chair. She wondered what had caused James to light the fire at his house. There must have been other incidents, an existing condition, a first cause. Iris would like to talk about the circus, his adoptive parents and his mother.

'What?' said Iris. He'd talked; she hadn't been listening.

'He tried to kill me.'

'Who?'

'Zeus. He calls himself Zeus.'

'What's his real name?'

'He didn't say.'

'Are you Zeus?'

'No.'

'Would you know, if he is inside you?'

'I don't see how he could be.'

'Do you ever have blackouts? Missing time?'

'Yes.'

'So you can't be sure he's not in you?'

'I can't answer that. No one could answer that.'

Iris smiled. 'Are you a Martian?'

'No. I know I was ... kind of living him. Living the character. I ... yes, I see what you mean. He drugged me.'

'Oh?'

'He came into the hospital room. They moved me, after you left. He came in and gave me an injection.'

'What does he look like, the man who calls himself Zeus?'

Iris found herself holding her breath. Pavlovic had so persisted with his line of questioning even she was ready for James to say, 'He looked like you, Iris. Zeus is you.' How would she know if it was not knowable?

James said, 'It was mostly dark and I was drugged. He was kind of like nobody. Blondish. About my height. Fatter. Fuller than me. He made me sneeze. I was in his van, strapped to a wheelchair, my arms were gaffer-taped. I was still upset about the things I remembered about the kids. I was confused. I was still the Martian, the kids were screaming and you were kissing me, not Nisa, but I was in the back of a van. Maybe one of the containers of ether had a faulty top because I drifted, thinking about Nisa leaving me and the fire. Back in Australia I was a Martian. Strange.'

'You were in a van. Were you driving?'

'No. Strapped to a wheelchair. He was driving, talking in the front. At first I thought someone else was in the van, only I couldn't see anyone, it was only him talking and ... he was excited, angry. He was admonishing, admonishing the world. He was ... he called me "thing". "You will be famous, thing. You will be me. You will steal my fame but I will know. It should be mine." I kept passing out, I think. I also pretended to be out because I was working on the gaffer tape. It's actually harder than handcuffs because you can't get to it with your fingers. I used to get out of things as one of the acts in the circus, when I was small ... and break into places too, on the road. We arrived before I could do more than loosen it a bit by stretching it.

'He had trouble getting me off the van. He was grunting. He heard a noise and went off and came back. He said, "I put him down. Quick and kind. Put you down too, crazy thing." We are at an old church. A huge church. I thought this has to be a dream. He wheeled me down some steps. He kept talking and I kept pretending to be unconscious. He said, "I'm not going to bring it all in. It's not necessary to make the trick work." He talked about you, Iris.'

'Really?'

'Yes. He thought they might have seen things under the school they shouldn't have because Iris came and stopped it. He thought you'd done something to make the school go wrong. He got angry with you. He said you were dead. He ... he has lots of different feelings about you, I think.'

'Oh. Hmm.' As Frank said, he was a fan, or a competitor.

'He explained everything in detail, like the whole thing was how to put a clock together, describing what each thing's function is. I was a thing with a function. He said, "They have to see you. This cord you have to hold. Do you understand? I know you're awake. I only gave you three point five milligrams. You have to do your part. You won't suffer. I could make you squeal and quiver and cry and make your eyes go wide with soul pain, do you know? Do you know how long I could keep doing it? So, you be a good thing. Hold this." He plugged the extension cord into a wall socket, laid it out to the wheelchair. He poured water on the ground, on the stone pavement. He cut the gaffer tape.

He had a knife. I thought of getting it but I sneezed. I couldn't help it. I sneezed and sneezed again. He jumped back, holding the knife up. "Crazy Martian thing. You are going to be me." He was going to electrocute me, you see. He talked to me like I was a monkey or a moron. I couldn't stop sneezing. He is boring. Tiresome even when about to kill you. "You need to stand in this puddle and pick up the cord." He flicked the power point switch, careful to jump back. "You need to stand and grab the cord." Lights started flashing. They flashed on a wall, making the glass jars pulse blue. I wasn't certain whether I was having another hallucination. He went to the steps. I kept my feet up on the rubber footrests of the wheelchair. Do you know about electricity and earthing? I knew it was a long shot. I put my hand in my pocket. I was hoping it'd go down my side. As long as it didn't pass through my heart. As long as the amps were right. It's strange, isn't it, Iris?'

'Strange? What, James?'

'I was ready to die in my home and here I am trying to live under that church.'

'Yes. Maybe it's a good sign, James.'

'Anyway, I leaned down, not touching the floor or the metal of the wheelchair. He screamed, "No, not that way!" I grabbed the cord. Poof, here I am, crashed to Earth again.'

'It's a long journey, James. Longer to go.' Iris patted him on his leg.

'Ow.' He said it distantly. His eyes were closed.

'Sorry.'

'Don't let them cut off my leg.'

'I won't. Can we talk about dates? Do you feel up to dates and where you might have been?'

'No. Later. Too tired.'

'You sleep. I will be back later.'

Iris stood, spinning around to the audience. Frank leaned in the corner, his chin in his hand, looking at James. John nodded to her. Pavlovic stood in the doorway, his arms folded across his chest.

Iris said, 'Toxicology?'

'The lab.'

'If he has the same tranquiliser in him as the two attendants at Fieldhaven?'

'It could have been self-administered,' said Frank, to John, not to Iris. 'Time is unaccounted for between the zoo and the church. He might be acting it out, even in his head, a projected battle between the dominant identities. They are each trying to destroy the other. The incident in the church may well have been James Jules trying to stop James Zeus from killing again. He may have been trying to sabotage the Zeus identity's latest plans to kill, literally undoing the other's work while he's in control of the body.'

Iris said, 'Frank, it is not him.'

Frank barely glanced at her before turning back to John. 'I'm not convinced.'

Iris asked Pavlovic, 'Does his description of Zeus fit the descriptions of the fire inspector at the Zorro fires?'

He thought. He nodded. 'Out please. Everybody. Let's not have these conversations in front of the suspect.'

The cameramen were packing up. James appeared to be sleeping. His heart monitor seemed stable. She wondered if anyone watched it for jumps like a rudimentary lie detector.

Iris said, 'Are you posting a guard?'

Pavlovic said, 'Yes.'

'He's still in danger now he's seen him.'

'Under police guard in a locked room.'

Frank and John were in a discussion down the hall. Iris went to them. John said, 'We never asked the question: are you Zeus? Mrs Foster asked it.'

Iris said, 'Are you going to talk to him again?'

John said, 'In an hour.'

Frank wouldn't look at her. Iris said, 'Frank, how do you prove you don't have something you are not aware of?'

Frank said, 'This is why it is up to others to investigate and assess, not the patient. Qualified people who are not emotionally involved or sick themselves.' He still didn't look at her, even though he'd tried to wound her deeply.

Chapter twenty-five

Iris found her way to the public cafeteria on the second floor. She needed to be back at the room in an hour to listen in on the next interview. Through the glass doors leading to a balcony Iris saw it was dark outside. She grabbed a sandwich in a plastic wrapper, was about to order tea when she overheard the lady behind the servery explain that the water was off. She bought bottled water, found a seat.

Iris felt certain James was not Zeus. She was fairly sure Frank had been blinded by the excitement of discovering a multiple identity case. She didn't blame him. She didn't blame anyone for hubris or seeking the limelight. She would like to ask James about the circus. She suspected it had happened there or at the adoptive parents' house. Iris suspected the circus with its itinerant crowds and workers. He'd seen something or done something in KL that brought back whatever had happened to him when he was a child. Something triggered the breakdown in Kuala Lumpur. Something James did not want to face. Trauma causing further trauma.

Iris called Mathew on her dump phone. She got his answer service. He would still not recognise her new temporary number, she supposed. 'Hello, Mathew. I'm caught up at the hospital interviewing James Jules. I will be late. Sorry. I was thinking. When this sorts itself out, shall we hop on a plane and go see Rosemarie? See you soon. I love you.'

Iris noticed the battery was low on the phone. Time to demand her old phone back from the police.

She worked on the sandwich. The bread was damp, the lettuce dry.

She thought about Zeus. If James was not Zeus, then why did Zeus want to kill Iris at the zoo? Was she still in danger? He must have followed her in the past, which was why he knew so much. She recalled the CCTV footage of Zeus at the zoo. He disconnected the cylinders with familiarity. The sedative used on the hospital workers was an animal tranquiliser, Pavlovic had said. James sneezed around Zeus, he said. James was allergic to dogs. There were dog hairs in the truck at the school. Animal hairs. Different animal hairs. Not solely dog?

Iris rang Pavlovic. He answered straight away. 'It's all right, Iris. I don't think you could possibly be working with James. I'm convinced.'

'It's not why I'm calling. Zeus works with animals. Maybe he's from the zoo. No. He's a vet. The dogs he took to case the school. One was bandaged. You can see he doesn't treat them like an owner. He's taken them as cover.'

'The tranquiliser.'

'Yes.'

'The ether too. Chuck said it is used in ... He'd be familiar with the depot or whatever. Would know the drill.'

'It fits. You're looking for a vet. He has a bad record too. His animals die or have strange lingering illnesses. A cluster of unhappy animal owners. It's perverse yet also perfect. The triangle. Animal cruelty, firelighting, trouble in his past. It's the sociopath triangle. It's a brilliant cover for his animal torture. Blond, bland, meticulous, bossy ... oh, shit. He's a sociopath, a sociopath with a narcissistic personality disorder.'

'What?'

'I think it could be one of my patients.'

Silence on the other end of the line.

Iris said, 'Are you there?'

'Yes. Who?'

'Dr Hampton. His name is Paul Hampton. He fits the description, Stuart. He's strange in the right way. I'm not saying it's definitely him. I am saying definitely look at him.'

'On it. You got an address?'

'Call you back.'

She telephoned Charles Koch, was put to his answering

service. She talked quickly. 'Charles, it's Iris. I need you to check your files again. Back in the Springsteen spree was there a young white boy say about fourteen years old named Paul Hampton? Maybe he used a different surname. Paul Hampton – he would have been about fourteen or fifteen. Urgent. Um, call Pavlovic with what you find, my phone is dying.'

Iris telephoned Mary, hoping it was a late practice evening.

'Park Psychology and Healing Centre.'

'Mary, it's Iris Foster.'

'Hey, how are you?'

'I don't have time right now, Mary. Can you give me Paul Hampton's address?'

'Checking. You going to see him? He has been calling a lot. He got quite abusive when we explained you'd left.'

'Listen, I'm about to run out of phone battery. Can you give any addresses to a Detective Stuart Pavlovic?' Iris gave her the phone number. 'Mary, it's urgent and really, really important. Okay. Inform Patricia he may be dangerous.'

Iris's telephone shut down. She hoped Koch would get her message, although the files weren't important now. If only she'd seen them herself. His name might have jumped out. If only she'd considered the people in her practice. The people in front of her. His desire to show off to her, while fooling her, while pumping her for information about his case. Iris gasped at the realisation that if Zeus stole her laptop he conceived his idea about James as scapegoat from reading Iris's report.

Iris became distracted by another commotion at the counter. A doctor in greens demanded coffee. A cleaner called, 'The water's off on the whole floor.' Someone else said, 'The whole hospital.'

Iris peered at the smoke alarm in the corner of the cafeteria roof. She couldn't see a green light. Iris went to the corridor where she found another fire detector on the hall ceiling. It did not appear to be working.

She scanned the corridor of the concourse level. People were buying things from the florists and newsagent. Visitors meandered on their way to and from patients. A nurse moved with normal haste. A maintenance person was unlocking a panel.

Iris went to him as he checked the tap. Iris said, 'You need to go down to the mains. You need to also alert people about the fire alarms.'

He stared at her, confused. He appeared to be Sri Lankan, which meant he might have a PhD or no English.

'I think the hospital is under attack.'

He said, 'I'm maintenance. The pipes.'

Iris saw a bulge in his buttoned top pocket. She pointed, said, 'Can I borrow your lighter. Lighter?'

'No smoking.' He returned to the cabinet, closed it.

'I'll give you twenty dollars for your lighter.'

He glanced at her purse.

Iris produced a twenty dollar note.

He shrugged. He didn't mind making money from a crazy patient. He produced a disposable, traded. He put the money in his pocket before he said, 'No smoking.'

Iris went along the corridor until she found an open hospital room. The patient was in her thirties, her hair done nice, her nightie covered in pink roses.

Iris said, 'Hi, is your phone connected?'

'The phone works okay. The television won't get all the stations.'

Iris scanned the ceiling until she saw the sprinkler. It was an old room in an old hospital. She got the visitors chair, pushed it up against a cabinet with a shelf of flowers.

'What procedure are you in for?'

'Tubes tied.'

'Can you walk?'

'Yes.'

'You might want to get out of the hospital. Go down the main stairs. He can't block those.'

Iris put the cigarette lighter up against the mercury ball connected to the sprinkler. She flicked to make a flame, let it lick the mercury ball.

'What are you doing?' called the patient. She pressed her call button.

'Cover up. If I'm wrong, we are going to get wet. And Fire and Rescue will come.'

The mercury heated until the glass burst but only a dribble of water trickled from the pipe. It was residual with no pressure. No alarms sounded in the corridor. Maybe a light might blink on at the nearest fire station or call centre.

Iris climbed down, went to the lady's telephone.

She gave a short scream, cowered.

A nurse came in. 'What seems to be the trouble?'

'Her,' said the patient.

Iris said, 'I think there is going to be a fire in the hospital.'

Iris dialled out, then triple zero. 'Emergency Services, which service do you require?'

'Fire and police. There's a fire at Royal Hospital.'

'Nearest corner?'

'It's Royal Hospital! Top of the hill, next to the church.' She glared at the nurse, demanded, 'What's the street outside the ground floor entrance?'

The nurse said, 'There's no fire. There's no alarms. There's no fire here.'

'She lit it. She lit the sprinkler on the roof with her lighter,' said the patient.

Iris spoke into the telephone, 'Can you connect me to the fire communications centre?'

'Where is the fire in the hospital?' asked the emergency operator.

'I assume on the ground floor. Low, so it burns up and traps everyone. The basement. Start in the basement.'

The nurse said, 'Madam, there's no fire.' She pushed a button on her pager.

Iris said, 'Yes, call security. You had a code orange on Sunday night. Well, it's going to happen again, only this will be code red, if you have anything higher than orange. An actual fire with no warning.'

'We just got back in,' said the patient.

The com-cen operator said, 'We have no alarms showing at that location, madam. Can you reach a fire extinguisher?'

Iris said to the telephone, 'This is Iris Foster. The alarms are out. The water is off. The suspect for the gymnasium bombing is in this hospital. I believe a fire is about to start in the hospital, if it is not already going. You will want every available fire appliance, police dogs, rescue. Send soldiers. I know you are recording this conversation. Play it to anyone in authority. Now!'

Iris spun to the nurse, who'd gone quiet. She said, 'Security?'

'They aren't here yet.' She shrugged. They were not necessarily swift at the best of times.

Iris said, 'Where's your nurses station? Take me.' She turned to the lady in bed. 'If you can walk, I suggest you get dressed and leave the hospital.'

A ripple of commotion started in the corridor. People were moving with purpose and moderate urgency. Perhaps they had discovered the fire.

'Something is up,' said the nurse, looking back at Iris with wariness.

Nurses and civilians were standing at the lifts. The arrows were out. The lifts were not working.

Other nurses and a doctor were in a mild flap at the nurses station.

Iris said, 'We need security.'

'Have you seen them?' said the sister on the telephone.

'Who?'

'They've broken out of the prison ward. A policeman has been killed. All the patients from the secure ward are roaming the hospital.'

'The lifts aren't working,' said the doctor tangentially.

'I believe there's going to be a fire. You need to alert whoever you need to so you can go to code orange again.'

They gaped at her. Iris could spend days trying to convince one of them to get her to the person in charge, repeating the ludicrous tale thousands of times along the way.

The sister on the phone said, 'Oh my god. One of the criminals has a hostage. He's got broken glass and he's got a doctor hostage.'

Iris left them, studied the corridor again, noting the emergency exit.

Iris went back into the patient's room. The patient had gone. Iris went to the window to look out. She could see the street below. A small fire appliance was idling down in the street. Iris got magazines from the patient's table, tore pages, scrunching them into a pile of paper balls on the ledge of the window. She lit the paper under the curtains, got wrapping paper from the flowers and a plastic bin, added them to the flames which quickly raced up the curtains.

Satisfied with her alarm beacon, she left the room, shouting, 'Fire. Fire. Fire!'

Iris headed down the fire stairwell. It was busy now the lifts were out. Hospital staff were heading up and down. A woman in a hospital caterer's uniform rattled at a door marked EXIT on the ground floor. 'It's stuck.'

Iris said, 'Go out through the lobby. Prop this door to the lobby open so others go that way too.'

Iris continued down. She wasn't sure what she was looking for, but it was somewhere in the basement. At the bottom of the steps was a door marked MAINTENANCE STAFF ONLY. It was unlocked. A maintenance worker in tan-coloured clothes lay on the concrete floor inside the room. Iris felt his neck for a pulse. He was breathing.

Across the room was another red door, which Iris tried. It opened to a huge concrete room full of green generators, which sat on concrete risers painted yellow. Pipes painted blue rose to the ceiling where conduits and pipes wound across the fluorescent-lit ceiling. It was like being in the engine room of a vast ship.

Grey cabinets lined the wall where Iris entered. A small sign said ELECTRICAL. Nearby was the fire alarm system, housed in a red metal cabinet. The cabinet door was open. Iris peered at dials and switches, realised she didn't know how to restore the system.

She made her way through the turbines. They hummed rather quietly, smelt faintly of warm plastic and oil.

She came to more doors. CHILLER ROOM PLANT. CHEMICAL STORAGE. OVERFLOW BASEMENT LABORATORY. EMERGENCY BACK-UP GENERATOR. Iris found the red pipes with their red wagon-wheel taps and water pressure gauges belonging to the fire sprinkler system. She was about to search for the tap to turn the water flow back on when she saw another body.

She saw his legs first and rounded a generator to find a security guard near the lifts. A fire extinguisher lay next to the body, blood covering the blunt end. The lift doors were propped open. Drums were stacked in the nearest one.

'Aviation fuel.'

Iris spun to see Paul, behind her, dressed in the tan clothes of a maintenance worker. He wore glasses and a brown baseball cap. He also carried a large set of keys. 'This fellow here unlocked all the doors. I have locked them again,' he said, annoyed. He tossed the bunch of keys at the security man. They bounced off his body, jangled across the floor. The side of the man's head had been bludgeoned. 'I'm not ready. It needs to be done properly and you keep rushing me.'

Iris tried to smile.

Paul said, 'You should be dead.'

'I'm too smart for you.'

'No one is.'

'You know I am. It's why you fear me.'

He met her eyes with a moment of doubt before finding his scorn.

Iris thought about his case, their sessions. She thought about Paul's mother, the glitches in his social interactions, his desire to talk, the possibility every second he could be delayed, more people might get out of the hospital.

'Aviation fuel? I'm supposing it's not commonly available in most hospitals.'

'You say things in a stupid way. Do you know?'

'I hadn't thought about it. Possibly yes?'

'Not possibly. You try to make jokes. For no reason.'

'You don't like jokes, do you? It takes too long to work them out, to adjust to the expected response and then deliver it, fake the mirth.'

'Shut up, Iris.' Paul reached down to a small knife holster on his belt, pulling out a diver's knife. It had a large blade, serrated on top. 'Come this way.'

He directed Iris into the doorway marked EMERGENCY POWER GENERATOR where more drums were on a flat trolley. The drums were marked DIESEL.

'It is easier to pull rather than push.' He pointed her to the trolley.

'You said aviation fuel.'

'Yes. Don't believe what is says on the packet. See. A joke.'

'How?'

'How am I going to burn down the hospital?'

'I'm guessing the lifts will take the fuel. How'd you get it in here?'

'I came here while they were evacuating. Confusion, then quiet. While you were at the church, meddling. They use diesel for the emergency generators. Pull.'

Iris manoeuvred the trolley with difficulty, dragging it out through the door and towards the lifts.

'The lifts connect to four wings, the shaft is the centre of the H shape. If it ignites on level three, it should spread outwards. With no water, and a lot of chemicals and plastics, it should be self-sustaining. If I can generate sufficient initial heat, like the planes in New York. I was going to use diethyl ether, except the experiment at the school proved it too unstable.'

'You want the numbers.'

'Five floors multiplied by four wings. Incapacitated. Beds, wheelchairs. Only narrow steps clogging. They are still confused and tired from leaving and coming back.'

'You're going for a record. You want the glory.'

Iris stopped at the lift. James was inside, dead or unconscious, his arms taped to a wheelchair next to some drums already loaded.

Paul said, 'Stupid thing.' He was looking at James in the lift. He still held the knife.

'They know it's you, Paul.'

'Who?'

'The police. I told them.'

'We don't have to worry about him.'

'James?'

'The fat one. The one with the limp.'

'Charles?'

'My name was on his list. He asked questions about the old fires. He had no idea. He wasn't even armed. He came to the house. I put him down. Quite quickly.'

Iris took a big breath. Forced herself to stay sharp, not think about Chuck.

'With you gone too, and this thing, it can be neat again. Lift the drum and put it in the lift.'

'You're kind of stuck on the one plan aren't you?'

Paul's eyes flashed but the anger was gone in an instant.

Where were the fucking fireys? Where was security? Why were they taking so long?

'Move the drums into the lift,' he ordered calmly.

Iris tried to wrestle with one of the drums. She couldn't even budge it.

'You're not strong. You're useless. Stupid. They won't come yet. They are too busy searching for the Martian and dealing with the escaped criminals, getting in each other's way. Guinea pigs squeal in a special way when there is a fire in their cage.' Paul stood looking towards the basement ceiling as though listening for squeals.

Iris took a step away and he reacquired her. He put the knife in his holster. He said, 'You wouldn't get halfway to the door before I would catch you.'

'I'm trapped. I can't escape.'

He studied her. Iris guessed he was imagining hurting her, in quite specific detail, but he shook the thoughts off, grabbed the top of a drum, twisted it off the trolley. He half-rolled, half-walked it into the lift, pushing it in next to James.

Iris glanced down to the dead security guard. She didn't dwell on his face. He wasn't armed. She said, 'I have told other police it is you. I've given them your name.'

'You're lying.'

'You may as well let it go. You won't hide anything. We know. We know it's you. You're too fancy, Paul. Too set in your ways. You over-think it. There's too much foreplay and masturbatory self-touching as you set the fire up. It takes too long. You fuck like a Chinaman.'

'What?'

'A joke. You don't like jokes, I know. This one is about you. You. It was in a film. *Chinatown*. The detective, Jack Nicholson, tells about this man who has a problem. He's a premature ejaculator.'

'I'm not. I can control that.'

Bingo. 'It's a joke. It's not about you in that way. I'm sure you're a magnificent lover, Paul.'

Paul stood in the lift, staring at her, trying to work out what she was doing while also assimilating having multiple buttons pushed. It was like he was being nipped by tiny ants.

James moved behind him. It was done so quickly Iris wasn't exactly sure what happened. He moved, then he was still again, slumped in the wheelchair in the lift.

Paul saw her glance. He turned to look at James before stepping out of the lift.

Iris said, 'So, he goes to his friend and he says, I can't satisfy my wife.'

'I can. You are being annoying, Iris. You need to move on.'

'His friend says, well what the Chinese do is they, you know, get down to a bit of in and out, but when the man feels like he's about to ...'

'Orgasm,' said Paul. It was a strange thing, the way Paul said the word, perhaps too devoid of feeling.

'He withdraws from her vagina. Excuse my rude language, Paul. And my racism. Not my joke. He withdraws from her vagina and he goes outside to contemplate the stars, the garden. He returns to his wife and he enters her again. Once again, when he feels he's about to ... orgasm, he withdraws to calm down.'

'You are completely off track, Iris. Again, you're obsessing over textbook inventions. If I was once a premature ejaculator, I am not now. It is merely a matter of control.'

'That's not the point of this joke.'

'It's not funny.'

'I haven't finished. Ha.'

'You are delaying me.'

'Yes. Exactly.'

'Are you trying to disorient me with dirty talk?'

'Is that what your mother did? Talked dirty, while she ...'

'Enough.' Paul moved with sudden speed. He pushed her back to thump against the side of a generator.

She gasped at the sudden pain in her shoulder. Wheezed, 'Did you kill your mother?'

'Yes.' He stood over her, his eyes cold.

'Why?' she whispered.

'She was bad.'

'December, two thousand.'

He looked at her, appraising. He was a little frightened of her again. Perhaps he always had been, possibly because of his mother.

'Why the can of Passiona? Was it her favourite? Or yours. After.'

'Stop.' He raised his hand, but only in warning. He didn't strike.

Iris wondered whether it might be possible to confront someone with their darkest issues to such an extent you could actually talk them into catatonia. The talking cure as talking weapon. Cause a kind of loop or brain freeze while the mind couldn't keep up with its own defences so started fighting itself.

'Sex with your mother was wrong but it wasn't your fault. You were a child.'

He sneered. His hand dropped. 'Stupid thing, Iris. Fault. I didn't come to you to be cured. You have no idea. I told you I blew up the school and you thought I was talking about binge drinking. You stupid fool. Under your nose. My ... she ... we never had sexual intercourse. Wrong again.'

'Your mother did things to you. When you wet the bed. After you wet the bed she washed you, didn't she, and she ridiculed you for wetting your bed. She washed your penis and you got hard. It wasn't sex but it was confusing. She laughed at you, berated you. She washed you a lot.'

His hand shot forward, his fingers wrapped around her throat. One hand seemed sufficient to pin Iris against the generator, his fingers squeezing, his face twisted.

Her shoulder hurt again.

Iris had guessed close enough to cause him pain. She'd lit a fire, a blaze back behind his eyes, twisting on itself, sparking and burning up his own neural pathways.

Yet his hand kept squeezing, Iris could feel herself going. If she died, she'd go down swinging. Maybe it would be okay. A decent sleep, finally.

Paul stopped strangling her. He stepped back, started to twist around, twisting to get at his back as if trying to get at an itch. He turned and Iris saw a knife sticking into his back. His fingers got the handle, pulling it out.

Iris bent, grabbed the fire extinguisher from next to the security guard. As Paul rotated towards her, half-bent, with the knife, she brought the extinguisher down on his head. She felt it crunch into him, but it bounced back, got slippery in her hands so she had to grab it to her chest in a kind of hug. Paul was still standing in front of her, his head bent. She raised it again and brought it down on the side of Paul's head with all her might, falling with it as she did.

Iris twisted as she fell, landed heavily on her arse. She sat, panting on the cold, vibrating concrete floor of the hospital basement.

James was standing in front of the wheelchair in the lift, his bandaged left hand still taped to one side of the armrests.

Paul lay bleeding next to the security guard on the floor. Iris still held the fire extinguisher. She raised it above her head, ready for any movement. Wood splintered somewhere, doors cracked open.

Detective Pavlovic arrived first, his gun drawn. Firefighters followed, axes waving in vague threat.

He looked at James standing in the lift full of drums, taped to the wheelchair. He looked to Paul, his face covered in blood, then to the bloody fire extinguisher held above Iris's head. Iris watched him process the clues. She watched him raise his gun and point it at her. 'Put the extinguisher down please, Mrs Foster.'

Iris dropped it with a frightening hollow clang.

She said, 'For Christ's sake, Stuart.'

Chapter twenty-six

They found Charles's body in a workshop at Paul's hills home. The workshop was filled with timing devices, drums of fuel, electronics. Paul's wife claimed she had been forbidden to enter and never had. She had no idea Paul was a serial killer, she said rather blandly. He had been a wonderful father to his children, she said. Charles never received Iris's call of warning about Paul Hampton. He was already dead. He had been working his way through the list of fifteen year olds he'd finally gained from the Child Services department; working the case.

The map proved somewhat banal. All the fire sites covering ten years of increasing destruction and suffering were on a direct route from Paul's house in the hills to his veterinary clinic in a suburb ten kilometres away. He'd spot his next project and plan it on his way to and from work. It was simple, if you knew what and who were at each end of the line.

Paul hadn't given up many of his secrets in the hospital basement, although other records gave more later. His mother died in December. It had been logged as an accidental death while smoking in bed. They never discovered the significance of the Passiona can. They found some things in his files, other things they'd never know. He had been good at hiding.

Iris went back to work for the Arson Squad as a special consultant, with Mathew's blessing. She also worked with James to slowly uncover his childhood hurt. He'd been molested by an 'uncle', a boyfriend of his mother's, and he found a way to drift off and imagine himself somewhere else, on another planet, while he was abused. Many years later, James saw the uncle on television, famous for something else. It triggered a breakdown and a suicide attempt by fire. Some things don't heal on their own. They lie dormant waiting to metastasise, exactly like latent cancer.

Exactly like crimes against children. Most victims of child abuse suffered and struggled alone. They needed to be supported. They could be helped. Just not by Iris. She was not particularly good at curing, she'd found. She was a mildly messed-up person who'd been through some things she was trying to get over. Her life continued to be a work in progress. There were always people who visited their damage on others. If the damage involved fire, Iris would keep trying to put them out.

Acknowledgements

A good deal of research has gone into *Burn Patterns*, not least into fire investigation, narrative therapy and other psychological methods and post-traumatic stress. Yet no amount of secondary research can match the firsthand experiences and language of those working in the field.

I would like to give special thanks to Rick Curtis, a professional firefighter and fire investigator, for his close reading of the manuscript and his detailed terminology suggestions.

I'd also like to thank Judy Griffiths for her insights into the practices and philosophies of those working in the psychological health fields. The fiction of *Burn Patterns* has been strengthened by the 'reality checks'.

Any misunderstandings, manglings and mistakes are all my own.

It is wonderful to be working with Fremantle Press and the dedicated staff there. Cheers to Zoe Barnard, who has given valuable feedback.

Georgia Richter has been my editor once again and it continues to be a wonderful relationship, from my side, anyway. I thank Georgia for her sensitivity, artistry and massive patience. I continue to commit crimes against grammar.

Finally as ever, my reading family: Michelle, Jill, Les, Samantha and Frances who are subjected to early drafts. Also Bill and Lee for fruitful (and fruit-filled) discussions of my work. And Vivienne, Leonie, Meredith, Callum, Karin, Christian, Arna and David, for continued tolerance and occasional cheerleading.

About the author

Ron Elliott is a scriptwriter, film and television director and academic. He is the author of the novel *Spinner* and the fiction collection *Now Showing*, as well as 'The Lake Story', which was a finalist in the Carmel Bird Award for long short stories. Ron lives in Perth, Western Australia.

More great crime

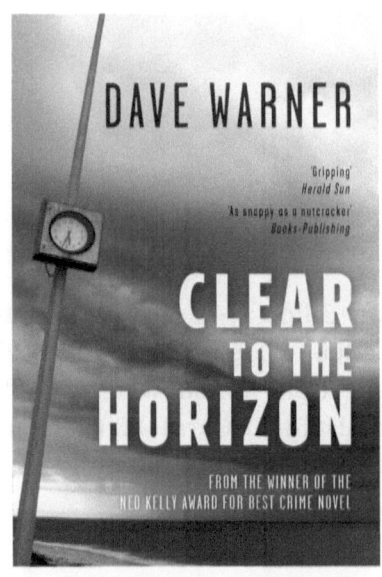

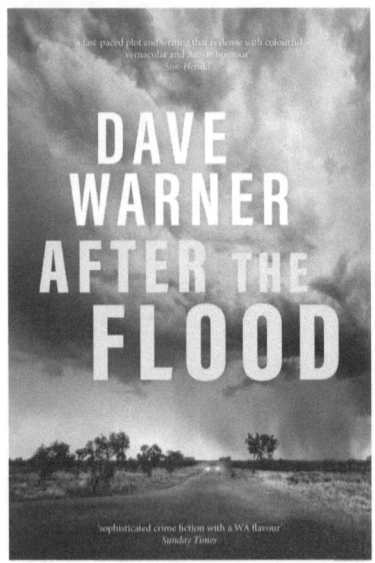

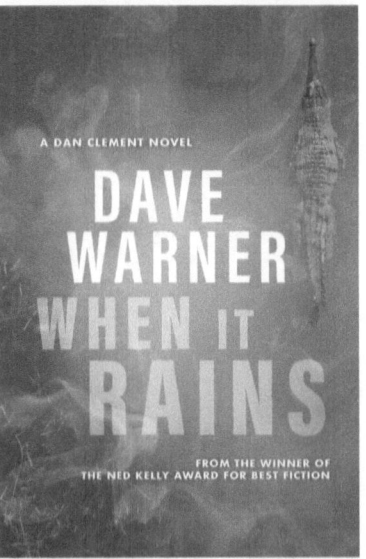

available from fremantlepress.com.au

from Fremantle Press

as ebooks and at all good bookstores

First published 2016 by
FREMANTLE PRESS

Fremantle Press Inc. trading as Fremantle Press
PO Box 158, North Fremantle, Western Australia, 6159
fremantlepress.com.au

Cover design Nada Backovic
Cover photograph © Jarek Blaminsky, Arcangel Images Ltd

 A catalogue record for this
book is available from the
National Library of Australia

ISBN 9781925163452 (paperback)
ISBN 9781925163476 (ebook)

Fremantle Press is supported by the Western Australian State
Government through the Department of Cultural Industries,
Tourism and Sport.

Publication of this title was assisted by the Commonwealth
Government through Creative Australia, its arts funding and
advisory body.

Fremantle Press respectfully acknowledges the Whadjuk
people of the Noongar nation as the Traditional Owners and
Custodians of the land where we work in Walyalup.

www.ingramcontent.com/pod-product-compliance
Lightning Source LLC
Chambersburg PA
CBHW030628030726
47497CB00006B/1687